THE LEGEND OF THE ISLE OF CATS

A man haunted by a murder journeys to a desert island to escape, and there he finds God and the treasure of forgiveness and peace.

THE LEGEND OF THE ISLE OF CATS

A NOVEL

AUSTIN ALLRAN

Redhawk Publications
The Catawba Valley Community College Press
2550 US Hwy 70 SE
Hickory NC 28602

ISBN: 978-1-952485-90-9

Library of Congress Number: 2022945463

Cover created by Ben Precup

Layout by Ashlyn Blake

Edited by Tim Peeler, Aurora King, and Robert Canipe

Printed in the United States of America

To order extra copies of this book, please visit Amazon.com or visit https://redhawkpublications.com

Contact the author at Isleofcats@gmail.com

Dedicated to the glory of God

and

in loving memory of my father and mother—and "Pip."

CONTENTS

PART 1
STARTING THE JOURNEY

PART 2
CELIA AND JENNIE

PART 3
THE REVERSAL OF FORTUNE

PART 4
THE PHANTOM

PART 5
THE LIGHT IN THE DARKNESS

PART 1

STARTING THE JOURNEY

PROLOGUE

Durham, North Carolina
1912

The upperclassman, a senior, wasn't really crazy, though some of his classmates had nicknamed him that behind his back. Tonight, he was the first to arrive for the poker game. Sitting down at a table in a dorm room dimly lit by gaslights, shadows fell across his brooding face with its short red beard. He wasn't one to talk often, but when he did, he expressed strange ideas, which were extreme and not viewed by most of his peers as normal. Nevertheless, he was cocksure and, in some ways worldly-wise, which projected an aura of authority that drew some people toward him.

One such person stood now in the threshold. A freshman, essentially a farm boy, he stood well over six feet tall, blond-haired, blue-eyed, a trusting sort. As he took his seat opposite the red-haired, older one, shadows crossed his face, as well. Best known as the kid who "lives off daddy's tobacco money," he'd never been away from home till this year. As a going-away present, to get him started in life, his father had given him a major cash legacy and an admonition: "Son, listen to me. This is your inheritance, your birthright. Manage it wisely. Make it work for you."

These words came back to him as he readied himself for the game, but for the last several weeks, rather than following his dad's advice, he'd been putting the money to work at this poker table. And Lady Luck had not been with him.

Next to enter the room was his friend from home, Junior, dark with a heavy shadow of beard, black hair, and though also a first-year student, he was not so trusting or naïve. As he took the third seat, his tall friend nodded with a smile, while the red-haired upperclassman remained expressionless except to stare at them both.

The last to arrive was a kid they called Bobo, recruited to the game by the red-head. As thick as thieves, these two palled around together, often playing cards while talking in hushed tones. Bobo reached into his shirt pocket and pulled out an unopened pack of cards, which he handed across the table to Daddy's Money. Then he pulled out a second pack.

Make no mistake, they all knew that playing cards of any sort was against school policy, but this rule had never stopped them before, and would not tonight. The rich but naïve farm boy opened the pack as the gaslight dimmed, then brightened, sending evermore shadows across his face.

Tonight, the sky was the limit.

Thus began the Legend of the Isle of Cats.

1.

DINING OUT

Sixty Years Later
1972

Sitting on a swivel stool at a greasy spoon diner called the Ham and Egger in downtown Durham, North Carolina, I began to follow the swift movements of an enticing waitress. She looked about my age, maybe 20, light brown hair, petite, graceful, pretty face, good figure. When she walked, she moved—contoured nicely in a tight yellow dress—in such a way that she was provocatively good-looking.

Her body language and eye contact suggested that she was flirting with me. She filled my coffee cup. "Are you a college student?" she coquettishly asked, not exactly batting her eyelashes, but something like that.

I smiled. "Yes." I had a feeling my eyes might be telling her I was feasting on her.

She sashayed off to wait succinctly on some other customers, then returned. "I forgot to ask you if you needed anything—sugar, cream?"

"Both." There was a motel not two blocks from here—Corolla's Motor Court.

Reputedly, it had a drive-through window where you paid and were handed a set of sheets after you answered the question, "By the hour or overnight?"

A hint of a smile appeared on her lips. "Really?" She *was* flirting with me. "Give me a second."

She returned with the cream and sugar. "Say when."

"Perfect," I lied. Actually, I preferred my coffee black. It was probably ruined, but who cared?

She smiled. "Good. I like to be helpful."

Then, abruptly there was another waitress behind her—new on the scene—much older and not smiling, outfitted in a white uniform.

The young one turned and handed the older woman the cream and sugar. "End of my shift," she informed me. A twinkle in her eye, she added, "But come visit us again."

I was ready to say, "For you, I'll do it." But before I could complete the thought, the new waitress said to her curtly, in a voice so loud I couldn't help but hear, "Go home and take care of your baby."

Reality check! I was way too young for babies. Babes, yes. Babies, no.

The young lady avoided eye contact with me, and I sipped my coffee, too sweet and full of cream to taste good, as I followed her with my eyes out the door.

I was not supposed to be here. It was 1972, and nobody walked to this place from East Campus because you had to go through five blocks that were prone to muggings, drug deals, and shootings. While the Ham and Egger itself was not inside that five blocks called No-Man's Land, it was on the cusp of a sketchy downtown. They say if you're from the campus, you might get beat up here.

So far, I hadn't been, but there was still time.

My name is Matthew Goodheart—my friends call me Matt—and I am a college freshman who two days ago got my second semester grades, and they're not good. Not good at all, a 2.7 as a matter of fact.

The night of the news, I didn't sleep well, or last night either, and now, Sunday morning, I was really tired. And had a hangover.

I got up this morning and worked on my Great American Novel. I've been working on it for years, and I'm almost done with the Prologue. I've promised myself I'll finish my bestseller by the time I graduate.

I've been promising myself for months that I'd get up on a Sunday and go to church at the Chapel in search of God and the actual meaning of life. I'd like to know both. All my life I've wanted to be a thoughtful, moral person—and a good Christian. Well, I am thoughtful, moral enough, and a Christian to some degree. When I was still living at home with my parents, I was a regular churchgoer.

I'm not a Dr. Jekyll and Mr. Hyde, but while my intentions are good, the nobler spirits never seem to get the better of me. Consequently, I'm not a candidate for sainthood—at least at this time.

Still, I'm always searching for the true meaning of life, reaching up to Heaven for God. To guide me. To rescue me?

Anyway, that's why, about an hour-and-a-half ago, I was sitting on a bench in front of the campus Chapel, admiring its awesome Gothic architecture and seeking divine inspiration. I was supposed to go to church, where I would find God. I'm looking for Him; I want to know Him. But then I stood up, and turned in the opposite direction and walked the forty feet to the bus stop. I caught the shuttle to East Campus, hopped off, and headed for the railroad tracks downtown.

Now I was sitting at the counter drumming my fingers as the waitress ignored me.

Problem is, I may just be a beach bum.

This struggle between the lofty, noble side of me, seeking goodness and excellence, and the bum-at-heart drifting from day to day easily distracted, is ever-present. How would Matthew Goodheart grapple with this?

And another mystery: How was I supposed to earn a living after I graduated? *If* I graduated.

And while I was at it, there was the matter of finding the perfect woman. I knew she was out there, and when I found her, I'd marry her.

Actually, I have a plan—go to law school after finishing as an undergrad, then practice law and get elected to Congress. Then maybe even Governor. But this news of my freshman GPA is not encouraging. At all.

I got here by walking on the tracks that run nearby the campus into town and beyond. I like trains, and I've heard it's against the law to walk on the railroad tracks, and I felt like doing something rebellious and maybe even a little dangerous; hence, I hiked the tracks through No-Man's Land. Anything to distract me from my situation. Instead of choosing to sit in a church pew and be in the presence of God and praying for Him to help me, here I was at this counter praying for this waitress to help me with a cup of black coffee. Was that a wise choice?

A little black dog, scared eyes, no collar, was outside the door. On the way in, I'd petted him, and I'd take him some food if I could get waited on. It's not like I'm exactly inconspicuous. I'm six-foot-six—but not tall and talented enough to play for the Blue Devils, which had been my dream from first grade through senior year of high school when I was accepted to Duke but failed to make the cut for the basketball team. I'm blond, blue-eyed, and rather frequently considered by the ladies to be handsome or cute or something like that. But now, considering the conduct of this particular waitress, you'd think I was invisible. Or worse.

They say on campus, if you make it through No-Man's Land to the H and E, even if you don't get mugged or anything, don't expect a welcome. So far, no surprises. Except for the cute, flirtatious waitress, now gone.

The current waitress, over fifty, over-worked and surly, fist on hip, finally asked, "Drink?"

A few smart-mouth responses came to mind, particularly considering my hangover, but my Southern manners prevailed. "Coffee—black." I added, "And some water, please." I handed her my nearly-full coffee mug.

Though I flashed my pearly whites at her, no smile in return. In her stained apron, she looked miserable. She looked devoid of soul, and that evoked my sympathy. So hoping to brighten her day, I smiled again. Considering I've often been told I have a great smile—and the fact that it had just worked effectively on her predecessor—I couldn't believe she didn't smile back.

It always amazed me when people drank coffee, ate a meal, and smoked at the same time. Like these two construction workers with buzz cuts sitting on either side of me. This place was open 24/7, and these two dudes must be charging their batteries for a Sunday morning roofing job at a factory.

I coughed from the smoke. This was Durham in the early 1970s, and it was still very much the Bull City tobacco capital.

I have to confess I've been known to smoke a cigarette now and again and enjoy doing it. I just don't do it while simultaneously eating grits, like these guys. While on the topic of tobacco, I might add this bit of minutia: It's been told in my family that one of my great-grandfathers made a fortune growing tobacco on a huge farm not far from here—and there are other parts to this story that are dark and better left to rest—though I'm a little sketchy on the details.

I guess at this point in my life, the rest of that story is not very important, but I'm thinking maybe *this* is: I have a girlfriend who I've been on-and-off in-love with since first grade. Jennie. She goes to Duke, too—same class as me. She's gorgeous. I don't know where that relationship is going to end up, but I've been all about her one way or another nearly my whole life.

I wasn't feeling too sure about a lot of things right now, but I did know that the month was May, and I liked the weather we were having. Seventy degrees, some humidity, and a blue sky. Made me feel like I was at the beach. Made me want to *be* at the beach.

Instead, I was choking on an overabundance of second-hand smoke and unfriendly company. But at least I hadn't been asphyxiated yet or kicked out. But there was still time.

Every table was packed with men, and they generally looked about as dour as the waitress. They didn't take to "Dukies" in these here parts.

In any event, I was kind of out of my element in bell-bottom jeans and a tight-fitting orange, brown, and yellow sunburst pattern shirt—not to mention my hair was long enough to annoy my father. After a year in college, I was looking kind of like a hippie, even if I didn't feel like one. When I walked in, I got a few glances, if not stares, but at least nobody asked me to step outside. I was taller than any of them. I might say to be fair that maybe my overall appearance was contributing to what I perceived to be a clash of cultures.

Even with all these heavy thoughts running through my head and no food to elevate my blood sugar level, I could still think about that little black dog, scared and hungry, wagging his tail when I petted him. I wanted to adopt him and take him back to the dorm.

I sat there jogging my knee, and after about a year, the waitress brought me some coffee and water and said, "Thang else?"

Probably—after all, this *is* a restaurant. "Two eggs—scrambled. Corned beef hash." I didn't care for ham, so I said, "Livermush." I added, "And a gravy biscuit."

She fixed her mean eyes on me and huffed. "What *number*?"

My eyes dropped to the laminated menu, which doubled as a placemat. What was this, a test? Hadn't I had enough of those where I'd come from? Hadn't I performed poorly enough on enough of those to torpedo my grade-point average—if not my whole life?

Huffing again, she shifted her weight. "Okay—*fine*. Ala carte."

Did that justify the death penalty?

"Also, grits—with butter."

Her eyes riveted on mine. She scribbled on her pad, then handed the order over her shoulder to the fry cook without turning around. The grill sizzled, grease steaming in a cloud to the ceiling, the odor competing with the smoke to fill the air.

I was a Southerner from a small North Carolina city called Hickory, no less; but at Duke that was out of place. The school was eighty-five percent out-of-staters and over-run with people from up North, especially New York and New Jersey. And you could rest assured that if someone was from up there, they knew everything. As a Southerner, I knew about grits. That's why I ordered them. The Yankees I knew on campus had never tasted grits but roundly condemned them anyway. Was that fair?

The guy beside me got up, paid his tab at the register, and left. He didn't leave any money on the counter, so I wondered if he tipped the waitress.

She brought me my ala carte blue plate and plopped it down in front of me, this time without making eye contact. I had to admit it smelled good and tasted even better, especially the gravy biscuit and corned beef hash, which had been fried a little crispy on the grill. The grits were perfect once I piled them with butter, salt and pepper.

I stood and looked quickly for the dog but didn't see him. As I sat down again, I thought of my friend Croom, a life-long buddy from Hickory who, like Jennie, was a fellow Dukie.

Croom told me yesterday that I couldn't adopt every stray dog that crossed my path. I think he meant that metaphorically.

He also kept telling me that before we graduated, he was going to go on an exciting adventure—maybe a journey—and that he was going to take me with him. So far, that hadn't happened, but we were only freshmen, so there was still time.

Regardless, I could go back to the dorm and tell people I'd eaten at the Ham and Egger, not gotten mugged, and the food was good. Maybe that would help improve relations between the students, who sometimes referred to the townies as Durmites, and the townies, who thought all Duke students were snotty rich kids in general and Northern preppies at worst.

After two semesters, reality had begun to set in. My grades were in the pits. I hadn't finished the Prologue to my Great American Novel, and I'd spent too much time partying. At this rate, I'd never get into law school, much less be elected to Congress and never mind the Governor's Mansion.

I had ambition; I just needed self-discipline. If I could concentrate on something—learn to know Jesus and trust God.

Nevertheless, I did like my freshman dorm. Everybody was interesting, including the Yankees. I was learning a lot about new things. Besides, beer was the international language, so everybody loved a good keg. I knew I did.

Still, there had to be more to life than just partying, cooperative dates, my Jaguar XK-140 convertible, and good professors at a highly-ranked private school. I could search high and low until I found the perfect woman of my dreams, but even that was not the ultimate point. It couldn't be. There had to be a true meaning of life for all of us. There *had* to be. That's what I was living for—to find the answer.

I finished eating, and my distraction for the morning was almost over. Except for getting back to campus. I stood, gave the waitress a gracious tip—though I can't say she earned it—and after paying at the door, went outside.

The air was humid and beachy and smelled like prunes—it's called tobacco. It felt so nice, and I felt sure I was going to embark on an adventure that would change my life. Maybe not today, but soon I would find the treasure I was looking for. If I searched long and hard enough, I'd find it.

I looked around for the dog but didn't see him anywhere. Instead, I saw a man standing on the sidewalk, unshaven, in tattered clothes, the whole nine yards. He said, "Scuse me, sir. Would you happen to have some spare change for some coffee?" Reaching into my pocket, I stopped. "Follow me." Nudging him inside, I led him to the place at the counter I'd just left.

As he sat, the two men on either side stared in stony silence, first at him, then at me, then at both of us. I said to the waitress, "Would you please give him whatever he orders?" I handed her ten dollars, knowing that would be more than enough to cover any of the numbers on the menu and still leave a big tip for her. She didn't exactly break into a smile, but I saw the start of one and did see a flicker of something bright in her eyes. That gave me a feeling of hope.

Outside again, I looked one last time for the dog. He was gone. That disappointed me, but maybe Croom was right. As I walked the railroad tracks the five blocks back to East Campus, the beachy weather took my mind off my grades and my anxiety about the future and made me want to go to the coast. After all, how could anyone be at the beach and not be happy? Besides, if I searched there in the right places, maybe I'd find something significant buried in the sand. A treasure of some sort. Or, even if I didn't find any sort of treasure at all, perhaps I'd discover something else—something quite different—that would still impact my life.

2.

ADVENTURE BOUND

Two and a half years later, I still hadn't discovered the true meaning of life, and I wasn't sure how well I knew God, but I *had* managed to pull up my grade point average. Plus, I'd met a girl named Celia, who I was pretty sure was *the* one. I met her my sophomore year through my friend Cindy, and we'd been off-and-on since. Summer of junior year, we'd been off.

But when summer was over, and school started back, Celia agreed to go out with me again. "Matt," she said, "I really missed you. I really did. It was harder for me to be away from you than I thought it would be." Then she kissed me. Then again. She'd never been more beautiful, and my heart melted.

By spring of my senior year, 1974, I had all sorts of plans for us. My head was full of weighty thoughts—and at least one question: whether to use a dinner coupon on a second beer—when my friend Croom sat down across from me at the table.

He answered the question when he said, "See this glass of

beer?" He set it on the table too firmly, and some of it splashed overboard. "It's for me. Go get another one for yourself because we have some serious talking to do."

Distracted from my reverie, I stood up, which, as sometimes happened, made an impression on those around me. Several girls at another table looked my way.

I smiled and returned with a glass of amber and sat down.

"Some serious talking," Croom repeated. My old buddy looked kind of like Edgar Allan Poe. Or maybe John Wilkes Booth—I wasn't sure which. But since it wasn't flattering to compare someone to an assassin, I never did. A girl once told him he looked like "a nineteenth-century English actor," and he liked that, so it was okay by me.

Regardless, it was a liberal time in terms of college, and this college being no exception, we could now drink beer in the main West Campus dining hall using the meal plan. That's what we were doing—drinking dinner.

Croom had some big plans he wanted to share with me, his latest idea for a grand adventure. "We have to go," he said. "It's a trip we have to take."

There was so much chatter and motion beneath the Gothic arches, I had to strain to hear him. "I don't have my sleeping bag. It's at home."

"You and me, Celia and Jennie. It'll be great. Our last spring break before graduation and maybe our last trip together, unhitched—well, at least Jennie and me." It was true. He and Jennie had wedding plans; Celia and I did not. He and Jennie had moved fast in their relationship; Celia and I were moving along in steps.

The girl of my dreams was proving to have a mind of her own. She wasn't just a beautiful brunette with big brown eyes and thick eyelashes; she was a princess aspiring to be an accomplished pianist. She was an intelligent, classy, strong-willed woman. I concluded that I'd met my match. But whatever it took, I intended to persevere. I knew a good thing when I saw it.

I wasn't as sure about the four of us on a trip together.

As I thought of Jennie, my mind began to wander back. I'd known her since first grade; I could even remember the first time I laid eyes on her, the very first day of school. We grew up together, from elementary school to college. We had a history.

Suffice it to say, it didn't work out.

So by our senior year, I could say to my oldest best friend, "It's okay. I'm okay with it. I'm over Jennie. Go ahead and ask her out." Now they were talking marriage.

As for Celia and me, I'd messed up with her, but I had this confidence in my heart that I'd win her back. That's where we were now. She missed me, and she'd agreed to give me another chance.

Croom was talking to me about his plans for the future: he couldn't wait to be a biologist. "And Jennie and I are going to have at least three kids. And how cool will it be for a guy to be married to a doctor?"

He leaned closer to me, contending now with the clamor. "She's such a booker," he confided. "Her nose always to the grindstone. Always a goal. I like that in her—I admire it—but that's another reason we have to go on this trip: to get Jennie out of the library."

Croom had a thick, dark mustache, and every once in a

while, he would pull the end of it when he talked. I thought he was funny; I always had. And he was loyal and had a lot of enthusiasm, especially when he got revved up about something.

He continued, "And this isn't just about getting Jennie out of the library. It's about you, too, good buddy. You need some help. You really do. You've become far too bookish, far too serious since the good ol' days of our freshman year." He grinned. "You used to be a party animal and a friend of the keg. Now look at you."

Glancing down at the glass of beer in front of me, I held out my arms on either side and looked at myself from left to right.

Croom asked, "What do you see?"

"A font of wisdom?"

Croom shook his head.

"A paragon of virtue?"

He paused a moment. "Maybe in another life. But for right now, all work and not enough play. Not enough fun. Congratulations again on the 3.6, but let's not lose our perspective." He had a point. Maybe this invitation was a sign that I was finally going to go on that great life-changing adventure I'd been looking for.

"We're going to the Outer Banks to explore," he said. "I'm not talking about places where Yankees and tourists go—I'm talking about a desert isle. There's this island called Hoophole. It's real isolated and rustic, three-and-a-half hours from the mainland by ferry. Hardly anybody lives there—no tourists. The only thing the islanders do is fish."

I was intrigued. "So that's where you want to go?"

He sat back, a twinkle in his eye. "Of course it is! It's a fantastic idea! I've spent a lot of time researching all this. What we need is an adventure. What *you* need is adventure."

Some of the smart alecks in my freshman dorm used to joke that "Life is too long," but considering that I was already a senior, I didn't believe it, though I thought it was a funny saying. What I believed was that life may be shorter than we think, and since I was in a quest for the meaning and purpose of life, I'd better get a move on.

"I have to admit I could use a change of scenery. But it's the girls. I'm not so sure it's a good idea for the four of us to head out on a trip like this. They don't know each other that well. Who knows what they'll be like on a camping trip."

"Jennie loves stuff like this. She likes to camp."

"Yeah, but what about Celia? And what about the two of them together—with us? This could get complicated."

He sat back but spoke loudly enough for me to hear. "The four of us are going to be friends for life, so we might as well start things off big, good buddy."

"I don't know, Croom. *I* want to go, but let's ask some other people, too. The more, the merrier. I've got my doubts about Celia and Jennie together for so long."

Groaning, he made a face.

I said, "My grandfather, the one who was a minister, used to say, 'Life is a collection of ironies—and one quick event in a person's life can change that person's life forever.' For him, it was a card game."

Before I could add that it was a card game right here at Trinity College, Duke, Croom interrupted me. "Anyway, as I was saying, it's not that first island—Hoophole—that we're aiming for. That's not our ultimate destination."

I raised my eyebrows.

"There's another island beyond it. A little island, totally deserted. The local people call it the Isle of Cats or, sometimes, Treasure Island. I don't know if there are cats there or not—or treasure. Who knows?—maybe Blackbeard buried some of his loot there. They say he did. He was all over those islands. Anyway, that's where we're going. We need a jolt from books and dull routine, and it might be the last chance we get for a while."

I looked at him, thinking how, on the one hand, I so wanted to go, and on the other hand, I wondered if it was a good idea.

"There may be pirates there, as well as gold." He smiled, *his* eyebrows raised. "So I'll be taking my knife."

He leaned back theatrically, pulled it out of his pocket, and opened it. Soon after, he closed it with a flair and returned it to his pocket. I could see us back in junior high and high school, him standing on the bow of the Dixie on Lake Hickory, slicing the air with a fishing rod, and yelling "Aaaarrrgh!" as Cindy Peppercorn—one of our classmates and a buddy—and I laughed. I shook my head, smiling.

I noticed a girl at the end of the table staring at him, then looking at us disapprovingly.

Croom smiled at her and waved. Her scowl melted, and she smiled back.

"You need to take one, too," he said.

"I don't have one. And it's illegal for you to be carrying that on campus, let alone brandishing it here in the dining hall. I don't care, but it might upset your parents if you get expelled."

"One of us has got to have some imagination," Croom said. "And I guess we both know which one of us that is. And you *could* do with a knife. After all, you *are* a cub scout."

"Eagle Scout. And like I said, I don't even have my sleeping bag here. It's at home."

"I've got one *for* you—a thick one."

"Celia doesn't have a sleeping bag. She'll never agree to this."

"I've got a sleeping bag for her, too. Even better than yours."

"She'll never agree to this. It's too rugged—too primitive. She's never been without electricity a moment in her life. How can she dry her hair?"

"You don't give her enough credit," Croom said. "No wonder she won't marry you—I wouldn't either—and I don't want you to end up an old maid. Jennie's all ready to go. I have a tent, too." Pounding his fist as the girl at the other end of the table looked at us again, he said, "Now call up Celia and tell her we're going to have the adventure of our lives."

3.

JUST US FOUR

When I called Celia, Croom was standing beside the phone. When she didn't say yes for me quickly enough, he grabbed the phone and talked her into it.

On Friday, the four of us loaded our gear into his dented, dirty Jeep. The next morning around five-thirty, still dark, we left Durham and headed to Raleigh. From there, we kept going till we hit the coast. By nine o'clock, we were at the sign for "Hoophole Island Ferry, 43 Miles." With ferry reservations for ten, we barely arrived in time, and the cars were loading as we pulled up. Around one-thirty, we drove off the ferry and onto the island.

Hoophole's "business district" was a small cluster of wooden buildings built on pilings over the water on the harbor side of the street.

Croom parked the Jeep on a sandy shoulder on the other side of the road and turned his head so he could speak to Celia and me in the back seat, as well as Jennie. He had spent some time on some of the other Outer Banks and Barrier Islands, so he was our authority and tour guide. "Hoophole's just a fishing village—no hotel, no restaurant, no shops."

I saw a General Store across the street, but we'd packed everything we needed.

Croom informed us, "Many of the islanders still don't have electricity or plumbing. Forget television."

I could see that Celia and Jennie were surprised. I knew *I* was. I'd spent a summer in Europe, but until now, I'd never been east of Raleigh in the state of North Carolina. Celia, Jennie, and I were out of our clime.

Croom was confident he'd make up for that. "Now that we're here, we've got to find our way to the island of the cats." He opened the door and got out.

Then me, then Celia and Jennie. I pointed to a small wooden building, no paint except for the words "The Fish House" above its open door in weather-beaten white lettering. "I'll go in there and ask for directions."

While Celia and Jennie waited by the Jeep with Croom, I crossed the street and ventured inside. Several men, dressed in yellow rubber jackets, pants and green rubber boots were chopping fish and squirting them with water. As I stood there, they ignored me, though I was noticeably out of place—not as a hippie, but as a different type of alien—in a button-down shirt, sweater with crocodile logo, sneakers and corduroy jeans. Still six-foot-six, I was larger than I was freshman year: summers working at my dad's textile mill on the construction crew had helped build an addition to the existing plant and additional muscles to my frame. I'd also spent part of last summer working on Capitol Hill as an intern. I enjoyed working at the mill, but I liked politics better.

I walked through the fish room, past the men in yellow cutting up fish, past a conveyor belt with fish traveling along it, past the faucets squirting water on the fish, over the wet floor, out the back door and onto a dock. A blond, sunburned fisherman about my age was pulling up in a small boat. Although he had to know I was there for a reason—I was standing right in front of him on the edge of the dock—he glanced at me, once, then refused to look again. As I stood in front of him, he began shoveling fish out of his boat onto the conveyor belt.

I was amazed that each fish had two eyes on the same side of its face. I stood there marveling at that fact. Finally, I asked, "What kind of fish are those?"

"Flounder," he said without looking up. Then he looked at me. "Where are *you* from—Mars?"

I felt kind of dumb. I'd never seen a flounder before, except filleted on a plate, served in a restaurant. No eyes.

"Hickory." Not that I thought he would know where that was. I added, "I guess that's about as far from here as Mars."

He stopped shoveling. "You want somethin'?" He looked at me critically.

"Yes," I replied. "Can you tell me how to get to the island of the cats? Treasure Island, they sometimes call it."

He snorted and twisted up his chapped lips to the side of his mouth. "You really *are* from Mars." I didn't say anything, just kept looking at him. "You can't go 'air," he said. Then, as if I'd walked off, he began shoveling again.

"Why not?"

He stepped onto the side of the boat, then up onto the dock. A water pipe and valve stood beside the conveyor belt with a hose attached. He turned the valve and began spraying the fish. Then he started the belt, and the fish moved into the Fish House.

Finally, he turned to me and said, "'Cause nobody goes to that oylet 'cept Roger Gaskill."

On the other side of the dock, about twenty feet away, two Asian men were stabbing flounders with knives. The guy in front of me turned off the hose. The two Asians jabbered back and forth. My cordial Viking friend looked at me and said, "Oin, oin, oh. Ah-so, ah-so."

I smiled. "Who is Roger Gaskill?"

After a prolonged silence with me not budging, he answered. "Boatman."

"The person who runs the boat from Hoophole to the Isle of Cats?"

"Yup. Lives ove' 'air." He pointed to the other side of the harbor. "Little gray 'ouse with one-sided roof." He paused for a moment of silence, then said in a deep voice, reverently, "No. Nobody ever goes to that oylet."

Without looking at me, he stepped back into the boat, unhitched the moorings, started the engine, and pulled out. He looked up at me and shook his head. I could only imagine what he was thinking.

I walked back through the Fish House and rejoined the others waiting for me beside the Jeep and told them what I knew.

Croom broke out in a hopeful smile. "So now we know where he lives. We're making progress."

I suddenly thought: he looks awfully preppy in that starched, pink-pinstriped, button-down shirt and sweater—as out-of-place as me.

"I have to say the fellow I was talking to wasn't very positive about our going over there."

Croom retorted, "So you've told us. You ran into a Negative Nellie. A *native* Negative Nellie. Not to worry. All the boatman can do is say no. But you never know till you ask."

Hands in the air, I shrugged. Celia peered at me from under her dark brows. Her eyes were beautiful but penetrating as if she sensed something was off here.

We got back in the Jeep and followed a dirt road along the shoreline to the other side of the harbor. Seeing a gray house with a shed roof at the end of the road, we parked the Jeep nearby, next to a chain-link fence, and got out.

"Look. An old cemetery," I said. "Maybe historic." Curious, we stood at the fence.

"Eight vaults above ground," Croom observed. "Brick and cement, nineteenth and early twentieth century. Looks like there's room for an even dozen—four to go." Shaking the gate, he found it locked. A sign attached to it, painted in black letters, said "JUST US," the spacing making it appear as two words, although we knew it was a family cemetery.

"Just us," Croom said cheerily.

"I don't know whether to be amused or creeped out," Jennie replied. "But the gate is locked, Croom."

"Private family property," Celia said.

Jennie pointed to the house nearby. "I thought we were here for *that*."

We walked the short distance to the dead end and knocked on the door, but no one answered. We knocked again. Then again. Finally, a gray-haired man with a sun- and windburned face and white-stubble beard came to the door, opening it partway.

"Don't take nobody to that oylet," he replied flatly.

Croom was persistent. "We'll pay you."

"Money ain't it. Don't take nobody to that oylet," he said more forcefully. He started to close the door.

Croom reached into his back pocket and pulled a bunch of bills from his wallet. The old man's eyes grew big, and the door opened. After he stared at the bills, he squinted suspiciously at Croom. "What is ye kids gonna do once you git 'air?"

"Just camp for the night," Croom replied. "We have a tent. You come back and get us tomorrow at noon. Is it a deal? Half now to take us over, the other half when you come pick us up?"

He frowned. "Only to camp. I mean it. Ye kids stay away from the 'ouse. Don't go near that 'ouse. Understand?"

He waited, squinting at us, till we nodded, then told us to get our things. He said it was okay to leave the Jeep parked on the side of the road beside the graveyard. Then he led us around back to where he docked his boat, *The Jolly Roger*.

We loaded everything in—sleeping bags, tent, backpacks, cooler—then I helped Celia into the front of the boat; Croom helped Jennie into the seat facing her. Then Croom got in; then I did. Finally, the boatman. "How long does it take to get over?" I asked.

"Bout an hour."

But once underway, it seemed longer. The water was smooth as glass, the sun bright, and the sky was a beautiful blue with only a few white clouds. Our boatman was silent and off-putting, and Celia, sitting beside me, seemed a hundred miles away, staring out onto the water.

Croom and Jennie, their backs to the boatman, looked natural together, ready for their wedding day, and now and again, Croom would kiss her lightly on her sparkling, blond hair—or cheek. But they didn't talk.

About halfway over, something happened. I sensed that the boatman seemed noticeably different, ill-at-ease, as if he'd suddenly thought of, or forgotten, something important. I nudged closer to Celia, noticing that her eyes were fixed on him, too. She took my hand and held it, then resumed her vacant stare off to the distant ocean. I nudged still closer and squeezed her hand.

"Penny for your thoughts?" I teased.

"Sorry," she said softly, looking at me and smiling. "It's just so quiet out here—and so far away. I feel lost in it." She squeezed my hand.

"Another penny for the rest of your thoughts?" I whispered. "What else?"

She looked at me with her big brown eyes. "Nothing." She snuggled closer to me, nudging playfully with her shoulder. "It's just that," she whispered, "all of a sudden, he"—she indicated the boatman with her eyes and a subtle nod—"looks so suspicious." She mouthed silently: *Creepy*. Then she said, "But it's okay. I'll get over it. Everything will be fine. We'll have a good time." She put her arm through mine.

I smiled. "Yes, everything will be fine."

With my thumb and index finger, I signaled Croom and Jennie, "okay." Croom raised his fist. After that, we said nothing, and as we continued onward, away from Hoophole and closer to the Isle of Cats, the boatman's unsettling aura made me wonder: What would we do if he didn't come back for us tomorrow—smoke signals? One uncomfortable scenario after another entered my head.

Finally, as we approached the island, I broke the silence by saying to the boatman, "It looks like the island is small."

He replied without looking at me. "It ain't 'at small. It's long. Shaped like the iris of a cat's eye, late-afternoon." He added, "Barren on both ends. Forest in the middle. We're approachin' the tip of the cee-gar."

Within minutes, we beached. It was three-thirty, an hour after shoving off.

Croom stepped off the bow onto the sand, and we handed him our gear. Then I helped Jennie and Celia off. Then I joined them.

"Don't ye kids forgit what I sayed," the old man growled again. "Ye kids stay away from the 'ouse. It would not do at all for you to be messin' round 'air."

"Don't forget: pick us up tomorrow at noon," I said.

Without acknowledging us, he started the engine, Croom and I pushed the boat, and he backed away from the shore.

We watched as he turned the boat around and headed back to Hoophole. What could possibly be such a big deal about a little ol' verboten desert island off the coast of North Carolina?

God only knew.

4.
THE ISLE OF CATS

We picked up our gear and moved away from the water, up the beach to where the high tide could not reach.

"The sun will set in three hours," Croom told us. "Let's set up the tent before we do anything else."

I said, "I think before I do anything else, I've got to have some bug spray." Thankful I'd worn long-sleeves, I was rubbing my ears quickly with my fingers, slapping my hands, fanning my eyes and nose. "This is awful," I mumbled to Celia as she fished in the duffle bag for the spray. Thankfully, she'd remembered to bring it since I had not.

Croom said, "Keep moving. That's the only way to keep them off. Create a breeze. That's the key. Walk. Do things. Move. It's only bad like this because there's no breeze."

Jennie, like Celia, wearing a sweatshirt and jeans, slapped the back of her legs. "Do they bite through clothes? What are these things?" she groused, shuddering all over. She kept tossing her hair around, trying to keep the bugs off. "They're horrible!"

"No-see-ums," Croom said.

Jennie grabbed the bug repellant from me and began spraying herself from head to toe.

"I'm just thankful I'm wearing jeans and long sleeves. And I hope to God this spray works." She brushed one swarm after another out of her strawberry-blond hair with small hands as lightly freckled as her face.

With Croom's direction in setting up the tent, we had it up and had all our things inside in fifteen minutes.

He unrolled his sleeping bag with Jennie's help. They left hers rolled up, tossed to the side of the tent. Celia saw to it that both of our sleeping bags were unrolled, side by side, with space in between. I could take a hint but wasn't offended: the fact that she'd agreed to come on this little over-night with me at all was pretty impressive. We were a couple once more.

Outside the tent, Jennie was being tortured by the bugs. "Damn it, Croom, will you do something about these freaking vultures? I can't stand this! What am I supposed to do—go back inside the tent, zip up the netting, and stay there?"

She slapped the back of her neck, tossing her long hair, then rubbed her hand underneath the collar of her sweatshirt. Mumbling a few curses, she said something about how she'd rather be using her time constructively—studying—any way but this.

Croom ducked out of the tent; Celia and I followed. The second we were out, the no-see-ums were again all over Croom and me.

Oddly, though, they didn't seem to be after Celia. "Funny, they're not bothering *me*." She smiled and added, "I guess I don't taste good."

Ignoring her, Croom stuffed a piece of bread in his shirt pocket. "We'll just have to walk. It's the still air—that's what we have to get away from." And he was right: the bugs weren't so bad as long as we kept moving, though, for a while, they followed us like a small, invisible cloud.

The island ran east-west in a narrow strip. Except for dunes covered in sea oats, it stretched out before us, nothing but barren sand; then a mass of trees and undergrowth, a maritime forest, separated our line of sight from the other end of the island. We walked along the beach, my arm around Celia's shoulder, Croom's around Jennie's. As we walked, I could feel Celia relaxing, and she smiled as she moved closer to me.

An array of sea creatures littered the line of the tide. A dead hammerhead shark had been grounded on a sandbar when the tide receded, and Croom, the biologist, pulled out his pocket knife and began to dissect it. Jennie stood attentively beside him. Finally, she said, "Let me have a go at it." He stood up and handed her the knife. Dropping to her knees as we all watched, she completed the operation as skillfully as a surgeon. Inside the shark lay a skate, undigested.

"Voila!" she crowed, flipping it out and inspecting it in the chyme as I watched in admiration. Celia grimaced.

"That's neat," I said, marveling at the way the skate was whole.

"Pretty amazing," Celia agreed as she walked off. Then, at a distance, holding a stick, she jumped back from something she'd uncovered in the sand. "And what do you think about *this*?" The three of us joined her. "What I want to know," she asked, "is what are *these* things doing in the sand?"

Croom, retrieving the knife from Jennie, used it to jiggle about in the sand until he'd uncovered parts of a skeleton. "Looks like cat bones, except they're too large. Hmmm." He scratched his head. As we walked on, he and Jennie debated the issue: they were supposed to know about such things. The bones of wild ponies? Not on *this* island; the ponies were on Shackleford, and the skeletons were too small, anyway. I suggested dog bones, but what did *I* know? I unearthed part of another skeleton. Then another.

While we stood there pondering, a half-dozen swooping seagulls surrounded us. As they took turns dive-bombing our heads, at first, we laughed. Croom was happy to throw the pieces of bread he'd brought them. But their diving turned to pecking, and since we ducked and covered our heads but did not run, their attacks became more aggressive.

"We've invaded a nesting area," Croom yelled. "Run!" They followed us for a while, but once out of their space, the attacks stopped. "Nesting this early in the year is unusual," he informed us, once we'd stopped to catch our breath and regroup. "Then again, this is an unusual place."

Celia rubbed the top of her head and inspected her fingers. Blood. Enough to make her eyes wide. I could see tears in them. Wanting to comfort her, I put my hands on her shoulders. As I looked at her sympathetically, her eyes grew larger and her breathing slowed.

"Are you okay?" I asked, thinking maybe she was overreacting.

Then she gasped, pointing into the dunes. Not fifty feet away, a cat was prowling, and it wasn't ordinary, either.

The cat was huge—and misshapen. Then there was another one. And several more. Large, ugly cats. "This is incredible," she said, inching closer to me, holding my arm. "They're so *huge*. And where are they coming from?" In all colors, they appeared—black, brown, gray, orange, mixed. Some had stripes; some were mottled. All were prowling nearer now, their backs raised against us, tails moving slowly back and forth.

Croom said, "If I didn't know better, I'd guess they were wildcats—or bobcats. Look how some of them don't have tails."

Jennie pointed to one hovering nearby in the dunes. "Look at that gray one with the strange ears. He's only got one eye."

Celia averted her head to the side. "Don't stare. Don't stare at them. Just keep walking." Hanging onto my arm, she seemed needy in a good way, and I loved having her close to me.

The sun, a big orange-red ball, sank closer to the horizon, and the sky turned rose-red with purple flecks, like a peacock's fan. Off in the distance, gray clouds appeared in the sky for the first time all day. Fifty feet away, the cats prowled the dunes, eyeing us.

The water rolling up on the beach bubbled, scintillating in blue and silver sequins in the day's last hour of light. I was closest to the water and the first to take my shoes off. As we waded down the beach, acting like we weren't aware of the animals, I said to Croom, "I guess you didn't have any idea there'd be a bunch of over-sized, deformed cats prowling around here. So—should we be concerned, considering we're going to be spending the night in a tent? I mean, I hope they've had plenty to eat lately."

"Pfft! Not to worry, good buddy! Not even a lynx or an ocelot would attack a human, and these bad boys wouldn't want you regardless." Then he assured the three of us, "These felines look like over-sized house cats to me. Nothing exotic. Just great big, ugly feral cats. Maybe they've been isolated on this island for hundreds of years and have mutated. The wild ponies at Shackleford are the descendants of the horses brought by the Spanish in the 1500s. Who knows?—maybe these cats are the descendants of cats left here by pirates when their ships wrecked."

"Good theory," I said. "I'm holding out for finding some doubloons—or the King's treasure." That's right: I hadn't given up on discovering the treasure; it was still crucial to my life's quest—all a part of my searching. I added, "Or even just the bounty of a good merchant ship."

Jennie smiled. "Wouldn't that be something if we actually unearthed some treasure?"

She paused. "What do you think the story is with the house that's supposed to be here? It's hard to imagine a house on this island, but the boatman was emphatic."

Croom smoothed the end of his mustache with the hand that wasn't on Jennie's shoulder.

"Yeah. Stay away from the 'ouse, ye kids. What do you suppose that could mean—be sure to find it and check it out?"

Celia responded quickly, an edge to her voice. "It means stay away. This is enough of an adventure if we take it easy and play it safe." She added, "I have enough blood on my hands already–we don't need to look for trouble." She had her arm around my waist and tugged me closer. The sky had begun to cloud up as the sun turned redder. As we moved along the beach, several cats prowled near us up in the dunes, all ugly, misshapen in one way or another, and unnaturally large. They seemed to be following us, making us nervous, despite Croom's insistence that they were only curious, not hungry.

But when we realized that they were actually after the gulls, our anxiety lessened. As we watched, these excellent hunters stalked both gulls and sandpipers, bolted after them like bullets, pounced, then tore them up and ate them. I found it fascinating, though I hated to see a bird killed like that.

Celia looked away. "I can't stand to watch."

Jennie said, "It's just the food chain, nature's way. Everything has to die, one way or another."

Celia made a face. "Comforting thought."

"Well, at least the bugs aren't as bad now," I offered.

We were wading along the shore on a sandbar and hadn't been paying attention to the movement of the tides. "Maybe we should turn around and head back," Celia suggested. "It's getting darker. And I think it's getting deeper between us and the shore." She'd no sooner said this than the water rushed up around us, cutting us off from dry land. "I don't like this," she said. "It's too deep." She pushed against me uncertainly. "The water is too deep here. It's moving too fast."

The foamy tide moved in and out around us. We stepped from one depth to another with no warning, with holes up to our knees. Even with our pants rolled up, we were getting wet, and the water was cold.

"Let's get out of this!" Jennie urged. "The undertow's too strong."

We waded through the pool of waves back up to the wet

sand and put our shoes on. Then we walked on eastward in the direction of the forest as the sky grew cloudier and the sun dropped still closer to the horizon.

Something prowling about in the dunes growled, and Celia screamed, practically jumping on top of me. Then, off in the distance, through the dark mass of trees that separated the two ends of the island, I spotted a light. "The house, maybe?" I said. "Maybe a headless horseman, toting his lantern?"

"Ha ha, very funny," Celia said, clutching me, "I think we should head back to our tent. I really do. I thought this place was supposed to be a desert island; now, there's a light in the woods. If it's coming from the house, we promised we'd stay away. We promised."

"There's probably no point in going back," Croom said, "not before we get to the end. Why don't we just keep going forward and follow the shoreline? We'll end up back at the tent anyway, and we'll have explored the whole island. At this point, we might as well."

Celia looked at me. "I don't know if that's a good idea." Regardless, we kept on walking in the same direction, east, toward the ocean, and the solitary light grew stronger through the trees as the sun faded. The forest itself was beautiful in its own way—tangled, gnarled, green, and lush—but so dense it was nearly impossible to walk through, especially in poor light, so we simply walked around it on the beach next to the water. On the other side, the island was once again bare except for dunes and sea oats, like the side we'd landed on.

We continued walking east, following the shoreline in search of the light. Before long, the house appeared, first a gray blur with a light, then an image growing larger and less blurred as we approached, and finally, a faded edifice rising in a clearing surrounded by tall, grassy dunes.

"I'll be *damned!*" Croom exclaimed.

"That's amazing!" I affirmed.

A ramshackle mansion with an ornately trimmed front porch, a central four-story Second Empire tower, assorted turrets, ornate chimneys, lightning rods, and a wood-shingled mansard roof stood before us in the gloom.

"It looks haunted," Jennie said. "It honestly does. '*Psycho*'."

"I don't believe in ghosts! Superstition!" Celia shot back. Then she said flatly, "Even so, I'm not going near it, especially since we assured the boatman we wouldn't. We did assure him. We did promise."

The sky grew darker still, and it began to drizzle. At this point we could have turned back, but we didn't because the house was near the far end of the island and Croom—and I—were determined to say we'd walked the entire length, from one tip to the other. About ten minutes later, as we reached the island's eastern end, the temperature plunged, and it started to rain. Behind us, we could see the light in the tower of the house, above the encircling dunes.

"We could stand on the porch if we had to," Croom suggested.

"But somebody lives there," I said.

"I'm not talking about going *in*—just standing on the porch."

Within minutes the sky was almost black. The rain fell harder until it was driving us forward, with beads so large we could feel them smack our faces and hands. As the temperature continued to drop, what had started as a breeze turned into a gusting wind.

The wind was blowing so hard, Jennie was nearly knocked over. Regaining her balance, she yelled, "What *is* this? A winter storm in March? A tropical storm? We've got to get out of this!"

Thunder and lightning were crashing all around us, and I clasped Celia's hand to pull her along. Though I thought she might be crying, I couldn't tell for sure. A monstrous jag of electricity lit up the sky in front of us, and we cowered as a clap of thunder exploded over our heads. Instinctively, we headed for the house.

Croom yelled, "Go for the porch!" As if there were an alternative. With the wind gusting ferociously and the rain obscuring our vision, it was difficult to move forward. As Croom and I pulled Celia and Jennie along behind us, I could feel Celia's hand trembling in mine.

We seemed to be attracting the lightning and thunder, blasting over our heads simultaneously. I couldn't believe we'd gotten ourselves into this. We had no choice: it was either get to the mansion or be struck by lightning.

Eventually, we reached the outer perimeter of the dunes surrounding the yard. Then, as we made our way over the dunes, we beheld *it* as it confronted *us*: a mansion in the pounding rain and whipping wind, a silhouette that appeared against the black sky with each new blast of flashbulb brilliance.

As we ran up the steps to the front porch, I crossed myself, taking three steps at a time, pulling Celia with my left hand. Once all four of us were on board the porch, I subtly made the sign of the cross again. To protect us? To keep the evil spirits away? As a reflex subbing for a prayer? I knew God and I weren't that close, and I figured He knew it, too; even so, in my mind, going through the motions seemed comforting somehow.

We stood on the porch huddled together, soaked and shivering. We could have continued like that, cold and huddling, with the rain soaking us in slanted sheets, but at one of the sidelights vertically flanking the front door, a face appeared.

5.

LOOSE LIPS

The door creaked partially open. Inside stood an old woman, stooped, wrinkled and white-haired, wearing a shawl and a faded yellow dress that fell to her calves.

"What are you doing on my porch?" Her voice creaked, like her door.

I spoke first. "We don't mean to bother you, but we had no other place to run to for shelter."

Celia was holding my hand, and when a jagged line of lightning lit up the sky and a blast of thunder split the air, she flinched.

"Even so, you can't stay here." She nudged the door toward us.

"We don't want to stay here," I told her. "But may we please just stand on your porch till it stops storming? Otherwise, we could be struck by lightning."

"It's not going to stop storming. Not tonight. This storm

won't pass till early morning."

I shivered and looked at Croom, Celia, and Jennie. As we stood there, the woman opened the door wide. "Well, you can come in."

She wasn't scary, I assured myself. Just old. But the combination of her and the house made the situation forbidding and creepy. The sky flashed bright again as another clap of thunder broke over our heads, and as we cringed, I sensed that the storm was wearing us down.

In the foyer, a massive staircase ran straight upstairs to a balcony fronting several closed doors. Beyond the staircase on the ground floor was a wide hall, with rooms that lay on either side of it. The ceilings looked to be fourteen feet high. Above our heads, a huge chandelier clinked unlit in the storm's sound waves.

After the old woman said, "I'll get you some blankets," she walked into an adjacent room, with a candlestick and chimney in hand. We heard her unbuckle the lid of a trunk, then heard it squeak open. A layer of dust covered everything, and the air smelled dank and musty. We were dripping water onto a faded Persian rug.

"I guess she's just an old lady," Jennie whispered, her long, blond hair, usually shimmering, now a wet, bedraggled mass about her face and down her back. "Not crazy or anything. You know, not dangerous. No one else here in the house but her, I guess." Her eyes, a little larger than normal, traveled upstairs to the balcony, to each closed door.

Croom took her hand and held it. Celia's eyes were big as she squeezed my arm. I took her hand and held it, then put my arm around her shoulders, pulling her close to me. Her brown hair, shoulder-length and normally perfectly waved, was now as wet and bedraggled as Jennie's.

When the woman returned, she was carrying two wool blankets that smelled of dust and mothballs. One she handed to Jennie, the other to Celia. "Wrap up in these. Cover your heads. I'll go get two more."

When she returned, she handed one blanket to Croom and one to me. By the light of her candle, I couldn't help but notice her eyes: they were narrow and as green as a cat's.

She said, "Follow me," and turned her back on us as we exchanged glances behind her. By now, it was black outside, and as she walked out of the room, she left us in darkness. We could see her shadowy form in the light of her candle waiting for us in the next room.

We followed her through the drawing room beyond the foyer, into the dining room with stacks of dusty books and papers, and into a backroom on the side of the house. A burgundy-colored, cushioned bench ran around two walls, behind which were tall Victorian windows framed in heavy, dark blue draperies. Apparently her den, the room smelled of mildew and faintly of urine. Dust coated everything. Cobwebs clung to the chandelier, another ornate arrangement, also unlit.

At a small table in the middle of the room, she lit a lantern next to a vase of cattails, then walked past me to sit on the bench, leaving in the air a faint odor, fishy as well as old. "I can't see the sea from this room," she said. "It's too low, and the dunes are too high. But from the tower, I can see it perfectly. It goes on forever. I have to get up there, though, and it's a long way. This is my den. If you stay wrapped up, you can sit down."

"Thank you," I said, sitting—and the others followed.

A small cathedral clock ticked on the back of a pump organ that sat against the wall opposite us. Celia huddled against me, comforting me as well as herself. On our left, Jennie cuddled up with Croom.

The old woman sat perpendicular to them. "I don't keep cats in here. They used to be in here a long time ago, but now they like to be outside. They eat birds, sandpipers, gulls. And fish. I don't keep rats here—none at all. I don't like them." She began to cough. Then she stood up and walked out, leaving us in near darkness again.

"This is screwed up," Croom said. "I don't think we ought to be here. I'm getting some bad vibes. Something bad could happen."

"Like what?" I whispered.

"Like anything."

"What did she mean," Celia whispered, "no rats? If I see a rat, I'll start screaming. I mean it—I really will. Especially here in the dark. I'll scream; then I'll have a heart attack and drop over dead right here in front of everybody. I'm not kidding; you will see a heart attack."

We heard the old woman coughing in the next room. When she stopped, she returned to the den all stooped over with her candlestick in hand. "My name is Miss Smiley," she said as she sat down again to our left on the bench perpendicular to us.

"I'm Matt."

"I'm Celia." As she addressed our host for the first time, she gulped. Then she clutched the wool blanket at her neck with her right hand, her left hand still in mine.

"I'm Jennie."

"Croom."

"You're not supposed to be here," she said bluntly. "Nobody comes to this island. Not in thirty years. What do you want?"

"We don't want anything," I assured her. "Nothing at all." Then, my upbringing of good manners not forsaking me, I added, "We're sorry for imposing on you like this. We apologize. It was an accident. We were just looking for shelter—anything to get out of the lightning and rain."

"How did you get here? Well—I know. And I'm bothered by it. He shouldn't have brought you. He never brings anybody but himself."

"He did tell us not to come near the house," Celia offered. "He didn't think we would. *We* didn't think we would: we had no intention. It was the storm."

"But you *did* come," she snapped, a bit rudely, I thought. Lightning crackled against the windows as rain pelted the panes. Shadows flashed against the walls. "I'd offer you something to eat, but there's not enough. You can stay till the storm passes; then you have to go."

I wondered which would be worse—staying here all night or spending it outside in that torrent with cold wind and lightning.

Miss Smiley stood up from the window bench, walked to the table, picked up the lantern, and set it on the back of the organ. Taking a seat, she began pumping her feet up and down, up and down on the pedals. Then she began to play a cacophony of carnival music in the beat of a funeral dirge. Celia, the pianist, groaned at the back of her throat while the rest of us looked at the old woman, then at each other, shaking our heads slightly.

After a while, she stopped playing and turned her head, speaking to us over her shoulder. "I'm hungry. I haven't had my supper. You all stay here. Don't move. There aren't any cats in here. No rats, either."

She stood up slowly, steadying herself, and walked out of the room. We could do nothing but watch, amazed by the whole scene.

After a few minutes, she returned carrying two candlesticks, one in each hand. She set one on the small table in the middle of the room next to the cattails where the lantern had been. Then she walked out of the room again, carrying the other. The clock, our only company besides the storm, ticked off the minutes, but she did not return. Fifteen minutes passed. Then another quarter hour, which seemed like forever. We had no idea what to do, and none of us wanted to go snooping around in the dark for her: there was no telling *what* creatures might be lurking inside the house.

When she finally returned, shortly past nine, she was carrying her candlestick in one hand, a plate of beans and some sort of cooked meat in the other. I was hungry—and lightheaded—and as my head began to ache, I imagined hearing something in the kitchen, though the old woman was with us in the den. She walked over and stood in front of me, peering. "I've always appreciated good manners," she said.

Normally, I'd have appreciated the compliment, but at that moment, I had more important concerns. Low blood sugar, Celia having a heart attack, the four of us never seeing civilization again, et cetera.

After handing off the plate, our host shuffled back to the

kitchen, eventually making three more trips, each time carrying one plate until she'd served each one of us. We looked at our supper in silence. "Thank you," I finally said.

Then she made four more trips, returning each time with a half-filled glass of water so that each one of us had one. Little particles floated about in the liquid, then settled to the bottom.

We sat in silence as she retook her seat on the bench across from us. "I changed my mind about your eating. I need to eat at night, and I know you all must, too. This late, you're bound to be hungry. Since I already ate something in the kitchen, I wanted to give you some of it."

We didn't respond, and after a moment, she said, "Mr. Gaskill is my cousin—my first cousin. And my friend. I don't understand why he brought you here. I've lived alone on this island for over thirty years. No one comes here. Just him. He brings the food. If I run low, the cats share with me."

Celia looked down at her plate and groaned. I hoped she wasn't going to be sick.

"The cats can go in and out of the basement," the old woman continued. "Sometimes I feed them—sometimes they feed me. We help each other."

Celia moaned. Jennie put her hand to her mouth. "We should leave," I said. I set the plate on the seat between Jennie and me and set the glass on the floor at my feet and stood up.

Outside, the storm was still raging. A near-hurricane, maybe. The wind seemed fierce enough to take the roof off the house and perhaps knock out the windows. Though the windows were closed, the curtains and draperies to either side fluttered in and out like dark ghosts. In spite of everything, I wanted Miss

Smiley to ask us to stay. We could easily get lost—or struck dead—trying to find our way back, and there was nothing to go back to. Without a doubt, our tent was long gone out to sea.

She began to cough. I hesitated, then got up and stood by her until she stopped.

In a scratchy voice, she said, "You can sit down. I'm not well, but I can still get out some. I go out and dig around on the beach."

Celia bowed her head, looking at her plate, and set it on the seat. As I sat down beside her again, she took my hand and held it in hers.

"I haven't been feeling well for quite some time. Months—maybe a year or more. I can't see a doctor. No one comes here, not since the early 40s. Only Roger. And he shouldn't have brought you. If you don't want to eat, it's okay."

Because we didn't know what to say, we said nothing.

"I can tell about you children from your palms. Even if you don't talk to me, I can tell." She got up slowly, walked into the dining room, and began dragging a chair from the table into the den. I looked at Celia, then got up and carried it for her.

"There," she said, nodding at the little table in the middle of the room with the candlestick she'd set on it next to the vase of cattails. I set the chair at one end of the table. "Get another one," she said. A little bossy, I thought.

Croom got up and brought another chair to the table as she nodded, "Other side." Then she sat back down on the bench.

"Daddy experimented only on animals. Just small animals—rats and cats—that's all."

I looked at her quizzically—then at Croom, Jennie, and

Celia.

"No humans. Only the Nazis did that. Not Daddy."

I cocked my head, eyes wide.

"That's why there are all these cats on the island. Some of them have deformities they inherited. Some of their deformities come from inbreeding. He did research—here on the island, underneath the house—on rats and cats. Since you're here, would you like me to show you what's downstairs?" She started to get up.

Celia squeezed my hand. "No!" she blurted out.

The old woman turned and looked at Celia and sat back down. "Some of the equipment is still down there—the cages, I mean things like that. A few things the government didn't confiscate. They took the medical stuff, all his equipment. His records. The transmitter. They came in and exterminated the rats in '43. They killed the worst cats, but not all of them. That's why their descendants still run loose on the island.

"Daddy was a genius," she said. A burst of thunder broke over us, and a streak of lightning lit up the room like the flash of a photographer's bulb. Celia screamed and jumped off the bench.

"It struck us," Miss Smiley said. "The tower. That happens in these storms. The tower's the highest point on the island. That's why there are all those lightning rods on the house. He signaled from up there—a Fresnel lens. Still there."

"So *that's* why we could see the light," Croom said.

She looked at him. "What you saw, my boy, was nothing compared to its ultimate capacity—just a glimmer. With a generator, it was a great signal—in code—to ships. Now, it just reflects a kerosene lamp. If I could, I'd light it every night like I used to—for my father. That's not so easy anymore, though, even though Roger Gaskill does bring me kerosene."

She coughed repeatedly, then settled down.

"Daddy didn't just signal. He also used boats. It could be done, especially in the fog. I didn't know he was doing it. I was thirty then, but I had no idea. Signals and boats. Well, he did get caught."

"Caught?" Croom echoed.

"Caught," she replied. "Like a rat in a trap. He used to be at Duke. At the medical school."

Jennie, the pre-med student, gasped.

"He was one of the first doctors there, back when they were setting up the medical school in the thirties. They did a lot of lobotomies, thanks to Daddy. He did most of them; then it went out of style. Some people thought they terminated him, but that's not true. He quit."

"*Lobotomies*!" Jennie exclaimed.

"Of course!" she snapped. "But what he really wanted to do was animal research—his way. They put too many restrictions on what he could think, what he could do. He was a free spirit, a free thinker. Dr. Adolphus Zeno Smiley—you've heard of him? Or maybe not. Before he left the medical school, there was even a building named after him. A big, imposing one. Gothic. You couldn't miss it."

"I don't know of a building . . ." Jennie began. Then she stopped.

"Later, there *wasn't* a building named after him," Miss Smiley said.

She stood up slowly and unsteadily. I jumped up and offered

her my arm—as she blew out her candle, still on the bench—and helped her as she walked over to the little table with the cattails. She handed the vase to me and nodded toward the organ. "Set them there."

I walked over and set the vase down beside the lantern. As I rejoined Celia, Miss Smiley sat down in the chair to our right side of the little table, the candlelight illuminating her pale, wrinkled face and white hair.

"He did get caught," she said again. "That's why they sometimes call this island Traitor Island."

"*Traitor*?" Croom repeated. "Is that actually what you're talking about?"

She looked at Croom, ignoring him. "A lot of new people on the mainland who don't know any better think the natives are saying 'Traysure.' But it has nothing to do with Blackbeard. Or the other pirates who operated in these waters. The only thing you're going to find buried on this island is bones."

We exchanged glances; then Croom asked, "But what do you mean, *traitor*?"

"U boats."

"*U boats*!" I blurted out.

"Are you sh—kidding me?" Croom exclaimed.

She looked at him. "It wasn't as hard to get away with as you might think. The government even helped—unwittingly. 'Loose lips sink ships.'"

"I've heard of that," Celia said. "I've read about it."

Miss Smiley turned her tired eyes and face on Celia. "So you read. That's good. Good Americans—and the Outer Bankers were—didn't talk about all the ships being sunk by the Germans off their coast. And there were hundreds of them. If you didn't talk about the war here on the North Carolina coast, it didn't seem exactly like there was a war here."

"But your father," Jennie protested. "Your father, a professor at Duke, was . . . a . . . *traitor*?"

Silence.

Finally, Celia said, maybe partially to change the subject, "I've seen those maps of the Graveyard of the Atlantic in gift shops. They've mapped hundreds of Allied ships sunk off the coast here by the Germans in World War II—each ship by name, where it was sunk, in what year."

The old woman looked at her, and through her, off into the distance and into the past, as a lingering silence ensued. Then she looked to the side, away from us. "1942. It began early that year, January, right after the surprise attack on Pearl Harbor. Germany followed their ally Japan with a surprise attack off the coast here. I remember."

She paused and looked at us again. "So many ships sank, oil flowed onto the beach. The cats got in it and tracked it inside. It was a mess." She glanced at the Oriental rug beneath her feet, her eyes darting about the floor. Then her eyes returned to us. "At Pearl Harbor, nearly twenty-five hundred lives were lost. Off the coast here, thousands of lives were also lost and, yes, hundreds of ships sunk. Everybody knows about the first attack, but the attack here was kept quiet. I'm telling you kids, though."

For a few moments, we sat silent before Jennie quietly asked, "But your father, a doctor . . . he was involved in it . . . for the wrong side?"

"It was 'the Second Happy Time'—that's what Germany

called it."

We looked at each other quizzically.

"'Loose lips sink ships,'" she repeated. "Daddy was a free spirit. A free thinker. He had a different point of view—that's all. But he did get caught."

A loud clap of thunder exploded overhead, shaking us as the room lit up in a flash of light. We were jolted, then tried to relax as the room went dark again.

"I've endured these storms for over thirty years."

In the light of the flickering candle, her face looked extremely fatigued and unwell. She sighed deeply. "Daddy bought the island in 1939, but after he was found out and convicted, the government confiscated it, except for the house and the land under it. I don't think it's fair. He didn't get to live here long, and it cost him a great amount of money to build this house. Nobody wanted to touch Second Empire architecture in the thirties, and they had to bring everything here on barges."

"That's how they built the Victorian lighthouse keepers' house at Currituck," Croom informed us. "They precut and labeled the parts on the mainland, then brought them to the island by tugboat and barge and assembled them on site."

"At that time, he was at his peak, a wealthy man," she continued. "This was his life's reward—his castle—on his own private island. You kids should never have crossed the moat. Don't say you weren't warned."

"But it's government property—you said so yourself," Croom protested.

"It's not a park!" she barked back. "It's not hospitable. It's my own private prison. No one ever comes to this island. No one but Roger Gaskill.

"When the government took everything we had, they left the house and land under it for me since I had no place else to go and hadn't known anything about my father's work. He died in prison.

"I can tell fortunes," she said. "I can. I can tell my own. I told my father his. I've told my cats'. I can tell yours by reading your palms."

I thought about Cindy Peppercorn and what she used to say when we were in high school: "There are certain people who know the future, and if you can find them, they can tell you what it is. Then maybe you can prevent something bad from happening. Or maybe you can't. In that case, maybe, you might not *want* to know what is going to happen." Cindy also said, "But you have to be careful because these people may be for real or they may not be, and it may be hard to tell the difference."

As I looked at Miss Smiley's ghostly face above the candle, I shuddered. Wasn't it true that only God knows the future, because he knows everything? No mere mortal can see future events—wasn't that true? Sure, there were prophets in the Old Testament, but obviously she wasn't a prophet, and we weren't living in Old Testament times, anyway.

"I don't know *how* I can tell fortunes—I just learned on my own. I said I would live by myself for over thirty years on a deserted island—and I have. I have a prediction for my cousin, and it's going to come true very soon. I've given myself a prediction for me—and that prediction is going to come true this very evening. I can tell you kids' fortunes, too. That's my gift. I'll start with the young ladies."

Squeezing my hand, Celia winced and shook her head no.

Miss Smiley looked at Jennie. "I'll tell the girl with the fair hair her fortune first."

Croom grabbed Jennie's hand to his side, but she pulled it away.

"Come here," Miss Smiley said to her.

"Don't!" Croom said.

"Don't!" Celia and I echoed at the same time. But Jennie stood up, walked over to the empty chair, and sat down.

I didn't feel good about this—my conscience said it was wrong: it didn't seem "Christian" or something—but Jennie wasn't one to take orders. Never had been—and if *her* conscience was telling her, "No, don't do it!," she wasn't listening; she'd already sat down with the old woman. So what was I—or Croom or Celia—supposed to do?

6.

MISS SMILEY'S FORTUNE

Miss Smiley pushed the candle to her right and reached across the table for Jennie's right hand. Holding it in her own, with her thumb in Jennie's palm, she shook Jennie's hand up and down, then removed her thumb and inspected Jennie's palm, tracing its lines with the crooked index finger of her left hand. The old lady's hand was gnarled and rough and covered with spots.

Jennie's was soft and pink and lightly freckled on top. The light of the candle flickered in their faces—Jennie's young and beautiful, Miss Smiley's tired and sickly. The clock on the organ ticked off the seconds as the lantern danced shadows on the wall.

Finally, Miss Smiley spoke. "You will travel the four corners of the earth. You will be rich and famous and adored here and abroad, but luckless in love. You will win, and you will lose. You'll lose someone you love. Someone you deeply trust will betray you." She looked around the room as she said this. "Your mind will be poisoned with thoughts you can't control. You will show impulsive temper. You'll suffer until you wake up."

Then silence, so Jennie assumed it was over and withdrew her hand. She moved to get up, but Miss Smiley took her hand again. "And," she said, tracing Jennie's palm with her crooked finger, "something else: You will see murder."

Gasping, Jennie jerked her hand away, pushed the chair back quickly and stood up. Her shoulders were scrunched up at the neck. Her blanket had fallen to the floor; she picked it up and darted back to her seat beside Croom, a scowl on her face.

Miss Smiley looked at Croom. "Now you, the dark one who likes to talk."

"Don't do it!" Jennie blurted out. He hesitated, but no doubt felt an obligation after his girlfriend went before him.

He left his blanket on the bench, walked over and sat down. She took Croom's hand in the same way, first shaking it, held with her thumb, then traced the palm with her left index finger.

After several moments, she said, "You will be rich, but not as famous as the girl. You will be impulsive and show temper, but not as extreme. You'll be luckless in love until you settle down. You will be a loyal friend, but someone will betray you." Again, she looked around the room. Then she returned her eyes to Croom. "You will uncover a deeply hidden secret."

She paused, then added in an ominous voice, "A deep. And dark. Secret." Frowning, Croom withdrew his hand and pushed back his chair. "And," she said, pointing her crooked, left index finger at him, "you, too, will see murder." As he got up and rejoined Jennie on the bench, I saw his anxiety.

Next, Miss Smiley looked at me. I started to get up, not

because I wanted to, but because it only seemed fair considering two of us had already gone.

What was God thinking about all of this? I doubted God *liked* our doing this sort of thing; on the other hand, I didn't exactly feel like the Devil was leading us into it. It was more a matter of feeling the way I'd felt as a kid, taking my first dive off the high board as everyone watched: I had to do it because everyone else had.

Celia clutched my hand as if to glue it to the cushion, but I pulled it free and stood up. The bottom line was that it was my turn, and this crystal ball stuff—best viewed as a crock of superstitious nonsense—was not to be taken seriously.

I sat down at the table across from the old woman at the table. She took my hand first, giving the peculiar handshake, weak and clammy—then turned my hand over and around in her own. Her fingers were crooked and her long yellow nails curved downward like claws. She studied my face, her green eyes boring into mine. My breathing became conscious and irregular, my hand clammy like hers as she held it. For some reason, she waited longer before she spoke than she had with Jennie and Croom. Was this showmanship—or was she torturing me? My heart began to pound.

"You, my dear boy, tall and fair, you with the reserved manner and manners—you, who fancy yourself a good soul but who fear you are not—you, who, after all, are sitting with *me* now, searching for direction and answers—you will know love, and you will admire. You will win and taste victory." I started to get up, but she pulled my hand to keep me seated. "Not yet."

Then, as she'd done before, she looked around at the other

three and said, "You will be betrayed by someone you deeply trust. And you will lose. Tragically, you will lose a dear friend and suffer deeply because of it. Your mind will be haunted by thoughts you can't control. You will seek and seek. You will continue to search and search, yet not find. Then finally, you will—where you never expected." Having said this, she let go of my hand and my eyes. As I stood up and turned to Celia, I determined that, one, Celia would not do this and, two, we would leave now, storm or no storm. Things had gone too far.

"And one other thing," Miss Smiley said to my back, her tone of voice sharp. I turned and regarded her face in the candlelight. "You, too, will see murder." I turned back to Celia and threw my blanket onto the bench beside her. She fought for air, her hand spread open across her chest.

"Let's get out of here!" I said. She stood up and walked to me. I took her hand to leave—but pulling her hand away, she stepped across my path, tears welling in her eyes, and sat down at the table. I stood behind her chair, my hands on her shoulders.

"I can't think with you there," Miss Smiley said. "Go sit down." Then she began to cough.

Celia glanced at me over her shoulder, signaling me to retreat to the bench. Miss Smiley's coughing, apparently painful, went on a while longer before she finally regained her composure.

The delay only made it worse, and Celia closed her eyes as she offered the old woman her hand. But Miss Smiley said, "Open your eyes, child; I must see your soul, as well as your palm."

As Celia complied, a tear coursed down her cheek. Miss Smiley went through the same procedure: the weird handshake, the inspection of her hand, tracing the lines of her palm. Finally, she said, "You will marry someone you love right now. That person is in this room. You'll be rich but troubled in love until you settle down. You'll be impulsive and lose your temper. You will win, and you will be admired. You will be faithful and show strength in time of crisis." She looked around the room. "But you will be betrayed by someone you deeply trust, and you will see murder."

Before Celia could move to get up, the old woman let go of her hand. Then, pushing her chair back from the table and standing up, she announced, "Yours was the last fortune I will ever tell." Celia didn't move, so I got up, tugged at her chair, and we both returned and sat on the bench.

"It's all right that you didn't eat the food," our host said as she surveyed the four of us, silent and still in front of her, "even though I don't have much, and I offered it to you out of kindness. Even though you showed up on my front porch as an act of your own free will. It was your willfulness that made you do this, even though you were told not to—and you promised you wouldn't. Despite all that, even though you've refused my hospitality, I'm not offended. I have friends."

She walked out of the room again, carrying the candlestick from the table. But this time, she continued to talk to us. "I have friends," she repeated loudly enough for us to hear. We heard her open a door. Some minutes later, she came back in and walked over to us.

"Well, maybe it's not all right that you didn't eat the food. After all, it's a sin to waste." She stepped in front of Celia and reached for her plate. Celia handed it to her.

"I can't waste this food. My friends wouldn't like it, and

neither would I. I'm still a little hungry. Faint. I feel quite unwell." Carrying the plate, she sat back down at the table across from us. She picked up some meat with her claws, ate it, then hesitated. A strange expression came over her face, and it began to lose what little color it had had. Then it reddened.

As we watched, she stood, holding the plate with both hands and began to teeter back and forth. A great wave of apprehension rolled over me—a terrible, helpless feeling of anxiety. I sensed that something evil was about to occur, but I felt utterly powerless to prevent it. She raised another bite to her lips, ate again, and started coughing, her face contorted with pain.

"Who will help me?" she whispered—loudly enough that everyone of us heard. As she coughed again, we sat as if frozen in place, watching, not doing. When the coughing stopped, she relaxed her grip, the plate falling to the floor. Her teetering turned into stumbling forward, she reached out, apparently for me. She was about to say something but didn't.

She clutched my arm to stay afoot, and I felt her claws in my scalp as she yanked my head toward her, nearly pulling me off the bench. I stood up to steady her, but she collapsed in my arms. As I laid her on the floor as gently as I could, Celia came over and stood beside me. The old woman's face and lips were purplish red. My mouth and eyes agape, I stared at her purple face, transfixed.

Celia, Croom, and I knelt beside her. First checking for a pulse, I put my hands on her chest and began the compressions, one hundred per minute. I started to breathe into her mouth but changed my mind. Taking her hand, I looked up at Jennie, still standing. I began compressions again, one hundred per minute.

I checked her wrist again, and again looked at Jennie, who did nothing.

I stared at the old woman's face, at her eyes—a cat's eyes, an animal struck by a car and lying in the road—eyes half-closed, glazing over—dead, or dying. I looked at her mouth, her purplish-red lips, old and wrinkled. She smelled salty and musty, unclean. Blood was dripping down the side of her mouth, down her cheek, and onto the floor. I saw all those signs, yet I could think of nothing more to do than hold her hand, trying to comfort her, hoping for a miracle, Celia close beside me.

I looked at each of my friends' faces in the flickering light. First Jennie, still standing, expressionless. Then Croom, kneeling, intent. Then Celia, close by my side. And last, I looked at Miss Smiley, bidding her farewell. Then, hearing a slightly hoarse alto voice at the door to the kitchen, I turned. My heart stopped. Moving to check for a pulse once more, a final time, I let go of her wrist as one cat, then another crept low over the threshold into the room.

7.

ROMILAR

Cindy Peppercorn had been a friend of mine from junior high school and into my freshman year of college when we had a falling out. In junior high, I played on the basketball team, as did her next-door neighbor, and he introduced us. She was a year ahead of me in school.

She, Croom, and I used to pal around together—go to the lake and ski, and ride around in her Volkswagen Beetle.

She looked kind of like Peppermint Patty, the character in *Peanuts*—red hair, freckles—and while I was on-and-off-again in love with Jennie Boston till Celia came along in college, Cindy had never been anything to me but a pal-around buddy. I thought she was funny, and I appreciated what I thought was an uncomplicated relationship. Well, it turned out that I was wrong about the nature of our friendship. Unbeknownst to me, she was actually in love with me.

By no means was I in love with her, but she did make me

laugh—kind of like Croom. But I also found her interesting because she read a lot of books and developed a different way to look at things. Though some people thought she was trying to impress them by talking about what she'd learned from books no one else had read, I listened. For example, she had a theory about the history of civilization and numbers. She said the Black Death broke out in Europe in the 1300s because 13 is an unlucky number. It was predetermined, not accidental.

"And it was no accident," Cindy told me, "that Rome was founded around 500 B.C., and the Roman Republic lasted five hundred years, till Jesus was born. Then the Roman Empire replaced the Republic and lasted another five hundred years, till around 500 A.D. And," she told me, "it was no accident that the Eastern Empire lasted another one thousand years, falling around 1500."

She could cite all types of numbers in history that had predetermined significance. "Look at the Holy Roman Empire," she said. "The Pope crowned Charlemagne Emperor in 800, and the Empire lasted a thousand years. Napoleon and the French dissolved it in 1806."

She said it was no accident that the Holocaust of World War Il occurred so near the turn of the millennium. I wondered if history and life are predetermined by an all-powerful, all-knowing God. Or does it play out with a lot of uncontrolled luck? And if it's the former, how could God be all-loving and let something like the Holocaust occur? On the other hand, if evil and tragedy occurred by happenstance, not controlled by God, then how could He be all-powerful? Or—could the universe be ruled by a combination of God's sovereignty and luck? Was that even possible?

Cindy knew a lot, and she liked to talk about it, but even she didn't know the answers to some of my questions. She mostly liked to expound on the things she had thought through. I listened as she expounded on her cosmic theories, and I listened as she talked about her older brother. Cindy was an only child because one winter night Sim walked out into the snow barefoot and caught pneumonia. This happened after she had dreamed about him dying, but she didn't know what to do to protect him, so she didn't do anything. She was twelve when he died, and he was fifteen. He was a sleepwalker and was out in the snow for hours wandering around. His death was really weird because she'd dreamed about it beforehand and because her parents would never talk about it. This burdened her with sadness and guilt.

There was something more to it that she confessed to me: she believed she had another dimension, and since she had it, she *should* have prevented her brother's death.

I remember she said this about "sixth-sense" people: "There are certain people who can tell you about the future because the future is already out there. If you could find one of those people, or if one of them found you, she could tell you the future. But you might not want to know it. Beware of them because they might tell you something about the future that you'd rather not know. And you might be able to act on the knowledge—and make the outcome better—or maybe not. And," she said, "you might not be able to tell a fraud from a real sixth-sense person."

I guess that had been my warning, of sorts, regarding what happened to the four of us on the Isle of Cats. Too bad it didn't prevent anything. I guess that fateful night we followed the wrong influence—a dark one. When Cindy and I were still friends, I wasn't just someone she could talk to, a sympathetic ear; I was also someone with whom she could pal around and occasionally do something really off-the-wall.

There was the Train Game. Romilar.

I could tell this little story from my point of view, but Cindy Peppercorn never liked someone speaking for her and, after all, it's really her story and her game. She can tell it best:

"Let's do it, Cindy," Matt says to me. There's that twinkle in his dark blue eyes. He puts the bottle in his pants pocket. It's night, and the tracks are downtown. I drive. I have a little green VW, a '67 my dad gave me earlier this summer when I turned sixteen. We don't go to the tracks right downtown; we go a few miles out, where we can park in an empty lot at a furniture factory.

Truthfully, I think Matt's cute. He's kind of tough-looking in a gentle sort of way and has big, dark, soulful blue eyes. He's funny and laughs a lot in a deep laugh. I don't know what he thinks about me, except that we're friends. He's supposedly in love with Jennie Boston, but I refuse to believe it, and I haven't been above stretching the truth now and again to help keep Matt and her apart. It's for their own good: they're not meant to be together. But mostly, it's for my own good: I have plans for Matt and me. We'll get there. We sure will. Wedding bells.

Right now, we're into the Train Game. Romilar. I love trains, and so does he. I love the sound they make and the thought that they are always moving, going someplace far from here.

We get out of the car. Down the track, there's a light near

the street, but here there's no light except for a few stars. It's a black summer night, and the cicadas are chirping so loudly they could wake an old lady's corpse.

Matt pulls the bottle out of his pants pocket. He hands the bottle to me, and I take a big gulp. I know my mother likes the alcohol in this cough medicine; that's why she keeps it on hand in her bathroom closet. Then I hand the bottle back to Matt.

The night air is humid. I slap a mosquito on my leg and take another swig. Then Matt. Then me again.

We're halfway through the bottle when we hear the train rumbling off in the distance.

"Romilar for two Romanovs!" Matt finally says.

"Romilar for two Romanovs!" I say back. "Our toast."

My head swims. My stomach is queasy. Time to sit down. We sit on the ground like Indians, facing each other beside the track. The rumbling of the train is faint, away down the track, but we know it's only a matter of time. We're two-thirds through the bottle. "Now up!" Matt exclaims. We stand. We sway. I feel sick to my stomach like I've been in an airplane through a storm, in a boat on a rough sea, or on the parachute ride at the fair, right after the Ferris wheel. I feel sick in my head, too.

We can see the train now, coming down the track. It's black as the night—with a white eye.

"Now sit!" I command. We fall to the ground, side by side, sitting, Matt next to the track, facing the train, me, leaning on his shoulder.

Another swig each. Then another and another. The train wails—loudly as it passes through a crossing. The cicadas are drowned out while it wails. I feel the vibrations beneath me. My head is spinning. I feel like I'm connected to something bigger than myself. I rock gently back and forth.

"Now down!" Matt says. Matt lies down with his feet toward the train and his head away from it, so he can see it when it approaches. I lie down next to the track with my head against his and my feet stretched in front of me. Blind side for me.

The train is getting closer.

He takes a swig then hands the bottle to me over his head. I take the last swig and smash the bottle on the track. I'm thinking, *Romilar for a Romanov*! but I don't say it: my heart's pounding, and the train is roaring toward us.

It howls in the black night, blocking out all other sound. The ground rumbles beneath us, shaking the stars overhead. My heart thumps against my chest, and I clutch the grass and earth beside me. My feet and toes curl up. My right arm stays flush against my side, next to the gravel and ties. Near panic—and excitement—seize me, as a fit of nausea rolls over in a wave. I struggle not to vomit.

The train rushes past in a huge rumbling wave, the sides of the cars towering above us, blowing a fierce wind, the track heaving up and down, up and down, up and down. I feel my head exploding.

I do think of dying. I think of Matt and wonder what he's thinking. This is the train ride. This is the game and the trip. The rest of life does not exist as the train swooshes by us—nothing exists but the train itself. The seconds tick by—and the minutes—counted off by the thumping in my chest and the click-clacking of the rails. The whole earth trembles, then I see the caboose, a white light on its back porch.

I do think of dying. But now this is living!

I feel Matt's head move against mine, and I like that feeling: his head against mine as he sits up. I sit up, too. Matt begins to laugh. Then I do. But he's not smiling. I smile. Then he's smiling.

"What a rush!" he says.

"What a trip!"

Then we stand up. He's so tall. I'm reeling. He puts his arm around my shoulder for support. We don't do anything. We're mostly just friends. We get back in my car and drive around town for a while.

. . .

8.

MOMENTS IN THE CHAPEL

Well, that's Romilar, the Train Game, in Cindy's own words, and it helps explain how she saw me, which was different from the way I saw her. Funny how two people can seem to be connected in a relationship and yet be disconnected in reality.

Anyway, freshman year of college, Croom and I went to visit her, a sophomore, at Meredith College in Raleigh, and I ended up falling for Celia, who lived in the same dorm and who was playing the piano in the parlor when Croom and I walked in to get Cindy.

When I saw Celia there at the piano, apparently struggling to keep a lid on her temper as she made the same mistake over and over again, I thought, "frustrated, irritated, but gorgeous." Beautiful brown, shoulder-length hair, big brown eyes, beautiful face. Gorgeous girl. She could have stood in for Natalie Wood in *Splendor in the Grass*. I was in love.

It was love at first sight—or at least infatuation at first sight. I walked straight up to her as she played her Beethoven and complimented her on her piano playing, but I was really thinking, "Wow! You've got the most beautiful brown eyes. The most beautiful smile. Luscious lips."

"I'll never be able to play!" she exclaimed.

"No," I said. "You will! You have talent. But you have to have faith." I knew this to be true, even in those times that I might be lacking in faith myself. "You have to believe. Then you'll succeed—I promise." She looked at me as if she would burst into tears. Then she managed to smile, first wanly, then warmly.

Croom and I, with Celia and her roommate, ended up walking out of the dorm together that night for an impromptu hamburger downtown, leaving Cindy alone in the dorm. We'd asked her repeatedly to go with us, but she refused. For walking out on her that night, choosing Celia over her, Cindy's hated me ever since. And never spoken to me again.

I ended up marrying Celia, and I know that it was the best thing that ever happened to me. It had to have been God's plan for me to walk into Cindy's dorm and see Celia struggling with the *Moonlight Sonata*. Surely, anything that happens in Life that's that good—that fortunate—cannot be ascribed to mere Chance or Luck? Can it?

Some things may be luck, some not. For example, I didn't think it was luck that I was sitting on the front row pew in this little chapel—unadorned, interfaith—at the North Carolina General Assembly right now: Surely my being here had something to do with my own actions and God. Right now, I was alone.

A simple white altar—basically a cabinet—stood in front

of me on a raised platform, a simple wooden cross on top of it, a Bible opened up in front of the cross. If only life were as simple as all that! I come here several times a week, seeking answers, hopefully simple ones, because outside this room in the Legislative Building and beyond, life seemed anything but simple. Besides complicated, life seemed to be moving very fast.

It was 1981, seven years after the Four of us went to the Isle of Cats, and a lot had happened since then. I graduated from law school, got married, had a child. Last year, I was elected to the North Carolina House of Representatives, which was why I was here at the General Assembly. At the moment, I was availing myself of some quiet time between committee meetings.

Somehow, after that trip to the Isle of Cats, Celia and I bonded closely, continuing to date throughout our senior year. Then we both went to law school—Duke for me, UNC for her—graduating three years later. That same year, 1977, we were married, at twenty-five. We were celebrating our fourth anniversary this year.

Hard to believe we'd been married over three years. It seemed like yesterday that I stood in front of the altar of Celia's church in Winston-Salem facing hundreds of people, watching her walk down the aisle on her father's arm—to me—in a white gown and veil and train. I'd never seen anyone so beautiful. I was marrying a princess. That scene seemed now like a dream, hardly real. I closed my eyes to pray, but all that filled my head in this quiet room was a rush of thoughts and images.

The girl I was about to marry was so radiant that when she walked past, the people on the ends of the aisles gasped. The church was packed, and I was taking part in a storybook wedding: I was Prince Charming—or a prince of some sort—marrying a princess of the realm, the King's daughter.

The church was a colonial-style colossus, built mostly by Celia's grandfather and four other plutocratic families, as home to an Anglican congregation. Despite the pomp and ceremony, the Nightingales were grounded in old-fashioned American values. I was impressed that a family with so much money could be so down-to-earth. Mr. Nightingale faithfully taught an adult Sunday school class. I felt like I was marrying into a family of both societal and spiritual giants.

Not only was everyone in Winston-Salem and Hickory there, so were people from all over the state. The Governor and Lieutenant Governor, as well as one former Governor, one of North Carolina's two United States Senators, the district Congressman, all the local members of the General Assembly. Even more prominently represented was the business community. My parents had a lot of friends and connections, but the Nightingales had even more. And a much bigger family. We were a big deal in Hickory, but William and Angela Nightingale were a big deal in Winston-Salem, a much bigger city, and their name was prominently displayed throughout the community—Nightingale Planetarium, Nightingale Boulevard, Nightingale Performing Arts Center, et cetera.

In the family church that evening, they were carrying on a family tradition. Celia could take me around the city and say, "That's the warehouse my great-great grandfather built right after the Civil War for one of his first companies. And over there is the library my grandfather endowed." Nightingale Global Transport trucks were everywhere, reminders of her family's ubiquitous presence.

It was almost daunting to marry into a family like Celia's, even though I liked them because they were down-to-earth, gracious people, not stiff by nature. Angela, her mother, was an old-school, genteel Southern lady who was always supportive of me—and liked me. William, her father, clearly liked me, too. And they liked my parents and family. I couldn't have asked for better in-laws.

I also liked her brothers. William, Jr.—Bill—was the oldest. He and his wife Margaret were the heirs apparent, and they acted like it, maintaining a reserved, formal bearing. The middle brother, Daniel—Dan—was countrified, with glasses that slid down his nose and a folksy personality and sense of humor, giving the impression that he wasn't too smart. What people found out, when they spent time with him, was that he was brilliant.

The youngest brother, Robert—short, paunchy, and swarthy—didn't look like he belonged in the family. I liked all three of her brothers for different reasons—Bill for his sense of place, Dan for his creativity and unpretentious brains, and Robert for his lighthearted, quick wit.

Every time I saw Robert, he wanted to give or buy me a drink. The first thing he ever said to me was, "Anybody from a place called Hickory is bound to be a drinker." The next thing he said was, "Even if you don't drink now, after you marry my little sister, you'll have to." Then he confided, "Don't ever make her *really* mad. She's got a whale of a temper."

For her part, Celia rarely drank anything. Occasionally a glass of wine. And I'd never seen her lose her temper. "Her head is screwed on right, all right," my father said. "She has it together." I opened my eyes when I thought of my father: he was so pleased that I married Celia. And he was so proud when I won the election. Then I closed my eyes again, once more trying to pray. But all I could do was play host to another rush of thoughts.

Celia had given up the piano. I loved listening to her play, and I liked the thought of being married to a pianist, someone who could play a sonata or a concerto. The Nightingales had a grand piano in their music room, as did my parents in their recreation room at Stately Oaks, and Angela played well, wanting her only daughter to do the same. But as it turned out, Miss Smiley had affected Celia. After that trip, on some days when she sat down to play, all she could picture was the old woman sitting down at the organ to pump out her own funeral dirge run amok. There were weeks when this happened all too often.

Celia wasn't fond of funerals—who is? So it took her back a little when she first learned that Stately Oaks was across the street from a cemetery. Not that the house faced it, of course—the cemetery was off to the side and back from the street—and the yard surrounding my parents' home was large and full of trees.

Stately Oaks, the Goodheart Mansion, sat impressively atop a hill with a winding drive leading up to it. But the Nightingale estate, Nightingate, was on a whole different scale. Massive columns stood at the base of the driveway, along with a grand iron gate that swung open by remote. The house, built of stone, brick and marble, was stunningly beautiful. The first time I entered with Celia, a man wearing gloves, Baker, opened the door. The last time I was "home," a month ago, Baker did so again.

Every piece of furniture in the house, every painting, had its own history. A huge pool, surrounded by a broad, gently terraced patio, was off the back verandah, perfect for entertaining. Beyond the pool, and on either side of it, formal English gardens including a maze of tall boxwoods, dominated much of the lawn. Beyond that, the yard was flat and manicured, perfect for sports and play.

Celia had attended the private girls' school in Raleigh, St. Mary's, because her mother had, as well as her grandmother and great-grandmother. And several aunts and great-aunts. The Nightingales were big donors.

The family had an important heritage at Wake Forest, too. The largest building on campus was named—as one might have guessed—Nightingale Hall. I could be bold and so proud as to say my grandfather went to Duke—and graduated despite his debacle of a freshman year—but Celia could say *her* grandfather helped endow their hometown university. And yet, tellingly, she chose not to go there. Instead, she went to an all-girls college in Raleigh.

After graduating from Meredith, she went to UNC School of Law. I went to Duke. We were two lawyers from rival schools married to each other—a house divided.

All in all, I guess I had been intimidated by the whole Nightingale thing once it had fully revealed itself to me. And yet I pursued Celia. So three years ago, in a morning coat at the front of Celia's family church packed with hundreds of people regarding me, I sucked in a slow, deep breath to steady myself for her long walk down the aisle and the vows I'd soon be making. Yes, that scene now seemed like a dream.

I opened my eyes. Before me was the cross, the Bible, the altar. But I had not prayed. I hadn't been able to quiet my mind long enough to focus. I stood and walked out of the chapel.

The public area between the Senate and House chambers was a beehive full of people. A man with a smile on his face, a lobbyist, walked up to me with an outstretched hand and said, "Representative Goodheart, may I have a minute of your time?"

9.
THE OCCASIONAL HAUNT
1987

With the passing of six more years—which I was now in the habit of measuring by two-year terms in the General Assembly—I had been promoted to the State Senate.

Now "Senator Goodheart," I was yet again at the General Assembly—chapel, front row—availing myself of some solitary quiet-time in the middle of an otherwise busy day. Beginning next week, we were starting up our legislative chapel services again: all members of both houses were always welcome, along with anyone who worked in the legislative buildings, and guests. Legislators and other people volunteered to lead the services. One of the legislative secretaries, a sweet older lady with angelic eyes and disposition, played the piano, which was to my right as I faced the little altar. Having volunteered to lead the next chapel program, I hoped I came up with some inspiration soon because I already had plenty on my plate just being a legislator without trying to be a spiritual leader, too.

I'd always had a special interest in issues involving families and young people because I had a family and was young. When I was first elected to the House, I was the youngest member, and now, as I began my career in the Senate, I was the youngest member there. My first important legislative proposal had been to raise the drinking age from 18 to 21—my first term in the House. Considering I'd had my share of experience knocking down a few brewskies in school, I felt qualified to become paternalistic in outlook once I became an elected official. Was that hypocritical—or just typical? Or both? Hopefully, it was the right thing to do and would save a lot of lives. That was my motive, anyway. My legislation created quite a stir and didn't pass my first term. But the proposal did pass in my second term, so the drinking age in North Carolina was now 21. Did that make me part of the Nanny State? I hoped not.

Now I was working on legislation to create a Graduated Driver's License for teenagers under 18. The literature showed that lack of experience was the main reason for teen crashes and deaths—and car crashes currently were the number-one killer of teens in the U.S. A graduated license procedure would ensure more experience for the young driver, thus saving thousands of lives. To be sure, this proposal was also controversial, and there was not a single GDL law in the U.S. or anywhere in the world, as far as I knew. Still, I believed it was the right thing to do, so I was going to run with it. I needed to time it right, though. Timing was crucial in politics.

I'd just been sworn in, the day before yesterday. The whole week had been a whirlwind, and this empty chapel served me well as a refuge. I'd come by my new Senate seat by being elected to it, but the seat had opened up through a chain of events created by a tragic occurrence. In a shocking turn of events, one of the two U.S. Senators from North Carolina had committed suicide. The Governor then appointed as his replacement the Congressman from my Congressional district. The then-State Senator ran for the empty Congressional seat, thereby opening up his seat in the State Senate, which I ran for instead of running for reelection to the House. The political domino effect at work. So indirectly, a man's suicide had resulted in a promotion for me. Was that how life worked? Well, no one ever said life was fair, especially in the world of politics.

In front of me stood the same, simple altar, not altered since I first came to the General Assembly six years ago. On top of it still stood the same, simple cross, the Bible spread open before it. Why could life not be as simple as that?

I bowed my head and asked God to keep me goal-directed and on the right path. I asked him to steer me away from distractions and dark thoughts. I also prayed for inspiration for the chapel program I had volunteered to lead. Should I talk about God's Will, Free Will, and the matter of Luck? Maybe I should talk about man's search for the true meaning of life. Maybe I should talk about my *own* search. Or, maybe I should be less ambitious and just read some scripture along with some thoughts from a recognized preacher. Yeah, keep Me Myself out of this.

When I opened my eyes, my mind went back to my days in the House. I didn't actually start out as the youngest member. I started out as the second-youngest. But soon into the session, *the* youngest Representative got into an argument with the Senator from back home in his district and decided to burn down the Senator's tobacco warehouse. Arson will put a person in prison, and that's exactly what happened. So *then* I took the distinction of being the youngest member of the House.

I guess I was undergoing, right now, a trip down memory lane. Next, my mind darted back to the first day of Session, my first term in the House, my very first day as a Legislator, the day we were sworn in. Sitting in the 120-member House chamber—on the back row, required seating for the handful of us Minority members—I was thinking about the Representative several rows in front of me. I began wondering what it was like to have lived your life in Smithfield, North Carolina, and to have Ava Gardner as your sister, Mickie Rooney and Frank Sinatra as your brothers-in-law, and Howard Hughes as your sister's boyfriend between husbands. As I was thinking, the Representative from Smithfield collapsed from a stroke and was carried out of the chamber, dying a few days later. Ashes to ashes. Dust to dust.

Maybe in my chapel program I'd talk about how we never know when, or where, or how our number is going to be called, so we better be right with God all the time. The truth be known, what I really sought in life was to know God. I kept searching for Him; I kept seeking Him but continued to be distracted from that relationship I'd always craved.

On a positive note, I'd done pretty well in life so far: graduated from law school, was practicing law, and been elected to public office. And re-elected. I now had four children. I took them to church every Sunday with Celia, hoping to raise them as Celia and I had been raised.

I considered that a big step in the right direction. Even so,

I still didn't think I knew God or the meaning of life as well as I should. So when I was here at the General Assembly, I attended chapel every week and came here sometimes by myself seeking God. I was still listening, waiting, and searching—was still struggling with all that. I wanted Him to speak to me. I mean, *really* speak to me.

For her part, Celia had done well. She was a good mother and a good wife. She even managed to practice some law, and the two of us were thinking about going into the furniture business. I owed a lot of my success to her stabilizing influence, as well as the faith I did have, and the fact that my father's driven personality had rubbed off on me. I could have been a beach bum; it hadn't turned out that way. At least not yet. But despite all that good news, Celia and I and Croom and Jennie still had an issue with that night on the Isle of Cats. You might think we'd have gotten past that by now. Not so. Not sure why it still haunted us at times, but it did.

I stood and walked out of the chapel. The area between the Senate and House chambers was, as usual, buzzing with activity. A reporter, pad and pen in hand, made a beeline for me from across the quad.

After we talked for a while about some upcoming legislative issues, most notably rumors of my graduated license proposal, I headed for my next committee meeting, the Isle of Cats returning to my brain. This time, like most, nothing in particular triggered those memories. Was it guilt that worked like that? Maybe I should go back to that island, and face the scene of our misadventure head-on. Who knew what might come of that? Maybe I'd find the treasure I was still looking for. Then again, maybe I wouldn't. Maybe I would just go digging beneath the surface and uncover something else. More skeletons?

In the meantime, like a dark apparition, the haunt on occasion returned. And when it did, that dark specter could take on the light with a vengeance, scheming to snuff it out.

PART 2

CELIA AND JENNIE

10.
UNFINISHED BUSINESS
March, 1992

Five years later, Celia and I decided together *we'd* go back. We made the decision that we'd return to the vicinity of our misadventure—at least go as near to it as we were prepared to do currently in our lives. We wouldn't make a big deal out of "our return"; we'd just pay a passing visit along the highway as we vacationed on the Outer Banks for our anniversary.

Night surrounded us as my headlights lit up the road sign for "Hoophole Island Ferry, 43 miles." It was just as well that Celia was asleep as I passed the sign. By now, eighteen years had come and gone since she and I—with Croom and Jennie—had taken that road and gotten ourselves to the Isle of Cats. Today, March 12, 1992, was exactly that many years since the boatman took us to the island.

I knew that if Celia had seen the sign, it was as close as she would want to go. It was the week of our fifteenth wedding anniversary, and although we'd agreed to journey to the Outer

Banks, taking this route, we'd also agreed we wouldn't go *all* the way back—not all the way. This was as close to Hoophole Island as we would go, forty-three miles and a ferry ride away. Many more miles of sea roiled between us and the Isle of Cats. But I *had* seen the sign again. I wasn't exactly sure, though, why we'd been pulled face-to-face with this turning point. What exactly were we searching for? What exactly was the draw? And the draw*back*? Could it be that something was searching for *us*?

The scrub bushes and low trees of the maritime forest surrounded our car on both sides like looming black sponges. I shuddered slightly, thinking of our children so far away from both of us—with Tracy, their nanny.

Our first three children—Elisa, Bert, and Caroline—had been born in two-year intervals, a girl, boy, girl. Then, only one year after Caroline, Teddy had come as a surprise. Celia was a methodical planner, an organizer, and three of the four had arrived on schedule. Right now, all four of them were home and in their nanny's care, but inexplicably, I felt anxious for them.

At thirteen, Elisa was still a child, but not completely; sweet but moody and usually compliant, she could also be rebellious, unpredictably so. But she was my firstborn and a girl, and I loved her intensely. Bert, eleven, who favored me in looks, was the All-American Boy Scout, a "chip off the old block," people said. My basketball buddy and, more than that, my dependable son. Caroline, at nine, grew cuter every day, and people said we had better watch out: it would be "Katie, bar the door" for us with boys in a few years. Right now, she was a voracious reader, affectionate, and even-tempered. Teddy, my eight-year-old who still liked to jump from the low rungs of the stairs into my arms, had a mischievous side, and Tracy said, "He has his moments." My youngest favored Celia, and Elisa claimed I spoiled him.

Regardless, at times when I was away, I longed to be with them, almost to the point of aching, just wanting to hug them and assure myself that they were safe. When I was away from home, they—and Celia—always drew me back.

Right now, I felt drawn by something else, and I wasn't sure it was good. As I drove the flat, deserted highway, running in front of my headlights like a black velvet ribbon, a force tugged inside me, calling me back to the sign. When I turned the car around in the road, Celia woke up. Groggily, she asked, "Are we lost?" Looking around, all she could see was black scrub. We might as well have been at the end of the earth. Without replying, I drove back to the sign and dead-stopped the car, my headlights shining on the fluorescent lettering, "Hoophole Island Ferry, 43 miles." An arrow pointed the way.

"No. We're not lost."

Celia sat up straight. "Okay, I know we did agree to drive this highway, and now we're here. There's the sign—the fork in the road. But this is close enough, as we agreed: no going down that road again. Back to the main road, Matt."

Now I was glad Celia was awake. If she'd stayed asleep, I might have taken the turn, though no ferries ran this late, anyway. What good would *that* have been? With the sound of her voice, my strange apprehension passed. "I was thinking just of Hoophole Island. That's all. Not the other place."

"What time is it?"

"Nine-thirty."

"Would you like me to drive?"

I said yes and pulled over to the shoulder. We got out of the car, exchanging seats. Clouds scudded across the sky, obscuring then revealing a bright-orange crescent moon. Like a section of incandescent tangerine suspended in the sky, it shone warmly, then disappeared behind clouds, then reappeared. In the same way, hundreds of stars in view disappeared, then reappeared, then disappeared again. A cold wind blew in from the northeast, and it began to drizzle.

As soon as I slammed the door, Celia locked it. "Matt," she said, grabbing my hand, "I love you." Then she leaned over and kissed me. "I love you so much, and I'm so glad you're with me right now. I'm glad we're here. I'm glad we're doing this, but I have to admit, I think it's creepy out here in the middle of nowhere. This is not the place for your car to break down."

I returned the kiss, and leaning over, hugged her. "I love you, too. All is well."

Before she put the car in gear, she kissed me again, and I grabbed her hand, squeezing it. Still, we didn't talk about that trip—not tonight, on this isolated road, though we'd come this close to the turn-off to the islands. In fact, up until this dark stretch of highway and *the* sign, our vacation had been ideal—perfect weather, no stress, a romantic second honeymoon. Why spoil a good thing?

Now, with a dark forest surrounding us, gnarled by salt and wind, I thought back to that spring break weekend when the four of us went to the Isle. As the headlights devoured the road, I tried to imagine what the house might look like now, boarded up, falling in, haunted. I was thankful to have Celia's company, the company of my favorite person, my best friend, the love of my life. Because of her, beside me in the car, I wasn't alone with my thoughts: "You will see murder," I recalled the old woman having foretold us all.

"I was thinking about the kids," I said.

"They're good—they're safe," she assured me. "Tracy is trustworthy—the best. She would never let us down."

Right. Tracy would never betray our trust in any way.

The drizzle turned into a light rain, and Celia turned on the windshield wipers. The scrub shot past us as we headed west down the road with nothing but that neon wedge of orange rind overhead to lighten sporadically the cloudy, black sky.

Whenever we made a curve in the road, the headlights lit up the black tangle of bushes and trees and undergrowth, as if shining a floodlight on a thicket of twisted phantoms.

My thoughts ran from the thickets, to the moon and back to Celia. The old woman had said to me, "You will know love, and you will admire." She'd proved right about that; I loved and admired the woman beside me. And now, after all the years—and all that had happened—we *had* come back. We'd gotten that close. We'd confronted the sign, the fork in the road. That was something, in and of itself.

My thoughts ran from Celia, safe beside me, to that night. I don't think I could have done anything else to save Miss Smiley. Afterward, the four of us had a long discussion about calling the authorities, a discussion that turned into an argument and then a confrontation.

Croom said, "Let's get the hell out of here! Obviously, we can't report what's happened."

Jennie agreed. "Of course not. She's dead. We'll be dragged

into a trial. I won't get into medical school. *None* of us will get into graduate school. I mean, why are we here in her house—especially after that man told us not to come here, and we agreed? We're inside her house, and she's dead, for God's sake!"

She and Croom were standing on one side of the body, Celia and I on the other, facing each other in the mercurial light of lantern and candle. Jennie continued, "This is way too suspicious. We'd be ruined over nothing. It's not murder, but it could be *something*—involuntary manslaughter or something."

Croom agreed. "Right. Why did she die? Did she choke? A heart attack? We didn't exactly kill her, but we didn't do much to save her, either. What's the point of dragging in the police when we're absolutely at the wrong place at the wrong time?"

As I looked at them, I was seeing them in a different light, and it wasn't just the haunting light of the lantern and candle. In their shadowy faces, I was seeing drives and intentions I'd never seen before.

In Jennie, it wasn't just her good looks. If I'd found her incomprehensible before, now she seemed like a different person. In Croom, it wasn't just his amusing, adventuresome spirit, or the rational, even-tempered good judgment he'd so often shared with me over the years when we were being serious. I'd grown up since first grade with both of them, but I was seeing something new in them both.

I said, "To me, it's just the opposite. We *have* to report it. She's dead. It's a dead body. We can't just walk out of here and leave her. She died in her own home; they'll want to do an autopsy. There's a legal procedure that has to be followed."

Celia nudged closer to me, her hand finding its way again

into mine. "I agree with Matt," she said firmly. "Definitely. There's no question we have to report it."

"We can't just leave," I said again. "She's dead."

"You've got *that* right," Jennie snapped. "She's dead! And the four of us are inside her house where we are not supposed to be. We're not even supposed to be on this *island*."

"Which, as we now know," Croom said, "is owned by the federal government. So do you really want to be questioned by the FBI about a dead body? Who's to say the local authorities—I guess the sheriff—would not feel obligated to call them in? Do you really want to take that risk?"

"But we can't just walk out of here as if we'd stopped in for tea," Celia said. "We have to report what happened."

"That's the law," I said, "of both common sense and the state."

"Reporting it won't bring her back to life," Croom said in a low voice. "There's a time and a place for everything. This is not the time to play Boy Scout. This is the time to be reasonable."

He and Jennie stood side by side across from Celia and me, facing us off. Glaring at us. Someone had to make a move. I said, "Okay. Then there's no choice but to vote on it. We'll take a vote." The expression that appeared on Croom and Jennie's faces told me I was an idiot.

"Against reporting," Croom said. They raised their hands.

"*For* reporting," said Jennie. Celia and I raised *our* hands.

Jennie smirked and rolled her eyes. "*That* accomplished a lot."

Celia said, "So now what do we do?"

Croom pulled a quarter from his pants pocket. "We'll flip a

coin. I'll flip. Matt, you call."

I could hardly believe what I was hearing and seeing. We were ghouls at midnight, festive over a gravesite. Was I really in a dark room with only a lantern and candle, standing with three other people over a dead body, flipping a coin to see what we would do with it? How had we come to this? My eyes followed the coin into the air, then into the palm of Croom's right hand, then to the back of his left hand.

"Heads," I called.

"You lose," said Croom. I asked for two out of three.

"That's ridiculous!" Jennie shot back. "This is ridiculous! And not fair. You lost the call, *Matthew*—accept it. We don't report. That's it. Final."

But Croom looked at me, then at Jennie, then at me again. "We'll give you two out of three."

Hands on her hips, a frown on her reddened face, Jennie said, "I don't think that's fair."

But Croom stared at her stone-faced till she relented. "Okay—but let Celia call." Croom flipped the coin again. Celia called it, and won the call. Again, we were tied.

"Jennie calls the last one," Croom said. He flipped the coin into the air.

As he caught it, she called it. And won. "Game over!" she crowed. "Decision made. We do not report."

Still, in the calmest, coolest voice I could muster, I tried again. "Is there no way to change your mind? I really feel we should go to the authorities about this."

"We're not going to the damn police!" Jennie yelled. "It will derail all of our lives!"

"We voted," Croom growled. "It was tied. We flipped—not once, which should have been enough—but three freaking times because you insisted on it. You lost. Deal with it."

Silence.

"We can't be split on this," he finally said, his voice calm. "Friendship is friendship, and we have to stick together." He took a deep breath, then another. "First of all, good buddy, I apologize. Celia, I'm sorry. This is not the type of thing I deal with every day."

I lifted my hands, palms up. "It's okay."

"I'm sorry, too," Jennie said. "Besides, there is the possibility you *could* be wrong. Croom and I *could* be right."

I didn't think I was wrong, and I didn't think they were right. But I did think further arguing about it would not change anybody's mind. We'd decided, right or wrong.

Now it was time to do something besides yell and argue.

We washed the dishes and put them back on the kitchen shelf. We folded the blankets and put them into the trunk. We returned the two chairs to the dining room. We'd run the cats out of the room when they first appeared and had kept them out with our movements and raised voices, but when the storm stopped sometime after midnight, and we finally left the room for good, six cats loomed over her. We agreed that they were just licking her face…

We walked back to where we thought we'd pitched the tent and huddled on the beach, hardly saying a word till daybreak.

The old man picked us up at noon. Since we'd hardly spoken on the trip over, I guess our reticence seemed the same, going back. I wondered how much of this Celia was thinking about, too. But I didn't ask: until my turn off the main road, our trip had been a second honeymoon, regardless of any heavier goals we might have set for ourselves before we left home. The moon was so orange, the clouds so black, the silence so thick, the scene through the windshield gave me gooseflesh.

After eighteen years, it wasn't that often that the image of Miss Smiley's death face flashed before my eyes. Or the image of the cats surrounding her.

The boatman said nothing to us, we said nothing to him, and the authorities never questioned us. So we never knew how long it was before her body was found or what condition it was in when they found it.

For years I've had a recurring dream in two parts—a challenge like an exam that I fail under pressure, then the face of a corpse partially eaten away.

I could have defied our decision and gone to the authorities on my own, but that would have destroyed my friendship with Croom and Jennie. It might have harmed or destroyed my relationship with Celia, too, but what effect on those relationships it would have had, I will never know. So I traded doing what I thought was the right thing for friendship, going along to get along.

I know it was a corporate decision, but I'll always believe it was wrong, and it has always bothered me. It was the first time in my life I'd ever done something serious that I also thought was wrong. My conscience had said one thing to me; I'd done another. More than once I've asked myself: where was God that night? Where was He when I needed Him? But it was too late now to fix any of that. We're both forty years old—been married fifteen years. Too much water over the dam.

The moon had migrated in the sky and was a duller orange than it had been thirty minutes ago. The rain increased, and Celia, without speaking, reached forward and turned the heat up one notch.

After college, things didn't work out for Croom and Jennie as a couple. He ended up in Dallas, a biologist, and was recently named head of his department at S.M.U. Ten years ago, his father died, leaving him a fortune, not that he really needed it. He bought a huge house in Highland Park and lives the life of a wealthy, prominent academic.

After the Isle of Cats trip, Jennie became restless and had a hard time concentrating on anything. She became dissatisfied with school and couldn't sleep well. She used pills to help herself sleep. To her parents' dismay, she failed to take her finals, got incompletes in all her courses, and didn't graduate even though we were in our last semester of senior year.

She and Croom had a falling out, and he broke their engagement. She then took off for Europe and beyond. While there, she discovered she could sing—amazingly well. More importantly, she discovered that people loved to hear her. Actually, she'd always had a great voice, but her parents, wanting her to be a doctor, third-generation, rather than "an entertainer," had discouraged any interest she'd shown in cultivating her music.

Once home again, she entered some contests and eventually found herself on a nationally televised talent-search program. Jennie won the competition and became famous to millions of fans overnight. She was neither country nor western nor, at heart, a star, but those were the songs she performed best, and she became an immediate country-western superstar.

In college, she'd always had a serious side, as reserved as she was outgoing. I'd always known that. In the first grade, on our first day, there she was, sitting up straight, looking straight ahead, hands crossed properly on top of her desk. The cutest girl I'd ever laid eyes on, but a girl not frivolous enough to notice the likes of me. A girl sensitive enough to cry when Cleve, the class bully, made fun of her and incomprehensible enough not to thank me when I stood up for her and backed Cleve down. Jennie Boston. Two syllables in each name. Each syllable, three letters. Her parents had an orderly plan for their daughter.

Now she was, in public, all smiles and extroverted personality. Especially on the late-night talk shows. Now she spelled her first name *Jeni*. I often read the headlines in the tabloids on the stands at the supermarket when I ran errands for Celia. With four kids, you were running out of things often.

When I watched her on TV, I was filled with a mixture of conflicting emotions. I was astounded that this woman I knew so well—had known so intimately, had known since we were little children—was now an international personality keeping company with Hollywood jet setters. At the same time, I felt sorry about how things had turned out for her.

I knew that, in private, she mixed pills and booze.

After our last year of college, Jennie had moved from one boyfriend or suitor to another—and one rejected fan had turned into a serious stalker—but she never lost contact with Croom. After Celia and I graduated from law school and were married the same year, Croom convinced Jennie to come back to him. All their friends, including Celia and me, wondered whether or not they would ever get married.

The answer was yes—the year after Celia and I did. They bought a home in Dallas, but it wasn't a smooth arrangement, and both of them never sold their residences. Jennie had to travel a lot, even overseas, and Croom, having a demanding, stable job at the university in Dallas, couldn't travel with his wife for weeks on end and keep his academic position. They separated and reconciled, separated and reconciled, over and over again. Even so, through it all, she gave Celia and me every indication that the only man she'd ever really loved and had never stopped loving was Croom.

"I'm not sure this is where we should have come to get away," Celia said suddenly as if reading my mind. "I love the coast, and this has been a wonderful vacation, but I just don't like being *here*, so close. Now that we're back, I think we might have made a mistake."

Trying to be light, I said, "But didn't we say you're supposed to face your fears head-on?" I tried to laugh. She said nothing. Finally, I said, hopefully, "We've always wanted to go to Duck."

It was her turn to be flip. "Are we headed to Duck? Or are we just continuing our ducking?" But she didn't laugh, and her tone of voice wasn't funny.

I didn't know what to say, so I didn't say anything. Did she really want to turn around and pursue the sign? I doubted it.

She drove on in silence, and just to break the tension, I reached to turn on the radio. But she grabbed my hand. "Please. I don't want news. Why did we have to go on that trip? It's affected our whole lives, hasn't it?" I said nothing.

"In a way . . . in some ways . . . it's got us stuck," she said.

"We can't seem to totally escape from it, going forward—and we can't go backward and escape from it."

"It wasn't our fault," I said. "We didn't kill the old woman. We didn't want to leave her like that, and we didn't ask her to tell our fortunes. And we know that all those predictions will not come true."

"It just happened . . ."

"That's right. Life happens. Maybe all the fault—whatever there is—is with Miss Smiley. Maybe she did it to herself. Or sometimes things just happen, not always for, or with, a reason."

Celia did not respond, and I said, "I don't think that's inconsistent with God, do you?"

Again, she did not respond—the silence uncharacteristic for her—and as the minutes passed, the foreboding overtook me again, a premonition that something bad was going to happen. Or already had.

Despite Celia's protest, I turned on the radio. When I found a news channel, I stopped switching stations. First, world news from the BBC, then state and local news, the reports ran the gambit from Sri Lanka to Raleigh to sports and entertainment. Then we heard it.

"Jennie Boston has been struck by a car in downtown Dallas," the newsman said. "The pop star has been rushed to a hospital, where she is at this time. We are awaiting further reports regarding her condition."

I was stunned. Shocked. I couldn't speak. "Oh, my God," Celia said. "I can't believe it."

I surfed through the stations in search of further information. This time the report said, "Jennie Boston was struck by a car today and rushed to a hospital. Latest news reports are that the driver of the car may have hit her intentionally. Stay tuned for breaking news."

"I just can't believe that," I finally said.

"Why would anyone *do* such a thing? Poor Jennie! Who would try to kill her? I can't believe that this is happening," Celia said. "That we're here, hearing this news on the radio. It's too coincidental."

"Maybe it's not true," I said lamely. "You know how the media is with rumor."

"I'm just blown away by all of this," Celia said. "It's so dark out here—and the rain—I can't half see, and we're so alone out here. I wish we hadn't stopped at that sign. It's bringing everything back. Now this incredible, horrible news. Of course, I don't believe that old woman, that fortuneteller, is the cause. Not some old lady who made some crazy predictions eighteen years ago."

I channel-surfed until another station reported the driver had hit her accidentally.

"They're reporting rumors. She's famous, so they can get away with it."

"Of course, we don't believe there's any connection here and now with what happened eighteen years ago," Celia said. "Coincidences occur, even uncanny ones. Tell me you believe that, too, Matt: that *if* this is true, it's just a coincidence. Say something."

"We have to believe that," I said.

"And if there's any disbelief, we have to suspend it long enough to get all the facts."

As we drove on in silence, now heading north to Duck, it began to thunder and lightning, just as it had eighteen years ago. Today. The rain came at us in sheets, blowing first one way, then the other, pelting the car noisily. Celia slowed to a crawl. Up ahead, we saw a lighted inn: "King Charles's Inn and Tavern." Quaint and rustic, awnings flapping about on a saltbox. Celia pulled off the road and into the parking lot. "I can't drive anymore. Is this okay?"

"Sure," I said. "It's probably the only place between here and another fifty miles, anyway, and we shouldn't be driving in this storm."

She parked.

I reached into the back seat and handed her the umbrella. "Run on in. I'll get our things from the back and follow you."

She handed me the car keys and dashed inside.

I followed with the suitcases.

The lobby looked as though it had been built a hundred years ago and hadn't been touched since. It smelled like the sea and old upholstery. I rang the bell, and eventually, a man with gray hair and leathered skin appeared behind the counter, wearing a bow tie.

Handing me the key to the room, he said, "Down that hall," and nodded pleasantly. "And we have a nice tavern, paneled in oak." I looked at him. "Down *that* hall." He pointed in the opposite direction.

We unlocked the door to the room. The bed was so high it had a footstool next to the dust ruffle and had a canopy overhead. The rest of the room wasn't as fancy. A small sink jutted out from the wall with two separate spigots, and beside the sink was a washstand with a pitcher. A bathroom the size of a closet was in the corner. An old cathedral radio sat on a nightstand beside the bed. Celia slumped in a chair beside the washstand, as I started to say something, then stopped.

"About Jennie," she said. "This news—it's not a result of what happened near here eighteen years ago. You know we don't believe that connection. We are attorneys, Matt, and we'll find out the facts. Jennie will be okay." She turned on the radio.

I felt like I needed a drink. "Mind if I go to the bar for a nightcap? I'll look for a phone and call Croom. I'll call home, too."

"That's fine, Matt, but . . ."

Opening the door to the hall, I looked back at Celia. Sitting in the chair beside the nightstand, fiddling with her wedding rings, she turned the dial on the radio.

"Don't stay too long," she said.

Not to worry, I thought. What in the world could I possibly find in the bar that would make me want to stay?

11.
THE TWO-MARTINI LUNCH

I walked into the lobby and called Tracy on the payphone. Everything was fine at home. Then I called Croom and left a message on his answering machine.

I called the hospital in Dallas, confirming that Jennie was there and that she was alive. The woman who answered the phone said, "The staff has been instructed not to allow calls into the room, but you can leave a message." I left another message for Croom.

In the bar, dimly lit and trimmed in wood, paintings of ships adorned the walls. Rigging hung from the ceiling, and the shelves behind the bar itself were outlined on their edges in thick rope. With mirrors lining the back of the shelves, there appeared to be twice the actual number of glasses and bottles. Warm and comfortable now, after our drive in a chilly rain, I felt I was below deck in an old schooner. Only four other people were in the room—two couples, each sitting at far-corner tables. So I sat at one of the other corner tables, as removed from them as I could get.

The bartender, bringing me a scotch and water on the rocks, gave the impression he was open to conversation, but I needed time alone. He walked off and I took a drink of my scotch, wincing as memories flooded my head. Oh, Jennie. According to some news reports, at the time of the accident, she had had drugs in her bloodstream. One memory after another filled my thoughts. That's what the threat of someone's looming death will do to you.

Eighteen months ago, I walked into the Bellaventure Room of the Dallas Town Club to meet her for lunch, feeling a twinge of nervousness I wasn't expecting. She seemed just as nervous to see me. Extending her hand, she turned her cheek up for a kiss. She returned the kiss—and hugged me, sharing her perfume, too—a delicious mix of rose and other florals. Jennie was so good-looking, so alluring. Wearing gold jewelry, she was goddess-like in a blue-green dress plunging at the neckline and slinky on her svelte figure. Not in the least country-western. Her hair was long, blond, and sparkling. I kept reminding myself that I was there in Dallas on business, that Croom was my oldest friend, that I was married to the most wonderful woman in the world, and this person sitting across from me was just a dear friend.

As our waiter seated her, I said, perhaps a bit too enthusiastically, "You look *great*!" The first thing out of my mouth had sounded childish. Too late now. The waiter took our drinks order: a martini for Jennie, iced tea for me, no sugar. After he left, Jennie reached across the table. "Give me your hand, Matt!" She squeezed it, her diamond rings sparkling like her hair. Those huge rings had accumulated in number each time she and Croom had separated and reconciled. Right now, the two were separated again.

Her fingernails were long and painted green-black. New and oddly camp. She still had that strawberry-blond, freckled kid's face, though. She withdrew her hand and smiled. That was the smile I loved, the one America and her fans worldwide loved, too. Despite the viciousness and lack of ethical standards of the tabloids, which did everything they could to tarnish her image, she managed to maintain a wholesome persona on stage and television.

"How do you like my choice of restaurants?

"Any place is fine. Just as long as we can visit and not be bothered by people—especially the press."

"This is about as safe as you're going to get. Croom and I pay these folks well for the privacy."

I didn't know what to say. I didn't know much about their situation except that they were living in separate residences—again. I knew that whenever they split up, he always stayed in the house in Highland Park because he had paid for it, mostly with the money he'd inherited from his father, and she lived in a condo, which, according to Croom, was palatial.

"I'm going on tour in a week. To Britain and Germany. I guess it's not so surprising that the Brits like country-western, but it never ceases to amaze me how much they love me in Germany. Who would have ever thought it?"

"I would think they would love you *anywhere*. I know *I* would. Next time you go to Australia, can I go with you?"

She laughed. "I'm so glad I'm getting to see you before I

leave. How's Celia?"

"Good. Real good. She sends her best."

Because of the furniture industry, a unique connection existed between Dallas and Hickory. Four years before, Celia and I had started our company, Tavern Craft, naming it after Hickory Tavern, the original name of Hickory. As manufacturers of high-end furniture, Celia and I made trips to Dallas several times a year. This time Celia had a conflict, but she did know I was having lunch with Jennie.

The waiter, wearing a black jacket and white gloves, returned with our drinks and the menus. I sensed by the way he was looking at us—especially the way he was looking at Jennie—that he envied me for having lunch with such a good-looking woman. It was clear by his deference that he knew full well who she was.

Her favored downtown haunt, the Bellaventure Room, was an outdoor patio on the roof of a six-story building. Jennie said, "I like to come here. Of course, they know who I am, but it's a private club, so they respect my privacy. That's worth it. The management and the members understand the code, and that keeps this place in business."

"It's first class," I said. "Upscale but not stuffy. And the weather's perfect, with a clear sky the color of a Texas bluebonnet."

In the first week of October, the temperature was around seventy-five. A dry breeze gently ruffled the leaves on the trees and potted plants around us. An aroma of spices and cooked onions from the kitchen wafted through the balmy air.

"No humidity," I added.

She smiled. "Not like Carolina. It takes some getting used

to. On those rare days when it's really humid and dripping, I always think of home. I think to myself, 'I feel like I'm home again. Back in Hickory. Or at Duke.' It makes me homesick, really, and I wish I were home.

"I'm glad Celia's well. And the kids? How are they?"

"Good. Good. Growing like weeds. Bert is the steady one: straight arrow, straight A's. He loves basketball and playing with me. Teddy's learning. Elisa and Caroline are angels . . . What would you recommend?"

"Everything here is good. If you're in the mood for fish, the trout is outstanding."

We made small talk for a while, discussing the various entrees and side dishes. Eventually, our waiter returned and took our orders.

I straightened a bit in my chair. "Tell me about Croom. We're not going to be able to get together on this trip. I'm flying back tomorrow, and I haven't had a good talk with him in almost three months. I miss him."

Jennie looked to the side and lightly touched the back of her head. "I would say he's fine, considering we can't seem to live together, at least not for long. Not right now. He still wants me to give up my career. He's demanding about that. I know he loves me, and I love him, but he knew I was in the music business when he married me. He wasn't deceived, at least not by me. I'm an entertainer, and it's a tough business. You are 'on' all the time, working hard."

"I see you on TV all the time. Your success is dynamite, Jennie. The public loves you."

"I love the public. But it's very stressful. It's a tough life."

She sipped her martini. "I won't give it up, though. And I can't give it up. It's who I am. You know me, Matt. You've known me forever. As children. Teenagers. In college . . . " She paused and looked away.

Then she said, "Maybe Croom shouldn't have married me if he can't accept me for who I am. He seems different in a lot of ways. I look at you—you haven't changed a bit. You're still an Eagle Scout and just as good-looking as ever. You haven't aged a day! Not a pound overweight." She smiled. "Forgive me, but you're just a tall, athletic version of Dick Clark, with a deep voice. No gray hair. Same sweet smile. I wouldn't give up my life, but I hope you and Celia know how lucky you are."

"You're awfully kind, but there's stress on this end, too," I said. "Plenty."

"I guess it's not that easy being a Senator."

"And the father of four children, a husband, lawyer, and a businessman. Celia and I have banked a lot on Tavern Craft. It's making money, but it *has* to—we've got a lot riding on it."

"Really?" She seemed surprised.

"Yeah. My father sold his textile mill."

"Actually, my mother told me that," Jennie said. "It really surprised me. I thought the Goodheart's would own Goodheart Mills forever."

I made a fake smile. "I thought the same thing. I thought, how can I take over a textile mill and make a go of it in the world we live in now? I'm not Bert Goodheart. I don't have his instincts. His knack. On the other hand, I thought to myself, if I don't inherit that mill, what am I going to do with myself?"

I paused, then said, "Well, my father is a smart man, and he saw the handwriting on the wall. He got out while he still could and still make money. The textile industry is overseas now, and he got out at the right time. He did well, but there's no family business for me to go to work for in Hickory. So Celia and I are reinventing things. We could move to Winston-Salem, and I, or Celia and I, could go to work for Nightingale Transport, but Hickory is where we and our kids want to live."

"Homier than Dallas."

"Homier than Winston-Salem, even. Besides, Celia went to law school because she wanted to prove to herself that she could be independent of her family. She loves them—and just as important, she *likes* them—but she's her own person. So, since there's no Goodheart Mills anymore, Celia and I have our own business. We've got two really good people helping us manage our operation: Annie Jameson, our controller, and Andrew Templeton, our floor supervisor."

"You have to have people you can rely on."

"That is so true. We were fortunate that Andrew came to us from another company; he was dissatisfied and sought us out. And Annie came to us by way of introduction: her aunt, Ruth Ann Phipps, used to work for my dad for many years. When Annie's marriage ended abruptly, she went back to school and back to work. Ruth Ann called my dad about her. She's worked for Celia and me for almost two years now, and Tavern Craft is beginning to make money. It's hard work but a creative challenge, and we're making progress."

Jennie shook her hair and took a sip of her drink. "I can't believe you're doing all that and staying in politics, too. I can't believe you're in your sixth term. My mother says the women vote for you because you're so good-looking and charming. My father says the men vote for you because they trust you. Are you as unbeatable as they say?"

"I just do my job. I work hard—I'm driven for some reason—and the people are kind. But I'm boring compared to you. I think you're awesome. I still sometimes get twinges of stage fright before I speak publicly, even after all these years. That must sound ridiculous to you; I can't imagine performing in front of a screaming audience."

She smiled and took another sip of her drink. "I remember how you'd sometimes get stage fright in high school when you'd have to make a speech in front of the whole school. But now, you can get a standing ovation from five hundred people and hardly use notes. And you were *always* incredible on the basketball court, Matt! You have no idea how much I used to love to watch you play."

"You have no idea how much I used to love to watch you cheer—for me."

"Don't forget who pushed you into running for Student Council President."

"Cindy Peppercorn?"

She turned her head to the side, raising a shoulder. "Ha!"

I smiled as our waiter returned with the orders. Piping hot, the aroma was delicious. He set the plates down. Excellent presentation.

I offered a short blessing. Then, silently I prayed, "Dear Lord, keep me from being distracted. Keep me on the straight and narrow path."

It was almost hard for me to believe I was having a

conversation with the same person who, in cowboy boots, had appeared on David Letterman a couple of weeks ago and dominated the audience and host. Right now, she was so sweet, so down-to-earth, so Jennie. Not Jeni. And certainly not Jeni B.

"Will I be calling you Congressman Goodheart soon? Or Governor?"

"Don't know. Maybe. Maybe not. Celia and I will have to make the decision about running when the time comes. The Governorship is a statewide race. Talk about stress! And even though a Congressional race centered around my state Senate district is much less ambitious and probably a lot more realistic, once you win, Washington is hardball. In every way. The press scrutiny is relentless. I can't imagine how awful it must be for you to put up with the tabloids. How can you stand the paparazzi—or shouldn't I ask?"

Her face tightened. "You shouldn't ask. I can't stand them. I really can't. I don't mind publicity. In fact, I like it. All *'stars'* do. It's a necessity to keep an audience whose admiration you grow to crave."

She sipped her martini. "It's the lying I hate. It's not true what they say about me—about the pills. I don't abuse drugs. I'm not addicted. And Croom isn't perfect, just because he shows up at school on a regular, dependable basis, and the students like him. Sure the students and faculty like him. Why shouldn't they? He's likeable."

"I think so," I said. "And he's a whole lot more than that: he's a great friend, too."

"But just because he's been named head of a department at Southern Millionaires University doesn't make him Mr. Perfect.

What's harder, to be a professor or a star? You'd think it was the first time in the history of the world that a superstar had gotten lucky enough to be married to a wonderful college professor, elbow patches on his tweed jacket and all. I hate the tabloids. They're so dishonest."

She was so animated about Croom. Her face was even a little pink.

"So according to those S.O.B.'s who write the stories, I'm the hick cowgirl married to the intellectual Southern blueblood, Dr. Nelson Croom Westfall the fourth. How ridiculous is that? Matt, we're from the same hometown, for God's sake! His parents and my parents were friends for decades. His mother, Alice, and my parents are *still* friends. They're members of the same country club, the one *your* parents are members of. Not to mention you and Celia."

I continued to eat, hoping a lack of expression would not encourage her.

"Actually," she finally said, "there haven't been that many stories like that. I don't know why the premise bothers me so much."

"Jennie," I said, "no offense, but if I didn't know better, I might think you were actually a little jealous of Croom."

"No offense taken—I am jealous of him! He has an easier life than I've got. Besides, he has more friends. You know how people are always drawn to him. Look at *you*."

"Nobody has more admirers than you've got."

We paused so that our waiter could ask us if we needed anything.

I glanced his way. "Everything is good, thank you." Back

to Jennie. "I saw you on TV doing that special for Veteran's Day. When you sang that medley of patriotic songs, the stadium had a meltdown. The cameras focused on grown men with tears running down their faces. Some of it was the songs, but mostly it was the way you, Jennie Boston, sing. Your voice is warm—and accepting—just what they need. I'll admit, I was overcome, too, watching it on television. I actually wiped away tears in front of my kids." As I spoke, my voice cracked.

"You're awesome," I went on. "My kids can't believe you grew up in Hickory and even knew I existed. They have a hard time imagining that superstar Jennie Boston could ever possibly have liked their dad."

She didn't say anything.

More silence.

Finally, she said, "But you grew up, Mr. Mansion, Mr. Stately Oaks, and married a Nightingale." Then she sipped her drink and leaned back to let me think about what that not only meant but suggested.

I didn't respond. I waited for her to say something, but she didn't. She sipped her martini, then finished it. She still hadn't eaten very much.

I studied her beautiful face as she looked down at the table.

Then, I asked, "Jennie—are you happy? Do you like your life? Do you like the fame and fortune?"

"What kind of a question is that? I already told you I like it and will never give it up." She waved at our waiter, and he handed her another martini. She took a sip, then ate the olive. "Why don't you ask me if I believe in fortune-tellers? Or about my faith in God—how strong my faith is?" She took another sip. "Life is as it is. We've been through a lot together. Not just Croom and I. But you and I."

She drank half. "I used to know who I was. I was my parents' daughter; I belonged to my father and mother, Dr. and Mrs. Parker Boston. Then there was *that trip* we took—you know which one, the one the four of us don't talk about. Then Europe, then a singing career, and"—her fingers made quote marks—"'stardom.' And ever since then, I've been different. Sometimes, I don't know *who* I am other than what my handlers tell me I am and must be for tomorrow's audience. Even my doctor. I'm whatever my managers tell me I am. Jeni B. I don't know why I'm telling you this. I guess it's the alcohol talking."

"Then quit. Give it up. Croom loves you—I know he does—and you'd make him the happiest man on earth. All he wants is his wife—you."

"And who is that? That's the point. I can't give it up. I know I can sing—that's my gift. It's the only thing I know. It's what I am. I can't be a doctor *now*. I can't be a mother *now*. I can't sit at home, in Croom's house in Highland Park. I'd rather be back in North Carolina. I miss all the hills and trees. The mountains. The ocean. I miss my parents. I can't get used to how flat it is here. It's lonely. I couldn't live in Croom's house and play bridge and join the book club. And I can't be Croom's housekeeper . . . I can't even cook!"

"Why would you have to?" I said lamely. "With all the money you all have, you could have a house *full* of servants."

She slumped in her chair and looked at me with slit eyes. Then she sat back up, straight as an arrow, and took another sip of her drink. "Why didn't you call me?"

"What are you talking about?"

"You never called me."

"Jennie—*what* are you talking about?"

"Nassau. After that night, you never called me."

I couldn't believe this turn.

"Jennie—are you serious? That was eighteen years ago. A lifetime! You know why I didn't call you. I was dating Celia."

"You were *not* dating Celia. You *had* been dating her. You weren't, then."

She looked straight at me—and drank again.

"Are we fighting, Jennie?"

"I don't know—*are* we? We're not even dating. We're both married."

"I'd say that's a good thing."

"For *you*, I'd say so. For me, I'm not so sure. Croom and I do a lot of fighting. And separating—and making up. That's no way to live, and it's exhausting. I'm no longer six years old, sitting in your first-grade classroom. I'd like my life in music, but a reliable life away from the stage as well—a good reason to go home!"

"But Croom's a good person. I honestly don't know a better one—never have—and I know a lot of people. I know him inside and out, and he's always been there for me. Even in politics. *You're* a good person. You just need to be kinder to each other, though that's the hardest thing to do. You're both talented, interesting characters. Fascinating. Charismatic!" I smiled. "That's one of the reasons I like both of you. I'm none of those things."

"*Don't* B.S. me!" she said, shaking her head. "You never called me. I should hate you for that. At least tell me why. After all these years, I'd really like to know. You owe it to me to tell me." I set down my fork and drank some water. After one deep breath, I couldn't help but sigh.

"Okay. I'll tell you. Here it is . . . I liked you, my dream girl, my whole life. Your whole life you never wanted *me*—or at least you never acted like it—and you could have. So one time I didn't pursue *you*—I was caught up with Celia whether you think I was or not—and that's the end? *You* could have called me if you'd really wanted to. What does that say about *you*?"

"What does that say about *you*, considering the circumstances? I didn't invite you to that boat!" She swallowed the last of her martini, then slammed the glass down on the table. People were staring.

"Jennie, please. It wasn't like that, and you know it. It wasn't like that at all. You're under stress. Let's not ruin our friendship over our differing memories of the past. I think too much of you. I value our friendship too much. Please."

"Excuse me," she said. She stood up from the table, as did I in response.

"Excuse me, Matt. I'll be back in a minute."

When she returned, she had calmed down, but her face and eyes were red.

I looked down at my plate. My appetite was gone.

Finally, I said softly, "Are you okay?"

"Yes. I'm fine."

"Things turned out the way they should have," I offered quietly, almost whispering. "I married Celia, and I should have. You married Croom, and you should have. You two love each other—you always have. You're both wonderful people. You just have conflicting lifestyles. Lots of stressors; you just need to work at the relationship. You need to be kinder to each other—more understanding and willing to compromise."

"Thanks for the advice. Now I'll tell you the truth. What happened is that things have turned out exactly the way that old lady—that witch—said they would." She made a little laugh and shook her head. "I actually used to feel sorry for her. Well, not anymore. You didn't ask me if I believe in fortune-tellers. Well, not as a general principle, but have any of us really had a choice? She fixed all four of our lives. And her name was Smiley. So who's smiling now?"

I wanted to contradict her, but before I could, she said in a calmer voice, "Matt, I apologize. I was out of line. I don't drink much, and I've definitely had one too many. I've got to go. It's late. I've got to get back to work."

She waved at our waiter. He walked over, looked at her plate, hardly touched, started to say something, then looking at me as I subtly shook my head, said nothing. With a slight bow, he handed her the tab. She scribbled her name and stood up. I stood up.

"Forgive me for rushing like this," she said. "But the time has slipped away from me. I've got to go. Don't worry about me—I'll call a cab."

She grabbed her purse and walked out. I followed her blue-green dress and long blond hair, still sparkling, as she left the restaurant.

No, I wasn't proud of any of this, but I never claimed to be a saint.

In fact, I felt like a heel. Worse.

The next day I flew home.

12.
THE SPEAKEASY

Now, a year-and-a-half later, I was alone at a table in a tavern on the Outer Banks. I got up and moved to the bar. While I waited for the bartender, I absentmindedly observed again the way the mirrors lining the back of the shelves seemed to offer twice as many bottles and glasses as there really were. There were still only four other customers in the room—the two couples, each sitting at far corner tables—and the bartender, who still seemed like he wanted someone to talk to.

"Same?"

I nodded.

He filled a glass with scotch, ice, and water.

"So what brings you through here, this time of night?" He looked like a construction worker, about my age, who got off work and came over to his night job without changing clothes.

"That's hard to say for sure," I replied. "Hard to say. The rain. The lightning. The storm. The hour. All those things."

"A lady?"

I looked at him, surprised. "That, too."

"Always that—too. Who? The wife?"

"Not really. Not really the wife. It's more like the wife's friend—or *my* friend. Her name's Jennie. Jennie Boston."

"Hm. Like *the* Jennie Boston."

"Yep. Exactly."

"So why are you here? On a trip?"

"Ever heard of the Isle of Cats?"

"Sure. Everyone's heard of it. Nobody goes there, but everyone's heard of it."

"*I've* been there," I said. "That's the problem. It didn't turn out well."

"I could've told you that. It's off limits. The government owns it. That's where they keep the awfulest traitors—spies, people like that—the worst of the lot. So that's why nobody goes to that islet."

"Except Roger Gaskill—trust me, I know."

"Don't know Roger Gaskill. Who's that?"

"The boatman. He took us over."

"So what happened?"

"We left the island in a different condition than we'd gone to it—eighteen years ago." I paused. "Do you believe in curses?"

"No. So what happened?"

"We ran into someone unexpectedly. It didn't turn out well for the four of us—me, my wife, my best friend, and Jennie Boston."

"Just like *the* Jennie Boston?"

I looked up from my empty glass. "Right. Exactly like it."

"Fill 'er up?"

I handed him the glass. He put fresh ice cubes in it, filled it, then handed it back.

"A classic case of the astronomical rise to fame and fortune of a basically private—serious—girl. Never really comfortable in front of the cameras."

"I'm not sure I get it. Must be something else."

I took a sip. "We're trying to figure out what else." I watched him as he swabbed down the shiny oak bar with a rag. "It's been an eventful day, and I'm wondering whether we may be living under a curse, my wife and I, and our two friends. And I'm wondering where God fits into things. I'd like to know how it all fits together."

"I definitely believe in God," he said quickly. "He makes all things make sense. And I *don't* believe in curses," he repeated emphatically. "And you don't look like someone who does, either. Must be something else. You weren't talking about the real Jennie Boston, were you? Don't tell me you were actually friends with *her*?"

"Yep. We go way back, all the way to first grade."

"You serious?"

"As a heart attack. First day of school there she was, sitting up straight and proper on the front row, hands folded primly on her desk." He seemed to be listening to me. "She had blond hair, long and sparkling, a few freckles on her cute face." I admitted, "I had a secret crush on her all through grade school."

Under the influence of a little truth serum and a stranger I assumed, and hoped, never to see again, I confided, "At one time, in the past, she was more to me than my oldest friend's girl. A lot more. I knew her before I ever met my wife. She met me before she met my buddy. I introduced them to each other way back when—when we were kids growing up in the same hometown."

"Wow! You don't say."

I hesitated, and he coaxed, "Go on . . ."

"You know what it was like to be a thirteen-year-old kid."

He nodded.

"In the summer following seventh grade—for me, that was the summer of 1965—she showed up at the same resort in Myrtle Beach that my dad took us to every summer. I got to see her at the pool every day for over a week. Every day in a different bikini." I smiled. He nodded again. "We talked. Once, she even sat beside me on my beach chair, and we took turns putting suntan lotion on each other. I was thirteen and *in love*."

I paused for emphasis. "We went steady for a year in junior high, but a friend named Cindy managed to break us up." I explained parenthetically, "Cindy was in love with me."

Gesturing with his palm, he told me to continue.

"In high school, Jennie encouraged me to run for student body president."

"Did you?"

"Yes."

"Did you win?"

"Yes."

"Did you like the job?"

"Yes." I thought but did not say, "I was also captain of the basketball team, and she was head cheerleader and my biggest fan and supporter. When our eyes met as I played and she cheered, I could make every shot." I did say, "That was high school. Then we ended up at the same college."

"What about your oldest friend?"

"All three of us ended up at the same college. He and she got married."

"Him and Jeni B?"

"Right."

"Hmm. This is complicated."

I wondered if he was thinking, *royally* screwed up.

But all he said was, "So this news really *is* personal for you. I get it. Then for you, it's a double shame. A triple shame! What a waste! That lady could really sing. And she was quite a looker, too. I was a real big fan. It's pretty hard to believe she got hit like that. Just like that."

He snapped his fingers in front of my face.

Clearing my throat, I said, "What news do you have on that?"

"Just what I've heard on the radio. She ran out into the street from between two parked cars, and a car hit her."

"Was the driver charged?"

"No. They say it wasn't his fault. But they say she might have been under the influence of drugs—some type of prescription drug. They're questioning her doctor. He was supposed to be taking care of her, not filling her full of drugs. They were all legal drugs; he prescribed them. But it's a real waste. She was so talented. Now she's in critical condition. Stable but critical, they say. Do you want me to turn on the radio?"

Quickly, I shook my head. "*Fama fugit*," I quipped, but inside myself, in the pit of my stomach and the depths of my soul, I felt numb.

I slid him my glass. "Another one."

He looked at me. "Back in a minute," he said, leaving me for one of the other tables. I settled for the ice cubes, crunching them, till he returned.

Busying himself at the cash register at the other end of the bar, he didn't seem eager to get back to me. I held up my glass. "Again," I said, grabbing his attention. When he didn't respond, I shoved my glass as expertly as I would have executed a free throw and watched it slide straight down the middle of the bar, coming to a halt within inches of his right hand.

That got his attention. He poured me another one with a lot of ice and water, a little scotch, and brought it to me.

I stood up, wavering. Steadying myself on the bar, I sipped the drink. "It's a trip we've been taking for eighteen years. Eighteen good years—productive years—but something that happened not far from here, I don't know how or when or if it might end. Just hope it doesn't end badly. We occasionally think about that, my wife and I—not often, but sometimes—and today's news could be a bad sign. Because, you see . . ." I stopped.

My head was beginning to spin. I leaned against the bar. He was staring. "Because what?"

"Because . . . Miss Smiley said something . . . and she had a knack."

He looked at me quizzically. "Miss Smiley?"

"Fortune-teller."

"*Had* a knack?"

"That's right. Past tense. She's dead. The first victim of her own plot. She died on our *first* trip out here. You might say she was the first one of our slumber party to go. Jennie could be the second. I'm praying she doesn't die, for a lot of reasons. If she does, though, I'm afraid she might have been killed. Murdered."

He looked at me curiously.

Still holding the bar, I sat back down. "By the driver . . . or the doctor . . . or maybe even herself."

He cocked his head.

"She may be the second of us to go."

He was squinting at me. "Back in a minute."

He walked round the bar, first to one table, then the other. Both couples ordered drinks. I had developed a headache and was thinking I needed to be drinking water only—and getting back to Celia. Except for that, my thinking was none too clear. Eventually, he got back to me and gave me his attention again.

I was now in a talkative mode. "She was neither country nor western nor, at heart, a star. Never have I thought of her as country. Her mother was, and still is, a Southern lady. Voice like magnolias and molasses—genteel manners. That's the home she was raised in."

He was swabbing the bar in front of me but listening.

"But on those TV shows, you see a different person. They even changed the spelling of her name. Jeni B in the tabloids, on stage, on TV—all smiles and extroversion. Miss Personality. Coming on with 'Yaawl' and stuff like that. 'Yaawl,'" I said again. "That's such an exaggeration; it makes me sick. I'm surprised they didn't dress her up in cowboy boots, a vest, and a fringed skirt."

"I think I've seen a few of her performances like that," he informed me. "I thought she was hot."

I shook my head and groaned. "She acted like that because

the audiences respond to it; they eat it up." I took a sip. "The operative word for Jennie, though, is act. That's what it is—an act. In real life, she is a fairly reserved person—even was as a cheerleader in high school. In college, she was a booker. She got that from her father. He was a second-generation doctor. She was supposed to have been third-generation."

I paused. "But the old woman's fortune-telling intervened and took care of that, directly or indirectly, one way or the other. She claimed to hold the keys to our future, *all* of us." I let the scotch continue. "According to her, we're all going to be betrayed by someone we deeply trust, and we're going to lose. As if that were not enough, murder is in our future, too—and we've already been there once. We spent the night where we weren't supposed to go, and—well—no inquest, no verdict, but somebody did die. That dear old lady told us our fortunes, all right. Not so very far from here, either—out on an island. That's the point."

I added, "But not the main point. The most important point is that my wife and I don't believe in that stuff."

"Of course not. God is in control of the universe, not fortune-tellers." He paused, then asked, "Miss Smiley's the one who's dead?"

"Right. But when she was alive, she looked into the future and claimed to see ours. Now, this has happened to Jennie. Who would care what Jennie means to me? But I'll tell *you*. She is a good person. She always was. Hell, I don't know *what* she was—someone I placed on a pedestal, I guess. And then I . . . well . . . something happened between us."

"I thought you were married."

"I am. We've been married fifteen years, fifteen *good* years.

This week we're celebrating our anniversary."

"Is your wife here with you, now?"

"Yes, she is."

"That doesn't sound good."

"Sure it is. We're celebrating. And searching for answers. Searching for truth." I looked at him. "Searching for *God*—in all this."

Then I said, "We're learning things. And I need to get back to her; I've already been here too long. You see, one of the main reasons we chose to come back here was to prove to ourselves that we could—and *would*. But now that we're here, instead of everything being hunky-dory, instead of our searching and finding what we'd want, we're hit with something very different: this news—about Jennie. And let me tell you, the timing of this is not cool."

I looked at him again. "Don't get me wrong. I don't believe in curses, either. Sure, it could just be an uncanny coincidence. Probably is. But this awful news, exactly eighteen years to the day since those predictions—well—it gives me something to wonder about. That old high school friend of mine—Cindy—used to say certain people could know the future and predict it. What do *you* think?"

I paused, but not long enough to let him reply. I continued, "This *is* a bar, and I need to think some things through. Some things you just can't discuss until you've figured them out for yourself, first. Right now, I'm comfortable here, as comfortable as a person could be under the circumstances. I'm a paying customer, so I figure it's my job to talk; it's your job to listen."

"Okay by me, big guy. Since you're not driving anywhere,

want another one?"

"Yes, I do. Fill 'er up."

He filled my glass. I took a swig. "I'm very glad I married the person I married. I loved her then, and I still do. Very much. Jennie married my oldest friend. I'm thinking of him, too. But I'm also thinking of something else right now. Wanna hear a story?"

"Sure. That's what I'm here for."

"It's real personal, about Jennie and me. Not something I go around telling people."

"I'm used to it. Shoot."

I looked into the mirror straight ahead, at my face behind the bottles. I saw someone else, too.

A man had entered the room, walked up to the bar, and stood about five feet to my right.

"Hey, friend," the bartender said. "The usual?"

"Yes, if you would be so kind as to indulge me with a cup."

As the barkeep turned his back to pull a bottle from the shelf, the man said to me, "Nice weather we're having—eh? Just a little damp."

Apparently, he had mistaken me for someone who wanted company.

13.

THE BARTENDER LISTENS

I already had company. The bartender. And this guy interrupted my story. But rather than be rude, I said without looking his way, "I've seen worse—especially around here."

Rather than take offense, he said, "You're right, of course. It could be a hurricane. What's a healthy rain, other than healthy? Where would we be without it?"

Still looking straight ahead, I said nothing.

The bartender handed him a paper cup with a lid on it.

The man handed him some money. "Keep the change, of course. Good to see you as always, and I'll be shoving off now."

That's *illegal*, I thought to myself.

Tipping an imaginary hat, the customer said, "See you later, my friend."

The barkeep tipped back. "See you later, Rudy. And *thanks*!"

With that, he left.

"Rudy Casper," said the bartender. "Occasional patron.

Always a good guy. Good tipper. Always stops in if he's passing by here; he goes to Raleigh a lot to visit his daughters. He lives at Hoophole." I said nothing. "Rudy knows everybody, and everybody knows him." More silence.

"Hmm," he said. "So what were we talking about? Oh yeah, a story you were going to tell me about you and Jeni B."

"About Jennie," I corrected. "And me."

"Correct."

I glanced into the mirror again—there I was among the bottles.

He said, "I want to hear the story."

"Okay. Here it is, short version: Jennie, my best friend, and I went to the same college. Another girl, the one I eventually married, who is my wife now, she and I dated throughout our junior year, but she broke it off with me before the start of summer vacation leading up to our senior year. So that summer, I was not dating anyone."

"Got that."

"A different friend of mine, named Trevor, a member of the college sailing club, asked me that summer if I wanted to sail with the club to the Bahamas."

"Never been there, but I hope to, someday."

"Well, I'd never been there before, either, and I'd never sailed before, so it sounded like a great adventure, and," I admitted, "I've always been up for an adventure."

He smiled and gave me a thumbs up.

"I'll never forget how beautiful the lights of Miami were as we set sail from the harbor that first night. I sat on the bow of the boat with a gorgeous, olive-skinned girl named Melody. And while I couldn't help but be attracted to her company, I really wished my former girlfriend—"

"Now your wife . . ."

"Correct. I really wished *she* were there instead. This Melody girl was really good-looking, but I wanted my old girlfriend back. I remember a warm breeze floated over us, the night sky twinkled. Bear with me."

"No problem."

"Except for missing my ex-girl, I couldn't have been happier. A great trip. Anyway, we made it to the Bahamas, sailed around the islands, and spent one night in Nassau."

"The capital, right?"

"Correct." I continued, "That night in Nassau, I was shocked to bump into Jennie Boston in the casino on Paradise Island."

"I've never been to a casino."

"I hadn't, either. I was trying to take it all in—the bright lights, the colorful games, the glitz, the clinking sounds, the people."

"Sounds fun." He hesitated. "I mean, if you like that sort of thing. Me, I don't gamble. Don't believe in it. A person could lose a fortune."

"Yeah, they say that happened to my grandfather. But that was a long time ago, like eighty years, and at this particular time, I was enjoying myself. Including the free drinks I was being handed just because I was there."

"Doesn't work that way here."

"I know. Anyway, I walked up to the booth where it appeared you got coins or chips for the games and watched the man in front of me as he stepped to the window. When it was my turn,

I said, 'May I have some nickels, please?' and handed the woman behind the glass two one-dollar bills."

"Been some inflation since then."

"Correct. Anyway, she looked at me a moment—amused, I thought—smiled, and the nickels came rushing out in the tray at the bottom of the window."

I paused and looked at the barkeep. "Okay, this story is getting long, and I said short."

He made a brushing gesture with his hand. "Don't worry about it. It's a slow night. Only one couple still here. Then what happened?"

"I scooped the nickels into my bucket and was standing in the walkway between the machines thinking what I might do next when I turned around and bumped into—"

"Jeni B!"

"Jennie. She was in Nassau with her parents, who were back at the hotel. Of course, she was as surprised to see me as I was to see her. She squealed and hugged me tightly. It was like that time at the beach, only now we were older. I felt like I'd stumbled onto a hidden treasure. Like I'd accidentally found something I'd always been searching for."

He looked genuinely interested. "Hmm. Then what?"

"We started out popping nickels into slot machines as the hostesses made the rounds with trays of drinks, so we'd want to gamble more." I went silent while I thought back. "She sat and pulled the lever while I stood beside her. We traded places, and I sat down and pulled the lever while she stood beside me. Then she stood behind me, very close, leaning up against me. I couldn't ignore exactly how that felt."

He listened. Respectfully.

"We stayed at the casino a while longer and then walked out onto the beach. It was a beautiful night, one of the most beautiful I've ever seen, with a big moon and lots of stars reflecting on the calm sea. Then we went next door to a bar to dance. We danced for a while—I got to hold her close, something I'd never done before—and I asked her if she wanted to see the boat I'd sailed in on.

"When we got there, no one else was on board. That was a surprise, and I was not asking for anything to happen. I didn't think anything would." I looked at the barkeep. No change in his expression. "But somehow, it just did. One thing led to another. It's one of those rare encounters you never forget—or get over."

"And after that?"

"Back at school, I couldn't call her because if I had, it would have been all over with the girl I was trying to get back with—the girl I married."

"So it was a one-night stand?"

I looked at him critically. His tone had not been flippant or disrespectful. Maybe a poor choice of words, but at this point, I was hardly in a condition to pass judgment on anyone else's speech.

"I guess you could say that; I guess it could be viewed that way. But it wasn't that for me. Neither one of us was looking for a one-night stand. It just happened. And the odds of it happening, the way it happened, seem so remote, I've always felt like it was meant to be. Like maybe God had a hand in it. Maybe not. Maybe fate. Maybe not. Maybe luck. Who can know? But if God did put us there alone in Nassau that night, at the same time in the same casino, then why didn't things work out between us? What was the point?"

I paused while I reflected on that. "Regardless, I won my old girlfriend back, so I was okay with my best friend asking Jennie out. That's what eventually happened. They'd known each other from back home, too.

"He quickly won her over. He had a magnetic personality. Elan. Charisma. He was Errol Flynn."

"Who were you?"

"Jimmy Stewart."

"I always liked him. One of my favorites."

"Same here. Thanks."

"So, did your friend Errol marry Jennie?"

"He did. I already told you that."

"My mistake. This is the guy who is married to Jennie Boston—*the* Jennie Boston."

"Yep. He still is. But it didn't work out too well. It's hard being married to a celebrity, especially if you're not willing to give up your freedom, your own life, for her." As philosophically as the alcohol would allow, I said, "We all have to make decisions in our lives. Some are more important than others. Jennie may have made the wrong career decision. But that old woman had predicted it."

I looked him straight in the eyes. "What do you think about that—about predictions? Do you think a certain, special kind of person can really predict the future? Or do you think we bring that future on ourselves?"

"Me? I'm not superstitious. I don't believe in fortune-telling. The people who do that stuff are phonies."

"You sound awfully confident."

"You asked. Those people are phonies. They make general, sweeping predictions that could come true in the broadest sense sooner or later in most anyone's life. Those predictions are the ones the gullible person homes in on. Then, all the other predictions that don't come true at all are ignored. Some people just want to believe in that hogwash."

"Hogwash."

"Yeah, B.S."

I sighed. "This has been a long day. Regardless, Jennie's parents were right. Her father was adamant that she should be a doctor. He said it was in her genes. It seems such a tragic waste, this accident. She is a talented, gifted singer. Maybe she'll be okay. It's all so complicated. Have you ever noticed how the longer that you live, the more complicated life seems to be? I've been searching for the simple key to life, my whole life. The answer to life's mysteries. But the longer I live, the more complicated life seems to get. Why *is* that?"

"Because you know more?"

"Or less. I know what my wife is wondering. She sometimes wonders, half secretly, if we could be—I don't know if I have the right word—'*cursed*,' maybe—or that may be too strong. Under some sort of a spell? It's a hard concept to describe or define. She doesn't say so in so many words, but I know she sometimes wonders about it. She is now, because we're so close to the source, here, near the island, and then this sign, this seeming reinforcement, this seeming confirmation, in the accident. Not really proof—but evidence?"

I paused, cradling my drink in my right hand. "Not just my

wife and I—but all four of us—we're all in this. Yep, Cindy had warned me about people like Miss Smiley. Miss Smiley claimed to know how things worked, how they were *going* to work, and she told us. We took her life—sort of. She might've taken ours—sort of. She may take Jennie's for keeps."

I took another swig. "Jennie told me, herself, Jennie did, that she thought she might be murdered and that Miss Smiley was the ultimate cause. What do *you* think, now that you know the story?"

"I'm just a bartender, remember? It's not my place to judge."

"Fair enough. I have to admit I don't feel so hot."

"That's understandable, considering the circumstances. But I have a question."

"Shoot."

"Miss Smiley? I don't get it. Who *was* she—what makes her so important to the story?"

"She was the crystal-ball lady. The palm reader."

"So what happened to *her*?"

"Like I said, she died. Then a pack of cats set upon her, devouring her."

He squinted hard at me, then shook his head. "I have to go check on that couple in the corner."

"It was all part of the Plan. Not the Plan of Salvation, mind you. But a different plan—dark rather than light. The old woman's number got called first. Now Jennie's number may be up."

I paused to consider how my head hurt, my hands going to my temples. I smiled. "Don't take anything I say too seriously. It's the scotch talking. I won't talk about it anymore."

He didn't say anything.

"I want another drink."

This time, he ignored my request. "Was that a true story?"

I groaned. "No, I'm a fiction writer. I'm working on a novel. I'm here using you as a sounding board for the plot. Did you like it? Give me another drink, and I'll spin you another yarn."

"A tall tale?"

"About as tall as I am."

"I have to check on that table."

He walked around the bar, leaving me sitting there, alone and drinkless.

In a few minutes, he returned.

"Want some water?"

"Yeah."

He handed me a glass.

I drained it. "Thanks."

"Here's one last drink," he said, pouring me another one—water and ice with a splash of scotch. He set it in front of me. "On the house. Then maybe you ought to call it a night. It's good you're spending the night here."

I took a sip. "Thanks."

He moved on down the bar, then returned. "I'll be shutting down in about a minute."

"Take yourself," I persisted. "When you step outside the door, here—or crack a window—what is the first thing you hear? The crashing of the waves upon the sand and rocks. Does that *worry* you? No, not normally. Normally, you don't even think about it—it's something you take for granted. It's always there, isn't it? And it's mostly good.

"But what about the storm days in summer and fall? What happens when the hurricane comes in? And the hurricane does come in. It's only a question of when—and how much damage—how extreme the injury.

"But *you're* lucky: at least the ocean is natural, not plotting against you. And you could move away from it if you had to. Miss Smiley is out there, too—but there's nothing natural about it—and we can't seem to rid ourselves of it, at least not completely."

Now he was looking at me, listening. I chugged the rest of my drink. "But of course, you don't believe in this type of thing. Not *you*, smug and snug in your oak tavern."

His face turned dark. "You've had one too many, fella! You're drunk. No more for you."

I reached into my back pocket and pulled out my wallet. I handed him some twenties.

"Keep the change," I said, waving my hand. "I'd like to have another one."

He shook his head.

"I want another one! Except I might trip over a barstool walking out of here and split my head wide open. How good are you at stuffing brains back into a skull? Probably no better than I was at resuscitating Miss Smiley . . . an old woman . . . who somehow had power, yet looked at me pleading, 'Who will help me?' Or, I might make it to my car, take off down the road, and kill somebody. And it would be your fault because you allowed me to get drunk."

"Time for you to turn in. Past time for you to leave the bar." He started around the counter toward me.

"Not a problem," I said, palms in the air. When I stood up,

I was a lot taller than he was, but he was stockier—and sober. I stumbled against the barstool. I pulled out my wallet and offered him another twenty.

"You've already paid for the drinks," he said. "And given me a good tip."

"Take it," I said, handing it to him. "You've earned it. You're a good bartender." I was more wasted than I thought. I staggered from the bar to the lobby and from the lobby to the front door of the inn. My hand on the door handle, I thought, "Wrong way."

"Wrong door," he said, standing behind me. "I'll help you to your room." He led me by the elbow down the hall. I knocked on the door; he walked off.

Celia appeared in the doorframe. "You've been gone an hour."

"An hour is less than forever," I replied.

She looked at me. "What's that supposed to mean?"

"That I'm awfully glad to see you."

By the look in her eyes, I knew that, even though I was drunk, she didn't care. She wasn't mad at me. "You have the most beautiful brown eyes," I said.

She smiled and took my hand, pulling me toward her across the threshold.

The lock clicked shut after us.

. . .

When I woke up the next morning, it was to sunlight streaming in, blinding me, my head hurting. Last night had ended beautifully despite the bad news and the bar scene, but now I was paying again for the scotch. Celia had brought me breakfast in bed, including coffee, orange juice, and a newspaper. Eating anything was unthinkable, but I did gratefully drink the orange juice and coffee. I looked at the newspaper. Of course, one of the stories on the front page was about Jennie: JENI BOSTON STRUCK BY CAR, IN CRITICAL CONDITION. I laid it aside and groaned.

Celia was packed and ready to go, happy again like she'd been before we hit the highway last night near the sign for Hoophole Island. "I slept great," she said. "And it's a beautiful day out. I feel so bad about Jennie, though."

Eventually, I was dressed and packed.

At the front desk, we settled up with the weather-beaten man in the bow tie. On the way out, I glanced toward the bar. I'd been compos mentis enough never to give the bartender Celia's name—or mine—but that was about the only thing I hadn't said. Once more, I groaned.

Once on the road, it seemed irresistibly necessary to have the radio on, to hear the top-of-the-hour news about Jennie. Now we were in the post-accident phase, with gossipy speculation and questions from every commentator, so much seductive noise, so little information. Jennie was a friend, a person, a human being. She was a whole lot more than a news story, and I felt so bad for her and Croom. At the same time, I was grateful to know my children were all at home safe with Tracy and grateful to see Celia so happy again after being so distressed last night.

My head swirling with all these thoughts and pounding from my visit with the bartender, we continued up the coast on a trip that, in some ways, still seemed more surreal than real despite the sunny day.

Considering all that, I could only wonder what this trip had waiting for us on the road ahead.

14.

THE LOADED GUN

Celia and I listened to the news on the radio until the repetition of the facts about the car accident, Jennie's condition—the questioning of the driver and the questions about the doctor and his generous prescription policy toward drugs—became oppressive. Even the outpouring of emotion from her admiring public was being exploited for entertainment.

Since I had a headache, I asked Celia to drive.

As she followed the highway north to the town of Duck, we stopped a couple of times and got out to view the ocean to our right beyond the dunes. The wind had picked up just enough to stir up whitecaps, and over the water, seagulls by the hundreds swooped from the sky, dive-bombing the surface for fish. The air was nippy but comfortable.

The story in the morning newspaper said the accident had occurred in downtown Dallas. I knew the street, close to the

Dallas Town Club. Jennie had come running off the curb from between two parked cars, and the driver hit her with enough force that she was knocked out. Her injuries were critical, compounded by having prescription drugs in her bloodstream at the time. The driver wasn't charged. I felt awful. Soon I channel-surfed the radio again in search of some hopeful news until Celia said, "Matt, give it a rest."

When we got to Duck, we toured the rows of big houses set out in the sand, then traveled on to Corolla and visited the Currituck Lighthouse. Completed in 1875, the imposing brick tower had a grand cast-iron staircase spiraling around the interior from the base to the light, one hundred sixty feet up. Celia and I climbed the stairs, all two hundred fourteen of them, to the top. The view from the lantern room was a panorama of sea, beach, blue sky, and scores of white houses. But despite the scenic beauty, my heart wasn't in it.

"We need to head back," Celia said, reading my mind. "You're too preoccupied for us to stay out here and continue this trip." I smiled wryly and nodded.

"I know you want to fly out to Dallas to see Jennie and Croom. I want you to."

I looked into her deep brown eyes, so understanding, as she said, "We'll drive back to Raleigh, and you can fly out from there. I'll drive back to Hickory and spend the night with the kids. We've been gone a week; I miss them, and I want to see them. Just give me a day and night at home, then I'll fly out and join you."

"Are you sure?"

"I'm sure. Of course, I want to see Jennie and Croom. I just miss the kids."

I took her hand and squeezed it. "You're an angel." We headed back down the staircase.

When we got back to Raleigh, I booked the next flight to Dallas the following day. Celia took me to the airport and waited with me till the airline announced the boarding call. I looked at Celia apologetically. "I guess this isn't the best way to end a fifteenth-anniversary vacation."

"It's okay," she assured me, my hand in hers. "There's no way we could have known this would happen—and, Matt, I had a wonderful time overall. Thank you."

I gave her a hug and a kiss. "I love you," I said, then picked up my one piece of carry-on luggage. "I'll call you when I get there. Tell the children I love them."

"I love you, too. Be careful. Call me—and I'll see you soon."

I followed the line of passengers onto the plane and buckled myself in. Now settled, I gave in to a rush of memories. The last time I'd seen Jennie was three weeks ago. She and Croom were back together again, but she wanted to have lunch with me.

I called Croom to be sure he was okay with it, and he was. In fact, he encouraged me. "Please talk to her, good buddy," he said. "I'm worried about her. It's been difficult. Maybe your friendship will be a calming influence."

It was true: Jennie was not doing well. About a year ago, she'd decided she wanted to be a mother, at thirty-nine. She and Croom reconciled and were living together, and she became pregnant. Then she lost the baby. Devastated, she underwent counseling and also put a lot of trust and faith in one of her doctors, an old, gray-haired, courtly gentleman by the name of

Dr. McGregor, who had a small practice and made house calls to Jennie because he liked her, she paid well, and he knew she had special circumstances because of her celebrity. He always practiced with his wife at his side, as his nurse, and Croom became a patient of his, as well. He'd come highly recommended, and Jennie and Croom had nothing but the highest regard for him. One day, they received in the mail a short letter informing them that Dr. McGregor had retired and sold his practice. In that way, Jennie "inherited" a different doctor—Dr. Salafar.

Three weeks ago, I had lunch again with Jennie in the Bellaventure Room at the Dallas Town Club. It was the first time I had seen her in almost a year and a half since the time she walked out on me. This time she was a different person. She talked non-stop—not so much with me, or even to me—as *at* me. At first, I tried to carry on a conversation with her but then realized she really wasn't interested in what I had to say. So I sat and listened to her story.

"This new doctor was completely different from Dr. McGregor," she said, "even the way he looked. He was short, noticeably overweight, and had jet-black hair. Maybe dyed. I could see the top of a blue tattoo peeking up over his collar on the side of his neck. As well as I could tell, it was a cupid shooting an arrow into a heart, with a crescent moon off to the side. It was hard to tell how old he was, but I guessed about fifty."

She continued, "He told me he was in the middle of a bitter divorce with his wife who was back in Ft. Lauderdale with their two children. I told him I was having trouble sleeping, that I had a lot of thoughts I couldn't get out of my mind. The loss of my baby son. And all the lies the magazines and tabloids wrote about my miscarriage, and me, and Croom."

The doctor gave her a prescription for a drug that was supposed to help with obsessions and anxiety. After ten days, Jennie developed chest pain, and thinking she was having a heart attack, was taken by ambulance to the hospital. She was released the next day but had stroke symptoms that night, and Croom took her to the emergency room. Again, she was released the following day, after a battery of tests. She went back to Dr. Salafar the day after that for her two-week follow-up visit.

"He asked me how I was doing," Jennie told me. "I told him about the chest pain that put me in the hospital and the fear that I was having a stroke, which had put me back in the emergency room."

She told the doctor, "Two nights in the hospital in four days. And my thoughts are as bad as ever. Maybe worse. I feel like I'm speeding. No, I'm not doing too well."

"Do you think the medicine has anything to do with it?" Pensively, he tapped his cheek with his pen. "You need to double the dose. Double the dose, okay?"

Jennie did as he prescribed, and over the next four days, her behavior grew increasingly bizarre. "I'd never had more energy. My mind had never seemed sharper. As my mind raced, I'd leave the house at night and walk fast for hours," she told me. "I didn't think I could actually fly—only Superman could do that. Or Superwoman. But I did think I could outrun a car if I needed to. And I thought I may *have* to because *they* were after me. The same people who killed my baby."

Croom thought she was acting like a crazy person, and on Saturday, he put her in the hospital against her will.

"I hated that," she said. "All I could think about was the bars on the fifth-floor window and how I might somehow break out and scale down the wall like Spiderwoman."

Then she said, "I've thought about it a lot, and I kept a journal of those days and weeks. I fought Croom every step of the way into the hospital, but looking back on it now, I know he saved my life."

The flight attendant, a pretty brunette in her late thirties, stirred me from my thoughts. "Something to drink, sir?"

"Ginger ale would be good."

A young woman in blue jeans and a western-style shirt sat beside me. As she put down her heavily dog-eared paperback to order a Coke, she wafted her scent, smelling like a cosmetics counter. The man in the aisle seat, dressed in a suit and a tie and reading *The Christian Science Monitor*, ordered a beer.

I thought about Jennie's story of three weeks ago and also Miss Smiley's words spoken eighteen years before: "You will lose someone you love. You'll have poisoned thoughts you can't control."

I also thought about my conversation with the bartender last night, at least part of it, the part about whether or not God was in control of things, or if maybe someone—or some*thing*—else was. It seemed downright perverse even to suggest that Miss Smiley might now be exercising power over us—from the grave—but if her words meant nothing and held no power, how had she guessed things so well? Even if the bartender was right, that fortune-tellers make sweeping generalizations that can apply to anyone, then why did God, if He was in control, let bad things happen?—Jennie losing her baby, Jennie and this car accident?

Not to mention that the accident occurred on the very same day as our Isle of Cats fiasco and Miss Smiley's fateful words.

For that matter, where had God been that night we spent on the island? Who sent the storm that drove us into the house? How many times in our lives had we prayed, "Lead us not into temptation, but deliver us from evil"? Where was God that night when we needed Him? And where had He been when Jennie, on drugs, needed Him? I so wanted to believe He was there, all along.

Jennie had said to me, "It's hard for someone else to understand what it's like for a person to be under the influence of a psychotropic drug. The public needs to be protected from these drugs—they're really dangerous."

Regardless of her state of mind at that point, she did at least know that. And she said, "Matt, you're a lawmaker, the only one I know. One of the main reasons I kept the journal was to help people understand what I went through. I'm going to send you a copy. I want you to work for change. It has to start somewhere; it might as well be with you."

But she never sent me the journal. And things obviously had gone from bad to worse.

I should never fly coach: I was too tall; my knees were always crammed against the seat in front of me. At least the young woman beside me was petite, so she didn't take up much space. I thanked the flight attendant for the pretzels that followed the ginger ale, closed my eyes, then opened them to the window and clouds. I thought about how my dad used to fly us on the clouds when we were children and how, in his Cessna 310 "Sky King" plane, we could feel the clouds underneath us. Then my thoughts returned to Jennie—and her story.

Her attending physician, Dr. Adler, had changed the intake documents so that her commitment was "voluntary." So "Courtney Collins"—the identity they'd given her to protect her career—had voluntarily entered the hospital to receive detoxification from a legally prescribed drug.

"While I was there," Jennie said, "I kept waiting for Dr. Salafar to call me. I wasn't allowed to place a phone call out, but I so hoped he would care enough to call me." She added, "He didn't."

When she returned home from the forced hospitalization, she felt self-conscious and embarrassed about her experience. Croom said to her, "This whole thing has been really hard on me, too, and that Dr. Salafar needs to know what he did to you."

"What he did to both of us," Jennie said. "I could have died from that medicine. He could have killed me."

"That medicine" was something she wanted to know more about, so she looked for the pharmaceutical insert she'd placed in a desk drawer in the den. But when she opened the drawer, there was nothing inside but one of Croom's guns—a .38 Special.

"Croom was with me when I went looking for the insert," Jennie said, "and he opened the drawer on the other side of the desk and handed it to me. He'd moved it there because he didn't want it—or anything else—in the same drawer with the gun.

"I read the insert to Croom," Jennie told me. "You were supposed to look out for mental or mood changes, confusion, and trouble sleeping. I'd had all those symptoms in the extreme. I was a sleep-deprived wreck. But, according to the insert, there were a lot worse possible side effects.

"There were possible fatal syndromes. Symptoms could include blood pressure changes, agitation, hallucinations, other mental or mood changes. Bizarre behavior, chest pain. New or worsening agitation, panic attacks, aggressiveness, impulsiveness, irritability, hostility, exaggerated feeling of well-being, restlessness, or inability to sit still. Unusual or severe mental or mood changes.

"I'd had all those symptoms," Jennie told me.

The insert also warned, "Family and caregivers must closely watch patients who take this medicine." But Dr. Salafar hadn't told Jennie or Croom, and this was the first psychotropic drug either one of them had ever dealt with. The insert also said there must be close monitoring whenever a change in dose was made. Again, no warning from the doctor to the patient.

When Jennie and Croom called Dr. Salafar and told him what had happened, he responded dismissively. "You sound all right to me," he said curtly.

This angered Jennie. "I trusted you!" she fired back. "You could have killed me! I wasn't depressed; I was speeding. If I'd jumped out of a window and killed myself, you'd just have told everyone, 'She was depressed; she'd had a miscarriage.' Well, I wasn't depressed—and if I'd jumped out of a window and been killed, it would have been because I thought I was Superwoman and I could fly. Doctors bury a lot of their mistakes, and I'm glad I'm here to tell you and others the truth about what happened. It's been a horrible two weeks. You stole two weeks of my life and could have taken it completely."

Dr. Salafar replied, "Okay, I shouldn't have put you on that drug, and I shouldn't have doubled the dose, and I should have *closely* monitored you. And I should have warned you about the possible side effects."

He paused, then added, "So is that enough?" His tone had turned defensive and sarcastic. "Or is this about something more?"

There was silence between them for a few moments, then he blurted out, "So you want money! It's always the same. One little slip-up and—bam!—they hit you with a lawsuit. Well, I wasn't born yesterday. I've been around the block—with lawsuits."

"I can believe that," Jennie said. Silence on both ends of the phone.

Then the doctor said, "Maybe I can help you out with your bills if you sign a release. But I don't have a lot of money right now: the wife and the kids—not to mention my girlfriend—are taking it. Come see me at my office in a week. I'll have something for you."

A week later, Jennie and Croom went to see the doctor—not about money or any sort of legal action—but to get a sincere apology. "If he would have just acted like he cared," she told me, "like he was sorry. All I wanted was for him to say he was sorry and to admit he'd made a mistake—not dismissively, defensively—but in such a way that I would know he wouldn't make the same mistake again with anyone else."

As they walked through the door to his waiting room, they hoped for a positive conversation so that things would work out well.

"They kept us waiting for over an hour," Jennie said. "It was so rude, and I grew increasingly on edge. Finally, we were ushered into Dr. Salafar's examining room, where I sat for another thirty minutes while Croom, leaning against the wall, stood beside my chair. The longer Croom and I waited, the more frustrated and less charitable we became. Then, when Dr. Salafar entered, he walked straight to the window without looking at either of us.

"We're here—just as you told us to be," Jennie said. "We've come to discuss the matter we talked about on the phone and the dangers inherent in that drug and not properly monitoring its effects." He didn't reply.

Finally, Jennie said, "And your responsibility to your other patients. This could happen again, and next time your patient could die. Surely, you must be sorry."

"That conversation didn't go well," the doctor replied without turning around.

Croom said, "Well, I guess everyone was emotional. But there's no cause to be emotional about it today."

Jennie said, "Matt, this made me want to be conciliatory, despite everything. So I said to the doctor, 'Right. We just don't want this to happen again to anyone else. We think you realize you made a mistake, and we're sure you must be sorry.'"

She said, "Matt, I just wanted him to say he was sorry for what he did to me, and actually act like he cared."

Instead, Dr. Salafar turned around, glaring. "Was I under oath?" he demanded, his eyes intense. "I haven't admitted anything." He handed Jennie a business card. "Here's my insurance carrier. Give her a call. She's going to handle this."

"So on top of everything else," Croom blurted out, "you're a liar!"

Jennie said to me, "Matt, I could feel the bitterness—even hate—inside me. I reached into my purse and pulled out the pistol Croom kept in the desk drawer at home. I aimed it at Dr.

Salafar. Croom hit my arm, the gun fired, and the doctor, with mouth open, eyes wide, and his right hand over his heart, fell back against the window."

15.
FAREWELL

The flight attendant came by checking to be sure seatbelts were fastened and trays were up because we were landing in ten minutes.

I promised myself that, when I got home, I'd inspect the medicine cabinet to be sure I knew what was there and what the dangers were. I also promised myself I'd research the legislation governing the prescribing of controlled drugs. People were dying every day from painkillers. Now I was learning about psychotropics. As we started our descent, the rest of Jennie's story came back to me.

"Matt, you're shaking your head in disbelief. I know this whole story seems unbelievable. It seems like a bad dream to *me*. The gun discharged when Croom hit my arm, and the bullet flew past the doctor, lodging in the wall. I'm positive I would never have pulled the trigger on my own, but Croom *thought* I was going to shoot. What flashed through his head when he saw the pistol, he told me later, was the prediction made by the old woman. He thought he was about to see 'the murder' take place.

"When the receptionist and the nurses came rushing in, Dr. Salafar lied and said he was showing Croom his gun, and it accidentally went off. Can you believe that? He covered for us! He didn't want the police there any more than we did.

"Pulling a gun on somebody is totally not me. It's been the worst few months of my life: first, losing the baby, then all this. That's why I had to have a sane, stable person to talk to—someone I trust. You. All I want is some peace—some rest. I need to rest."

As she finished her story over lunch, Jennie said, "Matt, I really appreciate your caring enough to meet with me and listening so kindly. But I'm incredibly embarrassed about all this—the hospital, Dr. Salafar, everything. My parents and Croom's parents know about my hospitalization. Other than them, no one knows but my friend Camille, who was with me at lunch when I had the first attack of chest pain. She called the ambulance. No one knows the truth about the gunshot, either. Promise me you'll keep all of this to yourself—well, you can tell Celia. Swear her to secrecy, and I'll be okay with that. I know Celia would never betray a confidence. If she did in this case, it could destroy my career."

I promised Jennie I wouldn't tell anyone but Celia. I had a lot of things I wanted to say, but before I could speak, she said, "Matt, I shouldn't have blamed Dr. Salafar. *I* took the drugs; I'm an adult. My parents didn't raise me to take drugs."

"No, Jennie," I said, shaking my head. "Jennie, listen to me. That drug was legally prescribed by a doctor. He prescribed the drug. You didn't. He doubled the dose. You didn't. And he didn't sufficiently monitor the effect on you or give you or Croom any warning of the possible adverse effects. That's negligent." She looked at me silently, then lowered her gaze. Her lips began to quiver, and she burst into tears.

I looked at the young lady sitting beside me in the plane. She seemed so intent on the book she was reading. As the plane continued its descent, she looked up, and I said to her, "Excuse me, but you've been so engrossed in that book, would you mind telling me what it is?"

She looked at me. "It's called *Finding the Gold in the Garbage*."[1]

Well, for any number of reasons, that didn't sound like something I'd want to waste my time reading.

As if she'd read my mind, she smiled and added, "I know that may not be a very good title, but you shouldn't judge a book by its cover—or its name. It's actually a really good book—spiritual."

I was surprised. "Spiritual?"

"Yes. And deep. The point is that in life—as we live our day-to-day lives and as we face extraordinary events—we inevitably encounter a lot of garbage. But we have to find the gold that's hidden inside that garbage. It's there if we look hard enough for it. And have faith."

"The light in the dark, so to speak?"

"Yes, exactly. The gold—the light—in the darkness."

I could tell she wanted to keep talking, and I did, too, but the plane hit the ground with a thump, and our conversation was interrupted by a voice on the intercom. As soon as the plane stopped moving, seatbelts opened with a clicking sound, and the passengers around us began the dance to collect their things and exit the plane.

As the two of us remained seated, she said to me, “You should read it. It’s positive, spiritual.” She smiled. “It could have an impact on your life.”

She stood, and I noticed that from her necklace hung a small cross.

Now I really wanted to talk.

But the man standing beside her, aisle seat, handed her from the overhead bin her luggage. She thanked him as he stepped backward in the aisle so that she could get out in front of him. I grabbed my luggage and took my place in the aisle behind the man. His nice manners had separated her and her cross from me. As we exited the plane, she walked off and was absorbed into the crowd.

Outside the terminal, I hailed a cab and took it directly to the hospital. In the lobby, I called Jennie’s room.

Croom answered. “Thanks for coming, good buddy,” he said. “I really want to see you. Come on up.”

As I walked down the hall, I saw him standing a few feet from the room, a security officer standing guard at the door behind him. Croom came toward me and shook my hand and hugged me, but he looked awful.

Nudging me a few feet down the hall, he said in a low voice, “She’d become nearly impossible to live with. I couldn’t handle her anymore. I was scared of what she might do because her mind was so messed up, and the gun was the last straw. I was going to put her in the hospital again, but she had the accident before I could.”

"I'm so sorry, Croom. I came as soon as I could. Can I go in and see her? I'd really like to see her."

"Matt, you can go in and see her," he said, tears in his eyes, "but that's all you can do—see her. Jennie's in a coma."

For several hours, I sat in Jennie's room with Croom.

"She actually went back to Dr. Salafar," he said. "She went back to him partly to explain that although she pulled a gun on him, she had no intention of firing it and wouldn't have, except that I hit her arm—the whole thing was an accident. Her other reasons I don't understand.

"So what does he do? He talks her into more medicine. He's the one who put her here; that's who did this to her. When she started acting crazy again, and I found out she was back on medication, I was going to put her back in the hospital, but she was hit by that car. She was on her way to the Dallas Town Club—they'd met there a couple of times. I found that out after the fact.

"The whole thing is really bizarre. He really screwed her up with that drug. Why would she go back to that quack after his carelessness about her life had landed her in the hospital the first time?"

Croom asked me to spend the night at their home, but since he wouldn't leave Jennie, I spent the night in a nearby hotel. I'd called Celia earlier and told her Croom didn't expect her to fly out, at least not now.

I stayed another day, and night, just to be with him. Jennie's parents were in town, too, and at least one of them was in her hospital room almost round the clock. Croom's mother also kept a vigil with us. Jennie's friend, Camille, was allowed to visit. Except for her, though, the hospital staff kept non-family members away, and no one with the press was allowed on the hall. Flowers, letters, and gifts, delivered to the hospital by the hour, went to the house. Croom had hired the security guard who stood outside Jennie's door.

When her condition didn't improve after two days and nights, I decided the next morning to fly back to Charlotte. Having slept poorly since leaving home, I found myself nodding on and off during the flight, and when aided by a tailwind, the plane had landed early. I disembarked, fatigued and groggy. Celia hadn't arrived, and I took a seat in the waiting area. The longer I waited for her, the harder it was for me to keep my eyes open. I nodded, then sat up, nodded, and sat up. Then I dozed off. . .

The TV monitors set on the news channels flashed the breaking news about Jennie—"Jeni B."

She was dead.

The graveside service in Hickory was kept private—only family and closest friends were invited. Otherwise, it could have been a circus. The cars lined up in front of Jennie's family church, and then the small funeral procession began. Celia and I, both in black, drove in silence as we followed a somber parade behind the hearse and limousines carrying family.

We proceeded down Stately Oaks Avenue, passing in front of our own home, then passed Oakwood School, where I had first met Jennie on the first day of first grade. We passed Stately Oaks, the house where my parents lived, then turned into Oakwood Cemetery, where the entrance was guarded by two police officers, one at either side of the iron gates. We passed monument after monument representing generations of Hickory families. At the Goodheart family plot, we wove our way up the hill, finally arriving at the Boston family plot now covered with a tent.

Men dressed in black, wearing white gloves, first attended to the hearse, then the limousines of the family. Somberly, close family and friends gathered around the tent. This early afternoon in the latter half of March gave no sign of spring, so Celia and I stood huddled side by side. While the minister spoke, a wind quickened, and trees began to sway. Clouds overhead cast shadows along the ground, the sky darkened, it grew colder, and shortly a light rain began.

The minister recited the Twenty-third Psalm. When he finished and began reading other scripture, my mind wandered to our first day of school and finding Jennie sitting there on the front row. Her long, blond hair and freckled face told me she was a strawberry blonde, because that's what my mother had told me *I* was. She seemed perfect to me, her hands folded primly on the top of her desk.

In junior high school, Jennie had walked up to me at the beach resort pool and put forth the effort to be friends. When we were in eighth grade, we dated steady, but eventually Cindy Peppercorn managed to break us up. Other memories flashed through my mind, drowning out whatever the pastor was saying. Jennie, the cheerleader, cheering me on, on the basketball court.

The casino in Nassau. The boat.

The other boat.

She and Croom standing over the dead body of that old woman.

Jennie singing her heart out to a packed stadium.

Jennie on drugs.

Now, her own dead body. All that vitality vanished—with no child to remember her.

Why?

I could feel Celia shivering beside me. I moved behind her and held her close. She leaned her head against my chest.

It felt comforting—good—holding Celia close.

And that was important because as the trees swayed and the sky darkened and shadows crossed us, I felt another presence. One that was neither God nor good.

Miss Smiley might as well have been there with us. After all, she had predicted this turn. Winning fame and fortune. Losing a loved one. Betrayal by someone trusted. Poisoned thoughts—and murder. Why should the old woman not join us as a phantom-form today? Indeed, I felt her standing, stooped over among the mourners now, there with us, watching as they lowered the casket with our Jennie into the ground.

Suddenly light-headed, I watched, and shuddered, as family members dropped flowers upon her casket.

The sky grew darker still, and it began to snow.

White flakes swirling about, Miss Smiley looked at Celia and me, and moving away from the graveside mourners beside her, she headed toward us.

16.
CLOUD NINE

As Miss Smiley approached, she slowly reached out her hand to me. "Who will help me?" she pleaded.

Then the ground began to shake.

"Matt, wake up. Wake up." Smiling, Celia was shaking my shoulder. "Wake up, sweetie; you're talking gibberish in your sleep, poor baby."

I opened my eyes and looked around. Celia's pretty face, beautiful smile—the waiting area in an airport. A man in a suit reading a newspaper, sitting across from me. A young woman with a child on her lap, beside him. My one piece of carry-on luggage beside me on the floor. I shook my head, trying to clear it.

"Wow!" I said. "Am I ever glad to see you! Celia, what a dream!"

Sitting down in the chair next to me, she leaned over and kissed me on the cheek. I stretched my arms in the air and returned the kiss.

"By the sound of it," she said, "that must have been *some* dream!"

"I'll say—about as vivid as you can get. How long have I been asleep? I don't want to miss the plane."

"I don't know how long you've been asleep, but I don't think you're totally awake. You're not going to miss a plane: you're already back from Dallas—you're in Charlotte. I've got the car to take us back to Hickory. You really *were* asleep. Sounded bad, Matt."

I stretched my legs and sat up. "I dreamed Jennie died. When I landed here at the airport, I saw the news on the TV monitors. We buried her at the cemetery. Before that, we went to her funeral at the church. The service was really sad, and you and I cried through the whole thing. It was so real. It seemed like life itself."

I looked around, and the TV monitors were in the restaurants, none in the waiting area. I hadn't been in any of the restaurants, so I couldn't have seen any news reports.

"You must have been exhausted," Celia said. "I'm late—terrible traffic—so you fell asleep waiting for me. Just a vivid dream, a bad one. The good news is that I had the radio on in the car, and I didn't hear any bad news about Jennie."

"So Jennie's not dead? She's still alive?" I wasn't just thankful for the obvious reason, but also because I feared that if she'd died, she might not have gone to Heaven, and I would never have seen her again. "Thank God!"

Celia was smiling. "No change—that's what they're reporting. I thought you would be giving me a report about

Jennie—here I am telling you. But I'd say no news is good news."

I stood up. "I need to call Croom," I said, picking up my luggage. "Let's go find a phone."

Carrying the travel bag in one hand and pulling Celia with the other, we headed down the concourse in search of a phone. Croom picked up on the first ring. "Hey, good buddy!" he said, an unusual excitement animating his voice. "I can't tell you how glad I am you called. I already called you and left a message at your house. I've got some incredible news. Jennie's pulling out of it. She's opening her eyes and waking up!"

"Are you serious?" I exclaimed and looked at Celia. "Jennie woke up!"

Celia's face beamed.

"Croom, that's incredible! Thank God!" Dropping the phone, I quickly reached down and retrieved it from the end of the cord. "Sorry, Croom, I dropped the phone. Tell me what happened. What's going on?"

"All of a sudden, she just woke up. Not for long—just for a few minutes. Then she went back out. Dr. McGregor showed up this morning with Mrs. McGregor. He apologized for not being in touch with us earlier. He said he was sorry he had to sell his practice, especially on such short notice. He said he'd heard some bad things about Dr. Salafar and then the awful news about Jennie. He said he'd like to spend some time with her if the rest of us wanted a break, so he and his wife spent a couple of hours with her.

"When I walked back into the room, they were smiling. Jennie's eyes were closed, and Dr. McGregor said she was 'out' for the time being. But he said she'd come back if I'd just sit there patiently and wait for her. So I did, and sure enough, she opened her eyes. Just like that, she was conscious.

"He said she would wake up for short periods, then go back to sleep, then wake up. He said she would be confused and have amnesia that could last for weeks or months. He said it would be slow progress over months, but he believed she would slowly improve. But we would have to be patient.

"The other doctors came later and said they needed to be realistic in their prognosis; they shouldn't give us false hope for a full recovery after two-and-a-half days in a coma: she might fully recover; she might not. So we have a team of young and middle-aged doctors telling us not to have false hope—there's no guarantee of full recovery—and an old, retired doctor saying we should be hopeful, spend lots of time with Jennie—and pray. So that's what we're doing . . ." He paused, then spoke more slowly. "Will you and Celia pray for us, too? I mean it, Matt, we need you to pray."

"Yes, Croom," I said, and looking at Celia, "Celia and I will pray for Jennie and you."

"Thank you, good buddy," he said quietly and paused again. "Jennie has a long way to go. She doesn't seem to know what's going on at all. That's a little disturbing, I have to admit, but she *is* conscious—she's conscious right now. She might not be in a few minutes, but she is right now. I'll take that for a start. I sure will."

"Well, Croom, I can't tell you how happy and relieved I am. And Celia, too. She's right here beside me, listening in. We're in Charlotte at the airport."

"Let me talk to her," Croom said.

I handed Celia the phone. "Hey, Croom—it's Celia."

After a minute, she said, "Oh, Croom, I'm so happy." Her eyes began to tear as she listened to him go on. "I'm so happy," she said again. "We both are. We're with you. We're with you, thanking God every minute! You must be on cloud nine!"

17.

BETTER LATE THAN NEVER

Unfortunately, the euphoria only lasted about a week, then reality set in. Jennie had memory loss and confusion, and because of that, personality changes. So over the next few weeks, sometimes in the hospital, but usually at home with an attending nurse, she could be at times a demanding patient.

Her close brush with death affected all four of us. Croom was now a caregiver. Celia, now more conscious of the fragility of life, decided to return to the piano in a serious way while she still could, and I developed a nagging feeling that there was something I had to clarify once and for all regarding my relationship with Jennie. She'd nearly died, and I thought about Cindy Peppercorn and how she lived to regret not trying to prevent her brother's death. I was thankful for this second chance to clear up any issue that might remain with Jennie, and I figured I owed that to all four of us. It was only a matter of working out in my mind what to do—and when. In the meantime, I stayed in touch with Croom, wanting to be a supportive friend.

Being closer at hand, however, Dr. McGregor was proving to be his biggest support. An invaluable and unaffected source of inspiration, he had practically adopted Jennie—and Croom—or maybe it was they who had adopted him.

"Never give up hope," he said. "No matter how daunting things appear, no matter how inadequate you may feel at times, have faith and never give up."

In July, his wife passed away. He grieved openly and visited her grave often but never lost his faith or his willing spirit. He spent even more time with Jennie and Croom.

"Always hang on to hope and faith," was his way. "Good things will come to those who put their faith and trust in the Lord and are steadfast in Him."

Though I knew Croom was sometimes discouraged by the slowness of Jennie's progress—and her demands and at times difficult personality—he rarely let on. "We *will* make this work!" he told Jennie—and me—and everyone else. Then he'd thump his fist emphatically. "I'll stand by her forever!" he told Dr. McGregor and all of us. "No matter what." At the same time, he was always there for me, just as he'd always been, politically and otherwise, yet never asked for anything in return.

As for Celia, she'd decided that running a furniture company had grown too time-consuming and now wanted out of her management position and day-to-day operations. "I want to do some other things with my life," she told me, "while I still can. I want to do something creative, something inspired. I'd like to inspire others."

Though I understood and couldn't blame her, there was no way I could take up the slack at Tavern Craft, and Andrew Templeton, my head supervisor, needed help, so we turned over more responsibility to Annie, making her our finance manager.

Celia asked my parents if they wanted to give up the grand piano sitting unused in their basement recreation room at Stately Oaks. Delighted to pass it on to an appreciative heir, Celia got the piano, and by May, she had thrown herself into practicing several hours every day.

As for me, I'd learned from the experience of buying an old house in need of repair and renovation—our home on Stately Oaks Avenue—that I enjoyed restoring old homes. I bought two additional old houses and was now in the process of restoring them.

At the same time, while not practicing much law, I was still in the Legislature and had been for the last twelve years. From the beginning of my career, Celia had been supportive. She knew I'd always had a keen interest in politics, and she'd said, "Yes, Matt, I think you ought to run for the Legislature. You like people, and you're comfortable with them. You have an easy-going personality. People like you, and you're fair-minded. Besides, you've talked about running for office ever since I first met you. It was a college dream. That summer as a Congressional intern really gave you the bug. Now's your chance. Go for it."

She'd laughed. "I don't have the temperament for it. I lack the required patience, and I like to tell people what I think. I might go too far with that in a weak moment." Then she'd laughed again. "Worse than that, I might get really mad. I don't want to shock anyone."

I *had* been smitten by the thought of serving in the Congress, ever since a trip to Washington with my father when I was in the third grade. As for motivation, I got some of that from my father, who was a decorated fighter pilot in World War II and was hard-driving. Celia and my children also gave me motivation. I believed devoutly in the genius of the Founding Fathers and our Constitution and the basic goodness and greatness of America and her people. I might have been confused about some things but never about that. Political philosophy was easier than the meaning of life and understanding God and the cosmos.

Celia's nudging and support fit in with my childhood and youthful dreams and adult ideals, so I ran. In that first campaign, Croom had helped me, and I was amazed at his innate political instincts on a practical level. His advice and encouragement were unflagging and intuitive, and he was also a generous donor. I won by a large margin that first time and couldn't have had a better friend or supporter.

Now in my sixth two-year term, I was still motivated, and Croom was still faithfully with me despite his own complicated life. 1992 and Jennie's close call with death convinced me I had to be a better friend to both him and Jennie. And I wanted to be a better friend with God. I wanted a closer relationship. Life could be taken away from us at any time.

In July, not long after Mrs. McGregor died, we learned that Jennie was pregnant. Though she still had issues with memory and confusion, she was ecstatic with the prospect of becoming a mother, and Croom was equally thrilled.

My children were growing up. Elisa was now in the seventh grade, Bert in the fifth, Caroline in the third, and Teddy in the second. I now knew something of the challenges my parents had faced in raising four children, and also just how deep and abiding is a parent's love.

As spring turned to summer, Celia and I took all four children on a cruise to the Caribbean and Aruba. Then Celia and I took a ten-day vacation all by ourselves to St. Maarten and St. Bart's to make up for the fact that our trip to the Outer Banks back in March had ended prematurely.

We got to see our old friends again in the latter part of August when they visited us in Hickory, full of the news of Jennie's pregnancy. It was Jennie's first trip out of Dallas since she'd been hit by the car, and all four of us very much enjoyed our time together. Even so, I wasn't completely convinced that Jennie and I were totally where we needed to be, friendship-wise, because both of our last two meetings alone had not been happy, positive or comfortable. This was something I wanted to set right.

In the meantime, summer turned to fall, and in late September, Celia, having practiced for six months in our living room on her grand piano, gave her first concert in the fifteen-hundred-seat auditorium at Lenoir-Rhyne University in Hickory. On the night of the concert, she confessed, "Matt, your wife is scared to death." It didn't help her nerves in the least that my father, Bert Goodheart, was then serving the University as president and would be introducing his daughter-in-law. Nevertheless, she played beautifully and received a standing ovation and demands for an encore. The next day, Celia received such good reviews in the papers, it surprised everyone, most of all herself.

Outwardly, it seemed that everything was going well for

us—and Croom and Jennie, too—moving in the right direction, away from the pull of negative memories and toward a positive future. But six months after Jennie's accident, something still nagged at me. The dream I'd had in the airport before Celia woke me up, felt so real. Cindy Peppercorn had dreamed her brother died, but did nothing about it. I thought about Croom—and Celia—and how all four of us were linked by strong memories.

Jennie had received a second chance at life, but Cindy's brother had not. I said to myself, I'll give it a full year, till March of 1993, and surely, by then, the vividness of Jennie's "death" will dissipate from my brain, and the unpleasantness of my last two meetings with Jennie will be forgotten. But that didn't happen. The nagging thoughts wouldn't go away. I talked to Celia about it more than once. But because of all the demands on my schedule and Celia's, two more months passed before I could act.

. . .

May, 1993

Celia said to me by phone—she in Hickory, I in Raleigh for the Legislative Session—"You keep talking about going to see Jennie. I haven't seen her baby, and you want to go. You know I can't go with you: I have a concert in two weeks. It wouldn't be the truth if I said I'm not a little irritated. I am. But I also have a problem with my schedule, so I want you to go. I think you need to, and I'm not sure when I can get away."

I took an excused absence from Session on Thursday and flew out of Raleigh-Durham on the morning flight. Landing at Dallas/Fort Worth, I rode a shuttle to Highland Park, the long ride making me increasingly anxious.

"That house, there on the right," I said to the driver,

pointing. “The red-brick colonial.”

Wide and flat across the front, the house had a massive two-story gallery running its length, supported by huge round columns made of cement, four on each side of the front door. Not particularly imaginative style-wise, the house was nevertheless impressive because of its size. I paid the driver and got out.

In a navy-blue blazer and white slacks, I stepped onto the front porch and rang the bell. It was late afternoon, and since I’d called ahead, I knew Croom was still at the University. As I waited, another wave of anxiety came over me. Jennie answered the door. Dressed in a pink-silk, sleeveless blouse, and a black skirt, she looked lovely. She smiled, drew me in, and let me kiss her cheek, but she didn’t hug me.

We walked into the study and sat down on opposite ends of a sofa across from the fireplace. Croom’s animal heads still ranged high upon the four walls, but I noticed that they were now in competition with Jennie’s gold and platinum records and awards and framed photos documenting her success as a country-western superstar who had crossed into the mainstream. As we exchanged small talk, a young woman in a white apron entered the room and asked us, in a diffident Spanish accent, what we wanted to drink.

“Iced tea, Maria—sweet,” Jennie said.

“Tea, please—unsweet.”

After some small talk about the flight in from North Carolina, my family’s doings, and those of the legislature, Maria entered carrying a silver tray with our tea and a variety of small sandwiches, setting it down on the table before us. Jennie thanked her; Maria smiled and left. I stood to stretch my arms and legs.

"Sorry," I said. "I'm a little on edge. Not a bad trip in, but long."

I sat again, and we continued to exchange pleasantries about Croom, and Jennie's parents. Then the weather. "Unusually humid," Jennie offered. "More like North Carolina than Texas. You must have brought it with you. I like it."

"You look really good," I said; then, hoping to be less superficial, I added, "Happy."

"I *feel* good, and I *am* happy. Aren't you going to ask me about my baby?"

"Of course. I was hoping I'd get to see him. Celia can't wait to get to know him."

She smiled and pressed a remote on the table beside her. A few moments later Maria appeared, carrying an infant wrapped in a blue blanket. Jennie stood, and Maria handed the baby to her as Jennie beamed. Tossing her long blond hair, she hugged the baby to her chest, with his head resting on her shoulder.

"Meet Wes," she said, smiling at me broadly, tossing her hair again. Then she sat down with her eyes fixed on the baby. "Wes," she said, "this is our friend, Mr. Goodheart."

"He's beautiful," I responded. "Perfect! It's been a long time since any of mine were that little. You can forget what they were like at that age, so fragile and needy." Smiling, I held out my hands. She handed him to me. "What a good baby!" I said, smelling baby lotion. I held him for a while as Jennie, smiling, watched me talk to him and make funny faces. Soon, Wes smiled and cooed back at me, crinkling big blue eyes.

"He was born March 30th," Jennie said. "It took us a while to figure out what we'd call him. We didn't want to call him 'Croom'—too confusing. Or 'Fifth'—sounds like booze. Or

'Nelson'—too geeky. Or 'Nels.'" She laughed. "Too Old-World. We finally said, 'Wes, it is. Nelson Croom Westfall the Fifth'—Wes Westfall."

I'd heard that story before, from Celia, but never from Jennie herself. I didn't think I'd ever seen Jennie smile so contentedly in my life. She was radiant. She couldn't take her eyes off her little son, so I handed him back to her. He cooed, smiled, then hiccupped as she rearranged a small white cloth she'd taken from the end-table and placed over her shoulder.

I said, "He looks like you," then added, trying to be funny, "Thank Heaven!"

"Blond . . . blue-eyed." She glanced at me. Then she said, "Matt, I love being a mother. I can't tell you how much. I'd have four, just like you and Celia. I'd never set foot on a stage again. That's not where I want to be. This is where I want to be."

"*Never* again?" Somehow I was doubtful.

"Not at this point—I have no desire. I can't imagine I'd ever have gone that way in the first place if it hadn't been for . . ." She hesitated, searched my eyes, then said, "That crazy woman on the island we went to . . . with her predictions. She changed my life, and I'm not sure the direction was good. A year ago, I almost died. I was a breath away from dying. It's made me question almost everything, even my faith. If it weren't for Dr. McGregor—and Croom—I don't know how I would have managed." Suddenly, she'd gone all serious on me.

I took it as my segue. "It's made me question my life, too," I said. "And my relationship with God. I want to be a better person. That's what I want to talk to you about. That's why I'm here. But I've got to ask you first—I'm curious—why did you go back to Dr. Salafar the second time? I just don't get it."

She shifted her position, slightly nearer me. "I really do need to talk with you. Our last two meetings alone didn't go well, and I feel bad about that."

"So do I. I think we need to talk some things out."

"Me, too," she agreed. "But I have to tell you I'm a little nervous. I'm glad you're here, but in another way, I've been dreading this visit, wondering when it would happen, thinking about the best way to handle it."

I said, "We go back a ways."

"Let's not rehash the past—agreed?"

"Agreed."

She smiled. "No more arguing about the boat."

"Right," I said. "History."

"Okay. Good. But you asked me about Dr. Salafar—why I went back to him."

"Why *did* you?"

"Okay. I'll tell you flat-out. I went back to him the second time because I was weak—and confused . . . and because he had a strange hold on me."

I cocked my head. I was ashamed to think it, but I wondered if it was because she'd been involved with him. Croom had made me wonder that, regardless of whether or not he meant to. "Uh—a *hold* on you?"

"I was going through an awful time then, as you well know. I'd lost the baby, and Dr. Salafar had put me on that drug. Dr. McGregor seemed gone at the time, and I felt a dependency. I went back to Dr. Salafar for several reasons." She was not looking at me; she was looking at Wes. "To convince him I wasn't crazy, not an attempted murderer. Maybe to convince myself of that, too. My brain still carried the effects of that psychotropic drug he'd given me. And personally, he had a strong hold on me for some reason. Strangely, I trusted him. But looking to him was a mistake that nearly cost me my life."

She smiled. "I'm good now, though. I'm a new person. A mother and a wife, and I'm happier than I've ever been. Dr. McGregor is a man of true faith, and he's been a role model. He was amazing after Mrs. McGregor died. He was with her when she passed away, and he has no doubt that he felt her soul pass out of her body and ascend into Heaven. He grieved terribly for her because he missed her, and of course, he still does miss her, but he knows absolutely that she is with Jesus in Heaven. And he's looking forward to joining her there. Dr. McGregor's been an inspiration to Croom and me, both. I wish I were more like him."

After a moment, she added, "Then there's Dr. Salafar. He's fled the country, wanted for income-tax evasion. Fortunately, he seems so long ago, more than a year, and not so important now. The past is past. I'm content with the present."

She tickled her baby under his chin, and when he smiled and made giggling noises at peace again, she kissed him on the forehead. "I just wuv my wittle Wes," she said, kissing him on the nose and tummy.

At that moment, a bird—a big white pigeon—waddled into the room from the den, his head bobbing up and down as he came toward us.

My eyes wide, I said, "Jennie—there's a pigeon in here!"

She laughed. "He's harmless. He comes in to visit every

once in a while. Sometimes, he walks into the den from the patio if the doors are open, then he comes poking his head in here. He's a dove."

"You let it in the house?"

She tossed him a piece of bread from a cucumber sandwich. "I guess we shouldn't. Croom started it, though. Our dove walked into the den one day, and Croom tossed him part of a cracker. He gets a snack, then leaves."

He came within four feet of us, and Jennie tossed him some more bread. The bird was cooing, and so was Wes. I was shaking my head. "How do you know it's a dove and not a pigeon?"

"I don't know. But Croom and Wes and I want him to be a dove, so that's what we say he is." She tossed him two more pieces of bread. He poked and pecked on the polished wood floor until he'd eaten them, then he turned and waddled out.

"Aren't you afraid he'll fly into the den and mess it up?"

"I'm not afraid. Once he gets a snack, he leaves. He may not be back for another week—maybe never. Anyway, Wes likes him."

"Maybe Wes should have a puppy?"

"Maybe later."

"Jennie, that bird has distracted us. Are we avoiding something?"

She looked down and kissed Wes on the nose, and he burbled back at her.

"You know how confused I was—and why," she said. "This has been a year-long recovery. I've been practically sequestered for that length of time, and a person can do a lot of thinking, soul-searching—and praying—in fourteen months."

I guessed she was right, but all I ever seemed to do was drive back and forth to Raleigh, trying to keep my head above water. I prayed and soul-searched as best I could, but interstate traffic wasn't the best place for a retreat.

Then she threw me a curveball. "Would you like to talk some more about that Miss Smiley woman and all that?"

"Well . . ." I paused.

"What she's meant to the four of us—and all that?"

"That probably would be a good idea; sometime, we probably do need to talk about that. But for the moment, since I don't know how much time we have together right now, I don't want to get distracted from the real reason I came."

I paused again. "I've done *some* soul-searching, myself. And praying." I continued, "I need to do more. But I've done enough already to know that I had to come see you for the sake of honesty and my own peace of mind and because of how much you and Croom—and of course, Celia—mean to me. But I'm just not good with this type of conversation, less so than you are."

Her attention was off Wes, now, and totally on me. I said, "I'm not always the best at expressing how I feel."

Cocking her head slightly, she stood up and, carrying Wes in her arms, walked to the front hall. "Maria . . ."

Maria appeared, and Jennie handed her the baby. "Maria," she said, "put Wes in the stroller and take him to the park, please." She walked toward me and sat at the far end of the sofa, crossing her legs.

"I feel strongly, but I don't always do well with the words."

Jennie looked at me. "Matt," she said. "I got it in my head that I was being blackmailed. That was part of the paranoia under the influence of that drug."

"*Blackmailed*? About *what*?" I suspected Dr. Salafar was involved.

"About *you*."

Startled, I said, "Hunh? *Why*? We never did anything—wrong."

"That's how paranoid I was."

"Blackmailed by whom?"

"The paparazzi. I thought they had pictures of us taken when we were at the Bellaventure Room those two times. I guess I felt guilty as well as paranoid. It was the medicine on top of losing my baby. I was acting crazy and feeling cornered."

"But you went back to Dr. Salafar *after* that . . ."

"That was the drugs—and *for* the drugs—and the odd hold that man had on me. He was silently controlling. But I didn't feel paranoid about *him*; I felt paranoid about *you*. He came across as a safe harbor, even though it was his drugs that caused the paranoia that I needed a safe harbor *from*. Do you understand, now, what a hero my husband is? He saved me from all that—and gave me Wes, too."

"I've had a lot of time to talk to Croom," I said, "but he's never explained it to me like that. I understand it better now."

"Good. I wanted to tell you myself since some of it was about you. Events intervened, but I'm telling you now. Croom promised he'd let *me* tell you, and he kept his word. You know how he is, Matt: a lot more moral, a lot more sensitive than he lets on." Her voice broke. "The noble man, the loyalty thing."

I moved toward her.

She held up her hand, and I sat back down. Brushing her

cheeks, she regained her composure. She shook her head as if to clear it. "I'm okay. I said I wouldn't do that."

After a moment, all I could say was, "Wow! I'm blown away." With my hands on my forehead, I looked down. After a few more moments, I looked up. "Now I'm especially glad I'm here." I looked upward to the ceiling. "Thank you, God."

Then to Jennie, I said, "All the more reason for being glad I came."

"Are there other reasons?"

Again, I paused, looking away.

She smiled. "Go on. It's okay."

"Well, it's like this . . . it's been growing ever since your accident. I thought you had died. I believed you'd died. I had an incredibly vivid dream about it, your funeral with Celia and me crying, your burial at the cemetery—so messed up . . . Miss Smiley . . . was in attendance."

Jennie's eyes widened.

"Your death felt real. The drugs, the accident, your near-death on the eighteenth anniversary of our trip to the Isle of Cats: all of that's affected me. You know, like where's God in all this? We seem to know where Miss Smiley is, but where's God?"

I added quickly, "Don't get me wrong. I don't think about that trip all that often. I mean, I honestly don't. And those predictions do not—have not—controlled my life. It's just the rather amazing, coincidental timing involved. So it's been building for over a year as I've had time to think about it. I just wanted to be sure you'd had enough time to fully recover before I spoke with you."

Jennie stood up, walked to a wing chair across from me, and

sat down.

"For me, it was the accident," I said, "and the fact that I thought you were dead and I would never get to see you again. That strong shock can change a person. The dream I had of your burial seemed so real—along with the prediction—when I realized it wasn't true and you were alive after all, it was like you'd come back from the dead and given me a second chance. Given both of us a second chance. But it's taken me a year to get here."

"I'd say, Matt, longer than a year . . . for both of us. Maybe more like . . . the better part of our lives." She smiled kindly. "So let's just get this all out in the open right now, once and for all." Her voice was quiet and steady. "Yes, there have been two major events in my life that involved you. The first was what happened that night in Nassau. I promise that's all I'm going to say about it, and I'll never mention it again, but it touched me and linked me to you deeply. The second was what happened on the island. Both of those events changed my life—affected my whole life. Both involved you, the first for love, the last for something more complicated, harder to explain."

"What happened that night in Nassau, on the boat, that was significant for both of us. But it was a long time ago."

"Yes, Matt, a long time ago—and now, I'm happily married. Finally, I'm not just content—I'm happy—with my husband, with my baby, with my life."

"We're fortunate," I said. "Both married well to wonderful people." I paused. "It was believing you were dead. And the way Croom has been, and really *always* has been, so noble. I see that even more now. And the way Celia has always been there for all of us. Celia is noble, too. I'm the one who maybe hasn't always been noble . . ."

I paused again. "I've meant to come see you with this before now, but better late than never. Maybe, subconsciously I've been putting it off. But I hope this clears the air, makes things right, once and for all. I had to have this conversation with you, face to face, to set the record straight, once and forever, for the sake of all four of us. I'm searching, Jennie, for the right words to define us. This isn't easy—help me."

She smiled sweetly. "Just friends?"

"That's it—just friends."

"Oh, Matt," she said, shaking her head. She closed her eyes and looked down, then looked up. "Oh, Matt, my dear friend, I do love you."

In a low voice, I said, "Thank you."

We sat in silence for a while before she finally said, "You're welcome, beach buddy!"

I looked up. "*Beach buddy*?" I echoed. As she smiled at me, I thought for a few moments, then realized this was a reference to the summer before she and I went to eighth grade.

I smiled back. "Oh yeah, beach buddy!" I began to laugh, then Jennie laughed, and by the end, we were laughing so hard we cried.

Then we heard Croom whistling "Dixie." When he appeared on the threshold, he was carrying Wes like a sack of sugar, his baby blue eyes wide and happy at the sound of our laughter. Jumping up, I went to the door to greet them. Wearing an elbow-patched sports coat, Dingo boots and jeans—and mustachioed like a nineteenth-century English actor, he greeted me grandly—a self-styled *paterfamilias*. "Hel*lo*, good buddy!" he roared and gave me a firm handshake and hug as best he could. I smiled broadly and patted him on the back.

Then he sat down on the arm of Jennie's chair, one arm around her shoulder, the other arm still cradling his infant son. It was a beautiful sight, indeed, the three of them—father, mother, and child united and solid as a rock.

Smiling with relief at my two old friends, I took a deep breath and sighed out loud, as if a solid rock—a boulder—had been lifted from my shoulders, at last.

PART THREE

THE REVERSAL OF FORTUNE

18.

PREPARING FOR SPOOK NIGHT

I boarded the plane with a great sense of accomplishment and an even greater sense of relief. Now that Jennie and I both knew exactly where we stood, there was one less thing in life to distract and confuse. The air was clearer, the path narrower. I thought to myself on the flight back home, "God has blessed us. Life is good."

Before I knew it, spring turned to summer, and then to autumn. In October, when the leaves began to fall, Celia and I turned our thoughts to the end of the year and the season of holidays, the first being "Halloween on Stately Oaks Avenue," the annual event that transformed our street into a mini-Mardi Gras, minus the floats and outdoor alcohol.

This event had started years ago almost by accident. Originally, all the house decorating had been done to entertain the young children who lived on the street. Several of those were ours. Then the children from the surrounding neighborhood started coming to visit. In a few years, because of its well-decorated houses and the long sidewalks, the Avenue had grown famous for its Halloween hospitality. Now people came from all around, even outside the county.

Around two-thirty the afternoon of Halloween, 1993, I was in the front yard making final preparations for the *three thousand children* who would soon be coming to the street and my front door. The bushes were strung in orange and purple lights, with some green and other colors mixed in. Some of the lights were tiny jack-o-lanterns, some were flowers or fanciful creatures, and some were funny-looking faces. Regardless, nothing was neatly strung: I liked the "thrown-on" look for spook night. I had wrapped all the white columns on our front porch in black paper, like a Halloween barber pole, then spiraled some orange lights onto the paper to show up after dark.

With a bristling coat and huge eyes, a black cat hung from the doorknocker, looking like it had just seen a ghost. Ten different jack-o-lanterns, some real ones I'd freshly cut, some terra cotta or metal or pottery clay, sat on the front steps. Orange candles glowed in the windows, upstairs and down. Skeletons and ghosts hung from the ceiling of the porch, fluttering this way and that as they caught the October breeze. A life-sized witch dressed in black stood on the upstairs porch in the gambrel roof. A bucket of dry ice sat on the front walk, waiting to be activated at about the same time I lit the candles inside the ten jack-o-lanterns. Some of the creatures I'd hung from the trees in the yard were motion-activated and would move about and scream when anyone walked near them. I especially liked the faces that gave the effect of talking trees.

Having taken, as I did every year, some beer to my neighbors, we had already exchanged pleasantries. As we braced for the invasion, there was a special bond among us. "Are you ready?" was the question. "Ready for Halloween!" was the answer.

I had arranged a dozen lawn chairs, six on either side of my front walk, for the adult volunteers who would arrive in their costumes around six-thirty to help hand out the candy. Andrew Templeton had assured me he'd come over and help me wash the chairs, which had been sitting outside on the back patio since spring. He also would bring more beer and, later in the evening, go to the store for bags of ice. I thought it was about time for him to show up—I could use some help.

I knew Annie Jameson would arrive precisely at three o'clock, punctual as clockwork. She made the world's best lobster bisque, and everyone, starting with me, looked forward to it every Halloween.

Across the street, tarantulas, five feet in diameter, were suspended on cobwebs all over the front of our neighbor's two-story house. The house next door to that was held hostage by pirates; the house beside that one was cursed by a coven of witches. Our next-door neighbors to the left arranged things so that the children walked through a spook house before they got to the front door. The neighbors to the right had a Candy Land motif. Another neighbor had a black cat in the front yard the size of a parade float. The house beside that one had a yard full of talking gravestones, mummies, and werewolves.

Sure enough, at three o'clock sharp, a car pulled slowly up the drive. Our first visitor of the evening was Annie in her beloved, cream-colored 1978 Oldsmobile Cutlass, which she'd driven for the last fifteen years and which she washed every week whether it needed it or not. Teddy, playing next door and seeing the car, came running through the bushes.

In consideration of other cars that would arrive, Annie parked exactly where she knew she was supposed to, then set the handbrake. Teddy stood by the car as she, unbuckling her seat belt, looked in the mirror to make sure her rouge was sufficiently rosy on her chubby cheeks. Then she smiled, and he opened the door, and she got out.

Teddy hugged her. A third-grader, he wasn't shy about showing his affection if he liked someone, and he liked "Auntie," as he called Annie. "You know," he said, "like Aunt Bea."

"How's my favorite young man doing?" she said with a warm smile as she patted him on the head.

"I'm good, Auntie," Teddy said. "I hit a homerun yesterday and knocked in two people on base. Do you need some help?"

"I do," she said. "Someone strong, like you."

He beamed.

"Are Elisa, Bert, and Caroline home? I'd like to see them, too."

"No." Then he told her where they were.

"Well, sweetheart, you be sure to tell them I missed seeing them—okay?"

"Okay."

As I looked at their smiling faces, I thought how Annie seemed to have been born the age she was right now and never seemed to age. Five years older than Celia and me, she was barely an inch over five feet tall and rotund. She'd come to us recommended by her aunt, Ruth Ann Phipps, my father's long-time secretary, and for as long as we'd known her, her appearance had never varied—not her face, her hairstyle, or the way she dressed. Seldom in slacks, never in jeans, she wore a skirt and blouse to be casual, dresses to dress-up outside the office, and dresses at work. She was in a purple dress today, with small flowers on it.

Ever since I'd known her, she'd always worn rhinestone glasses and kept her brown hair pulled neatly in a bun, no variation, always adequate make-up on her face. She liked jewelry and wore several *large* diamond rings on each hand. I couldn't imagine her any other way.

"No, I don't dress up for Halloween," she explained. "I always come and go as exactly who I am—Annie. I don't do costumes."

Regardless, at Halloween, as at other times, Celia had grown to depend on her, and so had I. It was her dependability, along with her easy-going, methodical nature, that drew us to her.

"In the backseat," she said to Teddy. Then pointing, "Other side."

As she opened the door beside her, he opened the far door, and I watched with amusement as they loaded up with grocery sacks. "We've got it covered, sir," she said to me, nodding to the house, "if you'll just get the door." I grabbed the last sack of groceries and opened the back door.

"Annie, you're a dear," Celia said as we entered the kitchen. And taking one of the sacks, she said, "Here. Let me help you."

Annie replied, "That chili smells so good I can taste it. If it's ready before I leave, you can bet I'll sit down and enjoy myself. Maybe do seconds." Celia smiled.

Annie always left before dark, usually before the first

children arrived. Always on a diet, she said, "I can't hand out chocolate candy without eating some. Then I can't stop."

But we knew another reason she left before dark, besides her weakness for chocolate, was to avoid being around alcohol. Her husband was killed in an automobile accident with alcohol involved, and that tragedy had turned her into a teetotaler. Having never remarried, she was married to her work or whatever endeavor she undertook, whether it was master gardening or charity work or volunteering at the library.

She was pulling items from a paper sack. "I've got all types of cheeses, boxes of crackers, hors d'oeuvres." She pulled out a tin of cookies and held it up. "Iced Halloween cookies I baked and decorated myself. Still warm."

"Annie, you do too much," Celia said, shaking her head.

"Can I have one?" Teddy asked.

"As many as your mamma will allow," Annie said. "Your favorite, sweetheart—chocolate chip."

"Just one," said Celia. "Maybe two."

Annie arranged the items neatly, precisely, on the countertop, then adjusted and readjusted each one, ever so slightly, until they lined up perfectly. Watching her, Celia and I smiled with affectionate amusement. The checking and re-checking of things was *so* Annie, always conscientious to the point of being perfect. That was why she was such a good controller.

Annie pulled some napkins from the sack. "I've got napkins, orange and black, with jack-o-lanterns and witches on them. I even found some placemats the other day that go with the napkins. Cups, too. Half of them orange, half of them black. Perfect with the placemats. And lemonade and cranberry juice, just in case, and two bottles of wine, one red, one white."

"Oh, my goodness!" Celia exclaimed. "Annie, you've outdone yourself."

Though a teetotaler, Annie enjoyed giving wine as a present, particularly wines produced at local vineyards.

She shrugged. "Since I don't help with the candy—because I can't resist it—I try to help out in other ways."

Then she pulled out the items that *really* mattered: Tupperware containers filled with bisque. "The pink ones are lobster. The blue ones are seafood."

It made me hungry just thinking about it. I always ate some of Celia's chili because she made it herself, but I ate the bisque because it was the best I'd ever tasted. I smiled; Annie had everything we needed. Always efficient and organized, at play as well as at work, equally on top of things in and out of the office.

I looked at my watch. *3:20.*

The first children, the little ones, would arrive before dark, around five. An angel with wings. A fairy godmother with a wand. A knight. A robot. The next group would follow soon after—Kermit the frog, Minnie Mouse, a cowboy. Superman. The Scream.

By six o'clock, Celia and I would already have handed out candy to a hundred children. Shortly after dark, the other nine or ten couples would join us to help out, bringing bags of candy to stack against the foyer wall like a levee, as well as a six-pack of beer or a bottle of wine or Jack Daniels. Our guests arrived hungry, looking forward to Celia's homemade chili and Annie's bisque. Sometimes people joined us from the street.

By seven-thirty, the street would be a beehive of activity,

with many costumed children carrying jack-o-lanterns and paper bags. More than a hundred people might be in any front yard on the street at one time. By eight o'clock, the yards would be filled with thousands of people—children and adults—so much activity that, every year, first-time visitors were astonished. The houses turned off the lights between eight-thirty and nine-thirty. No answering the door after that.

In contrast, my parents, living at Stately Oaks, the house, had only a handful of children—brave ones—knock on the door. The house sat on a hill by itself. The distance from the driveway to the street was intimidating to children and parents. Besides, a huge cemetery covered the hill next to the house, on the other side of the street, and on Halloween night, the combined effect seemed more fearsome than inviting.

As I headed for the garage to fetch the metal tub for the beer, I glanced to the second floor of the house. That small porch in the front roof was a favored place of observation for our guests; they could stand beside the witch, dressed head-to-toe in black, and look down on the street and marvel from an elevated perspective at the sight of thousands of people, most of them the size of munchkins, dressed in costumes, walking around in the dark carrying sacks or jack-o-lanterns, many of them holding the hand of someone bigger.

Every year this amazed me. I loved it. Envisioning this, I thought how warm the afternoon was for the last day of October as I placed the tub on the patio. Where was Andrew with the beer and ice? And what about the lawn chairs? They still needed to be cleaned.

I glanced at my watch. And again.

Finally, Andrew showed up in his black Dodge Ram pick-up truck and parked beside Annie's Oldsmobile.

I let him in the back door—the kitchen, breakfast room, and dining room filled with the aroma of chili, melted cheese, black-eyed pea dip, and cinnamon cider. And Annie's bisque.

"Man, it smells good in here, Celia!" he exclaimed, and, seeing Annie, his face lit up. "Am I glad to see you! About that rush of orders we received last week: we've got to talk about me being able to get those orders filled and on what schedule. There are a few other things, too."

"Surely not right *now*, Andrew," Celia said as she stirred the crockpot full of black-eyed-pea and cheese dip. "Can't it wait till tomorrow?"

"Right now?" I echoed. "With a million kids to show up in a couple of hours and lawn chairs still waiting for us to clean—*Andrew*?"

"*I* don't mind," Annie assured us. "Business first, if it's important."

Andrew said, "Not to be a party pooper, but it is important. And Annie and I do need to talk."

"Not until you help me clean the chairs and take care of the beer. Then you and Annie can talk all you want."

"The beer's in the truck. Soft drinks, too."

Celia had made cider and brewed tea, so we would be covered as soon as we iced the beer.

Andrew, Teddy, and I brought the beverages inside, then walked out front to the chairs.

Andrew had been a star football player in high school and college. Because he was short and lightweight, a lot of people were surprised to learn that fact. But it wasn't his build that had made him a star; it was his speed and agility. He could catch a ball, outmaneuver, and outrun an entire field of bigger men. Now in his mid-forties, he was still physically fit and athletic, with the physique of a younger man and a youthful face. He coached Little League ball, and Teddy really liked him. Celia once told me she thought he was good-looking.

"He's our supervisor," I said.

"He's our supervisor, and I think he's good-looking," she replied. "Not as good-looking as you, of course." Then she kissed me.

Now he was helping Teddy and me scrub mold and bird droppings off the lawn chairs with Mr. Clean. When we'd cleaned the last chair, Annie appeared at the front door. "Excellent job, men," she said cheerfully.

Andrew replied, "Have a seat and we'll talk." He smiled and tugged at a chair. "It's clean as a whistle and waiting for you."

I said, "I'd like to join you, but Teddy and I have to make a trip for the ice."

Annie looked at me and straightened her glasses as she sat down. "Four bags."

I was glad to be reminded of the number we actually needed. Every year, I forgot.

Peering over the top of her glasses, she added, "But don't put it outside before four-thirty."

I signaled Teddy to come with me, and knowing Andrew was likely to leave about the same time as Annie, I said, "As always, thank you both very much for all of your help. We really appreciate it."

Annie smiled. "I won't leave until I've had some of Celia's chili—*and* pea dip. They're the best."

Andrew said, "I'm taking mine home, along with some bisque, both kinds."

Andrew and his wife, Susan, had three children, and in years past, since their home was on a quiet cul-de-sac, they'd made a point to come visit us as a family on Halloween night. Now, though, their children had aged out of trick-or-treating.

"You know we always have more than enough food for everybody," I said. "Please take some home. See you tomorrow—and thanks again."

When Teddy and I pulled out of the driveway, they were still talking. When we got back, they were gone. I wondered exactly what had been so terribly important that Andrew had to talk about it tonight, rather than let it wait until tomorrow at work. Well, I'd just have to ask them about that. Right now, though, I had a party to think about. I was looking forward to a fun-filled night.

19.

TRICK OR TREAT

Around four-thirty, I heard a persistent ringing of the front doorbell. Most unusual. No one ever showed up *that* early. My first thought was Tracy, but she never came to the front door, and I figured even she would not be arriving before five or five thirty. Celia heard the bell in the kitchen, and we walked into the foyer at the same time.

Celia had done a good job decorating—cobwebs on the chandelier, cobwebs on the staircase, some scary candelabra with flickering lights placed here and there. By dark, the foyer would look deathly spooky. We looked at each other: Who would come to the house at four-thirty in the afternoon when it was still completely light outside? If it were children, their parents had brought them too early, and they were ringing the bell too persistently. If it were grown-ups, they must be uninvited strangers. We had no idea who they might be.

Curious, I peered through the sidelight running vertically

beside the door—but what I saw out there startled me.

"*What*?" Celia said, standing beside me, holding a basketful of candy. I unlatched the door.

On the front porch, stood an old lady—white-haired, wrinkle-faced—wearing a faded dress falling to the middle of her calves. Celia blanched and set the basket of candy on the floor. The old lady held out a bag but didn't say anything. Her fingernails were long and yellow, like claws. Celia and I stood in the doorway, not moving a muscle.

The old woman peered at us, with the bag held out in front of her. Finally, she said, "Trick or treat. May I come in? I have a present for you."

Without speaking, Celia stepped back into the foyer. I followed. Taken aback, but trying to be polite and hospitable, I said, "Please come inside."

Our visitor stepped into the foyer and looked around. She glanced up at the chandelier covered in cobwebs, then at the cobwebs strung over the stair railing. Her eyes traveled to the doors off the upstairs hall. Then she looked at Celia, standing in front of her, dressed simply in black slacks and an orange blouse. "This place is scary," she said. We didn't say anything.

"I've come for a purpose, bearing a gift. But first, we need to visit. Mind if I sit down?" Celia and I looked at each other, and Celia's eyes returned to the old woman's hands and fingernails.

Without asking, the old woman walked into the living room but didn't sit down. Instead, she looked around, slowly surveying everything in sight. Celia and I followed her into the room. "Would you care to sit down?" Celia asked.

In front of the fireplace, a sofa and love seat were positioned at a right angle, a glass-top table in front of them. Celia's grand piano was at the far end of the room, in front of a large bay window that looked out over the backyard.

Finally, the old woman sat down on the love seat, setting her bag on the floor. We sat on the sofa. "I'm Matt—and this is Celia. But I guess you know that."

"Of course, I do," she replied. "And you know me. You've known me for a long time. You just haven't seen me in the flesh in the last twenty years. I'm here for a reason, with a gift."

"You already said that," I said. "So, are we supposed to guess who you are?"

"If you want to. Here's a hint. The last time we were together"—she looked at Celia and me—"things didn't go well. Things didn't turn out well. It was a bad scene, the way we departed. That was about twenty years ago."

A bad—truly scary—thought raced through my head. A scary thought that was ridiculous.

She added, "You haven't seen me since then, but I know you've thought of me. Both of you have."

Celia and I sat in stone silence.

Finally, our visitor asked, "Don't you recognize my voice?" We did not, and as we continued not to speak, the silence grew uncomfortable.

"Okay, okay. Enough. The costume's good, isn't it? Of course, I don't look this old in real life. I'm the youthful personage I always was."

All of a sudden, I knew.

"Okay, Matt, I can tell you've figured it out. It took you long enough. And, quite frankly, you both are as pale as if you'd seen a ghost. Seriously, the look on y'all's faces! And I can tell that Celia *still* doesn't have a clue who I am. My costume must be *really* good. What's wrong? Don't you like old ladies? I'm not a ghost, not a witch—much less, the devil—just an old lady. Innocent enough." She added, "I mean, my costume is."

She paused and smiled, not exactly pleasantly. "But, Celia, doesn't my voice give me away? I'm surprised. Surely, my voice hasn't changed that much. Well, obviously you're stumped. Stunned, by the looks of it."

"Yes," Celia said, "I'm stumped. Stunned."

"Well, what do you want me to do—take off my attire?"

Celia replied, "The mask will be sufficient."

"Okay, the suspense is too much. Here, let me remove this mask and wig." She pulled off her white hair, then slowly, carefully peeled off her face.

"Voila! It's just me—Cindy. Surprise! Youthful as ever!"

"Cindy Peppercorn," I said, sitting back on the sofa. "It's been a long time"—an understatement considering how she'd totally dropped me as a friend, hadn't spoken a word to me since that evening in the dorm my freshman year.

She didn't look like Peppermint Patty anymore, I thought to myself, although her short brown hair, now about half-gray, still had some red in it—and she still had freckles. Celia cleared her throat. "Cindy. Cindy Peppercorn. Yes, this *is* a surprise! Who would have ever thought?"

"Right. I can only imagine what you *did* think." She chuckled. "Anyway, here I am, your old friend. How many years has it been? I do believe twenty-two since we last spoke. But I'll be honest. You don't seem glad to see me. I haven't changed *that* much, have I? A few pounds heavier, maybe. Just a couple? But I've kept my looks."

Celia offered, "May I get you something to drink? Tea or water? Cider?"

"Not right now. Thanks, anyway. I just want to know about the two of you. How are you all getting along? I must say, the last time we talked to each other, I wasn't too thrilled with either of you. You remember: you left me alone in the lobby of the dorm back at college. You know, Matt: you came with our friend Croom to see *me*—then you and Celia left with Croom and Celia's roommate. Yeah, you just sort of dumped me there in the room, then walked out. You all but killed me. You probably thought I forgot that." She paused. "Or did you not even think about it?" I looked at her oddly, making a face.

"But today, I have a present for you, Matt. It's in my trick-or-treat bag." She reached down to get it.

I interjected, "Are you sure you wouldn't like something to drink? Maybe a glass of wine? Maybe something to eat? Celia's fixed a lot of food."

"Thanks," Cindy said, distracted from her bag. "But not right now. Unless you have some Snickers. I really like those."

"We do," Celia said, jumping up to get the basket of candy from where she'd set it on the floor in the foyer. She walked back into the room, holding the basket. "Here. Take as many as you like."

"Thanks, don't mind if I do." Picking through the candy with her claws, Cindy dropped a handful of candy bars into her bag and smiled. "Do you like my fingernails? They look real, don't they?" She looked at them admiringly, then looked around the room. "Hey, I like your place. Nice digs! I bet you can hear the trains from here at night. Remember when we used to play the Train Game, Matt?"

She stopped and held eye contact with me. "I'll never forget that. Have you ever told Celia about all the things we used to do?" She stopped again and looked at us. "I didn't think so. Celia, you probably wouldn't have married him."

"Actually," I said, "actually—"

She held up her hand. "No, no need to respond, not right now. I've got to say, though, I don't see how you do this Halloween gig—this Mardi Gras on Stately Oaks—year after year. It's over-the-top, really. A little daunting, if you ask me. I tried to drive down this street a few years ago on Halloween night—sorry I didn't stop by at the time—and, man, what a mob! How do you deal with it?"

"We have a lot of help from friends." I wanted to make conversation although—or perhaps because—the situation was beyond awkward. It was weird. "They come over and help us hand out the candy, and Celia makes dinner for them. We couldn't stand it if we had to do it by ourselves. There are so many kids, they'd work us to death." Then I added, disingenuously, "You're welcome to stay and help, too. The more the merrier."

"Thanks. I'll think about it. Hey, I like the way you two are dressed alike—black pants and orange shirts. How many kids do you have? It's four, isn't it? Where are they?"

"It *is* four; thank you for asking," Celia replied. "Elisa, the oldest, is at a party. The other three—Bert, Caroline, and Teddy—are at our neighbors who live behind us. They have two children the same age as Bert and Caroline, and the parents are giving some of the neighborhood children a party. Then Caroline and Teddy will go around the neighborhood trick-or-treating with Tracy, their nanny."

"You trust your children with a nanny? No one should trust *anyone* too deeply. You might get knifed in the back. Maybe you should think about that."

"We do trust Tracy," Celia said pointedly. "She's like a member of our family." Then she resumed: "Bert's going trick-or-treating with some friends. He's twelve and tall for his age, so it's probably his last year. Originally, that's all this was—a street event, then a neighborhood thing. It's just taken on a life of its own over the years. This is quite a surprise having you visit like this."

"I'll *bet* it is! Well, I don't have any kids myself." As she said this, we heard talk in the kitchen; then they were standing in the doorway—Bert and Teddy.

"Excuse us," said Bert. "We didn't know you had company."

Cindy craned her neck and looked him and Teddy over. "Don't mind me. I'm just a former friend, a blast from the past."

Celia said, "Come in and introduce yourselves."

"And who might you be?" Cindy asked as they stood in front of her.

"I'm Bert." He extended his hand. She shook it with her claws, and I saw him marveling at them.

"Teddy."

"Well, glad to meet both of you. I can tell you belong here. You"—she looked at Bert—"look just like your dad. And tall, too. Talk about a chip off the old block. And you"—she looked at Teddy—"look just like your mother."

Her eyes went back to Bert. "What grade are you in?"

"Sixth."

"Do you like it?"

"Yes, ma'am."

"What do you like about it?"

"Most everything. Especially basketball."

"I bet you play with your dad, don't you?"

"Yes, ma'am."

"Do you beat him?"

"Sometimes."

She looked at Teddy. "My, you look like Celia—but actually handsome. And how 'bout you? What grade are you in?"

"Third."

"Do you like it?"

"Yes. Most of the time."

"Do you play basketball, too?

"Yes, but I'm not tall enough yet. But I'm growing."

"You sure do look like your mother."

"I know. And Bert looks like my dad. I play Little League. Andrew's my coach. I hit a home run yesterday and knocked in two other people. I stole a base, too."

He looked at me. "Dad, can we get some candy? That's why we're here. They're running low at the party, and you and Mom will have all that candy stacked against the wall."

"Sure," I said.

"You can have two bags if you need them," said their mother. "There are two bags on the dining room table. But try not to eat too much of it. It'll make you feel bad."

"And we need to put our costumes on," Bert said.

Cindy asked, "What kind of costumes?"

"Superman," said Bert.

"Spiderman," said Teddy. "What are you?"

"An old lady."

"A witch? Or just an old lady? I can't tell. But I like your claws."

"I'm glad. You should have seen me with my mask and wig on. I think I scared your parents nearly to death."

Teddy looked at us—and frowned. "Then she must be a witch. Well, thanks for the candy—we need to go now."

"Well, nice to meet you," Bert said to Cindy, shaking her hand again, his eyes on her claws. Then he and Teddy walked out.

"Nice kids. Polite," Cindy said. "You know, I've always appreciated good manners." As she paused, I had a strange feeling I'd heard her say those last words before, but I wasn't sure when—or where. "Nice looking, too, but I believe that little one has a mischievous streak. You better keep your eyes on him as he gets older. I don't have any kids myself. But I *have* had three husbands. Would you like me to tell you about them? I'm going to because that will bring us to why I'm here."

I heard Celia quietly take a breath, then exhale.

"The first one, Ron, was a real looker. But that marriage was the Titanic—a real disaster. I believed in monogamy. We had that in common. It's just that, while I believed in monogamy with Ron, Ron believed in monogamy with every woman he could find.

"So the next time, I sought out a quiet type I could depend on. Well, I had no idea how quiet and dependable a type could be! After about a year, I got tired of talking to myself and waiting for him to say something back. When I left him, he didn't even say goodbye. He just smiled and waved.

"The third one, Phillip, was better than the first two. He was faithful—and I'd had more experience with men by then—and he wasn't a mute. But he got tired of listening to me talk—and one day, he told me to shut up. And I told *him* to shut up. After we volleyed that back and forth for a while, he gave up the match and walked out on *me*.

"So, after striking out three times, I decided to give up on men and try something different. I applied and got the job as director of a women's shelter in Richmond.

"I've been there a month, and I love it. Richmond's great. Really historical, really Southern, and they have some great monuments. Living up there, I try not to let life get me down. I try not to let irritating *people* get me down. Celia, take you, for example. After what you did to me in college, it was all I could do to share the same dorm with you."

"Oh, *come* on, Cindy," I said.

Again, she held up her hand to stop me. "No, Matt, calm down and let me finish: I survived. I made my own way."

"I can see that," Celia said.

"And I can see you've got a piano," Cindy riposted. " I guess that baby grand cost you a pretty penny."

Celia corrected her. "It's not a baby grand. It's a nine-foot Steinway, and it actually didn't cost us anything. It was a gift from Matt's parents."

"*Really*? How generous. Do you still try to play? Honestly, I always thought you had a modicum of talent if you would just apply yourself—and relax. I remember you trying to play that piano in the lobby of our dorm back in college." She laughed. "You used to get *so* frustrated—I was always afraid you would blow a gasket. Do you remember? That's what you were doing that night Matt came to the dorm for me and left with you: you were playing the piano. Trying to, anyway. Talk about being on edge." She stopped talking. I shifted on the sofa, putting my arm around Celia's shoulders.

No one spoke. Then I said, "What has this got to do with your husbands and why you're here?"

"So," she said, "Celia, do you still play? I think you should. I think you have talent."

"She's still playing," I said. "And she definitely has talent. She performed a concert in Charlotte a few weeks ago in front of a huge audience. They gave her a standing ovation."

"No kidding? I couldn't perform in front of a bunch of people if my life depended on it. So—Celia—if you're brave enough to do *that*, why did my costume scare the you-know-what out of you? Seriously, you and Matt both looked like you'd opened the door on a ghost. Did you think I'd come back from the dead?"

"Do you really want to know?" I asked.

Celia cut her eyes to me.

"Of course. Let's hear it."

"Do you remember," I said, "when we were in junior high and high school, and you used to tell me there was a certain type of person who could predict future events? You said, 'If you can find one of those people, she can tell you about the future. If you know the future, then maybe you can do something to change a bad outcome so that the bad thing can be prevented.' But you told me to beware. You said, 'But you may not *want* to find a person like that because that person might know things you'd be better off not knowing. Besides,' you said, 'she may be a phony—or she may be real—and you won't know which she is.'"

"I remember that very well. I usually don't forget things that have been said. So what happened? Did you find someone who could tell you about the future?"

"That's it. Exactly. She looked just like you in that costume."

"Well, I'll be damned!"

"And, when we saw you on the porch, it was obvious to me Celia was thinking the same thing. It was a shock when we opened the door—and there she was—or, rather, there *you* were—standing on our doorstep waiting to be asked in. In real life, we were on *her* porch, and she asked *us* in."

"I'll be damned," Cindy repeated. "What did the old lady tell you was going to happen?"

"Nothing!" Celia blurted out. "Nothing important."

But what *I* was thinking was quite different. I was thinking about what had happened to Jennie, just as Miss Smiley had predicted—the poisoned thoughts, the loss of someone she loved, even being betrayed as she had been by Dr. Salafar. And Cindy had mentioned Croom, which made me think of what Miss Smiley had told him. He would "be rich"—and he *had* been, ever since his father passed away—"but not as famous as" Jennie—and that was true. And Miss Smiley had said he'd "impulsively show temper," and he'd done that, minutes later as we stood over her corpse. She'd said he'd "be luckless in love" until he settled down. He had been. Until recently.

Of course, the fact that someone had "predicted" those things did not mean the predictions had anything to do with what occurred later. Just words. Coincidence. Luck. Whatever. No one had been murdered. Including the old woman, herself. Certainly not Jennie. Or Dr. Salafar.

Such thoughts, and similar ones about Celia and me, whirled about in my mind. After all, the spit and image of Miss Smiley had been sitting in front of us only minutes earlier until she unmasked herself.

I said nothing.

Cindy looked at me as the wheels turned in my head . . . then at Celia . . . then at both of us. "Okay, fine—don't tell me. We won't go there. Everybody has a right to their own secrets." She shrugged. "Who doesn't have a skeleton of sorts tucked away somewhere in their past? Take me, for instance. Here's the deal. I had this dream recently about an old lady in an old house and four other people. You two for sure, and I feel pretty certain the other two were Croom and Jennie. Am I right?"

Reading our faces, Cindy answered her own question. "I thought so. That's how I knew how to dress. The dream was so vivid—the old woman was so vivid—it scared me wide awake, so I figured it would probably scare the hell out of the two of you if I paid you a visit dressed like her. And it did. You seem to be a little sensitive about this subject."

She paused to let that sink in, then she said, "You left me in the dorm that night, Matt. Am I being too sensitive about *that*? My third husband just did the same thing to me a few months ago, and now I've had this dream. It's all tied in together. Hence, my visit this evening."

"You can't be out of someone's life," I protested, "or the lives of two people, for over twenty years without a word of contact, and then just show up on their doorstep with a story like that, dressed in a costume intending to scare them. That's not normal."

"Who said anything about 'normal'?" She laughed. "Vengeful, perhaps. I don't claim to be perfect—do you?"

Celia and I looked at each other, and Cindy said, "Okay, I can tell by your faces that you're having trouble dealing with all this—processing it, even. So let me try to help you understand: Celia, when you moved in on Matt, I wasn't exactly thrilled, to put it mildly. I liked Matt a lot more than you ever knew, and that night changed my life. And not for good, either. Sure, I snagged three husbands after that, even though I didn't have money to attract them—or superlative looks. But I did have something else. I got right in the man's face and let him realize I was attracted to him and might be available. Once he took the bait, I reeled him in. Worked every time—except with Matt.

"Then, that night, you Matt, and you Celia—and Croom—walked out on me, leaving me alone in the dorm with nothing left to hold on to but a question: 'What had I done to deserve this?' I felt like you'd dumped my body on the floor and taken off. I felt like you'd killed me. And honestly, it's followed me all my days, even into my relationships with my future husbands."

She stopped, took a deep breath, and sighed. "But, hey, let's get off of me and back to you guys. Celia, one thing you have to understand is that I knew Matt long before you came into the picture, better than you did, and I knew Jennie, too. And I know this, Celia: Jennie was the one he liked best. That unrequited passion went back forever."

Shaking my head, I could feel the tension grow in Celia's body.

"Cindy, that is so silly," I said, still shaking my head incredulously, "worse than silly—crazy. You're talking about a long time ago—high school and college. And I—Celia and I—haven't had a thing to do with your marriages one way or the other."

"Whatever," she said, brushing her hand in the air. "Suit yourself. I see you still don't get it, but maybe it's not that important that you do. At any rate, that brings us to exactly why I'm here. I've brought a present for you from Jennie."

I shifted and sat up straight.

"I do feel bad about her accident. I wouldn't wish that on anybody. I read all about it in the magazines. Especially when I was bored in a long line at the supermarket. She seems to keep *People* and *National Enquirer* in business, not to mention all those other tabloids nobody knows the names of."

"Cindy," I said, "this has been fun. But I'm afraid Celia and I are going to have to cut this short. We've got a lot of company headed this way."

"I understand. I do think she's a super country-western singer. Amazing, really. Even if—in high school—she *was* sort of—well, standoffish. You know, too cool to move. Except when she was jumping up and down with her pompoms…cheering for *you*, Matt.

"But now that I really think about it, I guess 'too cool to move' was actually you, Celia, in college. Jennie was more like… Miss Popularity. She was never tops on my hit parade in terms of personality, but I'll give her credit for being able to belt out a song. And she's not scared of a crowd. Me—you couldn't get me in front of an audience full of screamers and get me to sing if you had to."

"Or play a piano in front of an audience," I said.

"Heck no! I'd rather be tied to a tree and beat."

"Some people may want to take you up on that," I said.

"Maybe. Anyway, my purpose in visiting is to give you the present, Matt. It's in my trick-or-treat bag."

She began to cough repeatedly. The old woman had done that, then fallen over dead. I stood up. "Are you okay?"

"I'm fine, really," she replied, waving me off. "It's seasonal."

Celia stood up, too. "Can I get you some water?"

"No, no. Sit down. Really, I'm fine. Every year about this time—I think it has to do with the time change—I get this cough. It lasts about a week, then goes away." She leaned over and pulled a manila envelope from the bag. "Well, here's the present, Matt." Holding it in her lap, she said, "It's actually from Mrs. Boston: Jennie wanted her mother to give it to you, herself, but you know she and my mother have been friends forever. So Mrs. Boston gave it to her and told her to give it to me so I could give it to you. Jennie gave it to Mrs. Boston a while back and said she wanted you to have it, Matt."

"Why didn't Jennie just give it to me, herself?" I asked. "She and Croom visit Celia and me every time they come home. Or she could have just mailed it."

"It was a good while ago that she gave it to her mom. Maybe her mother forgot about it. But at least it's getting delivered, now. Or maybe, you know, ever since Jennie's accident and the coma, she's had some post-traumatic amnesia—it's left her a little confused. Maybe that's the reason she didn't give it to you, herself. Her mother told my mother it's been really rough. Still is, at times."

"Actually, I don't . . . believe . . . it is," I said. "She's not confused at all now—not in the least. She knows exactly how she feels about everything important."

"Anyway, her mother knows you and I were great, close friends in junior high and high school—and even college. Ha ha!" She rolled her eyes. "So she and my mother, being friends, thought it would be nice for me to pay you and Celia a visit with this gift from Jennie. I actually agreed with them—I just had to pick the right time. That dream helped me." She held the envelope out in front of her. I stood and took it from her, then returned to the loveseat.

On the outside of the envelope in large script was the message: "Matt, this is from Jennie. I didn't open it. Margaret Boston." I laid the envelope on the loveseat between Celia and me.

Cindy stood up. "Well, that's why I came. Mission accomplished. Time to skedaddle." I heard Celia sigh out loud.

"I'm out of here," Cindy said. "I need to disappear before the storm hits the shore." She looked at Celia and smiled. We walked with her to the door.

I couldn't decide whether to force myself to be polite and thank her for bringing "the present," or not. I decided not to. I started to say, "Thanks for stopping by," but decided not to say that, either.

"Well, thanks for the hospitality," she said. "Now, I'll leave you two alone." We watched as she, in her drooping, faded dress, headed down our walk, the bag with a handful of Snickers in it, in one hand—her white hair and wrinkled face in the other.

We stood there, then looked at each other . . . What exactly had just happened?

20.

AFTER THE SPOOK

We no sooner went back inside than the first children showed up. Within the following hour or so, all the grown-ups came over; then Elisa, Bert, Caroline, and Teddy came home and helped the rest of us hand out candy. Some of the grown-ups were dressed in imaginative costumes, including Marie Antoinette, Count Dracula, and Van Helsing, but none compared with Cindy's Miss Smiley. That disguise—Cindy's visit—had affected Celia and me, overshadowing the whole evening.

At nine-thirty, we turned out the lights and brought in the jack-o-lanterns, and within an hour, after helping Celia and me clean up the kitchen, the last of our guests left. Once the children were in bed, Celia slumped on the loveseat in the living room. "This has been a long day!"

I slumped on the sofa across from her. "No joke. And Cindy didn't help a bit."

"She had a *dream* about the four of us in Miss Smiley's house? *That's* how she knew what to wear—in order to scare us?" Celia looked tired as she said this. "Matt, like you told her, that's not normal."

Clearing my throat, I made a face. "She picked through the candy for the Snickers."

Celia sat up. "And did I hear her right? Did she use the term 'vengeful'?"

I stretched my arms and legs and sat up, too. "That's what *I* heard."

"Maybe I'm just tired, but should we be concerned about that?" As she brushed back her brown, bouncy, shoulder-length hair, I thought how pretty she looked, despite the tiring day, the late hour, and the conversation.

I smiled. "I don't think so; it's not like *Fatal Attraction* or anything." I forced a little laugh. "Maybe we won't see Cindy again for another twenty-two years." Then I told Celia about the dream Cindy had when she was twelve, and her brother Sim was fifteen—how Cindy dreamed about his death and then he died and how Cindy never got over it.

Celia shook her head. "Such a strange person—to have dreams like that and not try to use them to help people—and in our case, just the opposite. And how strange never to speak to you again after that night in the dorm, until now. Like this. With a questionable motive. It's just perverse; it really is. When are you going to open that envelope? You've got to be curious."

I reached down and pulled it out from under the sofa where I'd put it before the first children rang the doorbell. I set it on the sofa beside me.

"Maybe I'll open it tomorrow," I said. "It's too late to look at it now."

...

The next day was Monday, and I was in my office at Tavern Craft by 7:30 a.m. I sat at my oversized wooden desk with my eyes on the large antique clock on the wall, watching and listening as the hand ticked away the moments. Minutes of my life slipped away, and I couldn't focus my attention no matter how hard I tried. Surrounding the clock were pictures of my extended family—parents and children—and photos of me taken with famous people: Presidents, Governors, U.S. Senators, Coach K of the Blue Devils, Billy and Franklin Graham. Plaques commemorating accomplishments and events hung on the wall, as well.

A while back, I'd promised myself I'd start each morning with prayer, giving God—and myself—some prayer time. Sometimes I managed to do that; sometimes, I didn't. Today I had not, and right now I thought about praying—I wanted to—but I couldn't even focus sufficiently to do that. Okay, I'd pray later. Maybe on my way to Raleigh.

Andrew and Annie had an appointment with me at eight-thirty, but all I could think about was the visit Cindy had paid Celia and me last night and what was lying in front of me on my desk. The manila envelope lay there, daring me to open it. The old woman had brought it and left it, then left Celia and me standing on our front porch, wondering what had just happened.

I looked at Mrs. Boston's note, handwritten on the outside of the envelope: *Matt, this is from Jennie. I didn't open it. Margaret Boston.* Part of me had wanted to open the envelope immediately, last night. Part of me did not want to open it at all. I figured Jennie could have given it to me if she'd wanted to, or at least mentioned it, and my instincts told me Cindy, unlike Jennie's mother, knew exactly what was in the package and had calculated its effect. It was like Pandora's Box: nothing good would come of opening it, but curiosity and temptation would make not opening it impossible.

Besides all that, Celia probably would keep asking me about it until I read it.

When the big hand on my wall clock ticked its way to twenty-five after eight, I knew I had exactly five minutes before Annie would knock on my door. I opened my desk drawer, took out the letter opener, and slit the end of the package.

At the table that night, Celia asked, "Did you open the package from Jennie?"

"Yes, I did."

"What was in it?"

"It looked like a daily log she made when she was in the hospital. Also, a recap of the days before she went in. She told me right after she got out that she'd kept a journal. I think she also said something about wanting me to see it, that she would send it to me."

Celia looked surprised. "*Really*? That's an odd present. Why do you suppose she would have sent you *that*?"

I put down my fork. "I'm not sure, but I think it has to do with my being a legislator and a lawyer. Jennie doesn't think the laws are tight enough regarding certain prescriptive drugs, which is easy enough to understand."

"I'm so glad Jeni B is well again," Elisa said. She liked to call Jennie by her stage name, though Celia and I never did. "I love her voice, and I hope she goes back on stage." An-eighth grader, Elisa made sure her friends at school knew Jennie was a family friend.

"I hope she goes back on stage, too," Caroline, my fourth-grader, said. "I like knowing someone who is famous enough to be on TV."

I looked at Bert, "How about some hoops after dinner?"

He sat up straight. "Sure, Dad!"

"Me, too," said Teddy.

That was the extent of Celia's and my conversation about "the present," and I set the package aside on the stack farthest from my desk blotter. Jennie and I had had a great visit in Dallas; we'd cleared the air and gotten some things straight that we should have gotten straight a long time ago. I figured I knew everything I needed to know about her, and I didn't need to know anything else. So the truth was that I didn't really *want* to know what was in her diary, particularly since it had been written while she was in the hospital because of drugs. In any event, it was old news. For all of those reasons, I doubt I would have opened the envelope after that, except that every-once-in-a-while Celia would ask me about it. In mid-November, I picked it up and skimmed it. It was an account of Jennie's days in the hospital—and the days preceding—but reading it seemed like an invasion of privacy. Again, I set it aside.

Thanksgiving came and went. Celia and I would have seen Croom and Jennie over Christmas, but they didn't come home because her parents flew out to Dallas to visit them instead. Mrs. Westfall flew to Dallas, too. It was Wes's first Christmas.

Before I knew it, New Year's Day, 1994, had come and gone, and it was March. I was appointed chairman of a legislative task force charged with investigating the State's epidemic in fatal overdoses from legally prescribed drugs and with formulating a package of legislative proposals aimed at reducing those fatalities. Celia saw my chairmanship of the task force as a reason I should finally read Jennie's journal.

"You need to read that journal, Matt," she said to me one Saturday night over dinner at one of our favorite local restaurants. The cuisine at TomTazz was excellent, and so was the atmosphere. Though the menu was pricey, the restaurant enjoyed a loyal patronage, and we always ran into people we knew. We'd stopped by three tables on the way in, and two couples had stopped by to say hello to us. Except for that, having come with no one but each other, we were enjoying a night out alone.

"Think of how much insight you could gain by reading that diary." Celia took a sip from a second glass of red wine. In the subdued light of the small chandelier hanging over our table, her dark brown eyes beneath her long dark eyelashes were almost coquettish. "I can't believe you haven't read it, already—carefully—all the way through."

I smiled. "I never thought of it that way. Not as a source of education, as a legislative tool."

"Well, sure," she said. "You've been asked to read a record of someone who was almost another fatal statistic. The drugs Jennie used were legal. Maybe what happened to her could have been avoided if there had been better laws on the books. You're in a position to make that type of change here in North Carolina."

"I never thought of it that way," I said again, "not so much that way as just something personal."

"Well, you should think about it as a way to educate yourself." She paused, then said, "If anybody can succeed at the Legislature against the combined weight of the drug companies, the pharmacies, and even the Medical Society if it proves necessary, it's you, Matt. You've always been a man of conviction—even a crusader when you believe in a cause—but you have to know what you're dealing with. You don't have any experience with drugs yourself, but you've got access to someone else's experience. A close friend. Why else would Jennie have wanted you to read her diary?"

"Okay," I said, "you've convinced me. I'll read it. First thing Monday morning."

I made a point to be in my office before anyone else arrived at work and picked up from the low-priority stack on my desk the package Cindy had so memorably delivered last Halloween. I pulled out the pages and set them in front of me. I had to be in Raleigh to chair a meeting of the Task Force the next day, so I intended to read the entire journal before doing anything else, then go home for lunch, pack, stop by the law office, and still get to Raleigh at a reasonable hour.

By eight o'clock, having read about ten pages out of a total of thirty, I stopped long enough to go through some mail and sign some letters. Then my secretary buzzed me. "Andrew wants to see you," Kathleen said.

"How long?"

"Hopefully, thirty minutes max."

I looked at the clock. A quarter past eight. I said, "I really need to read something as background for the Task Force meeting tomorrow. I've set aside this morning to do that, so ask Andrew if it's urgent. If not, ask him to wait."

"Will do," she said and hung up.

My eyes went back to my assignment. The thirty pages of the journal were typed, covering in detail a two-month period two years earlier, with bold headers running from January 10th to March 12th. I'd found the first ten pages rather tedious. I already knew Jennie's story first-hand because she'd told it to me, and this written account was not an improvement on that, though she'd included a lot of details, some of which I skimmed or skipped completely. I felt like I was back in school being forced to read an epistolary novel that didn't grab me.

Kathleen buzzed me again. I picked up. "Andrew says it's not urgent, but he does want to talk with you. Also, you've had a bunch of calls, one after another, starting with the Governor's office. Do you want them?"

I looked down. "Sure."

"Want them in the order they came in?"

"That'll work," I said, glancing yet again at the wall as the second hand ticked its way round in a circle, "unless there *is* something actually urgent."

"No emergencies, so I'll start with the Governor. They called in response to last week's court ruling to see if you'll be available, starting Wednesday, for a three-day, specially-called session to deal with redistricting in light of what the court said *this* time." I could see her, sardonic as Eve Arden in *Grease*, rolling her eyes as she emphasized the word "*this*." She paused for effect.

"You have seven calls from constituents, but I've already relayed those to your office in Raleigh. Amy will talk to you after she follows up on them unless she has to talk to you first. She may call you on the road."

She took a breath. "Celia called and wants to know if you talked to your parents about coming to her concert. She's already talked to *her* parents, and they will be there. She also wants to know if you can go to parents' night with her this Friday to visit Elisa's teachers." She paused again, then said parenthetically, "By the way, that will conflict with the session."

I didn't respond, and she resumed. "The party chair called and said the keynote speaker for the fundraising dinner on Thursday the 24th of this month just called and cancelled. The chairman wants to know if you can fill in.

"Senator Meade called and is requesting an opportunity to address the Task Force tomorrow. The President Pro Tem's office also called about the special session because they need to get a headcount to make sure they have the votes they need. Your law office called to be sure you *are* coming in today before you leave for Raleigh. And finally, like I said, Andrew does want to talk with you. He said it's important, and he'd like to meet with you by himself. He said he knows Annie will want to be in on it, too, but he'd like to make an exception this time. He didn't say why. *Even so*," she said, "if you can't see him now, be sure to call him today."

She'd barely taken a breath, so I did. "Kathleen," I said, "I've got to finish the assignment I'm working on: I promised Celia, and I've been putting it off too long. Tell the Governor and the Pro Tem I can be there for the session. Tell Celia I will not be able to meet with Elisa's teachers on Friday, assuming the special session runs for three days. And ask her if she would please call my parents herself. Call Senator Meade's office and ask him what he wants to talk about to the Task Force so I can include him in the agenda. Don't tell him I said it, but his subject needs to be pertinent to tomorrow's meeting; if not, we'll need to schedule him at a later time. Tell the party chair I can stand in for the keynote speaker. I'll talk about what's going on in Raleigh right now, including redistricting and the Task Force on drug deaths. Tell Amy she can call me on the road this afternoon. Tell the law office, yes, I'll be coming in before I leave for Raleigh. Tell Andrew I'll call him as soon as I finish what I'm working on right now."

"Will do."

I hung up. It was ten minutes till nine. I went back to Jennie's journal, and knowing the plot, skimmed the rest of it. Then I wrote out a half-page summary and took it to Kathleen to type up. It wasn't my Great American Novel—which, by the way, after all these years was only at Chapter Five—but at least I'd finished the reading assignment. The doctor—Salafar—had prescribed Jennie a psychotropic drug, then doubled the dosage. Then Jennie'd spent two weeks in and out of the hospital. Finally, after she went back to Dr. Salafar and he again put her on drugs, she was struck by a car.

I noticed Jennie had written a few complimentary things about me, such as her entry of Friday, February 21st: "Today I had lunch with Matt. I told him the whole story. Matt's wonderful, so patient, and levelheaded. And kind. He always has been. I love him. When I finished telling him my story, I burst into tears."

In other entries, she said Croom had saved her life, and she loved him. Her last entry was Tuesday, February 25th: "I met with Dr. Salafar today. He said I seemed depressed, so he gave me a new prescription." Two weeks later, on March 12, 1992—exactly eighteen years to the day since Miss Smiley had told our fortunes—Jennie ran out in front of a car and was nearly killed.

Two years had passed since then. At the end of the last page, she had added a handwritten note: "Matt, thank you for reading this." Then, she wrote, "Love you forever, Jennie." She had signed her name the way it was supposed to be spelled, the way it was when we were kids: not "Jeni," for "Jeni B," America's sweetheart, but "Jennie," as I'd always known her. That personal note was not pertinent to my purpose, so I omitted it from my summary, along with the other personal parts I'd read and about ninety-five percent of everything else.

I knew Celia would want to know what was in the journal, but being so busy, especially with practicing for her performances, she probably wouldn't want to take the time to read it. I attached my summary to the outside of the manila envelope, then rushed to the law office, then home to pack, putting the envelope with the summary on top of the bureau with Celia in mind. Once I got on the highway, I called Andrew and apologized for not being able to meet with him.

He said, "I was reviewing some orders we completed a while back, and I had some questions about the paperwork. There were some things I couldn't make sense of. I wanted to meet with you and talk to you about it, but since I couldn't, I met with Annie instead, and now I think I understand."

"Good. Thank you for doing that, Andrew." I was listening

to a radio program, and the host was talking about the state redistricting plan and the Governor's calling a special session because of the court ruling. Then the topic switched to the Task Force, and I listened as I heard my voice regarding the spike in drug deaths from accidental overdosing. "That's good," I said to Andrew, again. "I'm glad you met with Annie and got that straightened out."

After I hung up, I thought, *Andrew, bless your heart, you're a wonderful supervisor and friend, but if it weren't for Annie, I don't know how you'd manage.* Three hours and a series of phone calls later, I was in the parking garage of the Legislative Office Building, heading down the corridor to the elevator. Five floors up, as I walked into the office, Amy greeted me with a smile and a notepad of items I had to attend to, starting with the agenda for tomorrow's Task Force meeting. Then there was the matter of the in-box on the corner of my desk, staring me in the face with four different levels, the top being "immediate attention." It was overflowing.

"But before we do anything else, Senator Goodheart," Amy said, "will you please sign these letters?" She handed me the stack. "I'd like to get them out before I leave." I read over them quickly and signed them. As Amy left the office, I told her Good Evening, then leaning back in my chair, took a breath.

Now finally, I had some time to pray. I bowed my head and said, "Thank you, God, for this day and for being with me throughout." Then I thanked him for giving me the concentration to read Jennie's journal like Celia wanted. Despite everything, I had gotten that done. It was my good deed for the day, and I felt sure Celia would be pleased.

21.
THE MISCUE

I worked until nine-thirty, then called it a night, and was back at the Legislature Tuesday morning at nine. The televised Task Force meeting ran from ten a.m. until two in the afternoon. Senator Meade, eighty-years-old and wearing a salmon-colored bow-tie and, as always, a blue seersucker suit, made quite an impression speaking about people he was aware of in his district—no names, of course—who were addicted to various types of prescriptive drugs. Speaking in his genteel Southern drawl, he told the committee—and everybody else who was listening through the media—that he knew examples of people who had been prescribed sixty hydrocodone or oxycodone pills at one time. "That's excessive," he said. "And dangerous."

Then he surprised the committee with this proclamation: "Besides," he said, dragging out the "i," "you ah not sposed to use those drugs f' non-cansa-related pain, innyway. That's just inappropriate an' invitin' trouble."

By the next morning, Amy was receiving phones calls from across the state from people who wanted to tell their own stories publicly, usually family members who had lost loved ones to prescriptive drug overdoses. The special session, which convened that morning, overshadowed the Task Force, even for me, because, as Chairman of the Judiciary Committee, I was charged with handling the redistricting bills as they came out of the Redistricting Committee. Everything was televised. So it turned out to be a demanding week, with an especially hectic schedule, more issues and constituents than I'd expected, bill-processing deadlines, and lots of press.

All of our party caucus meetings were begun with prayer, and this week I'd been one of the Senators who'd offered some of the praying. Though it was a great way to start our meetings, sometimes even prayer did not keep a lid on tempers. Thank Heaven those meetings were held behind closed doors, no press allowed, guarded by the sergeant-at-arms staff.

I'd never seen tempers flare any worse in caucus than this week. In the most recent redistricting plan, Senator Gladden was the sacrificial lamb, as the only thing worse than being given a bad district was to be "double-bunked"—intentionally primaried—in a bad district. It was like forcing a fellow crew member to walk the plank.

On Thursday when he saw his new district for the first time, he stood up in front of the entire caucus, his face beet red, and smashed his fist on the table. He then exploded in a tirade peppered with expletives seldom heard at the Legislature, even in private. Fortunately, the walls of the General Assembly were made of concrete, and the caucus room was soundproofed. The other Senators and I shrank back in silence, eyes wide, as Senator Gladden, not the most popular among us anyway, proceeded to cripple any hope he may have had to be re-nominated.

By eleven o'clock on Friday, I couldn't wait to escape the Legislative Building. But even on the road, I hadn't escaped. I received some phone calls on the way home and was now feeling loaded down with the houses I was renovating—the sub-contractors, the deadlines, bills that had to be paid. Without Annie and Andrew taking care of Tavern Craft, I couldn't have managed. I couldn't wait to see Celia. I wanted to be with her and put all the rest of it out of my mind.

In Greensboro, I called home and left a message on the answering machine so she would know I'd be home around two o'clock and be there to greet me. Just east of Winston-Salem, there was construction and a wreck, just serious enough to stall traffic for half an hour. Still, I got home before three.

As I pulled around the back of the house, I didn't take the time to park in the garage at the back of the yard; I just stopped in the driveway and went inside. In the kitchen, duffle bag in hand, a smile on my face, I called, "Celia."

I walked into the breakfast room. "*Celia—?*"

Still no answer. I called her again. Maybe she hadn't gotten my message. I walked into the den, the living room, then the dining room. No sign of her. The doors to the sunroom were open, so I went out there, enjoying the flowers and plants and sunshine, but Celia was not there, either. I checked all over the downstairs, and no one was anywhere.

Standing at the foot of the stairs, I looked to the upstairs hall and called again, more forcefully. When I called yet again, my voice was louder still. But the only response was a dead stillness.

Opening the patio doors, I walked outside. Maybe Celia was tending the flowers, or visiting with one of her neighbor friends at one of the gates. I walked around the yard, but found no one.

Maybe she'd gone over to Susie's house. I followed the path through the woods and stood at the iron gate, surveying the neighbors' yard, but I saw no one in it. Back through the woods and home again, I thought how the tulips in our backyard were especially beautiful this year, plentiful and vibrant, surrounding the pond and fountain in the middle of the yard. As soon as I found Celia, perhaps I'd clip some of them and put them in a vase for her. She loved flowers.

When I got to the breakfast room again, the pleasant feel of the fresh outdoors in spring was devoured by a closed-in feeling, an uncomfortable aura. A strange silence, a feeling even of abandonment.

I walked back into the kitchen, intending to get my duffle bag before going upstairs. But first, I pushed the remote and opened the door to the garage: Celia's car was parked inside. Yes—she was home? I stood by the counter a few moments, considering things, looking at some of Celia's notes: errands that needed to be run, appointments to be kept, her practice schedule. Her practice schedule, again. Her practice schedule, a third time. But the living room was empty, the piano silent. Taking a breath, I moved to the foyer with my duffle bag. As I stood at the foot of the stairs, looking up, I was surprised to hear movement in our bedroom. I had to admit, it did disturb me, a little, hearing that muted sound of movement in the upstairs. I waited.

"*Celia*—?"

I felt sure she would have heard me. As I started up the stairs, she appeared in the hall. Standing at the top of the staircase, she was dressed in a white silk dress, reminding me once again of Natalie Wood at her loveliest. Relieved, but also confused, I so wanted to embrace her that I broke into a wide smile. But she was glaring at me, an unguarded, fierce look in her eyes I'd never seen before.

I dropped my duffle bag. "What's wrong?" I said. "*What*?"

As she descended the stairs, I stepped back down and moved aside, my heart rate quickening as she walked past me. Then I followed her to the kitchen. "*What* is wrong?"

At the kitchen counter, she picked up a manila envelope. "This—is what." She waited. "Aren't you going to say something?" Her face was bright pink, her eyes penetrating.

"It was addressed to me." The second I said it, I regretted it. The adrenalin response had made me defensive, and there was no reason to be.

"Sure it was—from your girlfriend, old and new again! But you're the one who left it lying out as if you were daring me to pick it up and read it. And I think I have a right to natural curiosity." She was talking very fast. "How could I *not* want to know what Cindy Peppercorn dressed as Miss Smiley brought you as a present from Jennie Boston? I knew something was different. You've been moping around for weeks, preoccupied. It's like you're in a different world."

I shook my head as if to clear it. "I left that envelope lying out on purpose. Of course, I knew you'd see it. I even summarized it for you. I thought you'd appreciate my doing all that. Regardless, it's not very important; Jennie wrote it over two years ago, under the influence. If I'm moping around, it's because I'm overworked."

"You left the envelope out on the bureau in our bedroom. What was I supposed to do—settle for the summary?"

I was thrown off balance; I couldn't believe I was on the defensive like this. "You weren't supposed to do anything!" My tone had an edge to it, so I stopped long enough to ask God for a calm voice. More quietly, I said, "There was nothing to do, one way or the other. Did you read the whole thing?"

"Unfortunately, yes, and the unabridged version is quite different from the Cliffs Notes." Her face was now a deeper shade of pink, and I moved to the center of the kitchen to be farther away from her.

"The summary was for legislative purposes, too," I said. "Remember, you suggested it—for the Task Force."

"Oh yeah, blame me. You wrote the summary thinking I wouldn't read the whole thing. You could have had the common decency to hide the journal so I wouldn't see it. Instead, you left it out where you knew I'd see it and want to read it. That was so insensitive."

"If I'd hidden it, you'd have accused me of hiding something from you."

"Well, haven't you been . . . hiding . . . something? You've had the diary for almost five months. You knew I wanted you to read it—if for no other reason than to get it over with—but you didn't. You kept putting it off. Your procrastination in this and other things drives me crazy! Then you finally read it and just left it out for me with a cover sheet, leaving out Jennie's little love notes and a few other minor details. Do you have any idea how many times I asked you to read that diary?" Considering everything, I thought her question was mostly rhetorical, so I didn't say anything.

"And did you read it? No! Not for almost five months! Do you know how frustrating it is to be ignored like that?"

"I wasn't interested in Jennie's journal. Why didn't you just read it yourself?"

"How could I? It wasn't here. You had it tucked away in your office."

"You could have asked."

"You could have offered."

"So this is really about other things, not something Jennie wrote."

Her fists went to her hips. "What do you *think*, *Matthew*?"

"I don't really know *what* to think. You're confusing me." I paused, then said, "Okay, Celia, I actually did *not* read that stupid diary. Just the first ten pages, then I mostly skimmed the rest. I don't read other people's diaries. If Jennie wanted me to know something, she could have told me. And she *would* have. I don't need to read about it. And that diary is two years old, anyway."

"I guess it's just an old secret."

I shook my head. "Secret? What are you talking about?"

"I'll tell you what I'm talking about. That journal makes it sound like Jennie was, and maybe is, in love with you."

I shook my head, incredulous. "I don't believe I'm hearing this. That is not at all right. In fact, it's totally ridiculous. I've told you all about that last visit with Jennie—and Croom. Celia, that visit was a year ago—and that journal was written over *two* years ago!"

Shaking her finger at me, her voice loud and high-pitched, she said, "I'm not sure I care to hear what you have to say, right now. Do you know how much pressure I'm under with these concerts?" She picked up a pen from the countertop and slammed it back down. "And I'm the one who's home raising the kids while you're in Raleigh. I need your attention and support! I need you in my life! I have a life, too! Now I see the true nature of your relationship with her."

I raised my hands, palms up. "True nature? What?"

Her hands returned to her hips as she glared at me, her face red.

"Surely you're not seriously suggesting . . . ." I stopped.

She searched my eyes with her own. "I'm not sure what I'm suggesting. Except that Jennie's innermost thoughts suggest a type of intimacy."

"She may have written a lot of things in that journal. I don't know. But I do know she'd just lost her baby. She was on drugs. That's why Croom put her in the hospital! Celia—we're talking about someone who ran out in front of a car and almost killed herself."

"Oh, really? What about the blackmail?" she shot back. "What about the pictures? Answer me that! *That's* something new I'd never heard about before! You've never said anything about that! How could there be blackmail if there was nothing to hide?"

"There was never any blackmail. No pictures. Totally Jennie's imagination, with the drug she was on. Paranoid delusion. Celia, it's just common sense to understand that what Jennie experienced and wrote back then was under the influence of a psychotropic. I didn't include any of the personal stuff in the summary because it wasn't appropriate to my purpose. I should never have opened that envelope. I should have thrown it away."

Thinking she was going to cry, I stepped toward her—I just wanted to hold her—but her expression changed, and she started yelling. "I was a frustrated rich kid—the *perfect* frustrated rich kid—trying to play the piano, for God's sake. You made me feel beautiful—you even told me I played beautifully—and you seemed to believe it.

"You were cute—even handsome—and you pursued me from the moment you met me. How could I not like you? How could I not fall in love with you? You were even *smart*, for God's sake!

"I've got my biggest concert coming up and have been practicing almost non-stop for weeks. When I'm under a lot of pressure and stress, your procrastination drives me crazy! I asked you to do one thing—call your parents. But did you? No! I even had to call *your* parents about my concert! Can't you do anything? Sometimes I ask myself why you married me…Was it my money?"

Finally, as she took a breath, she paused.

I paused before I said, "I honestly can't believe you said that."

Though *my* voice was quiet, she responded, nearly screaming. "*I'm* your wife! I'm the one you're married to! I'm the one who's stood by you all these years—in politics, in everything else—had your children—and raised them!

"I'm sorry I'm not a famous star who can sing and be on TV and make the crowds—the *men*—swoon. I'm sorry I'm not famous and glamorous.

"Well, I've had it. *Had* it!"

She glanced at the countertop, picked up a coffee mug, and quick-pitched it, overhand, straight for my head. I ducked, and it sailed over me, smashing into the glass door of the china cabinet behind me and shattering them both to pieces on the floor.

22.
COMING TO TERMS WITH PIP

That evening in the kitchen with the children, my top priority was to maintain a cool façade. "Your dad did something I've told you never to do; I played with a basketball indoors. I was showing off for your mother, showing her how I can spin a basketball on the tip of my finger. My performance didn't go so well."

I glanced with a rueful smile at the cabinet's broken glass door. Elisa looked at me, then at her mother. Bert said, "*Daaad*!" Caroline raised her eyebrows. Teddy laughed, then made a face, frowning and pouty simultaneously.

That was Friday night, and Celia and I didn't speak a word to each other that evening. I slept in the guest room. Or tried to sleep.

The next morning, I got up early, feeling like hell and went to the office—both of them—as much to get out of the house as to go to work. I also wanted to call Jennie because I knew she would have to talk this all out with Celia. All four of us would have to talk this out together. At this point, I could only imagine what all Jennie had written in that diary because of that drug.

Well, this was my fault. I'd been assigned to read the novel, not skim it. I'd written my summary. Unfortunately, it was based on the skimmed version, not the whole detailed thing. Too bad. But I thought I knew what the greater problem was: Celia was stretched to the limit with all the demands she placed on herself and with her perfectionism at the piano, and that had made her ripe to believe the worst. On top of that, I was gone too much. And I was stretched thin to say the least. Finally, I had no doubt that my old friend Cindy Peppercorn, who'd always had a sixth-sense about certain things, had played us like a drum.

I'd get everything straightened out, but for the moment, I just wanted to get through the day. Celia's brother, Robert, had warned me years ago about his sister's temper, but until yesterday, I'd never seen it. Now that I had, Celia and I needed a cooling-off period more than anything else, so I avoided going home. I spent an hour-and-a-half in my offices, and after making a call to Jennie but failing to reach her, went to the pharmacy for some antacids and headache powders. I took Bert and Teddy to the Y, where we played basketball, and the boys asked me to prove I could still balance the spinning ball on a fingertip. I did fine but felt a shiver of guilt in the fun it brought.

I had my sons home by lunchtime but didn't stay for lunch. I dropped them off, parked the SUV in the main garage, went to the special-car garage, and got my green '55 Jaguar XK 140 convertible that still spun like a top and gleamed like an emerald—and headed, top-down, out to the lake, stopping at a hotdog stand along the way. Anything to distract my thoughts and get some distance.

Stopping at the lakeside park, I walked and jogged along the trail, concentrating on the path and my surroundings.

About an hour later, on my way back home, I drove past a supermarket. Seeing a cardboard sign on the curb, "Get Your Golden Retriever Puppy Here," I did a double-take and turned around. In the parking lot, a man and his wife were selling a litter of puppies. A small group of people were standing around a pen where the golden puppies, only a few weeks old, toddled about inside. They were adorable. I picked up one after another.

"Only these five are left unsold," the man said with a proud papa's smile. He was stocky, blond and sunburned, and his t-shirt said, "I like calling North Carolina home."

"Nine weeks old and looking for a good home," said his wife, who was also stocky, blond, sunburned, and wearing shorts. Her t-shirt said, "Welcome to New Hope Church."

"I'll sell you the pick of the litter," the man said.

I smiled back. "Have you got anything I can placate my wife with—for coming home with a puppy?"

"How 'bout some free dog biscuits?" He studied me, then asked, "Hey, aren't you in the government?" Squinting, he tapped his chin with his index finger. "The Senator, right?"

I extended my hand. "Yes—I'm your Senator. Matt Goodheart."

"I thought so. Glad to meet you. Hey, I voted for you. I vote for you every time you run. That's a lot of times. You're a good Senator."

I smiled. "You're mighty kind, sir. Does that mean I get a

discount on one of these puppies?"

He pulled his mouth to the side and scratched his stomach. "Heck, I'll *give* you the pick of the litter—what's left of it—if you'll give me that car of yours. What a beaut!"

His wife laughed. "I'll give you the *whole* litter."

Her husband said, "You need a bigger car than that, anyway. How do you get your legs in that thing?"

I laughed. "It gets harder every year. When I was sixteen, I didn't think about it."

"If you've had her since you were sixteen," the man said, "I guess you're gonna keep her. So we'll have to work out something else on the puppies. Seriously, we might be able to work out *somethin'*—on *one* of them little 'uns."

Shaking my head, I said, "If I were to take one of these puppies home, Celia wouldn't let me in the house." I thought, *If things are bad now, what would they be like if I came home with a dog?* To the man, I said, "You can't just come home and present your wife with a puppy you buy on impulse—not under the best of circumstances."

I looked at his wife. "Buying a dog is not like buying a dozen roses, and the maxim, 'It's easier to get forgiven than to get permission,' applies to some things, but not all things."

"Aw, come on," she said. "Who could resist one of these little fellers?"

"I'm in the doghouse right now."

"Oh . . . I see. Still, nobody can resist a puppy."

I could relate to that, and I took turns with *other* people as we picked up the pups. Before I knew it, twenty minutes had gone by, and I was still there, trying to decide whether or not to buy one, and if so, which one. I noticed that the people who stopped by to look preferred the puppies with the best outward appearance. One of the pups had a physical defect, a crooked tail. It also was the smallest of the five. None of the people who stopped by to look preferred that puppy, the runt of the litter. But, I thought, except for her funny-looking tail, she was awfully pretty—and she kept coming right to me. I couldn't help but think of Ellie, the stray collie mix we'd found under my dad's 1960 Thunderbird after a rainstorm. I was in early elementary school, and she was our first family pet. She and this one even looked somewhat alike.

"I think she has the best personality," the man said. "She's the most inquisitive."

Then he added, "We call her Crooky Tail."

Her brothers and sisters were bigger and had normal tails. While I held them, one after another, another customer bought one of her brothers. I wondered if I wanted a boy dog for a change. Now only one male was left, so if I did choose a boy, the little fellow still in the pen must be the one—even though, about fifteen minutes earlier, he'd peed on the asphalt, then sat down in it.

But it was a moot point because, no matter how adorable any of these four remaining pups were, Celia would never say yes, particularly now, when she and her artistic temperament were strung to the limit. Since I figured saving my marriage was a higher priority than buying a puppy on impulse, I got into my convertible and headed home.

I stopped along the way to eat—again, at the hotdog stand—so it took me about forty-five minutes to make a fifteen-minute trip. Starting up the driveway, I changed direction and backed out.

Back at the supermarket lot, only three puppies were left—the boy dog, a sister, and Crooky Tail. While I picked them up, one at a time, still weighing the pros and cons of everything, a man and his son bought two of the three, but of course not the one with the crooked tail, not the pure-bred dog with a defect. She was now the only one left out of the seven. Nobody wanted her. In college, Croom told me I couldn't adopt every stray dog needing a home. Well, it had been a long time since college, and I hadn't adopted a single dog. Not even that little black dog, soulful-eyed and hungry, sitting outside the Ham and Egger.

I said to the man and his wife, "How long are you going to stay here?"

The man answered, "Till we sell the last one—or sundown—whichever comes first."

"I'll come back before then if I can persuade my wife to agree."

An hour later, I was back, though I hadn't talked to Celia. And Crooky Tail was still there, all by herself. The man looked at me and shrugged. "Nobody wanted her. We were about to give up. We'll give you a discount off the price, for the defect. And we'll let you keep your car, since you're a Senator." I paid him and his wife the money—fifty dollars off the price of the others—and the puppy nobody wanted, and I drove home.

I pulled into the driveway, then into the garage where it was cool, and went inside the house, leaving the puppy on the front seat in a cardboard grocery box.

Inside, I looked around the house. I saw Celia sitting in the den, the only one at home. I walked into the dining room and sat down at the table. There, I prayed—a deep, sincere, humble prayer, seeking God's guidance and the peace I'd learned that only He can give if He's given a chance. This both calmed my soul and gave me courage. Entering the den, I sat down on the sofa across from Celia. Dressed in gym shorts and a t-shirt and sweaty from my day, I felt like I was walking into the locker room after causing the team to lose the NCAA championship in the last seconds by fouling out for swearing. But my prayers had prepared me, so I bent my head down so the coach could let me have it. I imagined the rest of the team was sitting in the room with us, watching me get ready to take a pounding.

"I didn't give you a chance to speak," Celia finally said. "Now, I wish you would. I want you to give me your side of the story."

I looked up, surprised, collected my thoughts, asked God for the right words, then said, "First of all, just to be totally clear, regardless of anything in that diary that you read—explicit, implicit, whatever—there is nothing at all between Jennie and me. Nothing." I then recapped the conversation Jennie and I had had that afternoon in her den when she introduced me to Wes.

"Second, that journal, which I admit again I didn't read much of, was the product of a psychotropic drug overdose—or allergy. And it should have been delivered to me two years ago or not at all. Preferably the latter. It's nothing now, Celia, but insight into the mind of a drug victim, just like you said over dinner that evening at Tom Tazz, when you pretty much insisted that I read it. And it's probably also insight into Cindy Peppercorn's sad ability to hold an irrational grudge. Other than that, it's nothing."

I continued, "And I apologize for not actually reading all of it. I told you I did, and I should have. If I'd done what I said, I'd have known what was in the diary, and I could have handled things differently. Better. I was wrong."

I leaned forward, my elbows on my thighs, my hands clasped. "I'm really sorry: I apologize for the part about the 'blackmail,' Jennie thinking the waiter took photos of us together at lunch. She was convinced he'd done that and sold them to the tabloids. But she only thought that when she was taking that medicine. It made her paranoid. I should have told you about that. I can see how that came across really badly, out of the blue. I'm going to call Jennie and Croom right now and get them on the phone."

I sat down beside Celia and picked up the phone. I called, but no one answered. "We'll try again later," I said. "It's important that we do that."

"I've been so stressed lately," Celia said.

"You try to do too much."

"We both do. Why do we work so hard?" Tears welled in her eyes. Her voice was unsteady.

I moved close to her. "Celia, does that diary really say a lot of awful things? I know there's none of that in the first ten pages. Just how out of her mind was Jennie at the time she wrote those recollections?"

At first, I thought by the look on her face that she was going to break down in tears. Instead, she closed her eyes, and I knew she was praying, as I had. In this way, she composed herself. "I did want to know what was in Jennie's journal and why she wanted you to have it. I wanted you to read it right after Cindy brought it. I wanted to clear up that whole mystery and forget about it. But you kept putting it off, and the more I thought about it, the more it stuck in my craw. Then when I finally read the diary myself, that part about the blackmail and the pictures—along with some of the things Jennie said, implicitly, I guess—made me start wondering. I started wondering if maybe that was why you kept Jennie's diary at your office all that time, instead of just reading it and telling me about it. I should've never thought such a thing, but the imagination can play tricks with your mind. And I haven't been sleeping well. Part of it is my perfectionism with the piano." She stopped.

Then she added something else I already knew: "Part of it is my need to be more than my last name." I knew she was referring to "Nightingale," not "Goodheart."

She confessed, "I'm always trying to prove myself. Always needing to prove that I am more than a prominent last name—more than just another privileged member of the Nightingale family. I've always got to prove that I can *do* something and not just *be* someone born to privilege. Then I started obsessing about things. All these things. I couldn't stop thinking about it. Between trying to be the perfect concert pianist and that stupid journal, I worked myself into a nervous wreck."

I took her hand, held it, and asked, "So now you believe me and not something you read? Are we okay?"

"It may be something else," she said quietly, looking away. Then she turned back to me, searching my eyes. "We're losing years together when we live apart so many days—and nights."

Her dark eyes—she'd never looked so beautiful. "You're the love of my life, Celia. You always have been." My eyes filling with tears, I quietly cleared my throat—all we needed now was for *me* to lose it.

"I'm so embarrassed," she confessed. "I'm ashamed." Again, she looked away. If she'd been looking at me, she might have read a questioning look on my face. I didn't say anything.

She said, "While you were gone, I called Jennie myself. I've already talked to her—and Croom—for over an hour. They are the nicest, sweetest people, ever—the best friends anyone could ever have. So understanding." Her voice cracked. "I can't believe I let myself get so overwrought, so emotionally out of control."

She burst into tears. I held her as she cried until she regained her composure. "After I read that journal, I even started thinking again about that old woman on the island and her predictions about betrayal. Cindy dressing up like Miss Smiley, based on a dream, and coming to visit us—I couldn't stop thinking about it, trying to figure it out. It was all too . . . I don't know . . . weird. Freaky. Supernatural." She added, "Wickedly perverse—contrary to good. Maybe even contrary to God."

She paused. "Is that too extreme, carried away? Regardless, everything taken together was making me crazy, and I took it out on you. I haven't totally lost it like that since I was in high school." She paused. "Croom and Jennie helped me so much on the phone." She sniffled. "Can you possibly forgive me?"

I touched her hand, then her cheek, then her lips. "Of course, I do. How could I not? I love you." I kissed her neck, her cheeks, her lips, as tears coursed down her face. She sniffled and smiled. For a while, we sat there together quietly, saying nothing.

Finally, Celia spoke. "Go upstairs and take a shower," she said. "I'll be up in a few minutes."

. . .

I had forgotten all about Crooky Tail, but an hour later, suddenly remembering that the pup was waiting for me in my old Jaguar, I said to Celia, "Sweetheart, I have something for you. A present. You'll never guess what it is. I'll bring it to you in the den."

Pulling on some jeans and a clean t-shirt, I walked downstairs to the garage and got Crooky Tail out of the box in the passenger seat. I set her out in the yard, then gave her some water. Cradling the puppy, I walked into the house through the back door and then to the foyer, where I stopped. Celia was in the den, waiting for me on the sofa. "Close your eyes," I said. "Don't open them till I tell you to."

I walked into the room and stood in front of Celia. "Don't open your eyes until I count to three." I held the puppy out in front of myself, so close to Celia she'd see how irresistible her present really was.

"One, two, three!" I said.

Celia opened her eyes.

"Meet Pip!" I said.

23.

AN INFORMAL LUNCH

Celia hesitated—no smile, no reaction. Nothing. Then she reached out and took the puppy, hugging it to her chest. When she looked up again, I saw Celia had tears gathering on her cheeks.

"Pip," she said, "you're adorable!"

I'd given Crooky Tail the name as I drove her home from the supermarket. Although it was obvious to me that "Crooky Tail" would not do, what would we call her? I kept thinking about how today's events had been rather impulsive—going out for a drive to get away from Celia, then coming home with a puppy as a present for her. Just like that! Impulse purchase—impulse present. I-pip. "Pip." That would work.

We spent the next couple of hours playing with our puppy in the backyard, like two happy children. Then, late in the afternoon, we got serious and decided to call Jennie and Croom again, so that all four of us could talk together. But this time no emotion, no outbursts. Just conversation.

Jennie explained, "I gave that journal to Mom early on when she and Dad were visiting us in Dallas. She was supposed to get that to you, Matt, right then. I wanted you to see it for legal purposes, I was so upset with Dr. Salafar. But just as much, because you're a lawmaker, the only one I know. Something needs to be done about all these drugs—psychotropics, painkillers—they're dangerous and too available, and there's no accountability. I still hope you'll do something, Matt—change has to start somewhere."

She continued, "In hindsight, I should have redacted anything personal, but my judgment wasn't the best, to put it mildly. Croom was living with me, poor thing, so he understands."

"Trust me," Croom interjected. "It wasn't easy."

Then Jennie said, "When I didn't hear back from you, Matt, I assumed you weren't interested, so the journal didn't seem to matter, especially with all the other issues going on in my life. I assumed wrong, and I'm sorry."

I apologized to everyone for not doing something definitive with the envelope as soon as Cindy brought it to me. "I should have called you immediately," I said to Jennie, "and asked you about it—why you sent it, what you wanted me to do with it. Shunting it to the side for five months proved to be a mistake." I added, "Not to mention skimming it rather than really reading it."

"There's no telling how long Cindy held onto that journal," Celia said.

Jennie concurred, "Cindy managed to get her revenge on all four of us. Clever—beyond clever. If she's dreamed about *that*, I hope she's happy."

"I just played right into her hands," said Celia, "when, in my worst moments, I was superstitious enough to entertain thoughts of the 'betrayal' thing."

We all understood, because it was part of our bond. And I sensed that we all understood, now, at a deeper level, that forgiveness was part of our bond, too, as well as our challenge going forward. Then we talked about Pip and the children and some more about the misunderstanding, offered a few more apologies, and by the time we hung up, we were laughing and planning our next visit.

The children, all four of them home before dark for dinner, could not believe their dad had gone out and bought them a puppy. Last to learn of the news was Elisa, who walked out onto the back patio to see what all the excitement was about. Teddy was rolling around in the grass—with a live ball of fur.

"A puppy!" she squealed. "Is it ours?"

Reaching down for Pip, she picked her up, hugged her, and put her on her shoulder, her blond hair snuggled against the puppy.

"A family pet! We have a pet!" she exclaimed.

I'd never seen her happier.

Though still a little skeptical, Celia seemed hooked, too.

It had turned out to be a pretty good day, after all; our marriage was saved, as well as our friendship with Croom and Jennie, and our children were delighted as they played in the backyard with a puppy they never expected to have.

. . .

Over the next four-and-a-half or so years, as we watched our children growing up, I continued to renovate and sell old houses and practice law part-time, while Celia had become increasingly successful as a concert pianist. At the same time, I continued to serve in the State Legislature and was involved in a series of demanding and trying campaigns. I was surprised—and disturbed—to see how money, and raising it, had become ever-increasingly important to campaigning. For some candidates, raising money was all-consuming. That phenomenon in American politics, even on the state district level, was shifting the power away from the people and the grassroots and toward big-money special interests. I remained "old school," emphasizing personal relationships instead of fundraising, but the down-side was that it took a lot of time.

Thank Heaven for Andrew and Annie. She'd become indispensable to Celia and me as the de facto manager of Tavern Craft Furniture, and Andrew was excellent as chief supervisor. Under their care, our company continued to expand and turn a respectable profit. While they held down the fort at work, Tracy, our faithful nanny, held it together at home.

On the political front, Celia and I had friends, Croom special among them, and we had detractors, and there were also "friends" who dropped away, but through it all, we had each other.

When the Legislature was in session, I spent Monday night through Wednesday night in Raleigh, coming home to Hickory late Thursday evening. Always there to greet me at the door, Celia kept Pip at her side.

At home, Celia and I made it a point to walk together daily for exercise. Before beginning, I stood against a wall of the sun porch and stretched. After some days of watching me do this, Pip began to stretch *with* me. She would even stretch on command, in preparation for our walk. We walked almost every day, or evening, weather permitting. Sometimes we walked in the daytime, down the street to Oakwood Cemetery where several generations of my kinfolk lay buried. When Celia and I, or the children, visited their graves, Pip went, too.

Stately Oaks was across the street. So sometimes when Celia and I were walking the roads through or around the cemetery, we'd cross the street and walk down the secluded road in front of the home place where my parents still lived, and go in for a visit. My mother still greeted me with a hug—Celia, as well—and my father greeted me with a handshake, Celia with a kiss on the cheek. Pip got a dog biscuit after *she* shook hands.

When I was growing up at Stately Oaks with my parents and three siblings, our front door was answered by Stanza, our housekeeper, just as Baker answered the door at Celia's homeplace even now. Stanza was like family to us, and one of my favorite memories of her is described by my sister BeBe, a teller of stories:

"It happened at Stately Oaks, at the front door. Mom and Dad weren't home, and Stanza was staying with us. I was thirteen and you, Matt, were ten. The front doorbell rang, and we went with Stanza to answer it. When she opened the door, a man was outside on the front porch. I could tell immediately by the expression on Stanza's face and the way her body tensed up, that something was wrong.

"What I remember most about that man was that he had a patch of white gauze taped over one of his eyes. And he was dirty, scruffy," BeBe said. "He hadn't shaved, and he had dirty hands and fingernails. Some of his teeth were rotten, some missing. He reminded me of a pirate, except that his patch was white instead of black, and he was dressed in overalls"—something you didn't often see in town, just out in the country.

"He said, 'Who's home? Who's here?'"

BeBe said he seemed drunk. She figured if he were any closer, she would have smelled him.

"'No one's home. No one's here but me,' Stanza said. 'Go way. Get off this porch.'

"He moved forward a little, toward the door. 'Don't make no never mind to me if nobody home but you. And *her*.'

"When he said *her*," BeBe said, "he was looking at *me*. I shrank behind Stanza, trying to pull you with me, Matt. But you stood there beside Stanza and shook your fist at him. He wasn't one bit scared of you, though, and he asked if he could come inside. Stanza said no and started to shut the door. But he pushed the door open and forced his way inside the foyer, so she told us to run to the kitchen. We did—and when she rejoined us a few moments later, she was standing there holding a switchblade at her side.

"I have no idea where that switchblade came from," BeBe said. "It was like it came out of thin air. But when Stanza needed it, there it was."

I guess I cherish that memory because Stanza was our salvation in time of peril, as children.

Another unique memory comes from what we called "the bug truck." On certain hot summer nights, the bug truck drove slowly down the street spraying a cloud of pungent insecticide all over everywhere, to kill the mosquitoes. You could hear the truck a block away with its roaring blower and see it moving slowly down the street surrounded in a cloud of thick, gray fog. Whenever we heard it, we sprang to our bikes—me, my brother Stuart, neighbor kids—so we could follow behind it in the stinking fog, the older boys, the really daring ones, even grabbing the back of the truck. Back then, there wasn't much to do in Hickory, so you had to create your own fun. Besides, without the insecticide, the mosquitoes were horrendous.

When I was in high school, some of my friends liked to kid me by referring to Stately Oaks as "The Goodheart Mansion." All those bedrooms, ten bathrooms—and an elevator! For years I had recurring dreams centered on that house. In each dream the house took on a different form and appearance, and the context of the dream changed, but it was always in essence the same house.

One time I dreamed an old, white-haired woman was living there when someone else died inside the house. I could never tell who the deceased was, though. I didn't like those dark dreams, because at their core I sensed an omen of some import. While I was in college and law school, I must have dreamt a variation of the "house dream" fifty times.

But I hadn't had that dream in years.

There were other interesting houses in my life, too—I had restored some of them myself—with Pip accompanying me to work in my pick-up. For example, the Whitener house, a few blocks away, was a large, rambling 1907 combination Queen Anne and Colonial Revival, known for its "secret" tunnel that ran from the basement under the front yard and then a ways under Stately Oaks Avenue itself. The owner of the house, a tavern keeper, had dug the tunnel during Prohibition as a place to hide his bootleg booze. The tunnel was full of oak barrels. Not only that, but in the basement floor was a well as deep as the four-story house was tall.

Farther down the street was a big, two-story brick house sitting up on a hill, its impressive porch supported by tall columns. Most people didn't know its history, but Celia and the children did because, when I was working in the house and they came to visit, I told them: "The man who lived here when I was a child hung himself. They found him hanging in an upstairs closet. He had a son who was crazy. He set a fire in Hickory High School, and his parents sent him off to live at Highland, the hospital in Asheville for well-to-do crazy people. That's where Zelda Sayre, F. Scott Fitzgerald's wife, lived after she went nuts."

"I know all about Zelda Sayre," Elisa said. "We learned about her in English class."

"In 1948," I said, "the year after my parents were married, there was another fire, this time at Highland Hospital, and Zelda Fitzgerald and eight other people died in it."

Elisa gasped. "He *didn't*!"

"The folks back home," I told her, "were always suspicious about the source of that fire." Elisa whispered, "You've got to show us the closet!"

Another time, as she and Celia and I went walking with Pip about the neighborhood, Elisa shared with me a curious theory she had about certain houses in the neighborhood, like the one where the man hung himself. According to her, "A house like that, with dormers in the attic—or a tower—might be haunted, because attics and towers are where ghosts live and ghosts like staircases, too."

Our own house, the Shuford-Allran house, a Dutch colonial built in 1925, had never given us a reason to think it was haunted. Quite the contrary, it was blessed; it had been a wonderful home for Celia and me to raise our family in, with a big back yard. Its only claim to eccentricity was that its basement walls, some of them a foot thick, were made of glass bottles as well as concrete blocks and cement.

Sometimes I took the family on riding tours. One of our more memorable stops was Old St. Paul's Lutheran Church outside Newton, the county seat. With a Pre-Revolutionary congregation, the church building itself, a white, two-story, box-like structure made of wood, was over two hundred years old. My mother's great-great-great-great-grandfather, the Reverend John Gottfried Arends, had been the pastor there from 1785 to 1807.

My family lineage had a number of preachers and ministers—as well as legislators—but the pastor who intrigued me the most was my maternal grandfather, Beauregard. He had gone to Trinity College—now Duke—starting in 1912, but he'd been expelled for gambling and lost his entire inheritance. Even so, he was readmitted and graduated late, becoming a Methodist minister "poor but educated," as my mother described him.

"Life is a collection—a series—of ironies," he used to say. And sometimes he would treat us to a homily. He also said that life was often unpredictable—"seriously so"—and that "In any person's life an event can occur in a twinkling—or within a short period of time out of the blue—and change that person's life forever." I guess I'd found out just how right he was. And so had Celia and Croom and Jennie.

My grandfather also said that life was an adventure—and more than that, a journey—and you had to keep searching faithfully, your whole life, and never give up; and if you did persist, you'd eventually find the Ultimate Truth. I felt like I was on that journey myself, faithfully searching for the Great Truth, the Answer to life's mysteries. I so wanted to find that ultimate treasure. I'd always thought Beauregard was interesting, and his philosophical nature and colorful past made me want to know more about him. Recently, I'd learned some things.

Four years since Celia had tried to do me in with a coffee mug—that occasion ironically bringing Pip into our lives—Celia's mother died. The year was 1998, October, and Mrs. Nightingale's death was very difficult for both of us, but especially for Celia. Her mother died unexpectedly in her sleep, and Celia, knocked off her equilibrium, was reeling from the impact.

The funeral was a major social event in Winston-Salem, with the family church so full, people had to sit in the balcony. Jennie and Croom flew home for the services, which were on Wednesday, and stayed six days in Hickory. On Saturday, Mrs. Westfall, a widow since Croom had been in graduate school, decided on the spur of the moment to have Celia and me over for lunch at her home—with Jennie and Croom—and my mother, with whom she'd been friends socially for over forty years.

At this luncheon I learned some new things about my grandfather, Beauregard—"Beergard," as his family pronounced it—as well as about Croom's grandfather, Croom, Jr.

At the last minute, I invited Teddy to go with us because he was at home and he'd asked Celia and me where we were going. "Croom's mother is having us over for lunch. Wanna go?" I didn't think he would, being a fourteen-year-old.

"Who else is going to be there?"

"Croom and Jennie—and Grandmother."

"Can I sit next to Jeni B?"

"You can sit beside *Jennie*," I said.

He smiled. "Okay—I'll go. Do I need to change?"

"Yes. Put on a nice shirt and some khakis. Change shoes. That'll work."

Celia said, "I'll call Mrs. Westfall just to be sure it's okay. But I'm sure she'll be delighted."

"Is Croom cooking?" Teddy asked skeptically.

"Probably," I said. "Still wanna go?"

"Is he a *good* cook?"

"I guess you'll find out. Go change."

At precisely noon, Celia, my mother, Teddy and I stepped onto Mrs. Westfall's front porch—and I rang the bell. We were greeted by the housekeeper, Sherissa Dodge, in her floral dress and white apron, who invited us into the foyer, then ushered us into the living room.

Mrs. Westfall appeared from the breakfast room, wearing a long black dress and a string of pearls. Her shoulder-length, blond hair looked as if it had just been coiffed. She had been a great beauty in her day. My mother was wearing a plaid blouse, a gray skirt covering her knees, a navy-blue cardigan sweater. The two of them were quite different and enjoyed each other's company immensely. Both of them had a great interest in, almost reverence for, their ancestry, which actually converged with a common ancestor in the mid-1700s; and both of them knew how to have a good time.

"Croom is around here somewhere," Mrs. Westfall said. "Croo-oom!" she called out. "Well, he'll get here," she said, laughing. "Why don't we sit down?"

We started to sit in the living room, furnished like a Victorian parlor in purple, gold, and pink, with ornate blue wallpaper. But Mrs. Westfall had a different idea. "No, no, not here," she laughed. "We're informal. In the dining room. I think lunch is ready to be served."

A young woman appeared at her side and ushered us to the dining room, seating Mrs. Westfall at the head of the table by pulling out her chair for her. "Just sit anywhere," Mrs. Westfall said. "Except for you, Marie, dear," she said to my mother. "You sit at the other end of the table."

I pulled out my mother's chair, then Celia's—then I sat beside Celia—as Teddy, tall for his age, took the chair next to Jennie's. He'd combed—and, I knew, tried to straighten—his curly, dark brown hair.

A white-laced linen cloth covered the table, and near each end, candelabra held four candles each. The places were set with silver and china, two forks for salad and entrée, another for dessert. Every place setting had two glasses.

I stood up again as Jennie, my beach buddy and now one of Celia's closest friends, entered the dining room from the breakfast room, carrying a large crystal bowl of salad. She looked as if she had dressed for a cover shoot, perfect in every way.

"Don't get up," she said, smiling. "It's just me—with the salad. I made it myself. Hope you like it." She placed it in the center of the table and sat down, giving Teddy a peck on the cheek. He broke into a broad smile.

"Croo-oom," Mrs. Westfall called out again. "Everyone is here."

When there was no sign of him, she said, "That young lady you just saw is Daniela. She's from Moldova." I knew that because Croom had told me his mother had an attendant-companion, a young woman who had been living with her since she fell three years ago. "I couldn't do without her," said Mrs. Westfall, "and thankfully, she doesn't talk much," she added with a laugh. "I'm so glad you could come for lunch," she said. "And Celia, again, I'm so sorry about your mother."

"Thank you. You're awfully kind to have us over. I'm very glad to get out of the house."

"Well, we *could* have lunch without Croom," Mrs. Westfall said, "but *he* has the food."

At that moment, Croom, wearing a big, almost mischievous, grin beneath his dark mustache, entered the room, carrying a steaming silver tray. "Hel*lo*, everybody," he said.

Setting the tray in the middle of the table beside the salad, he said, "Deer is served."

He gave Teddy a hardy pat on the back, then walked around the table, in his corduroy pants, plaid shirt, and cowboy boots to greet my mother with a hug, then Celia. "I'm glad you came over," he whispered kindly to Celia.

"Thank you, Croom," she said to him, smiling. "You're a dear. And thank you—and Jennie—so much, for coming to the funeral and the receiving and the beautiful flowers and memorial gift and everything else." Her eyes teared up and her voice broke as she spoke. "And thank you for having us over for lunch. I so need this diversion. I hope it's not too much trouble."

"Never!" Croom said. "I cooked the deer myself."

"He *killed* it, himself, too," Jennie said. "Quite the hunter! Sherissa did the rest."

Croom sat down beside Jennie and across the table from me, and Sherissa re-entered, pushing a serving cart. Starting with my mother, she began serving everyone, except Mrs. Westfall, who was served at the same time by Daniela.

"Croom," Mrs. Westfall said, "if you would say the blessing."

Croom returned thanks.

"Now," Mrs. Westfall said, "if you would help with the wine." She laughed. "Like I said, we're informal."

Croom got up from the table, then returned with a bottle of red wine. Starting with my mother, then *his* mother, he went around the table, serving each glass, except Teddy's, all trimmed in gold filigree.

Sherissa asked each of us whether we wanted tea, sweet or unsweet, then served it, after which Mrs. Westfall began chatting with my mother, reminiscing about the "fun times" they'd had together on their trips to Europe, and then the days when Mr. Westfall used to play golf with my father, and the years the two husbands served together on the bank board and church council.

One story followed another until Mrs. Westfall recalled, "When my father was at Duke, it was still Trinity College. He entered in 1912."

"My *grand*father was class of 1916," I said. "That's the same class. They were bound to have known each other, being from the same small town."

"They knew each other," my mother said.

Her father's college career was a sensitive subject with her, along with the fact that he hadn't raised her. When her own mother died soon after giving birth to her, he, already having three sons to raise by himself, informally gave up his baby girl to his wife's parents, so my mother was raised by her grandparents. She'd had a happy childhood, but she'd hardly known her father. When he'd lost his inheritance in college, one of the side effects later on proved to be losing his daughter.

My mother added kindly, "I've heard some good stories about my father and Alice's father in college." Alice was Mrs. Westfall.

Mrs. Westfall said, "I didn't know my father, either. He died young, in his early thirties. But I know he was expelled from college—for drinking and failing to attend vespers."

Teddy frowned.

Croom laughed. "Not to mention gambling!"

"There was some of that, too," his mother replied.

"That's what got *my* father expelled," my mother said.

I asked, "So—was my grandfather as wild and woolly as Croom's?"

Mrs. Westfall cleared her throat. "*Well*," she said, "although my father was expelled, he did get back into college, and he did finish, and he did become a doctor."

"But getting expelled wasn't the worst of it," Croom said.

"Not by a long shot," said Jennie.

Croom explained: "He didn't go back to Duke because they wouldn't readmit him, so he finished up—here's the awful part—at Carolina!" Laughing loudly, he hit the table with his fist, almost knocking over his wine glass. Mrs. Westfall began to laugh, too. Then we all did, including Celia, who had been quiet all day. It made me happy to see her smile.

"My grandfather actually graduated from UNC Medical School," Croom groaned.

The various expressions on Teddy's face told me that he too was enjoying this "grownup" conversation.

"And *my* father," my mother said, "ended up a Methodist minister. After making a terrible mistake that cost him dearly and changed his life drastically, he saw the error of his ways, and repented. He was readmitted to Trinity College and graduated."

"Life is a collection of ironies," I said. "And a life-long search. From lost boy to child of God."

"How could *he* get back in, when Croom's grandfather couldn't?" Jennie wanted to know.

My mother, who had loosened up considerably in the last half-hour with the help of the wine, blurted out, "My father repented—Alice's father didn't!"

We roared.

On a roll, she said, "He *needed* to repent. Not only was Beergard expelled for gambling and failing to attend vespers—just like Croom, Jr.—but also for swearing and watching a cockfight in Raleigh. Not to mention drinking. They didn't call him Beergard for nothing."

"Wow!" Teddy exclaimed.

"How do you know all this?" Celia asked.

I thought about how *her* grandfather, at about the same time in history, had been busy building Winston-Salem into a respectable community along with his parents and family.

"Family," Mrs. Westfall said. "These are the stories any family would keep alive."

"We can look back now," my mother said, "over lunch and wine, and laugh about it. But there's a lot more to it in *my* case. My father's early misspent college days caused him to—"

"Lose his inheritance," I chimed in.

My mother looked at me, not smiling. Raising her eyebrows, she spoke. "You be careful. You be careful with your own finances—don't be like your grandfather and lose everything. You look just like him, long legs and all. He was six-foot-six, blond and blue-eyed. A very handsome man. And he *would* have been very well-off."

I said, "I've always wanted to know more about that, about his losing his inheritance. How did it happen?"

"A poker game," said my mother. Teddy smiled, raising his eyebrows. "They were in a poker game—four of them—Croom Westfall, Beergard, two others."

"My father pulled out before the others did," Mrs. Westfall said. "But he got expelled just the same."

"My father stayed in," my mother said, "and he lost the entire inheritance my grandfather had given him when he left home for college—a lot of money—supposedly in gold coins. That's the story. I don't know how true it is, about the gold coins—he was not proud of his former life—his 'misspent youth,' as he put it. He never talked about it."

Mrs. Westfall said, "He lost the money to a student they called Hazy." She laughed and added, "Crazy Hazy."

"Hazy cheated," said my mother, taking the last sip of wine from her glass before Sherissa, who was checking the table, refilled it. Then she cleared and served each of us a glass of sorbet. "He cheated at cards—and stole my father's inheritance in a poker game," my mother repeated. "And *he* ended up a doctor, too—like Croom, Jr." She smiled and managed a little laugh. "Where's the justice?"

That made everyone else laugh—harder. Even Celia.

I said, "Wow! What a story! Why did I have to wait until I was forty-six years old to hear it?"

"Because it's a *sad* story," my mother said. "Nothing to be proud of. It didn't just change my father's life forever; it changed my life, too."

"A person could write a book about it," said Celia. I was happy to see her smiling and talking. "Maybe everything that happened was meant to be and was all for the best."

Jennie lifted her glass. "Let's toast to it. To the thought that all things happen for a purpose—and for the best. We just have to search for the good in the bad, till we find it."

"And never give up!" Croom said.

"That's right," I concurred. "Always search for the gold in the darkness." I was thinking about the young lady who sat beside me on the plane to Dallas, so engrossed in her book about Christian spirituality.

Celia raised her glass a little higher. "To the gold—the light—in the darkness," she said quietly but bravely.

We were silent momentarily, then Croom boomed out, "To fortunes lost, fortunes gained!"

"Great title for the book!" Celia smiled.

"I think I'll use it myself," I proclaimed, "if I can ever get past chapter five!"

Croom laughed so hard he spilled some of his wine on his mother's white linen cloth. "A best seller!" he exclaimed. "Hard cover!"

"Hear, hear!" his mother laughed.

"Hear, hear!" *my* mother laughed.

All around the table, we clinked our gold-filigreed glasses. Celia smiled and laughed with the rest of us, and it made me feel good, seeing her that way: she'd been so blue the last few days.

24.
DOG DAYS

That luncheon is a fond remembrance, but the next six months were hard. I think Celia was depressed without realizing it, and it took her almost a year—into 1999—to pull out of it. Angela's death was hard on both of us because it was the most significant, closest loss we'd ever experienced. We had some heart-to-heart talks about our faith, even questioning our beliefs. Was God really watching over us and our family? Did Angela, good as she was, *really* go to Heaven? Where was God in all of this? Though Angela's death created a void in our lives, by the latter part of 1999, we were doing better. Life was beginning to feel good again, and we began spending some time away from home.

We bought a house on the water at Bogue Banks, an island unusual in that it runs east-west rather than north-south along the North Carolina coast. In winter, the sun sets over the water, creating the most beautiful sunsets I've ever laid eyes on, this side of Puerto Vallarta. Elisa, Bert, Caroline, and Teddy, in a sense, grew up on this island beach because we visited as often as we could, despite the nearly seven-hour drive from home.

Sometimes I traveled to the beach with the whole family—sometimes I just took some of them. Bert, Teddy, and I played basketball in the driveway—and swam and fished. Sometimes I went with no one but Pip.

In her early years, Pip was an ugly duckling of sorts, but over time she had transformed into a swan—and she loved the water. Her crooked tail had filled out and become full of beautiful white "feathers" against the gold fur, and because her tail became so full, the crook in it was no longer noticeable. The imperfection had disappeared in several ways.

I enjoyed watching Pip romp in the surf: she had a beautiful gait on land, and in the water, she jumped the waves with energetic grace. She could chase seagulls for hours, pursuing them but never harming them; even if she captured one, she let it go.

Each beach trip, we made at least one trek from the house to the jetty. The Rocks were a string of boulders strung out into the ocean to prevent erosion in the inlet. Sometimes we found them deserted. Other times we had the company of fishermen using the jetty to get farther out into the ocean. Standing on The Rocks in patient silence for hours, they cast their lines again and again in hopes of a catch.

I liked to climb atop The Rocks and make my way out into the surf, waves lapping on both sides. It helped that I had long legs. For a dog to jump up on rocks, slippery with wet algae and maneuver from one boulder to the next was no mean feat—actually dangerous—but Pip had some pretty mean feet, and she followed me eagerly, every time—my constant, true companion.

Over the next few years, I often visited The Rocks, sometimes fishing with Bert and Teddy till sunset. We stood in awe of the sun, a great huge red ball, moving slowly but perceptibly downward in the sky to the ocean's horizon. Then finally, it would dip beneath the line of the ocean, extinguishing itself while creating in the blue expanse a masterwork of orange, purple, violet, yellow, red, and pink. Sometimes the sky was adorned with variable cloud formations, and other times was cloudless at the close of day.

Pip was always with me at The Rocks, patient and contented. It had come somewhat as a surprise that I had grown, over the years, so attached to her. It was the same feeling I'd felt for our collie mix, Ellie, when I was in elementary school, only deeper.

Celia was partial to the mountains, possibly because she'd never fully gotten over our Isle of Cats ordeal. Had *any* one of The Four of us totally gotten over it?

Over twenty-five years had passed since our fateful trip, and you'd think our recollections would have dimmed. Instead, at times the trip seemed more vivid than yesterday. It was as if the events of those twenty-four hours had been imprinted on our psyches, embedded in our brains.

Over twenty-five years ago, around the Ides of March, we'd had a corpse on our hands, but our anxieties had begun long before the body was cold. From the dunes, just looking at the house—a ramshackle mansion—had sent shivers through our bones. Going inside would have been unthinkable had the storm not driven us in. Why—*why*?—had we convinced that squirrelly little boatman to take us to the island? What had we been looking for?

No one should be put off a boat, alone, on an island. And even though there had been *four* of us, we were still alone. Quite. Yet, not quite. And then there were her predictions. And then she was dead. Her body lay on the floor, blood dripping down, eyes open, green cat's eyes, staring up at us. Large cats, strangely misshapen, lurked in the outer room. Curious. Hungry. That had been us, then: youngsters, curious and hungry for adventure and a good time. The night was all around us, and the room was dark except for the light of a candle and lantern. And sometimes lightning, as the storm still raged outside.

The smell of blood and the dank smell of mildew—and the faint smell of urine—permeated the room. The pump organ the old woman had played, and the table where she'd told our fortunes were without her, now. The smell of fear was with *us*, though, in that dark room.

Now and again, the lightning would shock our sensibilities—and thunder would break overhead—as if, at that moment, we might be struck. But for the time being, there we were. I, the tall blond guy who the old woman said was polite, could have been the brother of the gorgeous girl whose long blond hair was normally shimmering, but now was matted and tangled from the torrent. She was paired with the semi-swarthy guy with the dark mustache, the guy who resembled Edgar Poe, albeit a dashing version. He could have been the brother of the beautiful brunette with the big brown eyes, whose brown hair was normally as perfect as the girl's in the Breck commercial but now was as tangled and matted as the other girl's.

Had the four of us been related that way—two sets of siblings—it would have been bizarrely like the Bobbsey Twins on a misadventure. And it couldn't have gotten much weirder, more macabre than it was as we stood over the dead body, flipping coins to decide how to dispose of the corpse.

That ghastly decision, made with a series of coin-tosses as if we were ghouls at a midnight gravesite, along with the woman's predictions and everything else about that trip to the Isle of Cats, had on-and-off since then followed the four of us—and cemented a bond.

So, when certain things happened in our lives, such as Celia's "impulsively losing her temper," we might think about Miss Smiley's predictions. But when *good* fortune came to us, such as my winning an election or my bringing Pip home as a peace present for Celia, we tended to forget about old Miss Smiley. The good things we credited to God—the bad ones to ourselves. What did that say about human nature—or was it just *ours*?

Regardless, Pip was partial to the beach and had no clue about a deserted island inhabited by strange cats—and a stranger old woman. So there were days Pip and I spent on the coast that Celia spent at home. Because of these subtle disparate preferences, mine for the beach, Celia's for the mountains, over the years, my dog and I experienced the howling wind and rain of a hurricane as it battered the sliding glass doors off the balcony of our house; sleeping on the beach in the dunes of the state park, Pip digging a nest beside me and plopping down in it as I slept; the changing seasons, including winter, the time of the year of the most brilliant sunsets; and even an occasional snowfall.

Typically Pip and I arrived at the beach late at night after a long drive, often at midnight or later. A causeway connected

Bogue Banks to the mainland. As we crossed it in the car, a huge sense of relief invariably overtook me as I left the busy world on the other side. Pip knew the bridge. She stood up in the back seat, and I'd crack the windows for her to sniff for the scent of the ocean.

Except for the late-night lights of Atlantic Beach and Morehead City and Beaufort—and the heavens—all was dark as we crossed the water, and within minutes we were parked at the house. Even before unpacking, we went out to the edge of the surf, under the stars, under the moon of whatever shape and size, and I looked heavenward in gratitude while Pip dashed into the water, regardless of the time of year or temperature.

If we had only a sliver of moon, like a neon wedge of orange rind—or scant starlight because clouds scuttled across the sky like coal-dust pillows against the moonlight—it wasn't easy to see out on the beach. Sometimes my mind wandered, and I'd think of that night with Jennie at the beach in Nassau, but now the recollection was fleeting, a small piece of glass in a kaleidoscope, meaningless by itself, but beautiful as a part of the whole picture.

I had to keep an eye out for my dog. "You be careful," Celia warned me. And my mother had admonished me the same way about money, that day at lunch. And they were right: self-control and good foresight had to be my watchwords.

The house had a pool encircled by a cobblestone terrace with water quite blue. At night it scintillated beneath the light of lanterns as a waterfall cascaded from the top of a rock wall to the pool below. Sometimes I swam many laps from one end of the pool to the other, while Pip swam, too. She never tired. Or, late at night, I could relax and enjoy the sparkling light as it made sequins on the surface of the water, and once inside the house again, if the windows were open, I could enjoy the sound of the water rushing down into the pool.

Those days and weeks and years at the beach were some of the happiest and most productive of my life. Miraculously, I even finished a rough first draft of my novel, a hobby necessitating quiet time and solitude. Still, I wasn't satisfied with what I'd written: there had to be a *point* to it all—there had to be a deeper meaning. An ultimate truth. Writing helped me in my search, but simply writing had not unearthed that buried treasure I still sought.

Beach-time helped me regain and retain my sanity in a life that sometimes veered into the insane, often hilariously so. Sometimes I asked myself why I remained in politics, considering all the business and family obligations I had. Well, first of all, I believed I was doing God's work in serving the people. And secondly, I enjoyed it. I guess part of it was also the Eagle Scout in me. At any rate, I must have been doing a pretty good job because the people kept electing me by wide margins, and now they wanted me to run for Congress.

Then, Celia, who loved the mountains, helped me rediscover my childhood love of the mountains by encouraging us to take weekend excursions from Hickory to the High Country around Blowing Rock. And every time we went, Celia looked longingly at houses—so, for her fiftieth birthday, I bought her one, preconstruction.

Going to our mountain retreat became almost a weekend event to watch the progress as the walls went up, then the roof, then the interior. My favorite features were the two huge decks—

one on the first floor, one on the second—as well as a balcony on the third, all surrounded on three sides by a panoramic view of the Blue Ridge, stretching over sixty miles and six mountain ranges, all the way to Tennessee.

We liked to visit, at nearby Tynecastle, a tavern with an outdoor patio and karaoke on Friday nights. Pip liked to sit with Celia and me while I drank a beer, and we suffered through the singing, amused. Pip also liked lapping the last few drops from my beer bottle after I'd poured the rest in a mug.

. . .

The first Saturday in August 2005, Celia and I spontaneously decided to head for the mountains. Quite hot in the foothills of Hickory, we were lured to the cool of the Blue Ridge, gladly suppressing our dutiful instincts to stay home and work on the weekend.

As we packed up the SUV and headed up the mountain, Pip, our only "child" still at home now that the other four had moved on, jumped into the back seat. It seemed like a great day for hiking, so that's what we did, Pip tagging along or running ahead. That evening, we went to a restaurant we'd never been to before and had a leisurely dinner outside on the porch. We wanted the evening to be special because we were celebrating Celia's birthday two days before.

We did enjoy the evening—the food was outstanding, and so was the atmosphere—with a casual, gracious ambience.

"Life is good," Celia said. "I've never been happier." We toasted each other with champagne. Then she said, "I saw your mother's friend, Mrs. Tatum, downtown on Monday. Do you know what she told me? She said, 'I believe Matt Goodheart is on a roll. He just can't miss. Whatever Matt Goodheart touches turns to gold.'"

"And do you believe that?" I said.

Celia answered, "Of course. Because I believe in Matt Goodheart."

"And I believe in Celia Goodheart. I believe that for her, the sky is the limit. The Kennedy Center. Carnegie Hall."

"And for my husband—Congress."

"Is that what you want?"

"I want whatever *you* want."

"The sky's the limit," I said. "Whatever we touch turns to gold. If Mrs. Tatum believes it, it must be so," I smiled.

Celia smiled back. "And so does Pip."

Pip looked up from her place between us on the floor, then put her head back down on her paws. I held up my champagne glass. "To the future."

We tapped. "To the future," said Celia.

"To us," I said.

"To us," said Celia.

"And to Pip!" I added.

It had been a lovely summer day in the mountains—and a lovely evening. A perfect Saturday. A perfect way to celebrate a birthday.

25.

BY THE DARK OF THE MOON

Saturday had been ideal in the mountains celebrating Celia's birthday. When we arrived home on Sunday, the backyard was warm and sunny, with the fragrance of gardenias and roses. The fountains were flowing and gurgling brightly around the perimeter of our edenic garden.

After a fine day, around ten o'clock, Pip and I joined up for our evening walk. I hooked Pip onto her leash, and we headed out just as we had done thousands of times before. It was a calm, clear night, and the generous peace of a long summer to come was in the air. I could hear the wailing of a train on the tracks near the center of town. We walked past my childhood home—where my parents still lived—atop the hill. We passed the cemetery. After thirty minutes, we came to the section of sidewalk in which we'd etched Pip's name and the date—PIP 2004—a year earlier just opposite the tracks.

We loved the train, and we loved the tracks, too. We always

had. Cindy Peppercorn and I, back when we were friends, used to visit the train tracks; now Pip and I did. Off in the distance, way down the track, I saw a small bright light, the engine's eye, shining in the dark, then heard the tigerish hum.

"Pip," I whispered, "a train! There's a train way down the track. If we wait a while, it'll be here." We walked over to a guardrail next to the road, a grassy median between it and the tracks. I sat down, holding Pip by her leash a good twenty-five or thirty feet from where the train would pass. As I peered at the bright eye, it grew more distinct as it moved nearer, the deep purring of the engine growing louder. Pip pulled on her leash as the great iron dragon wailed out its warning, and the ground began to rumble beneath our feet. Finally, as the engine was nearly on us, its wailing split the night air. I stood up and waved to the engineer passing only a few yards away, the ground pulsating under us as Pip jerked on her leash.

Romilar, I thought—for just a second.

First, the engine passed, then one car after another as Pip and I moved to a nearby streetlight, where I stood and waved to the travelers I saw inside the lit-up cars. Who could know where those souls were headed? Windows filled with silhouettes, one after another, passed by.

Then the train slowed—and stopped. Efficiently, passengers got off and passengers got on. Jerking at first, and then rumbling, the train was moving again, as Pip and I watched and listened as a wailing pierced the air, warning any cars—any people—to stay away. Then the lights became one single light, the other one, the final one: only that remained. That light, too, grew smaller and fainter until it flickered, finally fading imperceptibly into the night, extinguished.

I let Pip off her leash next to the tracks in the deserted grassy area with plenty of room to play. While she ran about sniffing the grass like a hound, I dropped to the ground and did a set of push-ups. Might as well get that done now as later.

I put her back on her leash; we crossed the road and headed down the sidewalk toward a fenced-in warehouse guarded by Rottweilers. Once there, I let her off the leash again so she could run back and forth in front of the fence to the ferocious barking of the guard dogs. Once past the fence, I re-leashed her, and we continued on down the sidewalk. At the intersection at the end of the sidewalk, we turned around and headed back in the direction of home. On the way, I again let her off her leash to run with the big dogs.

Then we walked on. She crossed the dark, empty street back to the grassy buffer next to the tracks. She wasn't supposed to do that—cross unleashed to the other side of the street—so I called her. She ignored me, but I cut her some slack since no one was around but us. I called her again.

No response. The disobedience irritated me, but the place was deserted, and she apparently had discovered a scent that had a hold on her.

After she'd been allowed enough time to play and sniff around, I called her once more. I wanted her back on *my* side of the road, back on the sidewalk, and not across the street near the tracks.

It was dark out except for the streetlight overhead and the glow of the full moon. Again, I called, "Pip, come here, girl!" She was playing her stubborn self, looking up at me, then returning to her sniffing in the grass as if I didn't exist. I started walking away from her, glancing back, doing the psychology thing. Off in the distance on a downtown street, one car was heading in our direction.

I called her again. "*Pip*!" She looked up at me but did not come. It did cross my mind that if the car continued to travel toward us and went straight through the intersection instead of turning right or left, it would run between me on the sidewalk and Pip on the other side where she was busy sniffing around. I called her once more. Again, she ignored me. My eye on the car, I watched as it, instead of turning right or left, continued through the intersection. Suddenly, I felt an extreme pang of apprehension. Then, as the car held fast its approach, I saw—as my pulse quickened—Pip move off the roadside and into the street, beginning to trot in my direction.

The car was closer to me than to Pip, and I stepped off the curb onto the edge of the street, almost in its path, waving to stop it or slow it down. But passing by me as if I were invisible, the car kept going, and a tidal wave of helpless panic overtook me. If I yelled for Pip to stop or go back, I knew she wouldn't.

She was coming toward me. And the car was going toward her. In that instant, the only thing I could think to do was call her, hoping she could outrun the car. I did call her, and when I did, she perked up and ran faster, her head held high, her face smiling. At that moment, it appeared to me as if she were seeing me and hearing my voice again for the first time after a long absence: she was happy to see me, looking forward to being back on her leash, having me pet and hug her.

I heard a thump, but the car kept going. When the car's

shadow had passed beneath the streetlight, I saw Pip lying in the middle of the road. The old white car kept on moving down the street as if Pip and I were immaterial phantoms in the night. Never once did the driver brake, swerve, or slow down.

I knelt beside my dog as she lay on her side, looking up at me, her most trusted friend. Still alive, her soulful brown eyes open, looking up at me, she was asking me to do something. I lifted her head in my hands and noticed a small hole about the size of a button in the top of her head.

I looked at the two houses next to the tracks, hoping desperately for a miracle. Nothing there but darkness. I looked down the road: the car continued on; at no time did its taillights brighten. Not for a second.

In a state of helpless shock and horror, I tried to breathe air into her mouth. Even under the circumstances, I knew it was a stupid, futile gesture, but it was all I could think to do. No blood was visible, and she was warm, so maybe she was just stunned and resting. Maybe she'd move, then get up. After all, her gold fur was beautiful and warm. Utterly confused and totally abandoned, I knelt in the middle of the road over my dog. I felt infinitesimally small and helpless—totally alone in the world.

I called Celia on my cell phone. I told her where we were and that Pip had been hit by a car. As I waited and waited for her to arrive, Pip's energy and mine seemed fused in a wordless, elemental task. When Celia arrived, I picked up my dog—still warm, her eyes still open—and placed her in the back of the SUV.

An all-night emergency animal clinic was nearby, and Celia drove as fast as she could, me in the back kneeling over Pip. I heard her honk the horn protractedly as she raced through an intersection even though the light was red.

When we arrived at the clinic, I jumped out of the back of the van and ran inside. A man and woman were in the waiting area with a small dog on the man's lap. I was trying to retain a sense of composure in front of them, but all I sensed were the seconds ticking away.

"I need your help immediately!" I said to the young woman at the front desk.

"My dog's been hit by a car. She's outside—it's really serious!"

Two nurses came out to help—none too quickly, it seemed to me—one pushing a gurney. Once outside at the back of our SUV, Celia and I—our beloved dog just hit and suffering—tried to retain some decorum in front of strangers.

"She doesn't have a pulse," one nurse said, and Celia broke into tears.

"Matt, how many times have I told you not to let her off the leash?"

"Please don't say that," I begged. "Not in front of the nurses . . . and Pip."

Pip was dead, after all. The nurses stood with us momentarily, then retreated inside. Celia and I were desolate, alone together.

"Go in and ask them how much it costs to cremate her," she finally said. I went back in to talk to the young woman at the desk. She answered me calmly and professionally. I couldn't leave my dog there, though.

I looked at the couple still waiting with their small dog safe in the man's lap. It wasn't fair. I didn't believe what had happened—and what was following it so inevitably. We left,

Celia driving, and I was in the back of the van with Pip.

When we got home, we got out of the car, and Celia said, only, "I've got to go to bed. I have to get up in the morning and practice for my concert."

It was scheduled for next weekend—the pinnacle of her career—at the Nightingale Performing Arts Center in Winston-Salem. She went inside, the screen door closing behind her with a loud thud that beat against my ears. I felt totally alone, abandoned in a way I'd never felt before—in a way I could never have imagined.

By now, it was about eleven o'clock, with a full moon in the dark sky. Something ghastly had attached itself to every aspect of my existence. I went into the garage, found a shovel, and walked over to the magnolia tree to dig. I dug for twenty minutes, my heart pounding. It occurred to me that this pounding in my chest might cause me to have a heart attack, but I didn't care: finishing me off would simplify things.

Celia was going to leave me. Who could blame her? It was my fault. I'd killed my own dog—her dog—our dog. Our last child at home. If Pip had been on the leash, this wouldn't have happened. It was that simple. I'd heard of cases where the death of a child caused the breakup of a marriage. Even after decades. Look at all the problems it had caused Jennie and Croom.

Maybe *this* was "*the* murder," the one we'd all been on the lookout for since the trip to the Isle of Cats. Jennie had survived the driver of the car who hit and almost killed her. She'd survived Dr. Salafar and his drugs. He'd survived her and her gun. Now, this. Pip had not survived me. She'd been killed, the ultimate betrayal.

I went into the laundry room and pulled a black trash bag from the shelf. I couldn't just lay her in the ground. I couldn't. I went to the back of the SUV and attempted to put Pip in the trash bag. Her eyes were glazed now, and she'd left some blood on the carpet in the car. I saw this through tears that poured down my face.

She was too big. Pip was a beautiful, healthy, copper-colored, sixty-five-pound golden. I got another bag. With two, I was able to cover her completely.

I stood at the back of the van trying to concentrate. Now was the moment of truth. Should I bury her—or have her cremated? I tried to think. I tried to decide. I couldn't. If I could have summoned help from God, I would have. But He was not around. I was alone beneath the shadow of the dark moon. I tried to imagine what Celia would want, and I decided on cremation.

I had wanted to bury Pip. But when it was time to do it, I could not bury my dog—my friend—my child. Not like this. Not in a trash bag, in a shallow grave, with no one around. Not in the dark of the moon—like this. Abandoned. No family present. Nothing.

I couldn't find the keys to Celia's van, so I had to lift Pip's dead weight into the back seat of my car. I drove her back to the all-night clinic.

The young woman opened the door for me and had a genuinely sweet, kind, sympathetic expression on her face, as if to say, "I understand why you're back."

"I couldn't bury her," I said.

When I got back home, it was time to clean up the blood in Celia's car. I scrubbed the upholstery in the back of her van with dishwashing liquid and old rags, but the soap and water and blood created puddles of pink foam. When I looked up, my surroundings were alight with the glow of the full moon. I felt no God, but there could be vampires, werewolves lurking among the trees. This night was the worst of my life, worse than the worst bad dream because I could not wake up from it. It would not go away. Then there was tomorrow. I had an appointment—an interview, a consultation with a client—at ten o'clock. I wondered if I'd still be married then.

I thought I would be, but I understood Celia would hate me forever, or at least never forgive me. Who could blame her? I would never forgive myself for this night—why should she?

I was almost fifty-four years old. Out of all the things I'd ever done in my life, this was the worst thing I'd ever done. If only I could turn back the clock a matter of minutes—even a matter of seconds ... On the grassy buffer beside the railroad tracks, I'd dropped to the ground and done a set of pushups, something I normally didn't do till I got home. If I hadn't stopped and done them midway through the walk, she wouldn't have been hit. If I hadn't let her off the leash, she wouldn't have been hit. This was the crowning act, the most decisive act of my life. I'd killed my dog, and it had revealed me for who I really was, reckless and careless. A betrayer of a trusting friend.

My backyard Garden of Eden had become the Garden of Gethsemane, and, despite its lunar glow, I saw no light at all, only darkness. I wanted to speak to God—I needed to pray—confess—but I could not. I wanted to ask God for help, but I could not. I did not sense His presence, at all. Only a dark, empty desolation.

. . .

I washed out the rags in the sink with soap, put them in the washing machine, and started the washer. I was wearing a T-shirt my younger sister Kristen had given me a few years earlier as a Christmas present. On the front, it said, "Austin," as in Texas; on the back, it said, "Keep Austin Weird." I pulled it off and threw it in the trashcan at the side of the house. I took off my shorts and socks and washed them till all the blood was out.

I didn't know where to sleep. It was almost midnight. If I got into bed with Celia, it might make things worse. I decided to lie down in the spare room across the hall. I figured I wouldn't be able to sleep, but at least I wouldn't wake Celia. I lay down, but I had no idea where my life would go from here. I'd get up in the morning and go into work—keep my appointment—then drive to Raleigh for the Monday night legislative session.

Across the hall, through the closed door, I heard soft crying from our bedroom, like a child's whimpering. I got up, walked across the hall, opened the door to our bedroom and knelt beside Celia as she lay in the bed, softly crying. I climbed into bed beside her and tried to comfort her as best I could. I held her as she continued to weep gently.

"I'm sorry," I said through my own tears. "I'm so sorry. I'm so sorry. I'm so terribly sorry."

Then I lost it—and began to sob, wailing. Celia sat up in bed and held me.

Finally, she said, "You can't go to Raleigh tomorrow. You need to stay home."

"I killed her," I said. "I killed my own dog."

"You did not," she said. "She had a good life. She lived

twelve good, healthy, happy years. She had a good life."

I couldn't believe her kindness. She was talking about her dog, too—the dog who'd been her constant companion for twelve years, the one who'd slept at the foot of her bed—or on the bed—and protected her during all the days and nights I'd been in Raleigh for a session, the dog who'd kept her from being alone when her husband was gone.

The children had grown up and left home. The only one left was Pip.

Now she was dead.

We lay together for the rest of the night, quietly embraced. Waiting together for what the dawn would bring.

26.

SAVING STATELY OAKS

I kept my appointment at my law office but called in to the Senate for an excused absence for the nightly session. Monday sessions were usually short in content and duration and often perfunctory, but I did not like to miss them and rarely did. In this case, though, I agreed to stay home.

Celia suggested I go see someone for grief counseling and recommended a Christian counselor. I'd never been to a counselor in my life because, like a lot of other people, I considered it a compliment to myself that I'd never "needed" to. But in this case, I agreed. She called and arranged an appointment for the following day.

I sat in his office on a sofa across from him. He was sitting at his desk dressed in casual street clothes. Leaning back in his chair, he regarded me through glasses above a neatly trimmed beard.

"My dog was killed this past Sunday night. My fault," I said.

"I loved that dog—so did Celia. I liked everything about her. Her quirky personality. The way she looked. Her gold coat. The way she ran. I even liked the way she smelled, like an old-timey car—dusty."

I paused. He looked at me patiently. I continued, forcing a laugh, "The top of her head smelled like the old 1931 A Model Ford my dad kept in a garage in our backyard when we were growing up." I added, "She looked like the collie dog we adopted back in those days as a stray—our first childhood dog. Ellie."

I shuddered. We talked for a while. I told him how Pip was killed. "I called her, and she came running to me. That's when she was hit."

"I think better of you for doing something like you did in calling her," he said, "doing something to try to save her than if you'd done nothing. You tried. That's the important thing."

"I stepped off the curb and waved at the car, but it didn't slow down. I thought about jumping out in front of it to stop it, but the way he was driving, I think he might have hit me."

"He probably *would* have."

We sat in silence. Finally, I asked him, "Do you think dogs have souls? The Bible doesn't necessarily preclude that, does it?"

He answered without hesitation. "I wouldn't say that dogs have souls, but they do have personalities. Their personalities might well be in Heaven, along with the souls of people. God loves people; that's why He created companions for them. Dogs bring happiness and love. Whether they have souls or not, they have personalities. Look at it this way: why would God wish to keep them out of Heaven? What would be the point? Did they do something wrong to make them offensive to the perfect place? God can do whatever He wants to do."

He counseled me not to repress talking about Pip. "Some people refuse to talk about the loss of a loved one," he explained. "That's the worst thing you can do. That's like denying they ever lived. This death is part of her individual and precious story."

I thought about that—and kept thinking about it after I left his office: "This death is part of her story." And Pip's had been a good story for me to be a part of.

The following weekend, Celia performed at the Nightingale Performing Arts Center in Winston-Salem. The concert was not a disaster, but it was not a triumph, either. The reviews, at best, were damning with faint praise; at worst, they dared to use adjectives like "flat" and "uninspired." One reviewer wrote, "Not up to par for Celia Nightingale Goodheart—a disappointment for her first appearance in the grand auditorium bearing her family name."

Celia was crushed, and I blamed myself.

"It wasn't just weak," she said to me afterward. "It was bad. I could feel it. It was the first really bad performance I've ever given. How could I do that to Rachmaninoff? I felt like I was back in college. And my family was there—Dad—and Bill, Daniel, Robert, and the wives—all sitting there in their special seats on the front row. I'm just thankful none of the children came. Thank God Mother didn't have to endure that performance—or the reviews."

"It wasn't as bad as you're making it out," I said. "Celia, it was clear and precise, without a single fingering error to my ear."

"Oh, yes, Matt—precise and soulless. Good for me." Then

she said, "We thought we couldn't lose. We were on a roll. The sky was the limit. What has happened to us?"

I wanted to be supportive, to say something encouraging, but I couldn't forget Pip's death. Every time I closed my eyes or let my mind wander, her moment of death, linked to my failure to think ahead and act, flashed back to me. As a result, I couldn't sleep or think clearly. I'd heard of people getting PTSD from traumatic accidents, but that seemed too dramatic to result from the death of a dog. With all the pain and suffering in the world, how could I be so selfishly affected by the death of a dog? It didn't seem right. If I had true faith in God, then I should be able to fall back on that and pray my way out of these obsessive thoughts and images. Right?

I should have seen the counselor again, but it didn't seem "All-American" to be so weak, so I threw myself into my work instead. Between my house renovations—that always had to move forward to pay for themselves—my Senate seat and political obligations, and my law practice, I had a lot of responsibilities, a lot of demands on my time and resources. If it hadn't been for Annie and Andrew taking care of the furniture company, I don't know how I could have managed. I had a lot of money but also a lot of expenses and bills to pay.

On my first day back at Tavern Craft after Pip's death, I sat at my desk and rang for Annie and Andrew. Within seconds, I heard Annie's familiar knock and invited her in. She stood until I asked her to sit.

There was something about her that had a calming effect. I think part of it was how her appearance never seemed to change. As she sat in the chair in front of me, pad and pen in hand, she looked like Aunt Bea with rhinestone glasses, large diamond rings—genuine diamonds, none of them fake—and a pendant. Predictably punctual as well as dependable, I could always count on her. Organized, with a head for numbers, she was wise and, at the same time, ageless.

"This, too, will pass," she assured me. Then she talked about Buffet, her Lab mix who, when he was old and sick, left home one day and never returned. "I looked for him for weeks. I said I'd never give up. Finally, I did. I'm not married," she reminded me. "He was everything to me. Be thankful for Celia and your family. All I had left was loneliness and grief, but we move on. We recover. It just takes time."

Andrew arrived at the door as usual at his own pace, making me wonder how he ever got to work on time. Without asking, he sat down in the chair beside Annie and broke into a monologue: "We have too many orders promised to too many customers in too short of a turn-around time. With so much business, we ought to be hiring, but we're not even advertising for workers, and the workers we need on the floor have to be trained. It's a long process."

His tone and assertiveness made me think he was pointing a finger—at Annie or me, or both of us.

"Don't get me wrong," he then said. "I'm grateful for all the business, especially in this economy. We're blessed because we have a niche. But our workers require specialized skills. We can't survive in today's market like Hickory furniture did in the past, when we made everything here and everybody here made good money. You know how competitive it is now." He added, "It's the global reality."

I could hardly believe he was telling us that. It was like he was lecturing us. I looked at Annie.

"If you'll excuse me," she said. "I'll be back in a minute."

She returned with a stack of ledgers and files. Pulling out the shelf in front of my desk, she began to explain why the company was doing what it was, why it was on the proper schedule, and why Tavern Craft would be profitable by the end of the fiscal year. She concluded, "By year's end, we are on track to have our best year yet." She handed each of us a spreadsheet, as well as a timeline for decision-making, and briefly explained how Tavern Craft would get to its year-end goal.

Andrew, who was a superb supervisor but who spent as little time in an office as he could get away with, studied the handouts in silence. Finally, he said, "You're the controller, Annie. You know the business end from top to bottom." Annie looked at me but said nothing.

Andrew said, "I guess I'm just a little frustrated. It's my nature." He smiled sheepishly. "I should have taken more advantage of N.C. State when I was there. All I wanted to do was graduate and go to work. I should have been a better student."

Annie smiled. "You're a wonderful student. And the hardest worker at Tavern Craft. You guarantee our quality, and you deliver. That's why we're headed for the best year in our history. We will hire more people, but we have to grow carefully and not expand too quickly. Controlled, sustained growth is what we want, not debt that will put us at risk."

I said, "And all around us, furniture factories are closing. It's sad, but that's the reality. We may not be able to do much about globalization, but as one furniture company, we can fight to keep jobs here at home—and we can innovate—and that's what we're doing."

"And we're succeeding," said Annie. "It's important not to lose sight of that."

We talked a while longer, and before we adjourned, all three of us were sitting back in our chairs, pleased that we were once again in agreement.

In the first couple of weeks after Pip's death, I wasn't comfortable driving. Everywhere I drove, I saw cars around me as veering too close and going too fast, even being life-threatening. Stepping off the curb to cross the street also made me anxious. I had always assumed that cars were looking out for pedestrians and would stop if need be—now I wondered if it was more likely that I would be hit. I thought of the emotional turmoil Jennie endured after she lost her baby and was hit. I couldn't help but compare myself and then condemn myself, for being so negatively impacted by the death of "just a dog."

Then there was that old woman on the island, recurring like a bad penny. She'd said, "You will lose a dear friend and suffer deeply because of it." I knew there wasn't a connection there, but what was wrong with me? My confidence had taken a blow.

Now I didn't enjoy sitting on our patio at night, either. With whom would I sit? Celia was a pianist, not a sitter. Why would I want to sit out there by myself? When Pip and I finished playing or walking, she'd always lain at my feet in quiet fidelity and love. Now she was ashes in a box in a drawer on the sun porch.

And how could I walk at night, alone? What was the point? Where was the company? The night Pip died, when I heard

Celia crying to herself as she lay in bed, this is what she asked me when I first went in, "When you're gone to Raleigh, who will protect me?"

I knew she was thinking about the time Pip had protected Tracy and the kids. One night, around 3 a.m., when Celia and I were in Europe and Tracy was child- and house-sitting, our laid-back pet turned into a crazed beast. Fiercely barking, teeth bared, hair raised on her back, she ran up and down the stairs from Tracy's bed to the downstairs patio doors. Turning on the light, Tracy got out of bed and put on a robe. When Pip grew even wilder and scarier, Tracy called the police.

Our gentle golden, now a primordial attack animal, was so fiercely protective Tracy dared follow her down the stairs, accompanied by Bert. At the doors to the patio, Pip repeatedly attacked the glass panes, not breaking them, while brandishing her large teeth ferociously. The would-have-been home invader on the other side ran away in fear for his life.

By the time the police arrived, some fifteen minutes later, Pip had transformed again into her old self, wagging her tail as the officers petted her as they inspected the crowbar abandoned in flight as well as the damaged wood between the two French doors. As soon as possible, I had a security system installed, but alarms are not the same as a dog. With a dog, you get used to the companionship.

Days—or was it weeks?—after Pip's fatal accident, Celia looked at me with her lovely brown eyes and said, "It's like Pip was one of our children. We're supposed to protect them." She didn't mean it to hurt; she was grieving.

. . .

On occasion, it crossed my mind to wonder if my dog's death had been "the murder" foretold. And on those occasions, I hoped it was: just in case the old woman's predictions were going to come true, at least this—as awful as it was—had finally happened, and it was not a human being. Honestly, I would have cared a lot less if it *had* been a human like Dr. Salafar: it seemed to me that he was basically a drug pusher. Or at least an irresponsible, dangerous prescriber. And he'd almost killed Jennie . . . No, I didn't share these thoughts with anyone. But I admit I had them, bad as they were.

On the other hand, if this was not "*the* murder," then what awful fate might still lie before us—Celia, Croom, Jennie and me? And where was God in all this? Where did *He* fit in? Who was in control?

I saw the darkness plainly enough, but where was the gold in it?

The old dream came back. For years after our stormy trip to the Isle of Cats, I'd had a recurring dream: I failed a challenge under pressure, then the partially eaten face of a corpse loomed up before me, and I gasped for breath to awaken. Over the years, that dream had crept away. Now, to my dismay, it had returned. And the old dream about Stately Oaks came back, too. Something bad was going to happen there. Three months after Pip died, it did. My mother heard a crashing sound in my father's study. He had toppled out of his chair and was dead on the floor from a heart attack. No prior warning signs at all, so none of us got to tell him goodbye. Gone—just like that. It was Celia's mother's death all over again—except for me, much worse.

"He lived so long and seemed so indestructible," I said to Celia, "I think I expected him to live forever." His death seemed so unbelievable that I kept imagining he'd come back. Our whole family was in shock.

Nevertheless, we rose to the occasion of a formal receiving of guests at Stately Oaks, nearly a thousand people who lined up down the front driveway waiting to be greeted by my mother and our family in the living room. The next day, we rose again to the occasion of a funeral in our family church, the pews so packed with guests that chairs had to be placed in the side aisles. As I sat on the front row between Celia and my mother, my saving grace was the stained-glass window over the altar given in memory of my father's great-grandfather, one of the two original elders of the church when it was founded in 1869: I stared, praying, at the massive artwork of Jesus, "Standing at the Door and Knocking," grounding myself in an otherwise surreal setting, as I prepared to make the long walk to the lectern to deliver one of the eulogies.

That was November 2005.

In 2006, I was supposed to run for Congress, but things didn't work out well. Our string of bad luck, especially my father's death, had taken the wind out of my sails, and my Congressional campaign failed to get off the ground. I talked to Croom quite a bit during this time, and he said, "Follow your heart, Matt. That's what you're good at; you're at your best when you do that. What does your heart say?"

"My heart's not in it," I told my friend. "It feels kind of buried."

While Celia and I were dealing with Washington,

Raleigh, and political matters—not to mention her struggling concert career—my mother, now a widow, became increasingly disenchanted with Stately Oaks. With my father gone, it wasn't the same for her: Stately Oaks had been their home—and the home of their four children before that. Now she was living in "the Goodheart Mansion" alone, and things were different: the house and grounds, a seven-acre tract, were a lot to keep up—and *her* heart wasn't in it. I did what I could do to comfort her, but I found myself stretched to the limit.

As for the homeplace, she sold it to a couple from Florida and moved to a retirement village. The day the movers came to move everything out, she and I stood at a front upstairs window and watched the men below packing up the vans. I felt sick as if I were mourning in secret yet another death. What would my father have thought? I kept thinking about him, too, across the street in Oakwood Cemetery.

It was hard to think about him and how quickly things had changed: how people from out of state, from Florida, a childless couple nobody knew, were moving in and taking over.

The decision to sell lifted a burden from my mother's shoulders, but things didn't go well for the iconic landmark that had been our childhood home. By mid-year 2006, the first signs of the Great Recession were upon us, especially in Florida, and the new owner lost his job with the corporation that had brought him to Hickory. Having nothing to make the payments, he let the house go into foreclosure.

With no demand for such a large house in downtown Hickory, it sat empty for months, the grass and weeds growing up around it, making it quite a sight, the talk of the town. Eventually, the City had to order the bank to mow the grass because it had grown so high it had gone to seed.

A shutter tilted here, an awning torn there, a rotting eave, a fallen downspout—the driveway, which my father had kept meticulously manicured, growing crabgrass—and, worst of all, the fountains dysfunctional. What had been a monument to my father's success was now a monument to abandonment.

One night Elisa said to me, "Daddy, Stately Oaks looks haunted. You'd never think you and Grandmom and Granddad—and BeBe and Stuart and Kristen—used to live there."

"It's not haunted," I said. "It's just sad. It misses its family. Maybe sadness haunts it."

I felt a kinship to the house despite the strangers from Florida who were its last tenants, and since the house looked like it was headed to ruin, I stepped in and bought it out of foreclosure. For my father. It might have been a foolhardy thing to do, but I did it anyway. That's why I did it—that's who I bought it for: my father.

By February 2007, when I closed on Stately Oaks, Celia and I owned two houses in Hickory within six blocks of each other, a house in the mountains, one at the beach, and a condominium in Raleigh. That was a lot of houses—and a lot of upkeep—for two empty-nesters. However, in November, we learned we wouldn't be empty-nesters much longer. Teddy, our youngest, a college senior, called home with some news.

Two years earlier, when Pip was killed by the railroad tracks, I ran off track—and no matter how hard I tried, I couldn't seem to get back on. It had been two years of nothing but bad luck. I felt like I was in a tailspin, with the ground getting closer and closer. I wasn't sure what else could go wrong in my life, but I was beginning to believe whatever it was, was waiting to happen. My mother's old friend, Mrs. Tatum, said to Celia the day before Pip was killed, "Whatever Matt Goodheart touches turns to gold." Now, it seemed, whatever Matt Goodheart touched, turned to muck.

On November 15, 2007, Teddy called me and told me he'd been expelled from school. He chose not to tell me why on the phone, but considering how seldom students were expelled these days, I could only imagine the worst.

27.
THE CHRISTMAS COTILLION

On Saturday, December 8, Celia and I and our houseguests, Croom and Jennie—in Hickory with Wes visiting their parents for Christmas—had just returned to Stately Oaks after the Christmas Cotillion at the country club. It was a special Cotillion, the fiftieth anniversary since its inception in 1957—my parents, Croom's parents and Jennie's parents had all been founding couples—and tonight, the men were wearing tails and top hats, not just tuxes. At the receiving line for the secretly selected new members, we men tipped our hats to the initiates as we and our wives walked down the line and shook hands. Then we left our top hats at the coat-check room before we moved to the ballroom. As for the ladies, the code was clear: full-length gowns bought new each year.

Before the receiving of new members, we had drinks and hors d'oeuvres on an enclosed terrace. In this first half-hour of the evening, Andrew Templeton, my head supervisor at Tavern

Craft whom I'd invited in October to come into the business with me as a partner, sidled over as I talked to the Mayor and whispered that he had some news to share with me. I apologized to Mayor Bryant and turned to Andrew, as the Mayor, helping himself to a shrimp bacon-wrap from a tray interposed to us, took up conversation with the president of Hickory Trust.

Andrew, who'd insisted I hire an auditor to audit the books because he couldn't understand where the company's money was going, nudged me to a far corner of the terrace.

"How much did she steal from us?" I asked. "How much, Andrew? How much has she stolen from us?"

His head down, he whispered the amount. "Over a twelve-year period."

I covered my eyes. "Where does that leave us?"

"Probably bankrupt. We owe a lot of money."

At first, I couldn't believe it, but after his eyes made me believe it, I thought I was going to pass out, I was so light-headed and chilled. We sat and talked a while longer. I said, "All our employees will lose their jobs. What about their families?" In a daze, I walked over to Celia and stood beside her as she talked to Croom, Jennie, and Amelia Gates, an old friend.

For the remainder of the half-hour of drinks on the terrace, I hardly said a word. Then, at seven-thirty, the headwaiter rang a bell, and we moved to the lobby where the men checked in their formal hats, and everyone processed to the ballroom.

Everybody in Hickory was there. The four of us made the rounds; we must have talked to everyone, visiting table after table: Croom and I, the lifelong friends, with our wives—one, a Nightingale and a concert pianist; one, the famous Jennie

Boston—*the* Jeni B, Hickory's most famous person *ever*. Because it was a special Cotillion, a photographer worked the room like the cameraman on a cruise ship, taking pictures at the tables as everyone dined, toasted, chatted, and smiled—taking pictures as everyone, dancing and smiling, circled the dance floor. Every time the photographer snapped, we smiled real big.

After the evening had gone on for hours, with me smiling and trying to carry on bright conversation as my head swirled with one vision of doom after another, one dark thought after another, I eventually recalled the words, "You will be betrayed by someone you deeply trust. And you will lose." So Annie Jameson was that betrayer. In my kaleidoscope of dark thoughts, it was one more piece of broken glass, part of the puzzle.

When I could no longer stand it, I leaned over to Celia sitting beside me at the table we shared with Croom and Jennie and two other couples, both now on the dance floor. "We can't stay any longer," I whispered. "I can't stay any longer—I'm not feeling well. There's been some bad news. I can't tell you about it here—I'll tell you when we get home." I stood up.

From across the table, Jennie looked at me. "What's wrong, Matt?"

I looked away, averting her eyes. "Not feeling too well."

Croom looked at his wife, then at me, then at Celia. "What is it, good buddy?"

I pulled out Celia's chair, and she stood up. Then, exchanging glances, Croom and Jennie did, too. It was eleven o'clock anyway, so we drove back to Stately Oaks, the four of us hardly speaking as I drove.

Now, as I stood in front of the mirror in the upstairs

bedroom that had been mine as a youngster, but which Celia and I now used as our own when staying at Stately Oaks while the master bedroom downstairs was being redone, I felt sick to my stomach. My bow tie was choking me, and the cummerbund was squeezing the life out of me.

Having told me she'd be upstairs shortly, Celia was in the kitchen talking to Croom and Jennie. When I heard a knock on the door, I thought it might be Teddy. I walked over and opened it a small way. Croom looked concerned. "You okay?"

"I'm not good, but I can't talk about it right now, Croom," I said. "There's a lot going on, but we can talk later. I'll see you tomorrow."

I closed the door. After a night of saving face, I suddenly felt like I was really on the brink, having some major-league difficulty keeping a lid on.

Andrew and I had discussed options briefly. "You'll have to try to find a bank that will extend you more credit." He paused. "But Tavern Craft is deeply in debt. It's making money, despite the economy, but Annie's been embezzling from that income."

I thought about all the money I'd borrowed this year to purchase and refurbish Stately Oaks, on top of the money I'd borrowed for the other houses I was renovating.

"When everyone else was out-sourcing jobs," I said, "we stayed local. How could she stab all of us—me, the employees—in the back? Can we sue her?"

He shook his head. "Prosecute her criminally, but not sue her. I had her followed, and I found out today that she has a secret life: she's a compulsive gambler." He said, "Even if she still has any of the money she's stolen, which is doubtful, what about the day-to-day operations going forward? She's been running the place like a Ponzi scheme and keeping two sets of books. I was bringing the auditors in late at night—she has no idea we know what's going on. We've got bills stacked on bills that have to be paid. We're broke. We're worse than broke, wallowing in the red."

I looked at myself, a ghost in the mirror. If I didn't do something drastic to prevent it, I would blow apart.

The house was a wreck, anyway. By day, it was full of painters and wallpaperers on the inside and carpenters on the outside. We were having the floors redone, and dust was everywhere, despite all efforts to prevent it. Still, we'd wanted to stay here with Croom and Jennie. We thought it would be special, a celebration of sorts, saving Stately Oaks.

I looked out the front windows. It had started snowing, and I watched it fall in the yard and beyond, out in the street. The driveway, a winding horseshoe that moved from the street at the bottom of the hill upward in a great slope to the front porch, was transforming itself from black to white. The trees were collecting snow, too, and if the temperature continued to drop, they would soon be crystal fairy-tale configurations. The light from the period streetlamps illumined the snow as it fell, swirling around them to the ground.

At one time, I loved all of this. I guess, in all honesty, I rather worshipped it. Now, I wished I'd worshipped something else. Yeah, that's right. If I'd really been on a lifelong quest to find God and the true meaning of life, I seemed to have missed the boat.

I closed the shutters, then glanced at my tall hat and tailcoat I'd tossed on the bed. I took off the bow tie, the shirt, my dad's studs Mother had found for me in a box in his bureau when she was readying to sell the house. I put on a bathrobe, then took it off and put on jeans and a flannel shirt—and my jogging shoes.

As soon as Celia entered the room, I could read the concern on her face, though she was trying to lighten it by smiling. "I've been talking to Teddy," she said. She liked having him at home, in a resigned sort of way. "Croom and Jennie turned in; Teddy asked if we'd had fun at the Cotillion. I said yes, except that you weren't feeling well." I felt my face giving me away.

"Okay, Matt, what's wrong? What happened?"

I told her what Andrew had reported. I looked at her in her svelte black gown and her elegant diamond necklace and her hair specially coiffed for the evening and saw her expression change from concerned to tired, then to scared. I sat down in a chair in front of a window and put my head in my hands. Celia walked into the bathroom, and I heard the door shut behind her.

Well, this was it. My father was dead. I had killed my dog. My dreams of Congress—dead. The children were gone—except for the one who'd been expelled from college. Now I was going to lose everything I'd spent my entire life working for. Even my house. Everything I touched had poisoned everyone around me and blighted my life.

When I was twenty-two, my future wife, our two best friends, and I had had our fortunes told by an old woman who predicted the future in a strangely vengeful way. I didn't think any of us really believed there was a curse on us, but it seemed to me now that Miss Smiley's foresight had somehow gotten it right. How? Why? Regardless of the why and wherefore, it seemed that God had abandoned me.

When I was forty-five, a friend of mine, ten years my elder, said to me, "They say fifty-five is the advent of old age." I didn't believe him. Now fifty-six, I full well believed him.

There was a knock on the door. I got up and opened it.

"Good night, Dad," Teddy said. In his face, I saw an expressiveness I'd had when I was young. "I hope you feel better. Tell Mom I said good night."

I told him I would, but I felt numb as he extended his hand and I shook it, then drew him close and hugged him. In a flash, I was glad the other children had left home.

I walked down the hall. I wanted to go downstairs, just to be going someplace, any place except staying still. I couldn't stand the thought of talking with anyone—not right now. I couldn't even decide whether to use the back stairs to get to the kitchen or the front stairs. I was fairly positive I wanted to go to the kitchen, though.

I walked down the front stairs. They curved around as they descended, and as I passed by the wallpaper, with its embossed design of pheasants and flowers, I brushed some dust off the embossing. The stairwell wall was covered with portraits and photographs, sixty-five of them, covering six generations, and I was irritated that some of them were hanging crookedly. I wondered if there would ever be grandchildren—a seventh generation of photos and paintings—and if so, whether I would be alive to see them.

I'd asked Roberta, the housekeeper, to straighten the pictures and dust the frames, but here they were, crooked and dusty. Dust lay on the baseboard molding and the hardwood steps at either side of the carpet.

I was especially bothered by the fact that three large frames were crooked. One was of a great-great grandfather, Coatsworth Wilson, who had been a minister and farmer, serving in the North Carolina Legislature in the 1890s, followed by his son-in-law, John Edney Hoover. Another frame contained a 1770 parchment land deed signed by my ancestor John Alran, a Charleston plantation owner. The last of the three was a photograph of my grandfather Beauregard, in a bow tie for his senior class picture, Trinity College (Duke), 1916, who'd earlier lost his inheritance in a crooked poker game. A gambler, like Annie Jameson. Who got expelled, like Teddy.

Screwing things up seemed to run in my family, a genetic predisposition. So I'd come by it honestly, despite my Eagle Scout award and my longevity in the State Senate. I needed to put my portrait on this wall—I would make it the largest of any of them as a tribute to the biggest screw-up of all—except that I wouldn't be owning this wall much longer.

All the pictures would have to come down, for the second time in two years. Who would care enough to dust them then? I straightened the pictures as perfectly as I could. The public humiliation would be complete shortly after the new year. Hickory and Catawba County, not to mention the Senate district, would have a field day talking about it, as would the Senate itself. I could forget about being re-elected. I turned and blew the dust off the frames. But then it occurred to me, why should I care?

I walked through the dark foyer. I didn't want light because I knew the chandelier had dust all over it with webs hanging from it, too. I walked through the dining room but didn't turn on the light for the same reason. Besides, I didn't want light because the light was good, and the darkness seemed more appropriate. I walked through the breakfast room and into the kitchen. But this was not the kitchen I wanted to be in.

I wanted to be in the *downstairs* kitchen. So I walked down the back stairs to the basement. The downstairs kitchen was halfway down a long hall that led to the recreation room with its billiards table and shuffleboard court—the room where Celia's nine-foot Steinway used to be—and the elevator with its sliding metal door of collapsible triangles resembling an ornate cage. On the opposite end of the hall was the garage. The garage held my sacred car: the 1955 emerald-green Jaguar XK 140 convertible I'd had since I was sixteen. That would have to go, too.

In the downstairs kitchen, I did turn on the overhead light, but what I was looking for at the back of this cabinet was not a midnight snack, cookies or popcorn. I knew right where to find it, however, wrapped in a paper bag.

Bag in hand, I turned and walked out of the room, switching off the light, and retraced my steps along the hall, past the garage, past the room my father had used as a downstairs office, back up the basement steps, back down the first floor hall, through the rooms, up the foyer stairs to Teddy's room, where I saw him as my eight-year-old, sleeping, and where I kissed him good night and tucked the covers around his peaceful little face framed in Celia's brown curls. Only he was twenty-two—and returned to live at home.

I walked down the upstairs hall, past the door that had been BeBe's room, past Stuart's room, then Kristen's. I continued past the guest room where Croom and Jennie were staying. Then I walked to the guest room that was hardly ever used, opened the door and walked inside. Without turning on the light, I laid the paper bag on the chest of drawers. I stood there in the dark. Walking back into the hallway, I went into the room Celia and I were using.

Celia was lying on the bed, reading, her eyes red and puffy. She looked up when I entered.

"I don't know what to think, Matt, and I don't know how to think. Obviously, we have to talk about all this, but I'm not in any condition for that right now—it's just too late at night. It's all I can do to read."

"We've got to talk about it sometime, Celia."

"I can't tonight, I'm sorry. I have to try to get some sleep if I can. So I can think. There's so much to think about, I can't begin to process it now. Let's sit down tomorrow and talk."

"I can't sleep," I said, standing at the foot of the bed. "And I can't think, either. I've got to get away. I have to get out of here."

Now she stared at me.

"I'm going to the beach. To the house."

She sat up, her eyes widened. "That's six—seven—hours away. When are you thinking about going? . . . For how long?"

"Now," I said. "Tonight. It doesn't matter how far it is. I couldn't sleep if I had to. I've got to get away for a few days. I can't think here. There's too much going on. Too many distractions."

I opened the doors to my closet and pulled my duffle bag off the shelf. I put some clothes in it while she continued to look at me without speaking.

Finally, she said, "Will you call me when you get there?" She paused. "Or before?" In her voice, there seemed to be little more than exhaustion, and when I turned around, nothing in her eyes.

"Yes—I'll call."

I kissed her forehead on the way out of the room, feeling guilty on top of everything else. Still, the abyss that loomed beyond the edge of all this here was more threatening than the guilt was enervating. It was me—or them. I had to get out.

I walked back to the guest room that was rarely used and put the paper sack in my duffle bag with my clothes. Then I walked down to the garage and got into my Ford Escape for the six-hour drive across the state to Bogue Banks.

I had no thought of return.

PART FOUR

THE PHANTOM

✠

28.

THE PHANTOM IN THE GLASS

After about an hour or so, around one o'clock in the morning, having already passed several large, official highway signs indicating Nightingale this and Nightingale that, I pulled off the interstate in Winston-Salem at a truck stop. Men dressed in blue jeans and plaid shirts were sitting at the counter smoking cigarettes and drinking coffee. Kept hot in glass carafes on burners, the coffee, not fresh, had a sheen on its surface and a dark, acrid smell.

I sat down at the counter and asked the waitress, maybe five years younger than me, for a cup. "Here you go, honey," she said, smiling as she poured it.

On the wall behind the counter were three TV screens, one with the news, one with a sitcom, the one straight in front of me tuned to a channel featuring a classical violinist. According to the streamer at the bottom of the screen, he was performing Mozart, Mendelssohn, Liszt, and Dvorak. Celia, I thought absent-mindedly, also performed all of those composers.

Except for the ruffled white shirt, the violinist was dressed in black, head to toe, including large black frame glasses; and his long, straggly hair was black, too, parted in the middle. Russian, his name was Volkov. He played well, but mostly he made me think of Rasputin, and that made me think of Annie, my *own* monk behind the throne.

I finished the coffee, then asked for a large cup to go. "Here, hon," the waitress said as she handed it to me along with the ticket. "I gave you an extra-large cup. No charge for the take-out. Drive safe, honey."

I thanked her, left a tip, and paid at the register. A lot of strong coffee, but whatever it took to stay awake—after all, I'd barely gotten started on my overnight trip. I bought gasoline and continued to drive. Halfway to Raleigh, I turned the radio on to an ordinary news day in post-modern America. "Time to recap some of the nation's biggest news stories." Turning off the radio, I drove on in silence, the heater on and the cold night air rushing in, in a swoosh, through a crack at the top of the passenger-side window. It was not snowing, but it felt like it should be. Once I got east of Raleigh, the landscape became flat and mostly empty—rural eastern North Carolina—sparsely-situated houses connected by telephone lines and fallow tobacco fields.

Near Farmville, I realized I'd taken the wrong highway in Raleigh, adding an extra hour or more to the drive. I stopped for directions at an all-night convenience store. Waiting in the check-out line, I observed the cashier and the customer in front of me. The cashier had been listening to the same radio station I had turned off. As he made change, he commented on the news broadcast with the customer. "We definitely live in a world with a lot of screwed up people in it," he said. The man agreed, grunting once and nodding. Then he walked out with a loaf of bread, a bottle of orange juice, and some headache powders.

I moved up to the counter. Overweight, with a shirt that pulled on its button at his bulging belly, the cashier was wearing a brown leather jacket because it was so cold, even inside. His hair needed washing, and he was chewing tobacco.

"Some people just ain' no good," he observed. "Just bad people. Steal you blind. Knife you in the back when yer not looking. Just bad people. How else could they do the things they do to other people?"

"It's way beyond my comprehension," I said. Then I asked for directions.

"You go right down that road ove' yonder," he said, pointing out the window into the dark at the nearly deserted highway I'd just pulled off of. "Take the signs to Greenville, look for Kinston, and the signs to 70. You're supposed to be on 70, not 264."

He drew me a map. I'd missed Goldsboro completely. I thanked him, then followed the map to Kinston, turning onto 70.

About an hour and a half later, it was still not dawn as I crossed the causeway onto the island. I unlocked the front door and walked in, the house smelling faintly musty. Turning on the hall light and the heat, I deadbolted the door behind me. Walking down the hall into the great room, I sat down on a sofa facing the sea and dropped the duffle bag at my feet.

The front half of the room was round, surrounded in glass so that, during the day, the outside seemed inside, and when the sliding doors were open, you could hear the ocean. Now all the glass, naked of blinds, was mirrored. Reflected in each pane, I got up and opened a glass door, bringing the sound of the surf inside the room. With the remote, I turned on a large fan suspended from the vaulted ceiling. I felt like I was inside a boat, gently rocking on the ocean.

I'd been here before in December—with Pip—when a nor'easter had blown in. The wind and rain were so extreme that when I opened the sliding doors to the balcony only a few inches, everything that wasn't heavy or secured flew about the room. The wind and rain had been so strong I couldn't sleep because the sound of the rioting heavens, rather than being soothing or comforting, or even fascinating in its intensity, was simply brash, unpredictable noise, and I couldn't drop off.

The next morning, Pip and I went out to the ocean to walk and explore, discovering a beach drastically rearranged. Dunes that had been were no longer there. Large castaway hunks of wood and metal, possibly buried for decades, now lay exposed. The beach that had sloped in a gentle incline from the dunes to the water's edge was now a six-foot cliff, and a small inlet had been created. Debris, including wreckage from boats, littered the sand.

I sat on the sofa, observing my phantom self in the glass surrounding me. I dropped my arm down beside me, hoping to feel Pip's warm coat at my feet, knowing she would still love me, regardless of how I castigated myself. But only the inert duffle bag met my hand.

I rummaged around in the clothes, searching for the paper sack, the one I'd brought from home. When I found it, I held it in my hand for a while, inside the duffle bag, while I thought about things. The sea. The islands. That old woman's predictions. Murder. Then I took it from the bag and set it on my lap.

I sat there, a while longer, thinking about other things. God. Where was He, anyway?

Finally, I walked into the kitchen, sack in hand, and set it on the counter.

Pulling a glass from the cabinet and filling it half-full with ice cubes, I poured myself a Scotch on the Rocks. Then, the Chivas in one hand, glass in the other, I returned to the sofa and drank until I fell asleep.

29.

LIGHT—NO LIGHT

When I woke up the next morning around ten-thirty, my head was splitting. I could barely sit up on the sofa. What I saw in the bathroom mirror was a wan face and two puffy eyes, which I averted, feeling sick. Shuffling to the kitchen, I put the kettle on the stove for coffee, then turned up the thermostat in the hall. After putting away the Chivas and washing the glass, I changed clothes and put on a jacket. As I zipped it up, the kettle began to whistle.

Steaming cup in hand, I opened the sliding-glass door to the balcony and beheld a flawlessly clear blue sky and a panoramic view of the beach all the way from Beaufort Inlet on the far northeastern end of the island to the pier on the other side of the house, and on down the beach to the southwest. To anyone else, the day would have been beautiful. With the wooden railing to set my coffee on, I watched the steam rise into the morning air and caught its rich smell. Though it was the second week of

December, all I needed for warmth was the jacket. Out beyond the grassy dunes was the bare sand, and beyond the sand, the surf. The air was calm—no whitecaps on the water in any direction—the ocean scintillating with a surface of sequins.

At the Sound-side of the island, boats and yachts packed the marina, their white masts standing up against the blue sky. Beyond the white boats was the mainland shore covered with white, lemon, aqua, and terra cotta houses. Before me was blue sky endlessly high, resting on the horizon above the ocean.

To my right, the pier—an old-fashioned, wooden fishing pier, crooked and uneven in silhouette against the sky and water—stretched from the beach into the ocean, antiquated lampposts sticking up on its railing every few yards from shore to the far end. Few people were fishing on it now, though.

In season, it was covered with fishermen of all ages, shapes, and sizes. I had taken my children there to fish, all four of them at different times. Bert and Teddy entertained themselves for hours, though as a little blonde of only five, Caroline was scared of the boardwalk because it shook when the wind blew, and once, when bare-footed, she picked up a splinter from the weather-beaten planks. "Daddy," she said, "save my feet! Carry me!" I thought about how I carried her back along the pier, hoisting her onto my shoulders, her squealing with delight as she clung onto my forehead. I imagined her little hand in mine once we were off the pier and into the sand as I walked with her beside me, shortening my strides by half.

But mostly, now, I thought of Teddy. As a little boy, he loved to fish from that pier. The family stories we told about "Beergard" were funny, but nothing was funny about Teddy's expulsion from

Duke.

When he called me to break the news, I said, "Teddy, you were smart enough to get into the same school your father and great-grandfather went to. You know how proud that made me. Now this. Why?"

I leaned against the railing of the balcony and sipped my coffee. "It was out in the quad," he said. "In front of a lot of people, at night. It was a keg party, and things got out of hand. There was this guy, a kid from Winston-Salem in a different fraternity. He was really drunk and obnoxious, shooting off his mouth. When he found out who I was, he started razzing me about politics. He said he knew all about you and that you would never have been considered in a million years for Congress, not even for five minutes if it hadn't been for your money. He said you'd been born with a silver spoon and were a pampered prince and had never done anything in your life but inherit money. I told him that was a damn political lie and to shut the hell up. He said, 'So who's going to make me? You, Goodheart?' This was in front of a lot of people, including a bunch of my fraternity brothers and their dates, and he kept it up.

"Then he started in on Mom's family. He said everybody who knows anything about politics in North Carolina knows the Nightingales are the main reason you're a big shot in the Senate and why you keep getting re-elected. He said you wanting to be in Congress was a joke. I told him if he didn't shut up, I'd knock his teeth in.

"Then he said, 'I'd like to see you try. Even marrying a Nightingale couldn't make your father a success.' That's when I hit him, Dad. I'd had a couple of beers, but I wasn't drunk. I just didn't care about what could happen. He had *no right* to talk like that—no right at all, about you, or Mom or our family. I didn't knock him unconscious or anything; I just knocked him to the ground—and he's bigger than I am and a year ahead. Flat on his back. A perfect punch, and he deserved it and more! He should be thankful I stopped, then. I really *could* have knocked his teeth out! The guys started clapping and cheering—they loved it! But that's not why I did it—it wasn't for them.

"I'm sorry I got expelled, but he deserved it. What he said was lies, and, Dad, I'd do the same thing again, except for the drinking. I did it because some things are worth fighting for. You're the one who taught me that."

I thought about my life—now—and closed my eyes. How far would I go to fight for my company and my name? I couldn't really fault Ted for standing up for his family, but the result seemed like another failure to add to my list. Maybe it said more about me than it said about him.

I watched the seagulls sailing gracefully, swooping close enough to me to get my attention. I went inside, got some bread, and threw pieces to them.

To my left, a forty-five-minute walk down the beach was Fort Macon, a fortress the Yankees recaptured from the Confederacy and used as a prison for Confederate officers, my kinfolk. At the fort was a jetty running half the length of a football field out into the ocean from the beach. These boulders, protecting Beaufort Inlet into the port of Morehead City, were The Rocks I often visited.

I puttered around until lunch then made myself a sandwich. My head was clearing. Later I walked down to the beach where a breeze had blown in. Those who were out spoke to me in the brisk way the people on this beach do in winter. I visited the pier, no one on it but me, and stood against the railing, looking out into the ocean. The wind had picked up; whitecaps crowned the water. I could feel the air, humid and smelling of salt, ruddying my face. Standing there, I thought again about Celia, my children, my father—my life. At this point, how could I salvage it?

I thought about Annie Jameson. I thought I knew her. But no, she'd betrayed us, a compulsive gambler. Andrew was still trying to discover how long she'd had this secret life. She'd gambled and lost with my money and Celia's. Worse than that, with my children's money, their inheritance. Even if she'd been able to steal from *me*, her employer who trusted her, how could she have stolen money from my children, children she claimed to love? And what about the lives of so many fellow employees? Again, I thought about my life as it was and closed my eyes.

I felt I must go down to The Rocks; I felt drawn to them. On the beach, I killed some more time, looking at shells, waving to the few people strolling by. No one would be down at The Rocks, I thought: no one walks that far this time of year and The Rocks are not safe, anyway—hazardous to climb, slick with algae and saltwater, particularly when the wind is up and the waves are high, lapping at their sides, sometimes splashing over them.

I began to walk next to the tide, whitecaps now dicing up the sea, high waves crashing near me in the surf. I passed a few other people. When I got as far as Fort Macon, the beach was deserted.

I knew The Rocks, now in sight, straight ahead, would be slippery, especially those farther out into the ocean.

Even though it was daytime, if I looked carefully off into the distance, I could see the flash of light from the lighthouse on the neighboring island of Cape Lookout. That made me think, once again, of the house and its light on the Isle of Cats. "You will be betrayed by someone you deeply trust," she said. "And you will gamble and lose," she had also said. "And you will see murder."

As I stared, the light flashed again in the sky, then disappeared for fifteen seconds, then reappeared in a twinkle. That occurred several more times: Light, no light. Light, no light. Light...

I looked down the beach toward The Rocks, clearly in sight. I looked down the beach, the other way, toward the house. I looked at the light there on the island. Light, no light. Light... I looked again at The Rocks. Then at the light.

The old woman had said I would "tragically lose a dear friend," and I would "suffer deeply" because of it. Pip, for sure. But also Annie? And that old woman also said, "You will search and search, yet not find." I felt like I'd been searching my whole life, and now was farther away than ever before from finding the treasure. After a lifetime of searching for it, here I stood, empty-handed. I looked again toward the lighthouse. Light, no light. Light, no light. Light. . . Looking to the sky, I prayed a prayer, a fervent prayer—for help—and crossed myself.

The old woman also said that after I searched and searched and did not find, "Then finally you will find, where you never expected." I hoped that was a positive promise, rather than a threat. I turned and headed back down the beach toward the house.

. . .

Up at the house, I put on gloves and a hooded sweater beneath my jacket, made a cup of coffee, and went out onto the balcony. Leaning against the railing, overlooking a rough sea, I pulled out my phone to text Celia, noticing she'd tried to call me. "Will call you tonight. I love you."

It was too late now to leave for Hoophole Island, even if I could still catch a ferry. Once there, I'd have to find a boat ride over to the Isle of Cats and another back again to Hoophole before dark. Impossible.

I went inside, got online, and looked up the departure schedule for the ferry and directions for getting there. Since it left at ten o'clock in the morning and the drive to the ferry itself from Bogue Banks took about an hour and forty-five minutes, I'd leave tomorrow around 7:45. To be safe, I called and made a reservation.

I packed my backpack: two changes of clothes, a flashlight, water, some apples and energy bars, bug spray, my Scout knife, and a gun. I set out my clothes for tomorrow: long johns, jeans, a heavy flannel shirt, gloves, ski mask. I'd also be wearing a hoodie and heavy, rainproof jacket with a hood.

I threw a sleeping bag into the SUV, then went to the closest ATM and drew out several hundred dollars. Just in case, I drew out the same amount again. Then a third time. The rest of the day I spent walking on the beach. In the last few hours, as the ocean had grown calmer, so had I. The blue sky was filled with layers of pink clouds. At 5:15, the sun set, and fifteen minutes later sank below the horizon.

I drove to a hamburger joint for something to eat, checked again to be sure I had everything I thought I needed for tomorrow, then called Celia. It was a short conversation that didn't go as well as I'd have liked. Mostly because about all we talked about was Cindy Peppercorn. Her mother wasn't well, Cindy was in town visiting her, and she'd dropped by the house.

"I didn't ask her inside," Celia said. "She stood on the porch and told me she had a message for you. She said, 'I had a dream that Matt is near something he needs to find. But he has to go look for it. Tell him I came as a friend, for old time's sake, and he needs to go find it. Tell him I said: GO.'"

I asked Celia what time Cindy had come by.

"Sometime around two," Celia said. "She told me she wouldn't blame us if we didn't trust her. Then she started down the stairs, turned back, and said, 'Celia, when I was a child, I had a dream that something bad was going to happen to my brother, so I needed to protect him, but I didn't, and he died. Tell Matt I told you that. He'll understand because he knows what I'm talking about.' Then she left."

I told Celia it was around two o'clock, out on the beach, that I'd made up my mind to go back to the Isle of Cats. The phone was silent. Then Celia said, "Matt, all of this is really distressing to me. The news about Annie. Your leaving. Then Cindy comes here like this. I'm feeling overwhelmed by everything—and alone. I don't want you to do anything but come home," she said. "I need you."

"I can't come home until I go back," I told her. "I have to, Celia. Then I can come home."

. . .

I sat on the sofa and thought about things. The wind had really picked up again, and I could hear the surf roaring. Out on the balcony, looking into the black sky that on a clear night twinkled with a thousand stars, I counted only six appearing through the clouds. No moon tonight, and the air was freezing.

I shuddered, then turned from the balcony and went inside, sliding the door closed and locking it. I stood for a moment, still looking out, but instead of observing the vastness of the universe, and all that that implied, what I saw tonight was but that dim reflection: my phantom self, staring in at me through the dark glass.

Even so, this time, there was also something else. Despite the deep wanting, despite all the darkness, something dwelling inside me—or calling to me from beyond—hinted with an offer of something different: a faint ray of light, a glimmer of hope.

It was that that I would cling to in my journey tomorrow.

30.

NOBODY GOES TO THAT ISLAND

The seagulls woke me the next morning around six. I ate a good breakfast and was on the road by 7:45. About an hour later, I passed the sign, "Hoophole Island Ferry, 43," and arrived at the ferry a half-hour early for the ten o'clock departure. It was overcast and far colder than I'd expected, hovering around 35 degrees.

The trip over to Hoophole took three-and-a-half hours, so I had time to think. I sat inside to keep warm and looked out the windows onto the sea. Unlike the massive upscale ferries that cross the Chesapeake Bay, cruise ships, by comparison, Outer Banks ferries were modest and practical, large enough for about fifty-five vehicles packed in headlight to taillight—no frills.

I needed time with Andrew Templeton, my auditors, my accountants and outside counsel to try to save Tavern Craft. But I really had no hope for doing so, as it would take quite a bit of money. Without adequate time to devote to my law practice,

I'd never make it lucrative. Our house renovations made money only when I sold a house, and then not much. Upfront, I had to finance the purchases and renovations. My legislative income was little more than what the position cost me in expenses. The only business that really made money was Tavern Craft. If it went bankrupt as Andrew assured me it would, then I owned nothing of value but our personal residences. I'd even borrowed money to buy Stately Oaks and more to make repairs and improvements. Quite a lot, in fact.

Celia and I each had a wealthy parent—her father, my mother—but neither of us had ever wanted to ask our parents for money and never had. Among other loyalties, we each had three siblings, their spouses, and children to consider.

I'd accepted the fact that I'd so mismanaged my life that I was ruined. I didn't want to hate Annie, but I did. I knew if I encouraged my friend, Thomas Steele, the D.A., to go for the max, he would, not only to make an example of her to the public but also to exact revenge on my behalf. Okay by me. Hate and anger are poisonous, and I knew they'd poison me and everyone around me. How could I help myself or Celia or anyone else if I couldn't control my vengeful desires?

I walked to the rear deck railing so that the wind was at my back, but even with my hood pulled tight, the cold, damp salty air stung my face. Maybe the sharp wind would numb the poisonous ill will I was harboring for Annie. The surface of the water, the white-capped waves, and the many leagues I sensed below were cold—and so deep.

I needed to focus on what I was doing *at this moment*. I thought about the boat I was on and the ocean around and below it. I thought about where I was going, what I wanted to do when I got there with what I would find—Miss Smiley?—and whether or not I believed in "prescience," specifically hers. And if such prescience did exist, coupled with predictions or hexes, did it have any power to affect future events? Totally ridiculous!—and yet, I guess even thinking such thoughts showed just how low I'd sunk.

The ocean, grayish-green, was now spraying cold salt-water mist onto the deck. The sky was socked in with gray clouds. I'd seen some breathtakingly beautiful sunsets from ferry rides over the years, but there would be nothing to see like that this evening. I checked my phone, but somewhere over the ocean, I'd lost cell service. Shivering, I went back inside.

We landed on Hoophole around one-thirty, and it seemed to me the fishing village hadn't changed in thirty-three years. Though I had done so much changing and in some ways felt like a different person, Hoophole appeared to be trapped in a time warp. I remembered The Fish House from the first trip, so I went inside and asked where to eat. It seemed the same men still stood at the conveyor belt, dressed in the same yellow rubber clothes and green boots, chopping and hosing down fish. One of them about my age, blond, sunburned, and weather-worn, said, "Gen'ral Store," without looking up. I persuaded him to tell me where it was, still without looking up.

Down the block, the store was a wooden building shaped like a barn, once white, now faded. Over the front, double doors were painted in faded red lettering "Hoophole Island General Store, Founded 1880." I opened the door, a bell chinkled, and the wood-plank floor creaked with each step. The place had a good smell—an old but good mix of candy, popcorn, soap, leather, and coffee. And hot food. I looked at the menu on the wall over the counter.

Before I'd said a word, though, a three-hundred-pound man, not tall, who stood behind a huge, black antique cash register, said, "'Ave a seat—ove 'air." He nodded toward two tables. "Whilst I fix you an egg, cheese, and liver mush sandwich. There's water, soft drinks, and tea ove 'air in 'at cooler."

I pulled out a bottle of water, walked over to the tables, and after nodding to a man who sat at one of them and receiving no response, I pulled out a chair at the other and sat down. A woodstove close by kept the place toasty. I took off my hood and jacket.

Figuring I had nothing to lose, I said, "Excuse me. Can you tell me how I might get a boat over to the Isle of Cats?"

Cocking his head, he squinted and studied me. "Nobody goes to that oylet." Then he got up and walked out the front door.

Had the ferry been a time machine back to 1974?

The big man in charge, wearing a soiled, white chef's apron over his blue overalls, brought me my sandwich. As he set it in front of me, I could tell from the aroma that he'd put spicy mustard on it. I thanked him, then asked him the same question I'd asked the other man.

"You cannot go to that oylet," he replied. "Gumment property—off-limits." Then *he* walked off.

I finished the sandwich and sat a while, trying to think of what to do next. In the next hour, I entered every establishment open, then knocked on doors at random, getting the same response everywhere. I returned to the General Store and ordered another sandwich. As I was sitting by the woodstove warming up, the front door opened, clinking the bell.

"I'm needing a Coke, Jeffro," the customer said to the big aproned man. He paid him, the register clanged open and slammed shut, and he walked to the cooler, rooting around until he found an eight-ounce bottle of Coca-Cola. Opening it on the side of the cooler, he walked to the tables, stopped, and regarded me. "You mind?"

"Help yourself."

He was no taller than five-six, medium build, paunchy stomach, ruddy face, as if permanently wind-burned, with some red splotches and a few pockmarks. He had wavy, gray hair and a large nose. He looked older than me, but it was hard to tell by how much.

"You're not from around here," he said as he took off his jacket and pulled out his chair. I assumed that was obvious, and since I'd struck out using the direct approach all morning, I simply nodded. "I don't know you," he continued, "and I know everybody around here. I may not sound like these people, but I look like them. I'm one of 'em. They trust me." He paused. "Rudy's the name."

I didn't want company, and I didn't want conversation. All I wanted was a boat ride out to the island.

"Joe," I said.

"So—Joe—you want to go to the Isle of Cats . . ."

I cocked my head.

"You've asked half the people on the island—how could I not know? . . . Cup of coffee?"

"Sure."

"Anything in it?"

"Caffeine."

"That's all they serve here. Anything else?"

"No—that's sufficient."

He got up and brought me a cup—black—from the pot near the register. "On me," he said. "I got the sandwich, too."

"Totally not necessary, but thanks."

Flipping his hand, he sat down. I ate some of my sandwich and washed it down with a swig of water. Then I set the rest of it down. "I'm a student—an older one, but still a student—a biologist, working on my Ph.D. There's some unique wildlife on that island, and I'm planning to write a paper on it, maybe my thesis."

"You mean the cats?" he said, studying me skeptically. "Shackleford Banks has the wild ponies and is open to the public, but people rarely go there in the dead of winter. The Isle of Cats is restricted by the government, and nobody goes there, ever. Funny that you would want to."

"Nobody goes there—*ever*?" I, too, could be skeptical.

"Not in a long time. It's a bad place with a bad history. Even some of the cats are bad in that they have birth defects from inbreeding. The fed owns all but one parcel of the island, and the whole place is off-limits to the public. A traitor by the name of Smiley—Adolphus Zeno—brought the cats there to run experiments. He had a daughter who was an astrologer or soothsayer. He was a traitor."

He pulled a flask from the inside pocket of his coat and poured about a half-ounce into his Coke. "Sort of like Aldrich Ames, except that Doc Smiley supposedly wasn't a traitor for pay.

The treachery was in his heart. I only mention Ames because his mother lived in Hickory for years—and at the time of her death."

My eyes widened. She'd been a real estate broker, active in the community. A nice lady. Across the street from my law office was a micro-park named in her memory. I also knew that, mercifully, she'd never known anything about the secret, double life of her son, who was only exposed after she was gone.

"I imagine that *is* where you're from: border around your license plate." He paused, then added, "Rum and Coke. I talk better that way." Squinting, he peered at me. "I guess you *could* be a Ph.D. candidate. Maybe. That's coming from the only person on this island who ever earned a college degree: N.C. State, class of '65. But I doubt it."

"So I guess you're not going to help me get over there, either." I stood up and pulled my hood and jacket from the chair.

"I didn't say that—*Joe*. Take it easy."

I looked at him.

"Actually," he informed me, "I think we've met. You *have* visited the tavern at the King Charles' Inn—right?"

I said nothing.

"I don't forget a face—even a sour one I only saw in the mirror."

I sat back down.

"I'd be more willing to help you if you'd tell me the truth. Starting with your name."

"What difference does it make? Why would you care one way or the other?"

"I make it my business to know things. That's why I can help you."

"Joseph Jones. Joe. Is that all right?" He said nothing. "And now I'll tell you the *real* reason I'm here: I'm writing a book. Been working on it for years. Seems like a lifetime. A novel."

"*Really*?" he replied sarcastically, nursing his Coca-Cola. "What's it about?"

"This guy's been searching his whole life for something elusive like the ultimate Good—searching for Truth and a personal relationship with God. But now, having failed to find it, he's lived just long enough to completely screw up his life. He thought he had it all; now he has nothing."

He leaned back. "That's it? That doesn't sound like much of a plot."

"Maybe he'll do something else." I also leaned back. "Go to a desert isle and never return. Die or something. He has a big life insurance policy, so if he's dead, he's worth something. It's just alive that he's worthless."

"That sounds awful."

"Well, this is my first book, so I'm not too good at it. I haven't completely thought it out yet. Maybe the guy still has a glimmer of hope coming from someplace outside himself." I stood up, grabbing my hood and jacket. "Well, Rudy, it's been nice talking to you. Thanks for the sandwich—I gotta go."

I turned to leave, and he said to my back, "There are large cats on that island, wild ones"—I turned around and looked at him—"and they've been rumored to attack humans in winter when food is scarce. Maybe they'll kill the guy."

"I thought you said no one ever went to that…oylet."

"Some kids did thirty-some years ago"—I wondered if he noticed any reaction in my eyes—"and they were never heard from again."

"They should have been more careful."

"Being careful isn't it. It's the island itself. It has a corrupted Soul. Nothing good ever comes of being there. It's a bad place—a cursed place."

"I don't believe in curses. There's never been any evidence in my life—or in the lives of anyone close to me—that they work. They have no effect."

"Believe what you want to believe. But you shouldn't go to the Isle of Cats for any reason, and you do have one—it's your secret. You won't be able to get over there tonight, anyway. There're less than two more hours of daylight, and nobody will take you. Even if somebody did, what would you do once you got there—sleep on the beach? It's going to be in the twenties tonight. There are better ways than that to do away with yourself. And if you succeeded, who would finish your book?"

I pulled out my wallet and tossed enough cash on the table to pay for my sandwich and coffee. "Here. I don't want your help."

Ignoring the money, he replied, "Fine. Have it your way—it's your life." He paused. "So, go to the Queen Anne's Lodge—that's the only place on Hoophole that rents out rooms. I doubt you'll like it, but that's not my problem—and it probably beats your car. The beach is out of the question. Besides, your boatman lives at the Queen Anne. Name is Hank Phillagraw. He'll refuse to take you—and *keep* saying No—until you get the fare right. You have to incentivize him sufficiently; then he'll take you to the island."

He stood up, and putting on his coat, walked past me, clinking the bell on his way out.

31.

ALMOST A DREAM

I found the Queen Anne's Lodge, a white boarding house in need of paint, and parked out front. Crossing the porch, I opened the door and went in as a bell rattled inside. An unattended front desk faced me, and to the left of that, a hall and staircase. The rest of the lobby comprised a fireplace with an upholstered sofa and two chairs facing it—and a dark, round dining-room table with four chairs. In one of the chairs facing the fireplace, a man sat staring into the fire.

A pungent odor, musty and dank, of mildew and mold, dust, cigarette smoke, and burning wood permeated the air. Over the desk hung a painting of a ship tossing about on a stormy sea at night, the rain pouring while sailors on deck in yellow rain gear fought to save the ship as waves crashed overhead. The beam of a lighthouse shone through the darkness from a rocky shore. As I paused, my thoughts on the painting, the man stood up and disappeared down the hall.

Moments later, he reentered the room—a woman beside

him—and, as he lit a cigarette and returned to his chair at the fire, she walked behind the desk. Wearing an old brown sweater and faded black pants, she had a long, gray ponytail nearly to her waist, and her face, deeply-wrinkled, told me she'd spent years in the sun and wind.

"Room?" she said, pushing back the glasses on her nose with her thumb. No smile.

"Actually, I'm looking for someone."

She looked up.

"Hank Phillagraw."

She raised her eyebrows, cocked her head at me. "*Room*?" she repeated, this time louder.

I looked at the man sitting by the fire and found him looking back.

"How much?"

"How many nights?"

"One."

She told me, and I paid.

Putting the cash in the drawer, she said, "Sign here."

I signed: Joe Jones. She nodded his way. "Right 'air." She handed me a key. "Yer in number four, top of the stairs. Bath, end of the 'all. Cold breakfast in 'ere in the morning on the table. Need anything, let me know." Then she turned and disappeared down the hall.

I walked over to the fireplace and sat down in an upholstered chair that looked and felt as if it hadn't been cleaned in fifty years. The man opposite me—short, thin but wiry, unkempt, and dark from years of sun, probably ten years my senior—looked away toward the fire.

"Rudy suggested I come see you," I told him, and he glanced at me sideways from the corner of his eye. When I added, "about the Isle of Cats," he recoiled, grimacing, and turned away.

For the next ten minutes, I tried to communicate with patient coaxing, lulls of silence—and doses of cash. Every time I mentioned his ferrying me to the island, I expected him to say, "No," but all he did was shake his head like a recalcitrant horse. Apparently, I was talking to a man who had an abnormal aversion to human conversation or was a mute. But he never left his seat, so I persevered.

Finally, after I pulled one twenty-dollar bill after another out of my wallet, making various offers, I hit on a deal he liked. "How about two of these tomorrow morning to get us started," I suggested, "another two when we get to the island? Two more when you pick me up again at 3:15 to bring me back. And another two when we dock at Hoophole. And," I added, "two right now to show we have a deal." At this, he nodded, and I handed him two twenties.

By the time I left the lodge, my clothes smelling of its years of neglect, I had a sense of relief and gratitude. I spent the rest of the day's light driving around with the windows cracked and stayed out after dark as long as I could—anything to postpone spending the night in room number four.

The fire I lit in the hearth was the only source of heat in my room—no electricity—and the room smelled of charred wood and kerosene. The only furnishings were a nightstand topped by an oil lamp, a small chest of drawers, a straight-back chair, and a round, orange rug—soiled and frayed—at the foot of the bed. The mattress sank in the middle like a bowl. Not wanting to sleep in the sheets, I tried to sleep on top of the bedspread, entirely dressed, including my gloves and shoes, although I did remove my jacket and hood to use as a blanket. It was so cold, I even tried to sleep with my ski mask on, but its scratchiness made me take it off. The mattress made my back hurt, and because it was short, my legs went off the end. The key didn't lock the door, so I lodged the back of the chair under the doorknob. It wasn't that I didn't trust the boatman staying in the neighboring room, but I didn't want him visiting me in the middle of the night, sleepwalking or otherwise.

About halfway through the night, a storm blew in from the sea, pelting the side of the building with rain. The windowpanes beside my bed popped with water, and for a time, sleet and hail. The window creaked and whistled, and a tree branch scraped against the glass, hour after hour. When the fire died, I was left in darkness, nothing for company but the sound of the storm and the restless scratching of the branch. I think I finally dozed off around four o'clock and slept fitfully till six-thirty when I got up and went downstairs.

Now I was sitting at the prow of the boat, my back to the Isle of Cats, the boatman ferrying me across the water. I was cold and hoped I'd be able to warm up once I landed on the island and started walking. I couldn't remember how long the boat ride had taken thirty-three years ago, but I guessed about forty-five minutes to an hour. What I did remember was that Celia and I didn't talk much, the boatman had been as silent as this one, and Croom and Jennie, though they didn't talk much either, seemed very much in love. I also remembered that Celia and I commented that the boatman changed his expression and attitude midway across the water.

Right now, I was living in a torturous dream. What was I doing here? Out in the middle of the ocean, on a bleak, frigidly cold December morning—the boat bobbing through the waves, splashing me with spray—with a dour and squirrely little man I didn't know, and all for what? What did I expect to find?

A couple of years ago, it seemed I'd had everything anyone would want. Now, it seemed, I'd lost everything. Yesterday I'd felt determined to go back to the Isle of Cats. But why? What was I searching for? What could I possibly expect to find on that godforsaken island after thirty-three years? And what was motivating me?—a ray of hope, feeble and faint, or simply desperation? Now I was wondering if I'd made a mistake in choosing to go back.

All I wanted was Celia.

I pulled out my phone as if looking at it might magically revive it. *I'm about halfway to the Isle of Cats right now—in the ocean beyond Hoophole. If I don't call you before midnight, call the Coast Guard.* That was the message I would have sent.

As I looked beyond the boatman, back to the larger island receding in the distance, the reality of what I was doing hit home: I was going to the island no one ever went to, and I was going alone. Was that smart?

We beached about thirty minutes later. Out of the boat, I pulled my wallet from my back pocket. "Here's the other half of what I owe you for bringing me over. Be sure to be back two hours before sunset—by 3:15—same place. I'll pay you again, just as we agreed."

He looked at the bills, held them up one at a time to see

the watermarks, then buried them in his pants pocket, nodding once. He got back in the boat, and I shoved him off the beach. As I did so, my anxiety grew. The temperature hovered around freezing, and as I watched him motor away from the island, it occurred to me that if he didn't come back and the Coast Guard didn't find me for several days—assuming they were looking for me—I might die of hypothermia. I did have the insurance policy, though. This really *was* a desert island. Nothing here but sand, sand dunes and sea oats, and a maritime forest halfway to the other end. Then, of course, there was the house. From the get-go, I was on the lookout for cats lurking in the dunes.

It was low tide, so the beach was wide as I walked along the edge of the surf, scummy foam clinging to the beach in a ragged line. Because of last night's rain, the sand was hard and gray even beyond the high-tide mark, making it easy to walk. Some two hundred or so feet higher up on the beach, the sand was soft and white, difficult to walk on. Here, shell fragments crunched beneath my jogging shoes.

I'd made one feeble attempt at conversation with the boatman. "Has anyone ever lived on the island?" I'd asked him, hoping he might tell me about the current status of the house and any inhabitants. Who knew?—maybe a Ben Gunn lived there now.

Mirabile dictu, he'd actually responded. "I don't know nothin' 'bout that oylet—'cept yer not spose to go 'air. No one. It's a mistake to go. Bad will come of it. Always does."

Now I was here. Funny about the seagulls. On Bogue Banks, where our house was, the birds were so comfortable with people, they were attracted to us. If I walked down the beach, especially in winter when food was harder to find, they'd sometimes land within a few feet, looking up at me for a handout. Then they'd be joined within seconds by others surrounding me in a flock. Here, the gulls wouldn't come near—unless their nesting area was invaded. Then they'd attack.

I'd had the boatman drop me off on the near end of the island because, had I insisted he take me to the far end, he'd have known I had a reason; and what reason could I have had other than an interest in the house? And how could I have known about *that*? So my only plan was to trudge forward till I got to the house and find there whatever I could. Then get back to the pick-up point by 3:15, two hours before sunset.

I felt a drop of rain, mixed with snow, then another, on my face. If it began to rain in earnest, my only cover would be the house—just like the last time. I pulled the ski mask out of my pocket and put it on. Every so often, the sea foam clinging to the beach, trembling in the breeze, would break loose and float through the air in clumps of bubbles or run along the surface of the wet sand like tumbleweed. In the distance, a flock of gulls huddled close to the ground. I marveled at how some of them could hop around easily on just one leg.

Miss Smiley deserved what she got. Fortune-telling was illegal for a reason. It was cynical and wicked and cruel and could have a terrible effect on innocent people's lives. All four of us had on occasion lived under that woman's shadow for thirty-three years. We had felt the weight of her predictions. I'd won and lost, lost a dear friend, and been betrayed. There was the matter of murder. And now, at this moment, I was *seeking* as I suppose I actually had been my whole life, even before Miss Smiley came along.

I was eager to find the old house. I assumed it would be abandoned, and if so, I'd go inside, look around, and try to warm up. If it was not, I had a loaded gun, and I knew how to use it if I needed it. To my left, over in the dunes, I saw a large cat, then another, creeping around, eyeing me. Despite myself, I shuddered. If the boatman didn't return for me, I guess I'd have two choices: sleep on the beach with the cats and freeze, or spend the night in the house—also with the cats?—for the second time.

Now I could see, far down the beach—though it was hard to judge *how* far—the forest, straight ahead. I continued following the shoreline until the forest grew closer and larger. In another half hour, I reached the thicket of scrub bushes and gnarled, dwarfed trees, and continuing along the line of the surf, I walked around it. Three times I spotted cats, all of them large and misshapen, each one bolting away as soon as it saw me. Other times, I just heard them, creeping through the undergrowth.

On the far side of the forest—on the island's eastern half—I still saw no sign of the house situated on the point farthest out in the sea. I passed a vulture feasting on the carcass of a large seagull, pecking it to pieces. Would that be me if the boatman didn't return? Not a pleasant thought. Or would the cats get me first? Also, not a pleasant thought. I stopped long enough to inspect the skeletal remains of two different shipwrecks buried in the sand, maybe merchant marine. If they were casualties of World War II, I figured Dr. Smiley had had something to do with sinking them.

I'd walked for over two hours and was cold and tired, but still no house in sight. I stepped around a dead shark, mutilated by pecking, and a large dead seagull with its eyes and innards eaten away. Seeking dinner, sandpipers hustled around frantically at the edge of the tide as it came and went.

Since I was getting close to what I thought was the farthest eastern point of the island and still hadn't found the house, I began to wonder. *Maybe the house was gone?* If so, then here I was, after most of a lifetime of wondering, and all that remained to answer my questions was shifting winds and sand. Nothing at all. And in that, there really was something sinister about this island. Whereas on Bogue Banks, there'd been those times I'd experienced a closeness to God, a spiritual thing, here and now, it was more a sense of nothingness.

Whatever *had* been, seemed to be gone, as if the whole thing had never happened, as if the witch Miss Smiley had never said anything to me or the others, as if a dark habit of mind had made it up, then fed on the illusion. Had it blown away, sea foam and grains of sand on the beach? Had she been trying, instead, to help us, to care for us in her odd way on a dark night? Was the fortune-telling no more than an awkward entertainment of hers to pass the time?

I didn't want to leave this place with just as many questions as when I arrived. I wanted to find something—some answers. There had to be some sense to it all. There had to be a reason for things.

I kicked around in the sand, hoping to discover *something—anything*. Finally, I sat down near the edge of a small sand cliff with about a ten-foot drop, probably created by the waves as recently as last night's storm. The sky was cloudy, the day so bleak, the island so desolate, I felt like a mariner lost at sea. I wished again that Celia were sitting beside me—up close—keeping me warm. We could huddle together, the two of us. I'd left her so abruptly . . . Now that I was here and she was there, I wished we were together. We could think together, think what to do now. Now that everything had been lost at sea.

I got an apple out of my backpack and ate it, then drank half a bottle of water.

Thirty-three years ago, Celia and I and Croom and Jennie had been here together. Now, here I was again. Alone this time. Why? What had it all been for? *Mann tracht, un Gott lacht.* You do your castle-building, then the tide comes in and washes it out. That's it. That's all there is. We think we're so important—that there's so much significance attached to our actions—then we discover it's ephemeral. Ashes to ashes.

I watched the waves rolling in below me at the foot of the sheer. Finally, two rolled in at angles, and the "V" they created when they converged sent a wave crashing against the cliff, splashing spray over me. I jumped up, and out of the corner of my eye, saw a large cat lurking in the dunes. Waving my arms, I yelled, running him off. But then another cat appeared, and as I walked toward him, he hesitated, returning my stare, until I yelled and ran toward him, and he scattered.

Yet a third cat appeared. This time I ran toward him, yelling as I followed him into the dunes, and watched as he ran across an open expanse on the other side. Thinking it odd that three cats had appeared from the same location, I walked to the middle of the open area and stood there, thinking. I kicked around in the sand, wondering exactly how close I might be to where the house had stood or if I was farther away than I thought. The events of that night were vivid, at least in the way that my mind remembered them, but now that I'd returned to the far end of the island, the lack of evidence—the absence of anything but sand and sea oats and a ring of dunes—raised doubt.

I wondered if those three cats had been here for a reason, and if so, were there others of them nearby in the dunes? And if so, why? I continued to kick through the dry white sand, accomplishing nothing by this except to put more sand in my shoes. Cold as it was, I'd have to take them off and knock out the sand before I headed back.

When to head back? When to give up? I was about to that point, now—about to call it quits—but as I kicked through some more sand, I uncovered a patch of concrete surface. And the more I moved the sand, the more surface I found. If I could determine that this surface was large enough, it almost *had* to be the platform where the house had stood! What else could it be? I felt at once sadly disappointed to think that the scene of our momentous adventure was no more, but also relieved—even glad—to think that at least *something* might still exist to prove that my memories were tied to reality.

Considering the edifice, a three-story Second Empire mansion that once had been, it was surreal to discover nothing now but a concrete surface blanketed in sand drifts. Yet, if I was right, it was something: a foundation. Since this surface was the only concrete evidence, figuratively as well as literally, of what had happened here to the four of us, I stood atop it for a while, head down, eyes closed, and thought back as hard as I could to the events of that night. She'd taken us to her den, sat us down, made four trips to the kitchen for four plates of food and four more trips for the half-filled glasses of water. She'd told us her story and told us ours in future tense. She said Celia's fortune was the last she'd ever tell. She predicted all of us would see murder. Throughout the night, she'd coughed repeatedly, finally collapsing into my arms.

After she'd made the first trip to the den and served the first plate, I thought I'd heard sounds in the kitchen when she was in the den with us. The cats appeared soon after she died. Holding her in my arms, I'd thought about trying to breathe life into her mouth but changed my mind. I gently laid her on the floor and did the compressions. We watched her die. That first time the cats appeared, we'd run them off, then stood over her corpse in the flickering light, flipping coins. But as we were leaving, the cats came back and surrounded her. We walked out, assuring ourselves that they were only licking her face.

As promised, the boatman returned the next day and picked us up where he'd dropped us off. If only I could know if something else—anything—had happened that night. If only there were some way to know for sure.

Pulling out of my reverie, I walked about the sand some more, again kicking into it, hoping, maybe ridiculously, to uncover some sort of clue. If nothing else, I wanted to find the outer boundary of the concrete just to assure myself that I was indeed standing on the foundation of Miss Smiley's house.

Sure enough, the outer boundary lay exposed in numerous places, the sand not only having drifted on top of the slab but also away from its base: the slab, I discovered, lay on walls of concrete block. Walking the perimeter, about seventy by fifty feet, I was sometimes atop the slab with the drifts of sand higher than the surface, and sometimes I was beside the slab with the sand lower than its surface. I discovered in one of the foundation walls a small metal door leading to a basement. With the flashlight in my left hand and the loaded gun in my right, I crept in, causing about a half-dozen over-sized cats with odd ears and tails to rush out, hissing and baring their teeth, as I shrank away from the doorway, my back against the wall and my heart pounding.

The floor—what I could see of it—had been made of concrete, small drifts of sand covering it, and the unmistakable sour odor of cat hung in the air. I scoured the room with my flashlight to be sure there were no more cats, then returned the gun to my backpack. The floor had been dug up, and clumps of concrete lay everywhere. One corner of the room was filled floor-to-ceiling with a mountain of sand, and kicking around in it, I discovered a staircase buried beneath.

I walked the interior perimeter with my light. Besides the concrete-block walls, the concrete ceiling, and what was left of the floor, all I saw was sand, cobwebs, spiders and their desiccated prey, a few empty cages, some empty broken bottles, and the awful evidence that cats were making this space their home.

I wanted out. But first, I turned and walked the perimeter again, this time in the opposite direction, inspecting the walls, ceiling, and floor. Kicking around in the sand again, I unearthed some timbers, and upon inspection, discovered what appeared to be burn marks. I'd assumed a hurricane had taken the house, but now I thought maybe lightning had.

I shuddered when I thought back to that night when the four of us, just college kids, had spent the night upstairs during a lightning storm. Perhaps after all the intervening years of the

Smiley mansion being struck by lightning as the highest point on the island, it had finally received the fateful bolt that burned it to the ground.

In the light of my flashlight, I noticed something else: between the rows of concrete blocks, every once-in-a-while small crevices ran horizontally in the mortar, as if they'd been scraped out with a tool. I kicked over a few cages, kicked around in the sand some more, then took out my Scout knife and poked around in the crevices between the blocks. I was hoping for some sort of sign—a note, a confession, a clue—some sort of explanation for why Dr. Smiley had done what he did, but all I found were four small, slate plaques shoved sideways into four of the crevices, one in each main wall, so that they were lying flat, hidden inside like tiny caskets. I pried each one out with my knife. The plaques, about four-by-six inches and a quarter-inch thick, had sayings on them, painted in calligraphy.

I put them in my backpack—for Celia, Croom, and Jennie—the only tangible mementoes of the events here that had affected all four of our lives. The place smelled of mold, bird carcasses, and cat waste, and I was eager to get out; still, I scoured the walls, ceiling, and floor over again, as thoroughly as I could, hoping to find something else—a clear answer or clue. I pushed the sand around with my shoes. Except for clumps of broken concrete and a few more charred timbers, I discovered nothing more. At the cellar door, I crept out into the light of a cloudy day, grateful for the fresh air.

I was at the pick-up point on the beach by 2:45, relieved to be able to sit and rest. While I waited, I opened my backpack, drank some water, and looked at the four plaques—three from

Shakespeare, one in Latin—liking the thought that I had actual, physical souvenirs of our adventure. Even though I was positioned to lose my worldly possessions—as much of them as the court and creditors could seize—I'd still have these four plaques to hang on to as material evidence of my past life. I smiled to myself, wryly.

How odd that someone had placed them, carefully calligraphed, one poked sideways inside each wall, in the foundation of the house! Who put them there?—and why?

I returned them to my backpack and looked out over the sea. Off in the distance, toward Hoophole Island, I could see a speck in the water—a while later, a small boat. As I watched, it grew larger, and around 3:15, the boatman beached.

Relieved, I did thank God for this!

Pulling the boat onto the shore and hopping in, I handed the boatman two twenties and shoved us off with a paddle.

About an hour later, we were back on Hoophole.

32.

THE DEADLY FRIEND

As the boat pulled in to dock, I tried one last time to get the boatman to talk with me. He and I stepped out of the boat and onto the pier and, as he tied onto a piling, I said, "I walked all over that island, and I discovered only the foundation of a building with a basement. A lighthouse, maybe? Or maybe just a house. It looked like it might have burned down." I pulled out my wallet. "Would you happen to know anything about it?"

I handed him two bills. Holding them on either end between his thumbs and fingers, he again inspected each one for authenticity as I stood there waiting, hoping he would say something. Without even looking up, he shoved the twenties into his pocket. Then he turned his back on me and went back to tending his boat. My hands in the air, I said to myself, "I give up." So much for social graces. I shook my head and walked off.

. . .

My first stop was the Hoophole Island General Store, for the woodstove and something hot to eat. "Scrambled egg, liver mush, and cheese sandwich—and can you tell me where I might find Rudy, the man who was here yesterday?"

"Casper," the three-hundred-pound man in the apron said, "Rudy Casper. Troy 'is 'ouse. Two blocks down the road on the royt 'an' soyd"—he pointed which way—"look for the burgundy pickup truck out front."

"Much obliged."

I stood by the woodstove, warming up, and scarfed down the sandwich. Ordering another one, I ate it on the way out the door. If I hustled, I could get to his house and still make the five-thirty ferry back to the mainland.

After knocking on the door of a one-story cottage with the burgundy truck, I heard a dog barking; then a voice yelled for me to come in. Once inside, the dog—I guessed a cockapoo—jumped up, his paws on my knee, his tail wagging, his black-and-tan, furry face smiling. Picking him up, I hugged him to my chest.

"In here," the voice yelled to me again, and in front of the fire in his den, I found Rudy Casper sitting in a rocking chair, reading a book and sipping Coca-Cola from an eight-ounce bottle.

"What's his name?"

Rudy Casper smiled. "Henry."

"Who's he named for?" I asked, the dog licking my face.

"Himself. So you're back—all in one piece! Congratulations." With a nod and an outstretched hand, he offered me a seat. "Did you find the answer to all of life's mysteries?"

"Not hardly," I said without sitting. "I'm still left with a few cosmic questions unanswered, but I've got to make the five-thirty ferry, and before I leave, I wanted to thank you for helping me out."

"Don't mention it—I was bored. Since you're alive, I guess what I did was okay after all, though I did feel a little guilty about helping you get there."

"I wasn't eaten by a cat, a lightning bolt didn't strike me dead, but I do have a question."

"Okay?"

"Can I take Henry with me?"

"Not on your life. What's the real question?"

"Do you know what happened to the house that used to be on the Isle of Cats?"

He raised his eyebrows but did not smile. "How would you know there used to be a house there? Are you sure you don't want to sit down before you answer that question?"

Now was the moment of truth: Tell him, be honest, and maybe get some answers in return—or lie, leave the island, and never know. But before I was forced to reply, he spoke. "Look..." and setting the book on the end-table beside his chair, he said, "it's been almost thirty-five years. It's a felony, and you could still be prosecuted, but if you burned it down, I won't tell anybody."

"Don't be ridiculous!" I snapped in a low voice. I set Henry on the floor, but as I stood back up—my back and legs so tired and aching all I wanted to do was sit—he jumped back up on my leg, wagging, so I picked him up again, reminding me of how much I still missed Pip.

"Easy," Rudy Casper said. "I can get you all the answers you want, but not in time for you to make the ferry. And you'll have to spend some more time at the Queen Anne's Lodge."

I groaned.

"I knew you wouldn't like the place, but I'm afraid that's where the answers are."

We drove over in his pickup truck—the three of us—Rudy Casper, Henry, and me. On the way, he explained why it had to be done this way. "I can supply you with all the answers you want—through Hank Phillagraw."

I shot him a glance. "*Hank Phillagraw*? He couldn't carry on a conversation to save his life. He's a mute!"

"Trust me; he's no mute. He's just peculiar as hell. Never been married. Probably never been with a woman. He won't talk to a stranger without company present—someone he knows and is comfortable with. Even then, he won't talk much if he's getting a bunch of questions—unless he's properly incentivized. That's something he responds to. I supply the company, and—"

"I supply the money."

"A sufficient amount—he'll let you know when. Then he'll talk you to death."

I asked him how it was that Hank Phillagraw knew the story.

"Actually," he explained, "everyone on the island pretty much knows the story—by word of mouth, anyway—but Hank knows it straight from his own daddy."

"Who *is*. . . ?"

"Who *was* Sam Phillagraw, Roger Gaskill's best friend"—I recognized that name; I was glad he couldn't see the glint of recognition in my eyes—"his only friend—and drinking buddy. He's dead now. Like Roger Gaskill."

By the time we pulled into the gravel drive in front of the lodge, it was dark. The bell chinkled when we opened the door, the odor of smoke greeting us even before we walked in. Hank Phillagraw was sitting by the fire, smoking a cigarette. He got up, flicked the butt in the fireplace, and walked down the back hall, returning with the proprietress.

"Hey, Rudy," she said from behind the check-in desk. "Hey, Henry," she said to the dog he was carrying.

"Ms. Walken . . ." he replied, tipping an imaginary hat. "I think you've met my friend here, Mr. . . . Jones." This time she smiled at me—not much, but a little.

"We were wondering if, for a spell, we could avail ourselves of the warmth of your fireplace and den. We were thinking Mr. Phillagraw might enjoy some company."

"Room four, still good?" she said, looking at me. She pushed back her glasses with her thumb. I let her hand me the key and paid her.

"I'm glad you loykt yer stay last noyt," she said. "Anything I can do whilst yer 'ere, let me know."

"I'm sure your warm fire and cozy den will suffice," said Rudy Casper, "except that, while we're enjoying them, a moderate libation from your pantry would be most appreciated. I doubt I'll need a room myself—I'll go easy with the Coca-Colas." He reached into his wallet and handed her a twenty. "It's a tip," he said, meaningfully pulling the corners of his mouth up into a smile. "Keep the change. Just a little rum. And a little extra for our friend, Mr. Phillagraw."

She looked at me; I shook my head. I was still in remission after the scotch.

"Make yourself comfortable—I'll be back in a minute. Rum on the 'ouse, of course. 'Ow many Coca-Colas did you purchase? No matter—I got a fridge full."

Hanging our coats on the rack by the door, we sat down in the den—Rudy Casper across from Hank Phillagraw, either side of the fireplace; me, facing the fire, Henry jumping into my lap. The room, dimly lit by the fire and a small lamp on a corner table, reeked of stale smoke and dampness.

Ms. Walken brought Rudy Casper a rum-and-Coke in a stein decorated with the seven lighthouses of North Carolina—one also to Hank Phillagraw, with the pirate flags, making sure the right mug, with a little extra, went to the right person. She handed me a glass of water, no napkin.

For the first fifteen minutes, Rudy Casper talked mostly about the weather, comparing hurricanes over the decades by name—Hazel, Hugo, Bonnie, Floyd.

"Hazel was especially destructive in South Carolina, though she smashed us, too," he said. "She leveled most of Myrtle Beach. Floyd hit Cape Fear and hovered over eastern North Carolina for three days with continuous rain and flooded the whole region to the five-hundred-year flood level. It proved to be the most destructive event for the area since the Civil War." He added, "But I can tell you, there will be others—even worse—always will be; it's part of life here on this coast. Cape Fear—Graveyard of the Atlantic—there's a reason for the names."

I said, "Bonnie ruined the floor in the great room of our house on Bogue Banks when the rain blew in under the sliding-glass doors." I wanted to help make conversation with a personal note, though I ached from exertion and lack of sleep.

"So you have a house on Bogue Banks," Rudy Casper said. "Information."

"And Hugo, starting in Africa, made it all the way to Hickory and Charlotte. It tore off our sun porch and took down nine trees in our yard as it went through."

"Noted," Rudy Casper chimed in. Hank Phillagraw remained silent, facing the fire.

"Speaking of hurricanes," he went on, "it's a little-known fact, only recently proven through archeological digs, that for over two centuries, the descendants of early European settlers lived on Shackleford Banks until a series of hurricanes finally wiped out their towns. Then, around 1900, the last of those islanders moved to the mainland and settled 'The Promise Land,' which is still there in Morehead City."

"Wow!" I said, genuinely impressed. But Hank Phillagraw said nothing.

Then Rudy Casper changed the subject: "This establishment is named for Blackbeard's ship, the Queen Anne's Revenge, which eleven years ago was discovered buried in Beaufort Inlet after being down there almost three hundred years."

"Interesting namesake," I interjected. "Apt—at least the 'revenge' part." I looked sideways at Rudy.

"Actually," Rudy Casper said, ignoring me, "he named his ship to honor Queen Anne because, as a Jacobite, as were many *real* pirates, Blackbeard believed the British throne rightly belonged to the House of Stuart. Queen Anne, having died in 1714—three years before Blackbeard captured his ship from the French—was the last of the Stuart line. After her death, the throne passed to the House of Hanover, which was German. Anne, of course, was Scottish." He paused long enough to take a swig from his stein.

"He had a good point," I said.

"Anyway, Blackbeard ran the Queen Anne's Revenge aground off the coast at Beaufort Inlet in 1718, effectively sinking her. He went legit for a while because of a pardon by King George but soon went back to pirating again and was allegedly in cahoots with the Colonial Governor of North Carolina, Eden, who'd been approved for the Governorship by Queen Anne."

On a roll, he paused again, but only briefly. "But the Colonial Governor of Virginia, Spotswood, wanted Blackbeard killed. So Spotswood sent out an expedition, which caught up with him near Ocracoke Inlet after he'd been busy drinking with his cohorts the whole night before." He took a gulp from his stein. "Mmmm," he purred. "Aaargh. In the battle that ensued—really ferocious—Blackbeard was beheaded. The British then threw his body in the ocean, and it swam around the ship several times before sinking."

He leaned forward in his chair and took another swig from his stein. "That very last part's not true," he whispered. "It's just a legend that won't go away." Then, leaning back in his chair: "But it *is* true that the British sailed back to Virginia with Blackbeard's decapitated head onboard, after displaying it for a while on the bowsprit of the pirate's own ship so everyone would see it."

Then he stopped talking—and waited. Still, not a word from Hank Phillagraw.

I said, "That was really showing off."

Rudy Casper cleared his throat. More silence.

I added, "Did you know that Blackbeard was tall, with broad shoulders?" I sat up straight and stretched my arms out to either side, careful, though, not to disturb Henry. Hank Phillagraw pulled from his shirt pocket a cigarette pack and some matches and lit a cigarette. Henry repositioned himself more comfortably in my lap.

"I have a question," I said. "Was Governor Eden a Republican or a Democrat?" I glanced sideways at Rudy Casper, then out of the corner of my eye at Hank Phillagraw, who looked the other way.

"O-*kay*," Rudy Casper then said, "*Hank* . . . Mr. Jones—Joe—really appreciated that you took him over to the island and got him back safely and right on time. And he would be most appreciative if you would indulge him, a visitor to our fair island in want of a little company, in some friendly conversation."

Hank Phillagraw exhaled a train of donut smoke toward the ceiling. I leaned over—Henry looked up at me, then moved off my lap—as I pulled my wallet from my back pocket. Peeling off bills, I handed one to Hank Phillagraw.

With both hands, he held it out to the light of the fire, then shook it at his ear. "Sounds mighty crisp."

"Fresh off the press."

"Huhn! I may need a few more."

Each time I handed him another one, I felt closer to bankruptcy: the value of a dollar had gone up a lot for me in the last couple of days. Once I reached the magic number and the boatman had them safely buried in the front pocket of his jeans, I found out that he could, indeed, talk more fluently than I'd ever dreamed possible.

"So why did you want to go to that oylet? Well, I know. To search—that's why. You was searching for the answer. You was searching for the answer to the hidden traysure."

As a matter of fact, he was right. Only I wasn't looking for coins.

"Well, it's not 'Traysure Oylet'—it's 'Traitors Oylet.' There's no traysure there—jest the bones of traitors." Henry, now nestled in beside me on the sofa, lay his head on my lap.

"Nobody goes to that oylet—and ever returns. Nobody's gone there in thirty-three years, until today. The last four who did never came back. At least, not in the same condition they went over. They was cursed. Because the oylet be cursed—and so was they. Everybody knows that; that's why nobody goes. If I were you"—he turned to look me in the eye—"I wouldn't have gone."

"But I'm here," I reminded him. "Back safely—promptly—thanks to you. I'm a writer. Been working on a book my whole life. And you're right that I went to the island in search of answers, in search of the Truth. And you're right that I'm looking for the treasure."

Rudy Casper looked at me curiously. I continued, "I suppose we all are. I think it's part of the human condition. God made us that way, so I'm sure it's for a good reason. Anyway, I walked all over the island, exploring, and the cats, some of them, are living in what looks like the basement of a house that might have burned down. What happened to the house? Did lightning strike it and burn it down?"

He patted his front pocket.

You've got the money—now talk.

He blew another series of smoke rings into the airspace between us. His teeth were stained dark yellow; his face and hands were leathery brown. Wearing jeans and a flannel shirt, he had that in common with Rudy Casper—and me.

Hank Phillagraw stuck out the lower lip of his sun-browned face. "Some say so—that lightnin' burnt it down. That lightnin' struck it. That Mother Nature—God—killt it dead to the ground."

"How long ago did that happen?"

"Years ago."

"How many?"

"A lot of years ago, but they're wrong. It weren't no lightnin'. I know because I know all the facts better than anybody else because my paw told me, and he got it straight from 'is best friend, Roger Gaskill."

"Roger Gaskill?"

"Yeah—Miss Smiley's cousin. Miss Smiley, the old lady owned the house. She lived there. Roger Gaskill was her boatman, the only one who ever visited her, the one who brung her food and kerosene and wood and medicine and stuff."

"What happened?"

"That's what I been tryin' to tell you, but you ain't givin' me a chance. Folks who think lightnin' struck the 'ouse and burnt it down—they're wrong. It weren't no lightnin'. 'Ouse was burnt down on purpose."

He paused. "Roger Gaskill did it. He set the 'ouse on fire."

I tilted my head. "The boatman? Why would he have done that? Why would the owner's own cousin have set the house on fire?"

"To kivver up the evidence."

"*What* evidence? What are you talking about?"

"*The* evidence—the evidence that he murdered her. He were in the 'ouse—don't you see?—the noyt them kids showed up. He poisoned 'er with cyanoyd that was kept in the basement—always 'ad been. Her father 'ad it. Roger knowed it was 'air, and he come upstairs with it an' 'id in the 'all next to the kitchen. She fixed some supper—and ate some of it 'erself because she were hungry, then took a plate of it to one of them kids. When she left the kitchen 'at first time with the food, right then, that's when he poisoned the food. That's royt—with cyanoyd. It'll drop you like a shot."

Poisoned thoughts! Murder! I shook my head as the wheels turned inside.

"So he jest killt 'er. She dropped dead, right 'air in the middle of the floor. Murder. Later, he dug up the basement, lookin' fer the traysure that weren't even 'air. But he didn't know that till after he dug fer it. All he knowed was that he were poor, and he thought she were rich because she lived in a big 'ouse and 'er father were rich. He thought 'is uncle buried 'is money to keep the gumment from takin' it iffen they found out he were a traitor."

As he talked, he grew animated, using his hands and leaning forward. He flicked the butt of his cigarette into the fire, spraying burning ashes around the hearth. He took another swig of rum. "Y' see, if he hisself could be talked into bringin' a bunch of kids over in 'is boat when he weren't spose to—jest for money—then they moyt git somebody else to bring them back in somebody else's boat, or maybe they moyt bring theirselves—

and they knowed a lot—they knowed too much. Or maybe they didn't know nothin'. Or maybe someone else moyt come besides them. No one was spose to go to that oylet. No one but Roger Gaskill. But they did—a bunch of kids—four, it were."

He sucked in his breath. "He had to kill 'er. Otherwise, someone besides hisself was going to find the traysure." He paused. "'At's what 'appened. And what Roger thought. Then he burnt down the 'ouse with 'er in it. No traysure. Jest her. Dead. Murdered. He couldn't jest leave 'er loyk 'at, laying 'air, dead on the floor. 'At would be stupid."

That's exactly what *we* did, I thought. "How can you possibly know this?" I asked.

"Simple—don't you see? My paw told me—and he knowed everything because, loyk I'm tellin' ya, he and Roger Gaskill was best friends."

"And drinking buddies," added Rudy Casper.

"Royt. Because Paw were his best friend—'is only friend. But him and Paw is dead now. And so is Miss Smiley. And Doc Smiley, her father. The 'ouse is burnt down. Them four kids is long gone. Probably dead, too. From the curse she laid on 'em. Who knows? Anyways, everybody on this oylet knows what 'appened, because everybody involved is dead or gone, now, so it don't matter if everyone knows. No traysure. No Roger. No Miss Smiley. No traitors. No 'ouse. Naught there but cats and bones and sand and ghosts. Wind and ocean. Ships passin' up and down in the noyt, loyk they say."

So many thoughts were churning in my head. "Is there anything else? Is that the whole story?"

"What more d'ye want?" he said quickly, rubbing his pocket.

"What do you mean by 'the curse'?"

He lit another cigarette and leaned forward toward the two of us. "The curse she put on them four kids. I'm sure my paw sayed there was four—two boys, two girls—and Roger Gaskill also sayed to my paw that he heard Miss Smiley putting a star-cross on the feelings between one of the boys and one of the girls because they wasn't meant to be together."

"A star-cross?"

"Yeah—you know—a curse. Roger, he heard her mumble it in the kitchen. She sayed it on the two blond kids."

"Oh my God," I groaned—and felt gooseflesh on my arms and neck. Rudy Casper fixed his eyes on me. "Just on *two* of them?"

"All four of 'em got somethin'," he said, "but only the two blond ones got the star-cross."

You, my dear boy, tall and fair, she'd said to me before she told me my fortune.

"But the whole oylet of cats, I believe, done be some cursed. Them cats—huge 'n' fierce—be the work o' the divel. Everyone on Hoophole knows that. That enough fer ye?"

He didn't wait for an answer.

"Ain't that—and murder—enough? He'd been waitin' fer years for the old lady to die of old age, so he could dig up the loot 'er pappy done buried in the basement. On 'is way boatin' over to the oylet with them kids, it suddenly hit Roger that he were messin' up bringin' them over, but they was already well on their way."

I remembered Celia, as she sat beside me in the boat, whispering to me that the boatman's expression had suddenly changed and he seemed different—"creepy," she said. That stuck in my mind, because otherwise she and I barely spoke on the boat ride over, and the change in the boatman's expression and demeanor is something we both noticed.

"So he dropped 'em off, headed back to Hoophole all scare't, got close to shore, and boated right back to the Oyle and docked the boat behind the 'ouse. Back then there were a slip back 'air. He secured the boat where it were safe. Then he snuck into the basement usin' the outside door, an' 'id there, then moved upstairs an' 'id in the 'all. Whilst she were takin' the first plate of food to one of them kids, he got 'is chance to poison the food. That's some of the poisoned food she, her very self, ett awhilst later because she were still hungry, even though she'd done ett some food earlier *before* he put the poison in it."

It's a sin to waste, I remembered her saying as she collected our plates. Then she ate some of the food with her claws. I could hear her and see her now.

"Roger heared the whole thing, 'air in the 'all next to the kitchen—or even right in the kitchen—'cause he crept around, just like one of 'er cats. He 'id in the basement past midnight, waitin' for the storm to break. When it finally did, them kids left the 'ouse, headin' for the dropoff point. When the water were calm, he boated back to Hoophole, from the east end, where the 'ouse were, in the dark. Them kids was walkin' back along the other shore on the other side of the oylet headed west. They never seed him; he never seed them, neither. But he knowed where they was headed. Roger, he waited back at Hoophole till the royt time, then boated back to the oylet, beachin' 'is boat exactly at the time he'd promised. Then he took them kids back. Do y' git it?"

"Yes," I said, "I think so. But what about the house? When did he burn it down?"

"He waited a few days fer that, to set 'er afire. He wanted it to be droy. That noyt, there'd been a helluva storm. Not just rain. Huge wind blowed up. Torrent, like a nor'easter. And lightnin'—lots of it. That's why people fer a long time believed lightnin' burnt the 'ouse down; that was before Roger Gaskill told my paw the truth. After Roger Gaskill died, the truth got out—understand?"

"Yes," I said. "I do, now. It's just a lot to take in."

"Whole story. 'At's it."

"I don't know," I said, my mind reeling.

"You don't know what?"

"I have to know for sure; I've got to ask . . . So, the kids didn't kill her, even accidentally? I mean, kill her even in the sense of letting her die accidentally? You know, by not doing everything possible to save her? They had nothing to do with her dying, one way or the other?"

At the same time, Hank Phillagraw and Rudy Casper cut their eyes to me, the same strange expression on their faces. Rudy Casper started to say something, then refrained.

Hank Phillagraw peered at me with squinted eyes as he blew another train of donut smoke into the air. Sipping from his stein, he continued to peer, and I watched as the rings drifted before my face. Then, one by one, they floated away as I waited for the answer.

33.

THERE WAS A MURDER

Hank Phillagraw snorted. "*What kids*?" Irritated, he flicked the rest of his cigarette into the fire.

"The kids you've been talking about. The four kids he took over in the boat."

"Of course not!" Rudy Casper said emphatically. "Where'd you get an inapposite idea like that? They were just a bunch of kids, probably college kids. What would have been a reason to kill anybody—a motive? Pfft! They weren't *crazy*—like Charles Manson and his family! Contribute to her death somehow? No. Let her die? No. She didn't die from a heart attack or old age. She was poisoned with cyanide. That's as deadly as you can get. There was nothing they could have done. They were just at the wrong place at the wrong time. There was a murder, but they had nothing to do with the killing. Maybe you've been watching too many of those forensic crime shows, Joe. Those four were just kids—I'm thinking college types. None too worldly-wise, either."

I felt my eyes tear up. I put my palm against my forehead and looked down at Henry. He looked up at me, his furry face smiling. "Here," I said, handing him off to his master. I stood up. "I gotta get some fresh air."

The two of them exchanged glances.

"Are you okay?" Rudy Casper said.

"Yeah." I stood. "I'll be back in a minute."

I walked out onto the front porch and stood against the post next to the stairs, looking out into the blackness of the street. Inhaling deeply, several times, I wiped my nose on my sleeve. Again inhaling the cold night air, I cleared my throat and walked back inside, my hands trembling.

I hadn't realized how dark it was *inside* the room. In the light of the waning fire, I walked straight to the fireplace, knelt, and stoked it with the poker hanging from the mantle. The fire blazed up, and I sat back down on the sofa, staring as it danced and crackled. Henry jumped off his master's lap, ran to my feet, and barked in his high-pitched voice until I picked him up. I could feel Rudy Casper staring at me, but he said nothing.

Finally, Hank Phillagraw said, "Yeah, like I done told you once't already, Roger Gaskill, her cousin, he murdered her, wantin' 'er money—the loot—the traysure. He thought, if them kids could get to the oylet, anyone could. Anyone could find the traysure. He had to git to it first."

I looked at the fire, then at Henry, the cockapoo.

Silence.

"Want some rum?" Rudy Casper asked me.

"No, thanks," I said.

"Well, *I* could do with a stein, don't mind if I do. Hank,

see if Ms. Walken would be so kind." Then he stood up. "Never mind—I'll take care of it. One for you, too, Mr. Phillagraw?" Rudy Casper said, accepting Hank Phillagraw's stein as it was held out to him.

Phillagraw took yet another cigarette from the pack in his shirt pocket, and we sat in silence as he smoked until Rudy Casper returned, a stein in each hand. Handing off the one with the pirate flags, he sat down. "This was Gaskill's thinking," he began. "'Why should all that money go to my cousin?—she'll never use it. She's never left the island, and she never will.' He said to himself, 'I do everything for her. Without me, she couldn't even live. She'd be dead. That treasure is nothing to her. I'm her cousin and Dr. Smiley's nephew. Since it's nothing to her since she doesn't want it, it ought to be mine. I earned it. Rightfully, it is mine.' That's the way he justified it."

"The treasure . . . ever illusive." Even to my ears, I sounded tired.

"Dr. Smiley's loot," Rudy Casper continued. "It was either all the money he'd made at Duke, helping set up the hospital in the thirties and giving people lobotomies, or bribe money he took from the Germans, though supposedly he didn't work for them for money. Some said it was gambling money, but nobody on Hoophole ever knew for sure—they just knew he was wealthy. Everybody always knows everything here."

He drank some rum-and-Coke. "He had to have stashed it somewhere, and considering his activities on the Isle of Cats, he'd never have deposited it in a bank; he was afraid it would be confiscated by the government. Everybody on Hoophole knew there was supposed to be treasure on the Isle of Cats, so of course, Roger Gaskill knew it, too. It's just that being Dr. Smiley's nephew, he was obsessed with the thought of it."

"Only they weren't no traysure," the boatman said. "But by the time he figured that out, he'd already killt 'is cousin and burnt 'er up in the 'ouse to hoyd the evidence."

"Still," said Rudy Casper, "there's a little more—right, Hank? Explain to Joe the part about how Miss Smiley *knew* she was going to be murdered."

My eyes jerked from the fire to Rudy Casper, then to Hank Phillagraw.

"Yep, she sure did." He flicked his cigarette butt into the fire. "Roger told Paw, who told me. She thought she might've heared somethin' in the hall and the basement, so she went around lookin' to check. She went downstairs. Roger was hidin' there, but she heared 'im, and she seed 'im, too. And she also seed the poison 'cause he'd done moved it, and it were out of place, at 'is feet. Roger, he knowed she'd seed 'im—and the poison, too—and he figured she knowed he'd poisoned the food when he had a chance. That were when she left the food in the kitchen the first time."

"But I don't understand—how could he hear everything that was going on, or so much of it, if he was hiding in the basement?"

"I thought I done explained that," Hank Phillagraw said impatiently. "He weren't in the basement *all* the time. Sometime in the hall, the stairs, the basement, even in the kitchen itself. Them kids might even 'ave 'eared 'im, too, despiten the storm. *She* did."

He pulled a cigarette from his shirt pocket and tamped it in the palm of his left hand. "Roger, he were eavesdroppin' on 'em, don't you see? He were eavesdroppin' and movin' around quick and sly—like a cat. He 'eared 'er kinda yell to them kids from the kitchen, 'I have friends.' Meaning the cats, Roger figured. But maybe she meant Roger hisself. Maybe the cats *and* Roger. Anyways, he hisself were creepin' around the place like a cat. It's jest that finally, in the basement, 'at's where she finally caught 'im—with the poison. Like a rat in a trap."

"So," I said, so tired I could hardly think, "she knew when those kids were there that she was being murdered *that night*?"

"Yep, sure did."

"Then, why did she let it happen?"

"'Cause *she* wanted it, too. She'd done been betrayed by someone she dearly trusted—her onliest friend in the world—and she were worn out. She'd been sick for about a year."

"Oh my God," I moaned.

"So, from Roger Gaskill's perspective," Rudy Casper said, "it was justified in his mind. From her perspective, it was self-murder, suicide, because she knew it was going to happen. And let it. After all, some thirty years earlier, she'd been betrayed by someone else she dearly trusted: her father. Now this—much worse—intentional."

I quietly groaned. So her death was a murder, after all—the one she'd alluded to so prominently in her predictions for each of us. But we'd had nothing at all to do with it, even through any act of omission. And our own murders? Was she predicting them, too? As awful as it was to acknowledge it, apparently so. But we'd escaped.

Again, I groaned. Then, exhausted, and before I realized what I was saying, I said out loud to myself, "And that's why she kept making the prediction . . . over and over again. Because it was imminent."

Dead silence ensued for several moments. Finally, Rudy Casper said, "Uhh . . . she kept predicting *what*?—murder? Did I hear that right? Is that what you said, Joe?"

He glanced at Hank Phillagraw, then turned his eyes back on me, the shadow of the flames dancing about on his ruddy face as he peered at me.

And that's when—and where—and how—I knew *he* knew: I had been one of the two star-crossed blond ones.

34.
REVELATION

I stood up. "Gentlemen, you'll have to excuse me. I'm so tired I can't stay awake another minute. I did some hiking today in the cold." I handed Henry to his master, then bowed slightly to Hank Phillagraw, and headed for the stairs.

The night before, I only slept a couple of hours, and my second night at the Queen Anne's Lodge was no better. I got up early the next morning to the squawking of seagulls, drank a cup of coffee, and ate a muffin alone downstairs, then drove to Rudy Casper's house.

Standing on his front porch, I knocked and heard Henry barking on the other side.

"Okay—look," Rudy Casper said as he opened the door, "if you're not going to level with me, I'd rather you not come in."

Henry scampered out, and wagging his whole body, stretched up to my knee. I picked him up. "Henry!" I said, holding him as he nuzzled my face.

"I think he likes you," his master said. "I don't know why."

"It's the nature of dogs; they're a good judge of character. Okay, I'll level with you."

His den was as inviting as the Queen Anne's Lodge should have been. The fire was warm and crackling—comforting after the cold wind outside—and the room reminded me of cabins in the North Carolina mountains. Spacious shelves stuffed with books and some framed photos lined both sides of the fireplace. I noticed a Bible, laced with bookmarks, on the coffee table.

"You've got a lot of books."

"I read, especially history. Lately, I've been reading about spies and traitors. That's how I knew about Aldrich Ames—and about how his mother, bless her innocent heart, used to live in Hickory. That's my life—reading. And when I'm not reading books, I read people. You're harder than most, with a lot of layers, but you're not as clever as you think you are."

"I'm not even as clever as *you* think I am," I said. "Far from it."

"Why don't you and my dog sit down?"

I set Henry on the floor, and taking off my hoods, sat in the upholstered chair, not the rocker with the book in it. Henry nestled down next to my feet. Rudy Casper offered coffee, but I declined.

I said, "Without your help, I'd never have found out the truth. I guess I owe you an explanation."

Rudy Casper looked at me from his rocking chair. "Yeah."

"First of all, my real name is Matt Goodheart," I began. "I live in Hickory, as you figured; I've lived there my whole life except for school. My wife is Celia. Since you figured out that I was one of those four kids, I might as well tell you that she also was one of them." Then I told him everything that had happened on the island that day and night thirty-three years ago. "So we flipped coins about whether to report Miss Smiley's death to the authorities and ended up leaving her dead body on the floor with the cats."

We talked about Miss Smiley for a while. He asked some questions, I answered them; I asked some questions, he answered them. After a few moments, he said, "I'm amazed to think that you were actually there that night and were directly involved. According to legend, you're dead. Legend has it all four of those kids suffered a terrible fate and died unnatural deaths, even though they did escape alive that night."

I didn't say anything.

"You've leveled with me," he continued, "to the extent that you have, so I'll do right by you, and I won't tell Hank Phillagraw or anyone else your name or what you've told me. I don't think it would serve any constructive purpose at this point in time, thirty-some years—"

"Thirty-three."

"Thirty-three years since it all happened. Besides, it's a legend now, and I think Hoopholers will be happier forever believing that the story of the Isle of Cats ends in a mystery."

He paused. "Do people really want to know what actually happened over at Roanoke Island four-and-a-half centuries ago to the settlers of the Lost Colony? Not really. They'd rather just believe they vanished after carving 'Croatoan' on a post. Hank Phillagraw will eventually tell everyone, one way or another, whatever it is he wants to tell—that you were 'one of the four'—

and that he, Hank Phillagraw himself, actually met you in real life and talked with you. He'll tell it however he wants to, but they're not going to learn your name from me—Joe."

"Thank you, Rudy."

"You're welcome," he replied simply.

Then I said, "Speaking of legendary stories, this thing about the Isle of Cats as a legend . . . You and Hank Phillagraw have filled me in on the facts, and I think I now understand them, but what I still don't understand is the other part, the legendary part." I added, "I know I'm asking you a lot of questions, but this is my big chance to finally get the answers."

"Fair enough," Rudy said, rocking his chair a few times. "But turnabout is fair play. After I answer your question, I've got a couple for you."

"Fair enough," I nodded.

"Okay, here we go. The Legend of the Isle of Cats includes everything that Hank and I told you last night. The island is cursed. Nothing good ever happens there. A traitor to his own country owned it. His daughter, a soothsayer, died in their house with the very cats he'd experimented on. The last four people ever to make the mistake of going to that forbidden place"—he paused and said parenthetically, "I'm looking at one of them right now," then completed the sentence—"had their lives ruined and died awful, unnatural deaths. The soothsayer didn't just die in the house; she was murdered. By her own cousin, her best and only friend. Then the murderer burned the house to the ground with her in it. It was a house of horrors. A place of darkness. The whole island is a place of darkness, with a heart of darkness. Just talking about the Legend brings shivers to the bones. That's why people turn away if you mention it: they don't want to talk about it. Much less go there. Nobody does. Ever."

I couldn't help but say, "Except me."

"Yes, you and a few others. However, there's sometimes more to the Legend than all that. Some people embellish it by saying that the government keeps spies and traitors imprisoned on the island."

I said, "Your friend, the bartender at the King Charles Tavern, told me that very thing—and that they were the worst of the worst."

Rudy nodded. "They're not just traitors and spies—they're killers, too. Some say they compete with the killer cats for food and control of the island—and that they all compete with the elements for life on a cursed place—and so no one ever goes there, or if anyone ever does, they never escape, or if they do, like those four kids, their lives are haunted forever by the curse, one way or another. *That's* why nobody ever goes there—no one with any sense."

With a faint smile, he added, "Present company excepted, of course."

Then he continued, "But as we know, Roger Gaskill did go to the island, over and over again. Until he went crazy with lusting for the money, then he murdered his own cousin, who was supposed to be his friend. And obviously, we know about the four kids. They were the only other ones ever to go to the Isle, and their lives were ruined because of it. They died unnatural deaths."

"Just goes to show how you can't necessarily believe a legend."

Rudy rocked back and forth a few times. "But there's a part

I *like* to believe: the Legend also has it, that if a person searches hard enough—and perseveres in the race, so to speak, and never gives up—finally he will win the race and find the treasure. It's out there, but it's buried, and it has to be found.

"Roger Gaskill believed *that* part of the Legend to the point that he became obsessed with it. So obsessed that he became willing to do anything, even kill a person, to find what he longed for. He searched for it so hard, his search became destructive, even destroying human life, and ended in evil and failure. He had the wrong ideas and looked in the wrong places. I like to believe this part of the Legend—about the treasure—but only in a positive way. Not in the way Roger Gaskill believed." He stopped rocking.

"So you believe there's treasure buried on the island?"

"I believe there's treasure buried someplace, but a person has to search for it with a right and positive spirit. If he does, the treasure's out there, waiting to be found."

He stopped talking, and I said, "I think that's why I'm here now—I'm searching for it." Then I added: "Miss Smiley said I would, but actually I'd been searching for it before she entered the picture, and there was nothing wrong with that. It was a *good* thing."

Again, he rocked. "That's good to know. I'm glad to hear it. I hope I've helped in some way, at least a little. I guess we're all involved in that search—sometimes a life-long journey—in different ways."

As I thought about that, he said, "Now, my turn for a question."

"Sure, go ahead."

"What do you do, now—I mean, for a living?"

That could have been a sensitive question, but Henry moved against my feet, like Pip used to do, then got up and looked at me. I picked him up and held him in my lap, giving me time to think about my answer. "I do a number of things: renovate old houses—and build furniture."

"So you're not a writer?"

"Only as a hobby. I guess I'm a wannabe—I write and stop, write and stop—but if I ever finish the book I'm working on, I'll send you a copy. The hold-up is the searching thing: I'm searching for something, which I know is..." I paused, oddly surprised at myself. "*God...I need God!*"

Rudy leaned back in his rocker, clearly somewhat taken aback, and proclaimed enthusiastically, "Well, God wouldn't hurt a bit!"[2]

Silence for a few moments as my revelation and Rudy's response resonated and sank in.

Finally, still a little surprised at myself, I replied, "And I want to find Him in such a way that I can speak and write about Him honestly."

He looked me straight in the eyes. "Then don't give up—don't give up searching."

I said nothing as I thought about that and let that thought sink in, as well.

Then I asked, "And what about you?"

He smiled. "I live on this island with my dog and my books." He paused then added, "I was born here, went to State, married Carlie, who was from Raleigh—and we lived there thirty years."

"What happened?"

He looked away. "She died. Cancer."

"I'm sorry," I said, thinking how fortunate I was to have Celia.

"Then I moved back here."

"Isn't it lonely? I don't think I could stand it full-time."

"I've been lonely since the day she died," he said. "But in that way, I'd be just as lonely in Raleigh. And have to put up with a lot of traffic. Here I live with my books." Again he smiled. "And God." He paused. "Besides, I actually like the islanders—I'm one of them though they aren't terribly sociable. And I've got two children and three grandchildren—all in-state—and they visit me pretty faithfully."

"And Henry," I added, looking down at my feet.

Still smiling, he handed me a four-by-six framed photo from the table beside his chair.

"Carlie."

"She's very pretty."

"Yes, she was. You sure you don't want something to drink or eat? Coffee? Cereal?"

"Well, maybe I will. Just as long as I make the ten-o'clock ferry."

"Cornflakes okay?"

"Just fine."

"Milk and sugar?"

"Just milk."

He got up and went to the kitchen, Henry at his heel. I walked over to the bookcase to the left of the fire and looked at the two shelves of framed photos. Carlie showed up again and again, sometimes with Rudy, sometimes with other people. Other photos I guessed were those of his children and grandchildren.

One photo really caught my eye because I thought I recognized one of the four girls in the picture. The four of them were standing side by side in sleeveless cocktail dresses as if dressed for a party, their arms around each other. He came back in with a mug of coffee in one hand, a bowl of cereal in the other. Setting them on the coffee table between the fireplace and the chairs, he joined me at the bookcase.

One by one, starting with Carlie, he named every person who was a member of his family.

"You're very blessed," I said, "and that girl right there"—I pointed—"the one standing beside Carlie, I went to high school with her."

"You're kidding! You two were in high school together?"

"I'm almost positive it's the same person; she looks really familiar. I didn't know her well—she was quiet—but I had a class or two with her, and I remember she was a really nice person." I thought a moment. "Audrey?"

"Yes."

"Now that I think back on it, we were on the newspaper staff together. She was quiet and nice—and smart."

"Wow," Rudy said, "it just goes to show what a small world it is. She and Carlie and the other two girls there were suitemates freshman year at State; I was a senior."

"Where is she now?"

"Last I heard, she was in New York City, a good position with a publishing house—a famous one, one of those everyone's heard of. After she finished two years at State, she transferred to Columbia and never looked back."

"Wow," I said. "She's never been to a single one of our class reunions, and no one ever mentions her. Ironic how things work out. Or don't."

"You sound a little wistful."

I looked at my watch and sat down again. "Thanks for the breakfast," I said as I ate the cereal. We talked some more—a little about Celia and our children, but mostly about Rudy and *his* family and *his* life.

I was glad we never got to the recent part of my life: the State Senator and lawyer part, the bankrupt part, not to mention the part about the other three "kids"—concert pianist, also bankrupt now; country-western star; university department head. I'd just mumbled something about the four of us living fairly ordinary lives, despite the Isle of Cats. I figured if he wanted to know the rest of the story—at least about me since he knew my name—and Celia, since he knew hers—he could find out on his own.

There was another reason I didn't want to bring him up-to-date. It wasn't just the bankrupt-failure thing; it was also that there was no real way a stranger would comprehend the effect Miss Smiley's words had on Celia, Jennie, Croom, and me over the last nearly three-and-a-half decades. You could tell a person that the old woman's predictions had followed us and come true, but what would be the point?

You could say, "I just found out she put a curse—a 'star-cross'—on Jennie and me that apparently"—Yes? No?—"affected our relationship for years," but what would be the point? How could Rudy Casper possibly understand the nature of that old woman's effect? I didn't understand it myself, so how could a stranger?

Right now, it looked like the crowning achievement of my more than five-and-a-half decades on earth was my being one of "The Isle of Cats Four."

"Gosh," he'd said after I finished my Isle of Cats expose, "so I'm actually sitting with one of *the* kids—thirty-three years later—right here in my own den."

I left it at that.

I did go to my SUV, though, to fetch my only mementoes, my only tangible evidence, of The Legend of the Isle of Cats. In front of the fireplace, Rudy looked at them. "Interesting," he mused. "Three of the plaques are quotations from Shakespeare. The fourth is written in Latin. So what do you think?"

"I haven't had time," I said.

Now, glancing at my watch again, I stood up and put on my hoods. "Thanks for everything, Rudy. I know Celia would really like Henry."

"You can't take him, Joe."

I picked Henry up to pet him one last time. He snuggled into my face with his cold, wet nose, and I gave him a huge smile.

Rudy said, "So you *can* smile."

I used to smile a lot. I handed Henry to his master. Showing me to the porch, Rudy shook my hand, then tipped an imaginary hat to me as I opened the car door.

"Don't give up the search," he said. "Stay in the race. Win it!"

I headed out in time to catch the ten-o'clock ferry to the mainland.

35.

ON THE ROCKS

Once on board, I kept checking my cell phone. About halfway to the mainland, I finally got service again, but the battery was all but dead, so I texted Celia: "Battery almost dead, am on the ferry from Hoophole back to the mainland. Will call you tonight. I love you."

Sitting in my SUV, my duffle bag on the front seat beside me, I reached in and pulled out the four plaques. I sifted through them, one after another, like a pack of cards.

As the calligraphy in places was scratched and worn, the plaques were sometimes difficult to read, but one of them read: "There is a tide in the affairs of men, which taken at the flood leads on to fortune. Omitted, all the voyage of their life is bound in shallows and miseries. On such a full sea, are we now afloat. And we must take the current when it serves, or lose our ventures."

Another plaque read: "If you prick us, do we not bleed? If you tickle us do we not laugh? If you poison us, do we not die?

And if you wrong us, shall we not revenge?"

The last of the Shakespearian plaques read: "The fault, dear Brutus, is not in our stars, but in ourselves that we are underlings."

The fourth plaque, in Latin, puzzled me. Bearing smudges and imperfections, it was the hardest to decipher, but as best I could tell, the words were: "Ad extremis," which I interpreted as "at the end of," and "terra," which I figured was "earth." Those words I surmised to mean "at the end of the earth." "Columna" looked like "column" or "columns." I'd have to look up the other words later. Maybe that's what the plaque wanted me to do since another one of the words was "thesaurus."

I put the plaques back in my duffle bag and, as I did so, accidentally touched the gun. It was still loaded. Looking around before I took it out to empty the bullets, I was startled by a knock on my side window. I jerked around to see a long red scar on the man's left cheek and a patch covering his left eye. In an instant, it flashed through my mind: Bebe and I, as children at Stately Oaks, a man pushing open the front door, then Stanza ordering us to the kitchen as she drew a knife. I put my hand back in the duffle bag and rolled down my window.

"Excuse me," he said. "Would you happen to have four quarters for a dollar—for the drink machine?"

"Uhh, sure." I opened the console between my seat and the passenger seat. "Just a second." Inside the console was a change holder, and I handed him four quarters for his dollar bill.

"Thanks so much," he smiled. "My wife wants a Pepsi."

Embarrassed, I said, "No problem," and relieved to see him walking away, I emptied the gun and locked it in the glove compartment.

Then I got out of my car and walked out on deck. I stood at the bow of the boat, leaning on the railing, breathing in the salt air and sea mist, watching as the waves crashed onto the deck. Yesterday I'd hiked the length of an island and back in near-freezing weather, with rain, snow, and ice in my face, and now it felt almost warm out here.

In about ninety minutes, the ferry docked on the mainland.

I knew the drive back to the beach house, at best another hour-and-forty-five minutes, would fully test my lack of sleep. But I made the trip even longer by stopping. At the halfway point to Morehead City was the only store en route, a mom-n-pop, where I pulled in and asked for a cell phone charger. They did not sell them. In Morehead City, I made three stops at convenience stores. No luck. I'd have to get home and charge the phone there.

By the time I got to the beach house, my body was exhausted, but my mind was racing.

Don't give up the search, Rudy said. *Stay in the race. Win it*!

A warm air mass had blown in from the south, and the temperature on Bogue Banks was breaking sixty degrees. Despite the spring-like, balmy air, fog hung over the beach so that I could hear the roar of the ocean but couldn't see it. My phone was dead, and now I couldn't find the freaking charger anywhere. I searched my duffle bag, my clothes, the house, retracing my steps. Maybe, in the state of mind I was in when I left home, I'd failed to pack it.

The more I searched for it thinking about Celia—concerned about what *she* might be thinking—the more agitated I became.

At least I'd texted her and told her I'd call her tonight. By that time, I'd have gotten a charger someplace and charged my phone.

Irritated with myself, I set the phone on the coffee table and went to stand on the balcony at the railing, looking out to sea. I was so tired I felt like a zombie, not even caring enough to take a shower or shave. Reminding myself of Ben Gunn, I turned and went inside to the kitchen, then returned to the railing with a handful of bread. I watched as one white gull sailed high in the distance. Breaking off a piece of bread, I threw it into the air and waited. Another piece. Then another.

Then, sure enough, fast as light, he was swooping down to me, catching the bread as I tossed it—rarely missing, his dives extreme. Then more gulls. Twenty, thirty of them. Pip had loved to chase after them on the beach.

Again, I thought of Celia. Then of Croom and Jennie . . . of how I'd left them, our guests, without saying good-bye . . . and the old woman telling our fortunes in the dark, then dying in the house with her cats surrounding her, eating her face. Now I understood that she *knew* she was going to die, poisoned by her last friend, her own cousin.

So all these years, we'd wondered if we'd been complicit in her death—letting her die or worse, and never reporting—now I, at least, knew someone had killed her. We'd also wondered about "the murder" that might occur later in our own lives; I thought maybe it had been Pip. Apparently, we'd seen it already that night in the house!

The ramifications of these revelations went on and on, including the fact that three of the four of us might have been murder victims ourselves. When Miss Smiley left the kitchen carrying a plate for "one of the kids," *that's* when Roger Gaskill poisoned the food. If we four had eaten the food Miss Smiley brought us, the last three of us to be served would have died with her in the house, leaving only one of us alive to deal with the aftermath.

As I threw more bread to the flock, I thought how graceful they were, these white birds, so competent, free, yet so in tune with their surroundings. To be *free, yet also in tune with one's surroundings* . . .

I turned, stepping back into the great room after the flock had eaten all the bread. They continued to circle for a while, some calling out to me to come back, then flew off.

Annie Jameson, whom I had trusted, had stabbed me in the back, robbing my family and me. And the people who to me were almost like extended family—my employees—would soon be unemployed.

I thought about Bert, my firstborn, my Eagle Scout, my straight-A student, the one who never gave me or Celia a moment's trouble. He had been destined to take over the family business, continue the legacy, make us proud—just as I had made my father proud.

Now I'd lost all that. I could blame Annie, but the judgment calls had all been mine. I was the one who'd trusted her enough to make her controller and then my de facto manager of day-to-day operations. Like grandfather, like grandson: Beergard had lost the inheritance *his* father had given him; I would soon lose the birthright my father had given me. Where was God in all this? Where was God when you really needed Him? And I did need Him.

Too many dark thoughts were crowding my mind. Something else I needed was sleep, something I'd lost over three days. But I knew if I lay down, my churning brain would keep me awake. If I walked down to The Rocks, I could clear my head—then I'd sleep.

At the beach, I collected some paraphernalia of the sea: a conch shell and various pieces of heavy salvage from ships lost at sea. My favorite was a small anchor encrusted with shells. I lined up my treasures on the beach and speculated which ones my children, when they were young, would have chosen as their favorites—and why.

I knew what I was doing, to time it just right. The sun went down at a quarter past five, and it took a good forty-five minutes to walk to The Rocks if the wind was against you—and it was. I wanted to time it just right.

I began walking alongside the foamy tide, with the fog rolling in from the sea. At times, the waves appeared as only a gray roar. Ahead, I saw a man with a black Lab. I observed them as we approached each other, the man throwing a ball as far as he could throw it out into the surf, the dog running in, then swimming after it and bringing it back, obedient and loyal. His master responded by stooping to pat the dog's head, neck, and sides. I thought of Pip, longingly.

After passing a few other people, I saw The Rocks straight ahead. On the horizon were fishing boats—boats full of fishermen, men who made their living from the sea. I saw the light from the lighthouse, guarding Cape Lookout. Light—no light. Light—no light. To my left were small cliffs of sand, cut out by the surf with each nor'easter. On top of the cliffs were sea oats, and back beyond that, the fort.

I kept walking. The surf was often more beautiful in the winter than in the summer, but today the fog obscured much of it.

Approaching The Rocks, I was surprised to see a small boat beached above the tide, surprised to find that there was someone else on the boulders—a man in a hood, fishing—but I couldn't see his face, and we didn't speak. My intent wasn't to talk—it was to get as far out on the line of the rocks as possible, as far as I could go into the sea. His intent was to fish.

The Rocks were slippery. As I proceeded, stepping precisely about the slick-algaed surface, I looked back at the fisherman. He cast, and I turned again to the sea, stepping forward one rock at a time. I looked back as he cast again, the waves from the inlet crashing up around me. Off in the distance to my right, to the southwest, the fog was lifting, and I could see a great ship passing by, decorated in elaborate rigging—not a pleasure boat, but a fishing boat. In front of me, the ocean, in unruly whitecaps, stretched on forever.

To my right, the horizon ran in a straight line, and above the horizon, the fog had lifted so I could see the sun moving downward, just perceptibly enough as it inched so close to the line that the shortening of the distance between the two could actually be measured by the eye. I looked away because the sun was a huge ball of bright orange light. The sky around it was orange and purple and rose, these rays emblazoning the blue background like a fan.

The shoreline, in that direction, was also brilliant orange. A wave crashed up around me, soaking my pants legs and splashing onto my face, the water salty and cold. Again, I looked at the sun, marveling, then turned away to behold the vastness of the sea. Here, I stood for some time, for it was safe. Then I glanced to my left, back toward the inlet—and the harbor where the fog still hung. The fisherman had disappeared.

The orange sun was fading to rose as the great ball of light had become a red half-moon, a yellow halo riding its outer rim. Over the ocean in the direction of the lighthouse, seagulls flew—and not far from me, a flock of them swooped in a circle about the waves, then, swooped down, their beaks plunging into the water.

Now and again, a pelican flew by, picturesque with its distended pouch full of fish. In the tide, sandpipers minced their way, to and fro, about the sand. As the water rolled onto shore, far down the beach, it was shimmering orange, then, closer to me, it turned to blue—metallic, scintillescent blue.

The sky, now, had changed color. The flecks of orange and purple were gone, and the whole fan had become a peacock display of rose petals in concentric half-circles, the rose-red sun its epicenter.

I looked back, searching the harbor. Still enshrouded in fog despite the great beauty of the scene to the southwest, it reminded me that knowing the truth about Miss Smiley's death made me feel in a way tricked, cheated by all those years of living unnecessarily under a cloud—all those years of not knowing the truth and sometimes imagining the worst.

The waves continued to crash about me, the sound of the breaking water reminding me of the roar of a train as if I were glued to the tracks as the train barreled down on me. Many times

I had stood on these rocks at sunset and felt close to God—sometimes with my children, sometimes with Pip—but as the sun sank now, I just felt full to bursting from exhaustion and my fogged-in, restless thoughts.

Once more, I looked back, searching again for the harbor in the fog. *Don't give up the search,* he said. *Stay in the race. Win it!*

As I stood there, the saltwater splashing about me on the slippery rocks, I looked down at my feet as a wave again crashed over them. The tide was moving in. I took a long step back toward the shore, stretching from rock to rock. Then another long step. And another. And another.

I hesitated, then moved again—and slipped and fell, landing on my tailbone. The pain that shot into the base of my spine was so acute I saw, quickly, blackness and stars—then I hit my head—and the stars faded and were extinguished, and there was only blackness.

. . .

. . .

. . .

.

36.
THE FISHER

Water was all around me as I sank, deeper and deeper. Drowning, I plunged. I was being pulled toward a black hole surrounded by a swirling ring of fire. This abyss became a long tunnel, and I was pulled downward through this black space. This would be my inescapable death, the place of the end, my life and all my being snuffed, extinguished like a computer with both its memory and power gone—forever. Nothingness.

§

But my direction changed, and I moved upward in the tunnel, out of the swirling ring of fire and upward in the water until a hand reached out for me. A voice said, "Do not fear. Do not be afraid."

He pulled me to the surface and got me to shore.

Then we went to higher ground, where I stood and watched, transfixed, as He transfigured into light. Growing brighter and brighter, the light became so brilliant it shone white[3] yet did not hurt my eyes at all. Intensely dazzling, it was the most beautiful light imaginable. I wasn't afraid; instead, I was drawn to it, warm and peaceful, perfect in its brilliance.[4]

The light asked me if I wanted to go with Him—to be with joy and peace forever with Him and the others—and I said, "Yes, I do. I want to very much. I want to go with you[5], and I want to be with the others."

I felt sure that my father was there, and Celia's mother, and Mrs. McGregor—and Pip in personality. I could feel the presence of all four of them, but of course, I wanted to be sure, and I wanted to see them and be with them. So I asked Him who the others were.

He answered, "Some you know, some you have loved and who have loved you. Also, great multitudes of beings you never knew or could have known, and which are different from what you expect. You must come with me to find out who is there."

I hesitated, not speaking, so He asked, "Why do you consider yourself unworthy—not fit to follow me?"

I did not answer—I could not answer, so the light said, "Matthew, Matthew, you have been worried and upset about many things, but only one thing is needed. You must choose what is better, and it will not be taken away from you."[6]

Then he asked, "So who do you say I am?"

I knew the truth, and I said, "You are the Christ, the Son of God, the creator of all things. My only hope, the only means of my salvation."

The light replied, "Who you say I am is true. And it is also true that you want to go with me, and yet I know you feel unworthy, still." He waited. "I want you to tell me why."

In awe—and shame—I could not speak. And regardless, I knew He knew the answer anyway. But He waited, so finally I said, "Sin. Sin is the reason I am unworthy to go with you."

The light replied, "Again, what you say is true. It is sin that you and all the other members of the human race hold in common. All were born sinful since the fall of the first parents."

I looked at the light, and the voice continued to speak: "Everyone has something in his or her past, and in his or her present. So does every tribe, every Nation. You have enough faith to have gotten you this far. So I saved you. You could have gone to the place of the dead. And you have recognized me—and acknowledged me. And yet you hesitate."

I knew the light knew everything about me, inside and out. I knew He knew my heart, my soul, my strength and my mind. And I knew that He loved me, in spite of all that He knew. If I'd never been certain of that before, I was now.

He said, "Your hungry soul, your searching mind want to know many things."

I said, "I have searched my whole life."

The light said, "That is true, but I was mostly elusive to you. You searched, but you had not found, and in certain ways, you had fallen farther away from me than ever. I had to let you fail in a worldly sense so that you could succeed in your search. I had to let you drown. I had to let you suffer so that you would be brought closer to me and feel more empathy for others. My love makes me want you close and dependent."

I did so love the light!

He said, "I know that there have been times when you have wondered, where was God that night? Where was God in the darkness? In the dark night of the Isle of Cats, in the dark night Pip was killed—when Celia's mother died. When your father died. When Jennie's son died. When she almost died. Now, when Annie, who claimed to be your friend and love your children, has thrust a knife into your back. Now, with the imminent loss of all your earthly treasure.

"Yes, many times you have asked yourself: Where was God? Where was I, the Light? And the answer is this: I was with you. I would never leave you or desert you.[7] Nothing can separate you from the love of God which is in me.[8] But because you didn't know me, you didn't recognize me, though I was with you."

He knew everything about me, inside and out. He said again, "Your hungry soul, your searching mind want to know many things. For example, you struggle with this question, which to you is a mystery: you want to know why bad things happen to good people—even worse: why God, if He is all-loving, allows evil to occur."

He was right. Of course I wanted to know the answer to that question, and the light explained, "God did not—and does not—create evil. Everything that God has created—and creates—is good. Evil comes from the corruption of good—and good things. God never *wills* evil. But He allows it, because evil, along with good, can result from his children having Free Will, the ability to think and make decisions. When that freedom is not grounded in moral responsibility, my child, freedom is destroyed and is replaced by enslavement.[9] This is Truth for the individual and also for the masses, the Nations."

Then the light said, "Matthew, if God had wanted to create automatons, He could have. Instead, He chose to create people—including you—whom He loves. That is why He sent me: to save people from themselves and the universality of their sin. That is why I was crucified, died—and rose again."

In brilliance, the light shone before me. Then He said, "But knowledge is not the basis for being here with me. Grace is. And the faith that goes with it. I am the provider of grace and faith. They are gifts from me."

He said, "If being in my presence, now, were based on sinlessness or merit, you would not be here. Nor would anyone else who is with me. All forgiveness is based on grace. Salvation is based on grace."

Again, the light said, "Everybody has something in his or her life for which they need to be forgiven. And something for which they need to forgive others. Upon their deaths, you treated Pip better than you treated 'that old woman,' as you sometimes refer to her. You were haunted for a while by Pip's death, partly because of guilt, but recovered. You were also haunted by Miss Smiley's death, partly because of guilt, but you are still not over it. Her predictions are not what primarily haunt you. The problem is not so much her words; it's that you left her body exposed to be devoured by animals, knowing it was wrong. That was your sin and the source of your guilt. It is not about killing her, which you did not do."

Still, my silence continued, and He said, "You've asked yourself how anyone could be so cold as to hit a person's dog in front of that person's face—your dog Pip—and kill her and drive away, heartless and unfeeling. But you watched a person die in front of your eyes, then walked away from the body, not so much as covering it, not owning up, and leaving her exposed to be eaten by animals."

I hung my head, ashamed. I could not look up. I could not face the light.

"And your more general sin?" He asked. "I will tell you. You have worshipped false gods instead of me. And I will tell you that all of those gods taken together amount to nothing. All your successes came to nothing. And Matthew, was not Miss Smiley at times more your spiritual guide than I was?

"What has she done for you?—filled you with anxiety, emptiness, failure, and guilt? I, on the other hand, only offer you victory and eternal life through my grace. And the victory I have to offer is sure and certain."

Judged, I stood before the light, looked up and asked, "What must I do to be forgiven?"

The light answered me. "Matthew, my child, still you do not understand. You have paid for your sin partially through your guilt and suffering, but that partial payment is never complete—not for you or anyone. Penance never is. But because of God's love and mercy, I have paid for your sin in full, through my death and resurrection. You must accept that—and believe. You must believe your own profession of faith in me. Then you will be able to forgive yourself. And after that, you will be able to forgive others."

He paused, burning brilliantly bright. "You need to forgive Miss Smiley for what she did to you and for what you *think* she did to you. And you need to forgive the others in your life for what you consider to be their betrayals. You think you've been betrayed, but the real betrayal is betraying me by not forgiving others for what you think they've done to you."

All I could say was: "I'm not good enough to be here."

Still patient, He replied, "As I have said, no one is. Yet many great multitudes of beings are with me. Your faith has gotten you this far because I died for the sake of your soul, as I did for theirs. My grace is for all those who believe. My grace is for the beings I choose. Stand before me as a child: helpless, dependent, bringing nothing to the table—hopeless, except for me. That is what it means to be child-like in your faith. I am the only means of expiation, of salvation, the only key to hope. And again, I assure you, the victory I offer is sure and certain—and eternal."

More than ever, I was drawn to the light, which emanated perfect love. "I want to follow you and be with you forever." But a part of me lingered.

So he said, "Then tell me why you hesitate, even though you long to go with me."

"What about Celia?" I asked. "What about Ted and my other children? What about the things in my life that are broken, the things I need to fix? I want to go with you, to be with you forever, but I don't want to leave Celia and the others behind, with things the way they are."

He admonished me: "A part of you thinks *you* accomplished all the accomplishments you've had on earth. But I'm the one who created it all. And I can take it all away. I can take what I give, and I can give what I take. In the twinkling of an eye. I am the sovereign Lord."

Then the light said I could go back because it wasn't for

myself that I asked. "Do not fear," He said. "Do not be afraid. You will have the insight to do the right thing. Walk with me, confident and humble, and you will be inspired to know what to say. After all, it's not so much that you found me, but that I found you. I was always there for you—though you did not know it—carrying you when you couldn't walk on your own."

I began to float, and He said to me in parting, "You can do all things through me, and I will never leave you or forsake you. Nothing can separate you from my love."

Then I floated away. In the radiant air, looking down, I saw my old, restless self, down there[10] on the beach as I lay at the foot of The Rocks. And I looked down on my bodily self as a hooded figure hovered over me.

I wanted to go back to the light, and to the others who were with Him because I knew without a single doubt that they were full of love and peace and joy, and because I wanted to see who they were and be with them—and especially because the light was all-good and loving and held nothing against me at all for anything I'd ever done or not done. I was sure of that. I wanted to be back there, with Him, among the others—except that Celia was still on earth, and I felt bad to leave her because she needed my help and love, and I hadn't said goodbye.

He knew everything about me—and understood it all—without my even telling him. And it broke my heart to be pulling away from Him[11] as I floated over my own self and looked down and now saw the gray-hooded man over my pale body, there on the shore.

Cold and soaking wet on the beach, I first felt Pip licking my face. When I opened my eyes, all I saw was the sky. Where was she hiding now? Ah, it was only the tide brushing and leaving the side of my face.

Night was coming on, joining the fog.

I didn't move. Looking into the sky, I tried to think—where was I? What had happened? I shivered.

Lifting my head, I saw about thirty or forty feet in front of me the line of rocks I had climbed, stretching from up the beach to my left, into the ocean on my right. Between the rocks and me, a small boat was beached above the tide. As the tide edged up my way, I propped myself on my elbows, looking about. I saw, about a hundred-and-fifty feet away, the same fisherman, casting from the rock farthest out in the ocean. I wanted to sit up, but propping on my elbows was all I could manage. As I regarded him, he turned, glanced at me, then returned to his fishing.

I continued to stare at him, so cold my teeth were chattering, and as I did so, I saw his dark form against the fading sky move slightly. Then he stepped, one rock to the next, as I had done, but unlike me, he did not fall. After he reached the far end of the line of rocks, opposite the ocean, he stood for a while, then stepped down onto the beach, but because it was getting dark, I could not see his face. It was odd; he stepped down to the sand and stood there—in front of The Rocks—his fishing rod held vertically beside him, a hood about his face.

I felt drawn to him. He began walking toward me, slowly—my heart now pounding—his approach at once awesome and repellent. Fearsome yet welcome. Paralyzed by confusion, my heart pounded harder. I stood as he slowly drew close.

"You fell on the rocks into the sea. I saw you fall and go under. You were drowning. I fished you out and dragged you to this safe place on the shore."

I was amazed and could not move or speak.

Finally, I said, "Thank you. For saving me."

"Can I take you some place in my boat?"

"No," I replied. "Not now. I need to go home."

"You can get home on your own from here?"

"Yes," I said. "I can get home."

I wanted to say—or do—something more, but I couldn't.

Then he turned slowly and walked away toward the skiff, hood covering his head, rod at his side. He stepped into his boat and rowed out into the sea. Shivering, I watched as he and the boat merged into the darkness and fog, then disappeared.

I headed back down the beach away from The Rocks, taking the longest strides I could take and choking back tears.

§

As I unlocked the door to the house, my head was spinning. I had been hurt, yet saved, too. Walking into the bathroom, I looked in the mirror. Blood was dripping down my right temple, and a knot had arisen on my head. Removing my wet clothes, I discovered scrapes and bruises down the right side of my body. How he fished me out and got me safely to shore, I could only imagine. Still shaken by what had happened, I showered in hot water, dressed, and walked into the front room. I couldn't stay seated, though, because of the pain in my tailbone.

Opening the door to the balcony, I stood at the rail and looked into the night sky—the diamond stars sprinkled on the black vastness of the universe. Hardly more than an hour earlier—

it seemed like forever—I'd seen other stars and descended into a different black space. Then I'd been saved from the sea and led to a place of love, peace, and joy. I'd felt the essence of death, but had no fear of it at all, now, because I knew what it was—what it meant—where I'd been—and I would gladly go there again.

Now I closed my eyes, bowed my head, and for several long moments, remained in awe of the night, in awe of the day I'd just had, and in awe of being alive. Then I prayed a deep, humble prayer of gratitude to God, thanking Him for saving me. I knew I'd spent a time in an infinitely better place but also knew I'd been allowed to come back for a reason—a *purpose*.

When I opened my eyes, I gazed again into the countless twinkling stars. I now knew personally who had created every one of them—and me—and everyone and everything else—and I knew He was with me, now.

I'd searched and searched and not found, but I'd stayed in the race and kept searching. I'd stayed in the race, and it was not so much that I found Him as that He found me.

Yes, I'd won the race, but it was He who had carried me, not my own self; and I had Him to thank, not my own self—and now, I couldn't wait for tomorrow.

PART FIVE

THE LIGHT IN THE DARKNESS

37.

STRAIGHT TALK AT OLDE TOWN

The next morning, the sun shone brightly into the great room, the sky was crystal blue, the sea calm. When I opened one of the glass doors, predictably there came up to me the gentle, perfect rhythm of the surf.

I was a new man.

Last night, I'd walked inside from the balcony to call Celia, but remembering my cell phone was dead, I'd walked into the bedroom and lay down. I fell asleep instantly and slept for twelve hours. Now, I searched for the phone charger until I found it buried in an inner zipped pocket of my duffle bag. Had I placed it there for safekeeping, or was I just addle-brained when I left home? Regardless, I was able to call home by the time I'd showered and shaved.

"Celia . . ." I said.

"Hey, Matt." Her voice was receptive. And relieved. "I've

been worried."

"Celia, the most amazing thing has happened. I want to tell you about it."

"Please—I want you to."

"But I don't want to tell you over the phone. I want to tell you in person. If I leave soon, I can be home in seven hours."

"No," she said. "I'll meet you halfway."

When she walked in the door of our condo in Raleigh, it was the best sight I'd ever seen—this side of Heaven. Hugging as if we'd been apart for a year, when our eyes met, she burst into tears. "I missed you so much—and I was very worried." She raised her hand and touched my head.

"What *happened* to you?"

"I've got so much to tell you."

We talked about my slipping on the rocks, nearly drowning and dying, and what happened afterward, the fisherman saving me.

"Matt, I don't know what you're more excited about—being fished out of the sea and not drowning—or sensing you were dying and going to Heaven."

"Heaven!—that's the best thing for sure! But being given another chance here on earth—starting with you—that's an incredible gift I'm truly grateful for."

The morning after the Cotillion—Sunday, December 9th before Croom and Jennie left for Dallas—Celia had apologized to them, saying, "Matt was called out of town on a business emergency."

Now, I apologized to Celia for packing up and leaving her

so abruptly.

"It's okay." Then she surprised me with an apology of her own: "I'm sorry I left you alone the night Pip was killed. I've been meaning to say that for a long time. I should have. I was wrong not to."

I felt tears in my eyes. "Thank you for telling me now. It means a lot. I really felt alone."

"That was *my* version of packing up and leaving. It was the best I could do under the circumstances—and it wasn't very good. I let you down."

"So we're both human and have made mistakes. But the past is past"—my voice cracked—"and all is made new."

"Matt, I love you so much." She began to cry, too.

After our tears, we talked about the Isle of Cats—and, finally, our finances. She could tell that something about me had changed. "You're so full of life," she said, "yet serene."

She insisted I go to the doctor, which I did, receiving a clean bill of health. "That's quite a knot," he said, "but no concussion." He gave me a special back pillow to sit on to protect my spine.

Over the next two days, we went to visit Elisa, Bert, and Caroline, all living in Raleigh. I hugged each of them a little tighter, a little longer, and told them with a new intensity how much I loved them.

When we got home, I spent the whole day with Ted. He and I made a pact we'd work together to get him back in school, then we went to the Y to celebrate. Getting up a game with some guys already on the court, I caught passes with ease, sank my free throws, made three-pointers, and dribbled circles around several of the boys.

The next few days, there were heartfelt words among Ted and Celia and me—lots of love—some tears.

Now, I really wanted to see my old friend, Croom, again—and Jennie: I couldn't wait to tell them everything that had happened.

So when they returned home on December 21st, Celia and I invited them to meet us for lunch at The Brewery in the Olde Town section of Hickory. Here, the sidewalks were brick and the buildings dated back to the years after the Civil War when capital had returned to the South sufficient to build again. I assumed the restaurant would be full of people I knew, but that was okay: I *wanted* to see friends and constituents.

With shiny dark wood walls, the eatery was a local institution with a bar so glossy and clean, it shone. Behind the bar was a massive mirror, and overhead, the ceiling was hung with hundreds of pewter mugs individually engraved with the name of the customer who owned each one. The walls were decorated with framed hand-painted pictures of local historical sites. Stately Oaks, even though it wasn't especially old, was included among them simply because it *looked* iconic. Booths lined the walls and were so full of people you could talk as loud as you wanted, and no one could hear you.

Today, a large Christmas tree covered with ornaments and lights stood at the back of the room in front of the window that faced out onto Trade Alley.

When I, "the Senator," as tall as Abraham Lincoln, and Celia, as fetching as Natalie Wood—and Croom, still looking like a nineteenth-century English actor—entered the restaurant, we were overshadowed by Jeni B. In public, she could still electrify a room with her looks and presence. She could wear anything, even heavy winter clothing, and look stylish, and her smile was charismatic. Plus, she'd cut her hair to shoulder-length, making some people wonder who she was. We were having great fun!

While people turned and whispered, the hostess ushered her and Croom to a booth, and I went from table to table speaking and shaking hands, Celia smiling and chatting at my side. The knot on my head was pretty obvious, so I joked, "Celia was aiming for my eye—and missed." Everyone, especially Celia, thought that was funny. By the time she and I got to the booth, a small group of people were standing around it, talking to Jennie and Croom, Jeni B happy to sign some autographs.

As it happened, the hostess had seated us at the booth that had the large framed picture of Stately Oaks featured on its wall.

"The Goodheart Mansion," Croom quipped, cutting his eyes to it as we sat down. "Did you call ahead for your own private booth?"

"That's actually one of the things we want to talk to you about," I replied as Jennie talked to a young couple and their two small children, then signed an autograph.

When the last of her fans had left us alone, I spoke. "I'm glad we could have you stay over with us the night of Cotillion, even if I did leave unexpectedly. But there was a reason."

"That was obvious," said my old friend, pulling playfully at his mustache, "it just wasn't obvious what it was."

"I'm glad you could spend the night at *Stately Oaks*," I emphasized, "because we're not going to own it much longer. Unless I can pull a rabbit out of my hat, we're going to be broke."

Croom jerked back his head, a twinkle in his eye. "What's

that supposed to mean? A Nightingale and a Goodheart, broke? That'll be the day. It would be more likely for you to be *dead*."

"Well, that's my other topic today, Croom."

The waiter appeared, handed us our menus, and took our drink order—hot chocolate for Jennie and Celia, coffee for Croom and me.

I began by telling them the whole story about our old family friend, my dad's long-time girl Friday, Ruth Ann Phipps, and how she'd recommended her niece to Celia and me when we needed someone dependable and competent to work for us at Tavern Craft.

"Ruth Ann trusted her," I said, "and we did, too. Ruth Ann passed away two years ago, so she'll never know about all this. As for us, we never suspected a thing. It seemed like everything Annie ever did was completely trustworthy."

Sighing, Celia slowly shook her head. "Yeah. We trusted her, all right. And she went from secretary to bookkeeper to controller to embezzler." She paused, then said, "Andrew Templeton, our head supervisor, who also would have been our partner, checked with the D.A. this week, and Annie Jameson *is* going to be arrested and charged. The D.A. wants to make an example of her, so she'll likely be in Women's Prison a long time. All of this is going to hit the papers in the next few days"—she rolled her eyes—"and we can't wait. What fun! Just the Christmas we were hoping for."

"We've met with the auditors, our accountants, and outside counsel," I said as the waiter served our drinks while Croom and Jennie looked at us incredulously. And in silence. I sipped my coffee. "Minus a miracle, we're almost surely going under—it's only a question of when. *That* was the news I got at Cotillion right after we got there—it definitely spoiled my evening."

"I don't believe it!" Jennie said. "I *can't* believe it!"

She waited, but neither Celia nor I spoke.

I saw Jennie gulp, then she said, "How could anyone *do* such a thing? Especially an old family friend! I've heard you talk about Annie Jameson for years! She *couldn't* have taken *that* much money!"

By the expression on his face, I could tell Croom understood and believed. "What a fraud! What a *thief*!" he mumbled. "For God's sake, ask your parents for help."

I shook my head. "I'm not asking my mother for money—I won't put her in that position. In the first place, she's a widow—she needs to feel financially secure herself—and my father left his estate to her, not to his children. In the second place, I know how she is, and she wouldn't be able to give me a dollar without giving the same amount, equally, to all four of her children. It would take so much to bail me out, by the time she gave all that, times four, she'd be broke herself. Better me than her."

"I'm not believing this," Jennie repeated, shaking her head.

In silence, Celia and I peered at her.

"So—you all are, *serious*?"

"I cried for three days," Celia said, "while Matt was gone. I'm okay now, though." She squeezed my arm. "I'm going to be poor, but I have my husband, and I have my health."

Croom pulled at his salt-and-pepper mustache. "What about your dad? Good Lord, he has a 130-foot yacht docked at New Bern—though he hardly uses it."

Celia shook her head. "I won't even ask. I'm not going to do that. I have three siblings, too—all men. All with wives. And that boat is owned by the corporation. I won't ask for a bailout from Dad. I wouldn't accept it if it were offered. I'd rather be broke than hated; and right now, we all get along with each other, my whole family."

The waiter returned to take our orders. Then Celia said, "Matt and I have talked this through. We got into this fiasco together. We're accepting responsibility for what happened: we should have been more careful, not so trusting. We'd rather be broke—and honest—than have money but a reputation as deadbeats. We're adults, not children, and we made our own decisions. My father is an incredible human being, but he's also eighty-six years old. Why should he be responsible for the mistakes of his adult daughter?"

"But Celia—" Jennie protested.

Celia shook her head and waved her hand No. "No," she said, "I'm not calling in my family to rescue me now. Matt and I could have moved to Winston-Salem and taken on that life. We chose not to. I think I've always felt a need to be something—hopefully, more—than a prominent, inherited last name. To be more than the Pappagallo outfit—matching skirt, blouse, and shoes—that I wore in college."

She said, "In Winston-Salem, I would've been 'a Nightingale,' or 'William Nightingale's daughter,' or 'Bill Nightingale's *only* daughter.' To be a good Nightingale, you have to love the name—and the status that goes with it. If you're not in love with all that, it can be more of a burden than a blessing. If I'd stayed in my hometown, I would've felt less like a person than a title; I'd have been a 'Nightingale'."

I'd never heard Celia talk quite like this. Certainly, not so freely. So openly.

She continued, "My life in Hickory has been less secure, less predictable, and more challenging—with an elected official for a husband, four children, and a career—but also more stimulating. I didn't want simply to *be*—I also wanted to *do*. My life with Matt has allowed—even forced—me to do things I wouldn't have done otherwise. It's been quite a challenge."

She leaned back. "But now"—she raised her hands, palms in the air—"I'm taking on the challenge of my life."

Moments of silence. Then Jennie said, "That's all well and good—admirable! But we'll help you out. That's what friends are for!" She sat up straight and crossed her hands primly on top of the table, making me at that moment see her again in the first grade, the first day of school. Now her voice was resolute, sincere, almost childlike and innocent.

"That's *it*!" Croom said, thumping his fist on the table. "We have plenty of money and only one child to share it with. You're our good buddies," he proclaimed. "We'll help you out, and you can pay us back once you're on your feet again. How 'bout that?"

I shook my head. "That's really sweet of you both—it really is—but you don't understand the depth of it: we're talking millions. We've put the beach house, the mountain house, and the place in Raleigh up for sale. We've priced them to sell, and if we can sell them quickly, we think we might have enough equity to buy ourselves three months. We're going to keep Tavern Craft running as long as we can, as much for the employees as for anything else. Can you imagine losing your job right at Christmas? Think of all those families."

Croom, cocking his head, looked at me agape but didn't say anything.

"*That's* your concern?" Jennie asked.

I replied, "So far, we haven't laid anyone off, but we're running out of time. In the meantime, we're talking to our accountants and bankruptcy lawyers."

I paused. "It's not that I've given up. I have not. And I'm not fearful. I'm not afraid of what lies ahead."

Celia nudged closer, right up against me, squeezing my arm. "We've just decided," she said, "we love each other for better or worse, for richer or poorer, and if we have to, we'll start over. Our children are grown—they can take care of themselves. As for us, we have each other, and we're going to start all over again—from scratch." She smiled. "After all, I do have a career."

I smiled. "All things work together for good, for those who believe and trust in the Lord." Croom and Jennie looked at me. *Where did that come from?*

"Right," said Celia, "If it weren't meant to be, why would that fisherman have been there to save Matt? God's not through with Matt Goodheart. And neither am I." Her voice was resolute yet warm.

They looked at us. "The fisherman?" Jennie asked.

I told them how I'd gone down to The Rocks and fallen.

"When I came to on the beach, it was like a miracle." I had their attention now. "I had no idea how he could have fished me out, as big as I am. I still don't. It's a miracle he was there, saw me fall, and saved me; otherwise, I'd have drowned. I didn't see him around anywhere, not on The Rocks, not anywhere, before I fell. I thought he'd left."

Then I repeated, as much to myself as to them, "I have no idea how he could have fished me out. I was *out cold*—under the water. I can't imagine how anyone could have done what he did. I was a dead man. It's a miracle."

Then I told them how I was drowning—and where I'd gone and who I'd seen. "I was being pulled into a black hole—the depths of Hell—but he stretched out his hand for me and said, 'Do not fear. Do not be afraid.' And he pulled me to the surface and got me safely to the other shore."

Croom and Jennie listened, expressionless and without comment. I continued, "He was a light so intensely brilliant and warm, it shone pure white, but I wasn't afraid at all. I was attracted to it. Then, the light asked me if I wanted to go with him, and I said, 'Yes. Yes, I do.' Because I wanted to be with Him and all the others who were there, some I'd loved and who had loved me. Also, I knew that, among the others, multitudes were different from what I would have expected because he told me."

Croom spoke. "Was that bad?"

"No."

"Was it disappointing?" Jennie asked.

"No. It was wonderful, a joy so wonderful it can't be described. I felt sure my father was there, as well as Celia's mother. Other people I'd known in life, too, like your dad, Croom, and Mrs. McGregor. I even felt that Pip was there, too, in personality, if not soul. But many of the souls would be different than I'd expected. But all good. He talked to me a good while and told me many things I needed to know. I very much wanted to continue, to go forward with the light. But I hesitated—and He asked me why. I said, 'But what about Celia? She needs me.' So He let me come back because I wanted a second chance, not for myself, but for Celia and other people. My employees, for example."

Croom and Jennie looked at me in silence.

"I was outside of my own body, you see, floating, looking down, and I saw the fisher in the hood leaning over me on the beach. When I came to, I was on the beach, near The Rocks. At first, I thought it was Pip licking my face to wake me up, and then I realized it was only the tide, and I was alone there. Then the man in the hood stepped down from The Rocks and started walking toward me. I stood as he approached, and he asked me if I was okay and if he needed to take me somewhere. I said, 'No, I want to go home.' Then he stepped into his boat and rowed off into the waves and the fog."

Silence still on the other side of the table. The waiter returned with our food, served us, and checked on our drinks.

"I'm not crazy," I said after he left. "It happened. All of it. And more. A great light. God. Just like I said."

More silence.

Finally, Croom spoke again. "How long were you there?"

"I don't know. It seemed like a good while. But it could have been only a matter of minutes. Maybe even an instant. There's no way for me to know. But I know the light taught me many things. He gave me a lot of answers."

Croom and Jennie looked stunned.

"I know what I saw—I know what happened to me. I experienced all of it. The most important thing is that I now have no fear—not of death—or, more importantly, of life. No fear of dying—no fear of living. Even impending bankruptcy and humiliation don't intimidate me. They're only money, pride, and reflected greed: false gods which, taken together, amount to nothing. The light told me I had to be faced with this reality so that I would come to know true success. Seeing the light—that's what matters. Life and love are what matter. God is what matters. He is forever. Here and now, and in the hereafter . . . . Say something."

"Well, blow me down with a freaking feather," Jennie said in a slightly hoarse tone. Croom remained in silence but wore a bemused little smile.

"Croom?" I prodded.

He leaned my way, an earnest expression on his face. "We'll figure this out, good buddy. We can do it. We'll do it together."

Celia said, "At this point, I honestly don't care about losing everything, not compared to losing my husband. He means more to me than all the property I ever owned—or could."

"And the children?" Jennie asked.

"I still have them," Celia answered.

"And what effect will this have on them?"

"They're all adults," Celia replied. "They have college educations. Except for Teddy, and we believe he'll be readmitted. We have faith they'll be okay. We never raised them with a sense of entitlement; we never spoiled them. They'll manage and succeed on their own merits—we know that."

Jennie and Croom just looked at her.

"When I realized I could have lost Matt, forever, I felt changed. I've done a lot of thinking. This whole thing has changed me. I not only feel closer to Matt, I feel closer to God."

"And dying and a gracious return have changed me," I said. "I know what I saw. What I heard. I know where I was and what happened. And it was good—*all* of it."

"Whew!" Jennie exclaimed, leaning back against the booth.

"*I'll* say!" Croom said.

Jennie sat up straight. "I feel like my life is changing, Matt; you and Celia are inspiring me." She thought a moment, then said, "That old Miss Smiley woman predicted I'd suffer until I woke up. I thought maybe that was a reference to my coma. But now I'm thinking maybe it means—meant—something else."

Celia and I glanced at each other but said nothing, and Jennie added quickly, "Sorry about that; it just popped out. This has nothing to do with her or all that. The point is, the two of you make me want to sing again." She looked at Croom. "Do you think I could do both, Croom?—be a good wife and mother—*and* sing for people?"

Croom grinned. Celia and I smiled, and Croom hugged Jennie's shoulders. "You sweetheart, Jen!" And we all laughed together.

38.
COMING CLEAN

Declining dessert, we finished lunch, and the waiter cleared our table except for our drinks. "There's no rush. Stay as long as you like, and I'll check back with you in a little while."

We thanked him, then I said to Croom and Jennie, "Let me tell you what else happened on my beach trip."

"Uhh, something *else* happened?" Croom asked.

"Good grief!" Jennie said. "How much can happen in one little trip to the beach?"

Celia raised her eyebrows. "Jennie, you already broached the subject. Get ready for this. He not only went back to Hoophole Island—he went back to the Isle of Cats."

Jennie's eyes grew huge; her jaw dropped. Dramatically, Croom raised both his hands, then hit the tabletop—loud! The people at the table across from us glanced our way.

"You *didn't*!" Jennie said, shaking her head.

"He did." Then Celia told them how I, out on the beach, made up my mind to go back, at the same time Cindy Peppercorn was on our front porch telling Celia to tell me to "*Go back there.*"

Jennie sucked in her breath. "Mental telepathy, on top of everything else!"

"When Cindy and I were in junior high school," I said, "she dreamed her brother was going to die. He was a sleepwalker, and the next night he walked out in the snow barefooted, caught pneumonia, and died a week later."

"I wonder why she never told *me* that," Croom protested.

"It was hard for her to talk about. I think I'm the only person she ever told. And that was years ago when we were kids."

"But she alluded to it when she was talking to me on the porch," said Celia. "She told me she'd had a dream that Matt was close to something important that he needed to find and that she felt a need, as a friend, to tell him he needed to go look for it. That it was important for him to *go back* to the island and look for it."

I drank some of my coffee. "I had to go back, not just for myself, but for all four of us. No one should let any one event in life have so much control over him or her—forever."

Jennie cleared her throat. "You mean the way that trip has had something on *us*, in different ways over the years, maybe even holding us down or back from our best contributions?"

Exactly, I thought. And that was why we were now going to talk this whole thing out thoroughly. Then I'd tell them what I'd learned from the light.

I said, "There has to be closure at some point. There has to be closure, one way or the other."

"So what happened when you went back, good buddy?"

I told them the whole story of how I had met Rudy Casper and how he directed me to a man whose father had been Roger Gaskill, our boatman's best friend and drinking buddy. How that man, Hank Phillagraw, took me over to the island where I discovered the house had burned down, leaving nothing but the foundation and a basement.

"I spent two nights at the hotel-from-hell, where the man who ferried me over to the island told everything that had happened that night we were in the house, facts the four of us never knew."

"Seek and ye shall find," Croom said. "Or something like that. Do you remember the old woman saying that?"

I nodded. "It was one of her predictions for me: 'You will search and search, but you will not find. Then finally, you will find—where you never expected.' You remember that, too?"

"*I* do—unfortunately," Jennie said. "Although I've tried almost everything, at one time or another, to forget that entire night."

"Then I remembered right. I never expected to find it from a drowning and rescue, that's for sure."

"I was supposed to uncover a hidden secret—a deep, dark secret," Croom offered.

Jennie looked at us as she thought about what we'd said. "'You'll lose someone you love,'" she then quoted. "My first son. 'Someone you deeply trust will betray you.' . . . Dr. Salafar . . . 'Your mind will be poisoned with thoughts you can't control.' The drugs and paranoia. 'You will show impulsive temper.' I could have killed a man with that gunshot. And so on. Including murder. I guess we all remember at least our own predictions. Too bad we didn't forget them."

Croom wrinkled his face. "But how could the man you just met possibly have known what happened?"

"Because his father, who was our boatman's best friend, told him everything."

Jennie looked perplexed. "But how could the man who took us over in the boat that day have known?"

I paused, leaned back in the booth, and settled my eyes on her and Croom. "Because he was in the house *with* us the whole time."

Again, Jennie's eyes grew huge. So did Croom's. Jennie hunched her shoulders and rubbed her arms. "Matt, that's terrifying!"

I explained how he'd dropped us off on the shore after deciding midway through the ride over from Hoophole that he'd made a mistake in agreeing to take us.

"Yeah," Celia said, "I knew at the time, there in the boat, that something seemed different—wrong—with him: about midway over, he changed his expression and seemed agitated. It was obvious to me, and I even whispered something to Matt about it."

Then I told Croom and Jennie how the boatman did motor back to Hoophole, but once there, decided to go back to the Isle of Cats, securing his boat behind Miss Smiley's house.

Croom nodded. "He would've *had* to secure it. Otherwise, the storm would've taken it."

"Exactly." Then I told them how he sneaked into the basement, using the same outside door I'd used myself. "Then he crept upstairs to the hall with the poison and went into the kitchen looking for the opportunity to poison Miss Smiley, eavesdropping on all of us. Finally, he hid again in the basement, overnight."

I told them how Miss Smiley knew he was in the house—because she'd heard and seen him hiding behind some boxes in the basement—as well as seeing the poison at his feet. "The four of us could have so easily been poisoned, too—all for the sake of the money he presumed she had. He was Miss Smiley's cousin and friend but thought her father's buried money should be his."

We went over the facts again and again. Celia said, "So she knew she was being poisoned."

Jennie shook her head in disbelief. "And she was poisoning *us*. So that means we didn't—"

"Kill *her*, in any way, shape, or form"—Croom finished the sentence—"regardless of a murder prediction. Just in case we were wondering." He paused. "But she *would* have killed *us*." He flagged down the waiter. "Could you bring me a beer, quickly? Whatever you recommend, the stronger, the better."

"Me, too," Jennie said, tugging at her husband's arm. "Oh, my gosh, Matt! Oh—my—gosh. That *was* the murder, all along! She predicted her own murder, knowing it was going to happen that night."

"Unless she was predicting *our* murders!" Croom exclaimed as he hit his forehead with the ball of his hand. "Yeah—*ours*! Talk about ironic! Sur-*prise*!" He looked around impatiently for the waiter. "Where is he with the beer?" Then back to us: "If we'd eaten that food, we'd have been murdered, too—right there in front of each other. So murder *was* committed that night, but we had nothing to do with it. Nothing at all. And there would have been additional murders—namely, our own—if we'd eaten the food she served us."

"So—she really was a witch!" Jennie said.

Being handed a beer by the waiter, she took a healthy drink without setting it down. Croom gulped his.

"And all these years I felt kind of sorry for her—in a certain way. I really did," Jennie confessed. "And I felt guilty about leaving her." Then, seeing the looks Celia and I gave her, she quickly added, "Okay—Croom and I did vote to leave her. Still, I've harbored a little guilt about the whole thing. How could I not?" She paused, then groaned. "What we did really was awful, wasn't it? Say it wasn't, but I know it was."

"Are you kidding?!" Croom responded, maybe a bit too loudly. "That bitchwitch would have killed us! And we're just now finding that out—after practically our whole lives."

Chugging the last of his beer, he slammed down the mug, then looked up, scratching his head. "But I don't get it. Why would she poison college kids?"

"Really," Jennie concurred. "Nobody could be *that* evil—so evil she'd murder four kids she'd never met before just for the heck of it."

The waiter came to check on us, refilling our water glasses, and I asked him for some more coffee, this time decaf. Celia asked for more hot chocolate.

"Hank Phillagraw said it was because she'd been horribly betrayed for the second time by someone she deeply trusted."

"I guess we can relate to betrayal," Jennie interjected.

"Yeah," I said, "I guess so. Anyway, her first betrayal was her father thirty years earlier; this betrayal by her cousin was even worse."

"She was old and sick and worn out," Celia said. "She didn't care about anything anymore; she just wanted to be done with everything."

I spoke next. "So when Miss Smiley whispered to us, 'Who will help me?'—those pitiful words that have given me some guilt—it didn't mean she thought she'd be helped or that she even wanted it. I guess she knew that the answer was: no one. Because no one could."

The waiter reached over and handed Celia a fresh cup of hot chocolate, then refilled my cup with decaf. Thanking him, I returned my attention to Jennie and Croom. "Rudy Casper and I talked some more about that very question the next morning when I went to visit him at his house. The night before, at the hotel-from-hell, I'd gone to bed and left Rudy in the lobby talking with Hank Phillagraw, so Rudy learned some things he hadn't known."

"So, what about her?" Croom asked. "Was she a mass murderer wannabe?"

My coffee was too hot, so I set it down without drinking it. "No . . . I wouldn't say she was evil. She was a spinster who'd lived alone for thirty-plus years on an island in a big, old house with some very bad memories. No one to talk to except a bunch of deformed cats. Her cousin was her only human friend."

"Some friend!" Celia said. Jennie shook her head.

"Before that," I continued, "she'd lived with her father, a German sympathizer—a traitor. She didn't suspect him; she idolized him. Her mother had died when she was a young child.

When her father was arrested and taken away, she was devastated. Her life was shattered. Under those circumstances, who *wouldn't* have been loony by the time we wandered into the picture three decades later?"

Celia said, "And that night, her cousin and only friend in the world betrayed her trust again like her father had done."

"But this was worse," I added. "Much worse because it was intentional. And meant to kill her. It's true she would have killed us, but over the years, we made her into what we chose her to be. We could have chosen something else."

"Okay. So, she was crazy but able to predict the future?" Jennie asked skeptically.

"I don't believe she could predict the future," I said. "She told her cousin, our boatman, that her father would go down in history as one of the greatest thinkers of all time. With Galileo, De Vinci, and Newton. Hank Phillagraw quoted those three by name. But Doc Smiley ended up dying in prison, disgraced and penniless. She got her own father's fortune *real* wrong. She even told her cats *their* fortunes."

Jennie nodded. "That's right. I remember she told us that."

"She was nuts," Croom said. "But she did a fine job on us."

Jennie groaned.

I reminded them of Celia's and my stay at the King Charles' Inn the night the media broke the news about Jennie's accident. "I remember the bartender, of all people, said of fortune-tellers the same thing Rudy Casper said: 'They predict in generalities so that they are bound to get some things right, and the predictions they get wrong tend to be overlooked.' Hank Phillagraw said Miss Smiley predicted she would live by herself over thirty years on a deserted island—and she did. That was self-fulfilling."

"So was her prediction for me," Celia said, "when she predicted, 'Yours will be the last fortune I will ever tell.'"

Croom rolled his eyes as he cleared his throat and said with a fake laugh, "I guess we could say it would be a self-fulfilling prophecy to tell four people as a prediction, 'You will see murder,' then murder them."

"*Really*," Jennie affirmed.

Celia and I said nothing, but our faces agreed.

Croom said, "Miss Smiley predicted we'd be betrayed. But who isn't, by someone, sometime in their life?" He looked at Celia and me. "Annie has certainly betrayed your trust, big time." Then he looked at Jennie. "Dr. Salafar betrayed our trust. And Miss Smiley herself certainly had been betrayed, so she was familiar with the concept." He thought a moment and said again, "I guess everyone is betrayed sometime in life."

"She predicted I'd travel the four corners of the earth and be rich and famous," said Jennie, "here and abroad. What about that?"

I looked at Jennie. "What is 'rich'? It's relative. You could have been 'rich' as a doctor—your father's not exactly poor—and you certainly could have done a lot of traveling."

"Okay, but what about being 'famous here and abroad'?"

"You made your own future—your own fortune," I said. "We all did. Annie Jameson has embezzled me into bankruptcy, but I should have paid closer attention to my business affairs and been a better judge of character. I spread myself too thin, with too many pursuits." I looked at Croom, paused, then said, "It was predicted you'd be luckless in love—I remember her saying that—and you *used* to be."

Croom nodded, "I'm bound to have had something to do with that. But I'm not luckless in love anymore."

Smiling sweetly, Jennie nudged close to her husband and kissed him on the cheek. Croom smiled real big—and sighed. "Not anymore—not by a long shot." Then he said, "But regardless, Miss Smiley could have, and would have, killed us. If there was one thing she could be confident in predicting, it was murder. *The* murder—murders. I guess by that night—in her last hours like you said—she just didn't care anymore."

We sat in silence; then I told them Roger Gaskill came back when it was dry and burned down the house.

"Her own cousin burned up her body. He burned up the evidence!" Croom boomed. The people at the table closest to us turned and stared. Then, more quietly, looking around the restaurant, "So—over the years, we've regretted and feared . . . a bunch of things we probably shouldn't have."

I nodded. "It looks like it."

"So, if we *had* called the police, what good would it have done?"

I was silent, just sipped my coffee.

Celia said, "Well, for starters, the police—actually the sheriff—would have gone over to the island right after we reported her death. That means Roger Gaskill would likely not have burned up her body in the house—and probably wouldn't have burned down the house, either—not with her dead and gone."

Jennie said, "Right—and there would've been a lot of questions to us."

"But we would have told the truth," said Celia. "We'd have said she dropped dead in front of us, probably from a heart attack, and there was nothing we could do to revive her. They'd have believed us."

"If they had, and left it at that, then no one would've ever known she was poisoned," Croom said. "Or, if they'd performed an autopsy, which would have been likely since she died in her own home, with us *in* it with her—on an island that was government-restricted, an island that nobody ever went to—they'd have found the poison in her."

Celia said, "We would've told the whole story as we knew it."

"But we'd have had a problem," Croom interrupted, "because we destroyed important evidence: we washed the plates clean—the ones with the poisoned food on them—and put them back in the cabinet."

Celia was persistent. "But we wouldn't have done that if we'd voted to report."

Croom was, too. "We don't know, now, *what* we would have done, then. We only know what we *did* do."

Silence, then Croom broke the lull. "So *if* there'd been an autopsy, the authorities would have had to accept that she committed suicide by poisoning herself, or charge us with the murder. Motive would have been a big issue."

He paused and rubbed his mustache while he thought about it. "Since the fed owns the island, federal authorities might have been called in—the FBI. An autopsy would've been crucial, and they often take forever in North Carolina. The investigation—the scandal—could have dragged on a year or more, easily, with us as the chief suspects. I can only imagine what the newspapers would have done with *that*—four privileged college students from well-to-do families kill an innocent old lady. A thrill kill. In the media, we'd have been guilty till proven innocent because that would have sold a lot of newspapers."

Celia looked at him critically. "You're getting carried away, Croom."

"I'm not so sure about that," he replied. "Having a Nightingale in the story would have sold more papers than having a nobody." Then he admitted, "Ah, hell, I don't know. But at any rate, Roger Gaskill obviously would never have said he went back to the island that night—and we had no idea—so he would have gotten away with everything, scot-free."

"He did anyway," Celia pointed out.

Another sip of coffee for me. "We could've at least seen to it that she had a decent burial."

"What makes you think she wanted to be buried?" Croom responded like a badger. "Maybe she wanted to be cremated—and that's what happened, more or less."

"Right," Jennie agreed.

"But even people who are cremated have their ashes disposed of properly."

To which my buddy replied, "What could have been more appropriate than to have her ashes—and her bones—scattered about the island she'd always lived on?"

Jennie took an exaggerated breath and sighed out loud. "This has gotten morbid, with a morbid imagination. Why is it that whenever we get on this topic, it always ends up morbid?"

"We don't ever get on this topic—we never have," Celia

corrected, "not the four of us together. We've never talked about it seriously and in-depth. The four of us haven't talked about it once since the night it happened. I think we were *way* past due."

"I'll drink to that," Croom said. "Or I would if I had any beer left. But before I flag down the waiter, I'm going to ask Good Buddy one more time: 'So, Good Buddy, what good would have come of it if we'd reported to the authorities?'"

Celia spoke instead of me. "Well, actions have consequences. So does inaction."

Jennie made a little shrug with a half-grunt.

Celia said, "Matt's grandfather, the one they called Beergard, used to say, sometimes an event in a person's life can occur in a twinkling, but it can nevertheless change that person's life forever. A coin toss happens in a twinkling."

Croom said, "So does a lightning bolt."

Jennie shrugged again. "I just remember the part about the two grandfathers getting expelled from college for gambling."

"But Matt's grandfather—unlike mine—lost his fortune," Croom added, "in the rigged poker game they were playing with the two upperclassmen."

"That's a great story," said his wife, "but right now, I'm stuck on this other stuff. I guess the bottom line is, we'll never know what would've happened if we'd reported her death. But what does this new information mean in terms of my whole life?"

Celia asked, "What does it mean in terms of *all* of our lives?"

"'*The* murder' was committed right in front of our own eyes," Jennie mused, still trying to understand everything, "unless she viewed her death as suicide and was actually predicting *our* deaths as the murders."

Her husband said, "Maybe her death and our deaths were all wrapped up in the murder prediction. Maybe she just wanted to show herself that she was a good fortune-teller."

Following a lull, Jennie spoke. "But Matt, didn't you say one of us had unpoisoned food?"

My coffee mug was empty. "Right. She took a plate of food to one of us, and while she was out of the kitchen at that time, Roger Gaskill poisoned the food that was left. I've thought about that fact a lot since Hank Phillagraw told me, and I actually remember *that night* thinking I heard something. I thought at the time maybe it was the cats, but now I know it was *someone* in the kitchen when she was in the den with us bringing in that first plate of food."

"Which one of us got the first plate?" Croom asked. "Which one of us would have lived and been forced to watch the rest of us Three Little Indians, as we were dying—and been forced to deal with the bodies?"

But before anyone of us could answer, a man and a woman walked up to the table and stood there, looking at us.

39.

BREAKING THROUGH

Though they had dead-stopped our conversation, they—looked harmless enough. The woman broke into a disarming smile and said, "Please excuse us for interrupting, but we wanted to tell you something."

Smiling charismatically, Jennie sat up straight.

The woman continued, "We're originally from Chicago, but we chose to retire here. We just wanted to tell you,"—they looked at Celia—"Ms. Nightingale—Mrs. Goodheart—just how much we admire your talent."

Jennie jerked back her head, her smile relaxing.

"Well, how kind of you," Celia said. "I'm honored."

The man smiled. "We've been to three of your concerts. We love music, and we love the piano. We have so enjoyed—so appreciated—and so *admire*—your interpretations. Your Beethoven's piano sonata number thirty . . ."

"Flawless," his wife said.

"Sublime!" he added, kissing his fingers. Then: "Sorry we interrupted your meal, but we just wanted you to know."

"That's just so kind," Celia said again. "Thank you."

Then the man added, "Oh yes, and thank you for what you do for us in Raleigh, Senator."

"Thank *you*," I said, bowing slightly at the waist. "That means a lot. Merry Christmas to you and your family."

"Merry Christmas to you, as well." They smiled at everyone at the table and walked off.

Celia grinned. "Miss Smiley said I'd be impulsive and show my temper—and I guess my sweet husband knows she got that one right." As Croom and Jennie looked at her knowingly, she giggled. "But she also said I would be admired."

"And be faithful and show strength in time of crisis," I added. "She was right about that, too."

"It almost sounds like you're arguing for her being psychic," Jennie said. "Don't do that too much."

"Regardless," said Croom. "Back to the conversation at hand. So, which one of us did the old woman serve first? Which one of us would have survived?" We looked at each other for an answer, but none of us could remember, not after thirty-three years.

"What does this mean in terms of my life?" Jennie repeated. "*All* of our lives?"

I was *not* going to mention what Hank Phillagraw said about Miss Smiley putting a "star-cross" on Jennie and me because I no longer cared. I was well over that now. But I'd mentioned it to Celia because in the last few days and weeks I'd wanted to tell her everything.

Everything.

And now she told Jennie and Croom. Jennie moaned, like I did when Hank Phillagraw told *me*. Her jaw dropped, and she hung her head, slumping her shoulders and covering her eyes.

Celia looked apologetically at me, then back at Jennie. "Sorry. Maybe I shouldn't have told you about the star-cross. But after all these years, I was thinking all four of us ought to know everything—get everything out in the open—and not keep anything from anyone else."

Jennie looked up, uncovering her eyes. "It's okay. I agree we need to get it all out now, once and for all. She referred to me as 'the girl with the fair hair.' And she said to Matt as she began his fortune, 'You my dear boy, tall and fair.'" Shaking her head slowly, she rolled her eyes. "So, is there anything more to this protracted horror story?"

Croom said, "Whichever one of us would have survived, can you imagine how different his or her life might have been?"

"The possibilities are endless," said Jennie.

"And no one would have known who poisoned the food; everyone would have assumed she did it." Croom paused. "But I still have to say, for someone who was crazy, she sure pulled off a damn good impersonation of a psychic."

"Psycho," Jennie whispered. "'You will have poisoned thoughts you can't control.' That was a very difficult time in my life."

"She told me I'd be a loyal friend, but someone would betray me," said Croom. Then he broke out laughing. "Don't worry, good buddy, I never suspected you!" Then he added, "But according to our witch, I *was* supposed to uncover a deeply hidden secret.

A deep, dark secret. If I have, I'm not aware of it. If it's yet to happen, should I live in dread? . . . What B.S.!"

Jennie and Croom, loosened up by the beer, took turns recollecting Miss Smiley's predictions and going over one more time all the facts of what happened in her house, then fell silent.

Finally, Croom leaned back, relaxed, and said, "Good. We've talked it all out. Everybody good now?"

I waited; no one spoke. I took a breath. Now was the time—time to test my wings. I said in a quiet voice, but one they could still hear, "When I drowned and was saved, the light said many things to me as I stood in His presence. And He told me He'd give me the insight and ability to share these thoughts with others. I want to share with you now some of what He said."

I waited; still no one said anything. I took another breath, then confessed, "He said, 'Upon their deaths, you treated your dog better than you treated that old woman. You think you have been haunted by the old woman's predictions, but it's not her words that haunt you. It's the fact that you left her body uncovered and exposed for animals to devour, knowing it was wrong. That was your sin. *That* is what haunts you."

I waited for a volley from across the table, but to my surprise, none came. Instead, Croom and Jennie, though they fidgeted a little, looked at me in silence.

"I asked Him how I could be forgiven for that sin in my life, and He said, 'If you weren't already forgiven, you wouldn't be here. You are forgiven by grace through the faith that you have. What you need is to forgive yourself.'"

Still, not a word from around the table. "Everyone has something," He told me. "Every individual, every tribe, every

Nation."He said that everyone must own up to that sin, accept the grace of forgiveness accomplished by His death and resurrection. Then forgive their own selves. Everyone, He said, is infected with the universality of sin. And He is the only remedy for that sin. Our only hope in life."

Since they were listening without speaking, I continued, "And beyond forgiving ourselves for what our sin has caused, He told me, we must forgive others. And He told me this: 'Your problem, Matthew, is that you have put your faith in the wrong things. False gods. You have searched in the wrong places. And there have been times when Miss Smiley was more your spiritual guide than I was.'"

Jennie and Croom, as well as Celia, were definitely listening, silently.

Again, I spoke. "He said to me, 'That night in the house, you were wrong to abandon and run and not own up.' The driver of the car who killed Pip did the same thing. So did Dr. Salafar. The light made me see that we all have sinned. He told me that what all mankind holds in common is the universality of sin. Miss Smiley, whose sins were her own, was a part of that universality, too." I paused. "The light made me understand this: what Miss Smiley did to the four of us was sinful. What we did to her was sinful. The light is the only provision for that sin."

Croom and Jennie, while they seemed in a way taken aback by me, surprisingly said nothing. I appreciated their silence—and respected them for it—and spoke again. "Then the light said, 'I died for all of that—for all of that sin.' Finally, the light said, 'You feel you've been betrayed, but the real betrayal is betraying me by not forgiving others for what you think they've done to you.'"

Speechless the whole time, Croom and Jennie looked at me. Then at Celia. Then at each other.

Jennie gulped.

Croom started to say something, then stopped.

Finally, he looked at me and spoke. "Okay. What about Annie?"

Celia turned and looked at me, too. All eyes on me.

I replied, "After drowning and being pulled from the sea and standing in the presence of Jesus," I replied, "there's only one answer: refusing to forgive is not an option. I forgive Annie."

Then I did not speak. Nor did Celia. Neither did Croom nor Jennie.

The Four of us—together sat silent.

40.
THE FOURTH PLAQUE

We sat together without speaking, long enough for the silence to grow a little awkward. Not uncomfortable, but a little awkward. I guess we had a lot to think about.

Finally, Jennie broke the silence. "Matt, when you were in Heaven, and the light—Jesus—told you that you held sin in common with everyone else on the planet Earth, how did that make you feel?"

"Yeah," Croom interjected, "how *did* that make you feel?"

Before I could begin to answer, Jennie spoke again. "I mean, I guess we'd all prefer to think that what we have in common with all other people is basic human goodness. You know, 'people are basically good,' and all that."

Of course, I knew what she meant. Of course, I understood.

But before I could answer her question, she spoke again. "But I have to admit, considering what I've been exposed to in the entertainment industry—not to mention the media—and what I've been exposed to specifically in the rock music industry, I'll have to say some of it comes across as pretty Satanic. Some of it seems downright Satanically inspired. Worshipful of precisely the wrong thing."

I'd never heard Jennie talk quite like this before.

Then she said, "I guess it's true that we're all sinful, no matter how hard we try to convince ourselves that we're not. I guess that is our real common denominator—rather than goodness."

Croom nodded. "Without the concept of sin and evil as a real force in the world, the worst of human history is difficult to comprehend. It's just too horrific. I mean, how can you explain the worst of man's inhumanity to man if no evil exists?"

Celia agreed, "The ultimate in sinfulness constitutes evil." But then she smiled. "But there's hope. There's light in the darkness. *The* light in the darkness."

The gold in the darkness, I thought to myself.

"So how did that light in Heaven make you feel," Jennie asked again, "when He reduced your human commonality to sin?"

"I was humbled," I answered. "He—the experience—made me feel humble. And connected. I felt connected in a good way with every member of the human race, because even though the common denominator sadly was sin, there was a cure: the light shining radiantly in front of me—hope itself—amazing grace—and that cure was available to everyone who will accept it. That's why He died that awful death on the cross and rose again."

They were listening, and I continued, "Because I was so humbled by Him and completely forgiven at the same time, I felt liberated. That's how I felt—liberated. And loved. Everything was perfect right then and there . . . except"—I looked at Celia—"I'd left someone behind without saying goodbye."

I paused, and then, to my surprise, Celia began to cry.

Then Jennie did.

I put my arm around Celia's shoulder, hugging her, as Croom did the same with Jennie. Celia composed herself. Jennie, too. They brushed away the tears. And sniffled.

Finally, Jennie said, "The light you saw in Heaven, Matt—the light you experienced—I want that."

"This is a lunch we won't forget," Croom said. "And by the way, if that light is being spread around, I'd like some of it, too."

We all looked at each other—in empathy. Then we smiled and laughed—not a lot, but a little.

I'm not sure where things would have gone from there—maybe we'd have gotten up and left the restaurant—but instead, three men in their early twenties who looked like college students stopped and asked Jennie for her autograph. The way they responded to her smile looked like she'd made their day.

"You wouldn't have had *that* happen," Celia said cheerily, "if you'd become a doctor."

"Rich and famous and *adored*," Croom teased.

"That's right," I chimed in, okay with the lightened atmosphere. "If it hadn't been for that stormy night on the forbidden island, you'd have gone on to medical school, moved back here to Hickory, and set up a successful practice, just like your parents always wanted. Nothing wrong with that. But instead, you accomplished nothing . . . except for international stardom . . . and bringing happiness to hundreds of thousands of fans in the U.S. and Europe."

"And Australia," Celia added, smiling. "And Japan."

"All things work together for good . . ." I said.

Jennie smiled back, her expression humble. "Okay, I think I'm getting this. It's going to take some time to think it all through—it's pretty heavy, but I think I'm getting it."

Croom made a pouty face. "Nobody gets excited to see *me*." Then laughing: "Except my mother!"

I laughed out loud.

"And Matt and me," Celia said.

"And *me*," Jennie added. "And Wes." Then she smiled and apparently couldn't resist saying, "And *Us Weekly*. And *National Enquirer*."

Croom rolled his eyes.

I smiled: it made me happy inside to see Jennie making light of the tabloids; for years, she'd only shown bitterness.

Croom made another face then rubbed the top of his beer glass till it squeaked. That made me feel like I was back in college. But older, wiser, not confused.

I said, "What I know for a fact is that God is always with us. Have no fear." I paused. "Hang on—let me go out to the car to get something—be right back."

I got up and headed out, stopping at a couple of tables to speak on my way, returning a few minutes later. We took turns reading the four plaques, passing them around to each other.

"What do you suppose it all means?" Celia asked. "Anything? Do you think they all work together?"

Jennie shrugged. "Maybe. Or maybe not. It could be that they're not meant to have an esoteric meaning. Maybe they're just quotable sayings to consider, each on its own, three being from

Shakespeare. But then"—she shrugged again—"they do mention the stars and fate versus will, poison, and taking advantage of life's opportunities at the right time—not missing the boat."

We talked for a while longer, each of us offering our own ideas on what the significance of each plaque might have been—or could be—and debating the question of whether Dr. Smiley created and hid them, or whether his daughter did, or perhaps someone else entirely. But mostly we talked about the words written in Latin.

I pointed to a phrase and said, "I think these words mean 'At the end of the earth'."

"I know what 'seputus' means," Jennie said. "It's like 'sepulcher.' It means 'buried'."

"'Est' means 'is'," Celia said. "So maybe something is buried at the end of the earth."

Jennie pointed to the word "columna." Wrinkling her forehead, she suggested:

"A column?—or columns?"

"A septic tank!" Croom boomed out, hitting his fist on the table and laughing boisterously. We all laughed at that, just as in college.

"Now look up 'thesaurus'," I said.

Jennie reached for her purse, but Croom beat her to it with the phone in his pocket.

"Tell Jennie what it means," I said.

"Hold on, good buddy—I have to find the definition in Latin." Then, looking up from his phone, he cocked his head in surprise, eyebrows high, eyes wide. "Well, whudda ya know? Doesn't that beat all?

"What?" Jennie said.

"Guess."

"Okay—fine. A book of synonyms."

He shook his head. "No. It doesn't mean that. It means—"

"'Treasure'," I said. "'Thesaurus' means 'treasure'."

Croom stood up abruptly, hitting the edge of the table, knocking over his glass and spilling the rest of his beer. Jennie rolled her eyes and, shaking her head, blotted the table with her napkin.

"We gotta go!" Croom announced. "We gotta get out of here—*now*!"

41.

THE KEEL OF FORTUNE

After leaving the restaurant, we stayed up the whole night, drinking coffee and brainstorming. Recreating every word we could remember about our conversation with Miss Smiley, we recollected that her father's name was Adolphus Zeno Smiley. And recalling the conversation the four of us had had with Croom's mother and my mother over lunch, we remembered Mrs. Westfall saying, "The student who cheated at cards was someone they called Hazy. Crazy Hazy." It wasn't much of a stretch to get from "A.Z." to "Hazy."

I reminded everyone of what Hank Phillagraw had said: "Everybody knew Doc Smiley was rich. Some said he made the money; some said he won it at cards."

"We'll look him up in the yearbooks!" Croom said. So we made two quick trips—Celia and I to my mother's house, Croom and Jennie to Mrs. Westfall's—and returned with our mothers' fathers' *Chanticleers*: my mother had some of the volumes from

1912 to 1917; Mrs. Westfall had some. Between them, we had all five years.

Sitting in the den, we pored through the volumes, and sure enough, we found him: a young A.Z. Smiley, in several group pictures with my grandfather and Croom's grandfather.

"He looks cocky," Celia said.

"That's funny," said Jennie. "I was thinking the same thing."

Over the next three days leading up to Christmas, we decided, after much thought and discussion—and prayer—that the three quotations from Shakespeare, while significant to the calligrapher, weren't the key to locating a spot on the island, and may have been created as distractions. In any case, the Latin phrase is the one we concentrated on. We decided "at the end of the earth" probably couldn't be taken literally because that could place the location anywhere on the globe.

"What kind of a clue would that be?" Croom asked. "So general, it's useless. So, the phrase must refer to a location on the island itself."

Then we decided the words probably didn't mean "at the end of the island."

I said, "That would be either of the two farthest points, east or west, or else the entire perimeter. And those 'ends' would always be changing due to the migration of the beach."

Miss Smiley had told us the government had confiscated the island, leaving her only the land under the house. So we came up with the hypothesis that "at the end of the earth" might mean her property boundary. We decided it had to have been Miss Smiley who calligraphed the plaques and placed them in the basement walls—and even did the burying—because the land wasn't parceled until after Dr. Smiley was taken into custody, tried, and the island confiscated.

What we were looking for—marked by a column—might be under the porch or just inside the property line.

. . .

The next four months were spent in planning and preparation. Then, on Monday, May 5, 2008, Croom and I, and Bert and Ted loaded our car with water, food, shovels, a deep-seeking metal detector, suntan lotion, bug spray, sleeping bags, four flashlights, and a tent. Pumped and ready for adventure, we then set off from Hickory to Hoophole Island, with a permit from the U.S. Department of the Interior allowing us seven nights and six days on the Isle of Cats, the island no one ever went to.

Unfortunately, we didn't get off to a good start. On the first day of the trip, we were stalled in traffic for an hour in route to the ferry by the malfunctioning of a drawbridge. As this caused us to miss the ten o'clock crossing, we sat for three hours waiting for the next one, but at one o'clock, the generator on the ferry wasn't working well enough to make the trip. By the time the crew fixed it, we didn't get to Hoophole till six in the evening.

Though we'd pretty much lost the first day, we did have a boat ready and waiting for us when we arrived. *The Keel of Fortune* was a white, thirty-foot fishing boat—nothing fancy but proven deep-seaworthy—with a deck large enough to sleep four men, plastic screening to keep out bugs, a fan strong enough to stir the air, a GPS system, and plenty of life jackets. The hold had two small beds, a small refrigerator, and a portable head.

The four of us, having spent just enough time on Lake Hickory to believe we could navigate a fishing boat, eagerly shoved off from Hoophole that evening to assure an early start the next day. With the engine running, the boat smelled of diesel at any speed, but she handled well and ran pretty fast, and we made it to the Isle of Cats around dusk and set up a tent.

Then we prayed, asking for blessings on our expedition. I led off, followed by Croom, and then by Bert and Ted.

It was cool that night. A full moon, stars, and intermittent clouds hung in the night sky, casting light on the water and beach. The lighted rigging of commercial fishing boats out in the ocean looked like pirate ships cruising for prey while a barge, pulled by a tugboat covered in bright lights, inched across the horizon in front of us.

We got up early the next morning and began our search and dig. Around noon, the wind picked up, so we took down the tent and stowed it in the hold. By one o'clock, it was so windy we thought we'd be blown away—still, we spent that whole second day searching and digging.

That night, a lightning storm raged on the ocean, so far out to sea, we couldn't hear the thunder. On one area of the horizon, for two hours, jags of vertical lightning shot downward from a huge, coal-gray cloud suspended in the sky, striking the ocean over and over. Hearing nothing but seeing the beautiful display of colors illuminating the sky, I stayed awake as long as I could, watching through the netting of the tent door as I lay in my sleeping bag.

The next day—our third—it rained for over an hour, so hard it forced us to wait it out in the basement beneath the foundation of the house after running the cats outside with threats and flashlights. Otherwise, we stayed away from the cats—and they from us—though their lurking presence in the dunes, haunting and surreptitious, was never completely out of mind.

While the nights were cool, the days were hot, and by the fourth day, despite all our efforts to prevent it with suntan lotion and bug spray every few hours, we were sunburned and covered with bug bites and almost out of food. Having spent three nights on the island, on the evening of the fourth day, we took an informal vote to go back to Hoophole, where I looked up Rudy Casper.

By this time, we looked like four broiled lobsters covered in sand and bug bites and smelling of sweat, insect repellent, and coconut. Rudy, as obviously surprised to see me and three other people on his doorstep as Henry was excited, said, "Well, blimey! Look at what the night sea's blown on shore—shiver me timbers if it's not a gaggle of landlubbers!"

While Henry licked my face, Rudy waved us inside, and we slept the next three nights under his roof. On the fifth day, we dug for eight hours, non-stop, till we were so sore we could hardly move. We concentrated on the area that would have included the property line, a quarter-acre square, measured from the center of the basement, but found nothing other than junk metal and ship salvage. By the end of the sixth day, after eight more hours of digging, we'd all but given up.

That evening, at Rudy's house with *The Keel of Fortune* securely docked, the National Weather Service issued an Emergency Alert: "Extreme tornado warning in this area from 7:00 to 7:30 EDT. Take shelter now."

"There's no real shelter on an island," Rudy said. "You stand in an inner hall with a pillow, away from the windows, and pray."

So that's what we did, praying aloud with me, again leading off, then Rudy and the boys, and finishing with Croom, who impressed all of us with his palpable sincerity. Lightning cracked around us over and over again as thunder shook the house and rain pounded the roof and windows like a hurricane, reminding Croom and me of our first visit to the Isle of Cats three-and-a-half decades earlier. Too bad we didn't pray the first time.

Even after praying, the closeness and violence of some of the lightning and thunder caused Bert and Ted to talk and joke nervously, with eyes wider and less confident than I was used to in my two grown sons.

Outside on the porch, we found Rudy's yard and the street under a foot of water up to the running board of his truck. It continued to rain hard for another thirty minutes, then rained softly but steadily all night.

The next morning, our seventh day, we got up and went to church with Rudy, driving through water most of the way, and arrived early so that we could spend quiet time before the service began, praying some more. Once again, we prayed for help with our search.

When Croom, Bert, Ted, and I returned to the Isle of Cats, we found that a piling had been exposed by the storm. *There* was our "columna," located behind the foundation of the house at the foot of the dunes at what would have been the back, left-hand corner of the property line.

As we dug down, taking turns, the moisture was sufficient to keep the walls of light-gray sand firm. Digging deeper, the sand grew grayer. When I jumped into the hole, it was almost as deep as I was tall, and the sand beneath my feet was dark and damp as I continued to dig. I was seven feet in the ground, at the bottom of the piling, when I hit pay dirt.

As I was unable to hoist the box over my head, we used ropes to pull it up. My heart pounded as Croom, Bert, and Ted, at the edge of the dig, lifted the box out, then pulled *me* out.

When we opened the inner box, we discovered two rows of Ball Mason jars. Opening one of the jars, I pulled out a twenty-dollar gold piece, "J.E.B." engraved on the back. My eyes wide, I was stunned speechless. I couldn't believe it. Finally, I said, quietly, almost breathlessly, "God answered our prayers!"

"God's intervention!" Croom exclaimed as we opened one jar after another but did not touch the other coins. "Pure gold," he marveled, "no corrosion. Looks like they may be in near-mint condition."

Hundreds of small gold coins were in front of our eyes, each without exception—we later found out—engraved with the initials shared by my great-grandfather and his son.

"It doesn't seem real," I said, slowly shaking my head, my eyes wide with amazement. I looked over my shoulder for a pirate—and out to sea, to the horizon, for a pirate ship.

"All the tales we've always been told about pirates' treasure," Bert said, equally stunned. "Captain Flint—fiction. Blackbeard's trove—real—but the Queen Anne's Revenge was nothing like this. *This* is incredible!"

"But now, for us," Ted said, "it's reality—real life."[12]

After motoring back to Hoophole, the first thing we did was call Celia and Jennie.

Then we went to Rudy's house. "This is almost unbelievable," he said. "Almost unbelievable. Praise God! I can hardly believe what I'm seeing. Traitors' Island is Traysure Island, after all. I promise I won't tell anyone till it's okay." I told him to hold out his hand.

"Here." I stacked three Liberties in his palm—clinking, one, two, three—then folded his fingers over them. "For everything you've done." For a moment, I saw tears glinting in his eyes.

Then the five of us, careful to handle each coin with gloves, created an assembly line, photographing and cataloguing, but dare not cleaning, all 1500 coins, about 150 from each jar. We spent the next five days doing this, each of us responsible for sixty coins per day. When we were through, they made their first appearance—with the lawyers—then with the numismatic team recommended by Cultural Resources. Estimated value: over ten million dollars! To that date, *the largest cache ever found on American soil.*

42.
LUCK OF THE IRISH

The press conference room at the North Carolina General Assembly was remarkably small—between thirty and thirty-five square feet—stuck in a corner of one of the four quads of the General Assembly building, a maze of sorts in which visitors often lost their way, not so much because of the building's size, but because all four of its quads looked alike.

On Tuesday, May 27, 2008, I was holding a news conference, and the room was so full of people, I knew the fire marshal would have turned some of them out had he been there. At the back of the room was a wall of lights—for the sake of the cameras—and in front of the lights were a half-dozen rows of chairs, with members of the press, cameras, and cameramen. On either side of the press, legislators stood in the aisles with members of the public standing at and leaning against the walls. To my left, the aisle was two deep; to my right, the entrance area was four- and five-people deep, and the rest of the throng were squeezed into the doorway and out into the lobby of the quad.

With all the people standing, crushed up against each other, the camera lights on the back wall, and the fact that it was almost June and there weren't enough air-conditioning vents for a room this full, the air was hot and stuffy.

In another time, the overflow crowd might have been drawn to my extraordinary legislation, but no. I knew the crowd was here to see Jeni B not only testify but bare her soul. Her subject was not exactly scandalous, but it was close. The room had begun to fill up before I arrived, and the crowd in the outer lobby included more legislative assistants and members of the general public than I'd seen at a news conference in my thirty years of serving.

Beside me at the podium, the sergeant-at-arms made sure the microphone was working properly and would adjust high enough for me and low enough for Jennie. Jennie was beside me, to my right; Croom, off to her right. Celia was to my left, the spouses with Jennie and me to show they supported us.

I was dressed as a Senator—dark suit, white shirt, conservative dark tie. Jennie was dressed in a suit. She had star-quality, regardless, and she'd been on the number-one-rated, late-night talk show just three weeks earlier—her first talk show appearance in several years—dressed the way her public expected. Her host, who had a reputation for being rough on female guests, did not get the best of her: she had been quick-witted, charming, and self-effacing in her humor. Afterward, she told us she'd done a lot of praying before making the appearance—and prayed right before going on the air—and it had brought out the best in her.

I had bared my soul to her, Croom, and Celia about our

impending bankruptcy, my drowning, being saved, and my trip to the Isle of Cats. Jennie was so impressed that she agreed to help me with my legislative agenda to reel in the proliferation of prescription drugs. Her helping me was appropriate: after all, taking legislative action on this subject was her idea, first. That's why she'd sent me her diary.

The pharmaceutical lobby had rallied in opposition, but I was tenacious when I wanted to be. I was not a born salesman like my father: I could never sell anything just to be selling it.

But if I believed in something, my sincerity was convincing, and people responded. On top of that, my Heaven experience had given me a huge new energy, some of which I seemed to be able to share with those around me. Having Jennie shore me up could only help, especially now that she and Croom seemed to be sharing this energy *with* me.

Except for that one late-night show—by contractual agreement, no mention whatsoever of drug use—Jennie'd been out of the public eye for the last few years, and now she was back. On *this* legislation. Everyone knew something pretty sensational was up.

Jennie agreed to testify, knowing it would give her publicity—negative perhaps, or not—about prescription drug abuse. After all she'd been through with the media before, it took real courage for her to voluntarily subject herself again. But now in her mid-fifties, she'd developed a genuine social conscience. Moreover, she said that I—and Celia—inspired her and Croom, to be better people—people of faith.

It was already five past ten, so I led off by thanking everyone for attending, then explained why the Legislature needed to make various changes to the law. I introduced each proposal with emphasis on the need to change the Controlled Substances Reporting System, the computer network that tracked the sale of prescription drugs.

"Accidental death from prescription drugs, by over-dosing and other accidents," I concluded, "is now the number-one cause of accidental death, having surpassed car crashes. We must control the proliferation of prescription drugs and the number of pills sold and readily available. Death by accidental overdose is now an epidemic, man-made, not just here in North Carolina, but all across the United States—and it is non-discriminatory. Victims come from all ages, races, ethnic groups, all socio-economic groups, both men and women. People don't intend to die from the drugs they're using, but it happens anyway: one hundred Americans accidentally die of drug overdoses *every day.*"

The press was attentive and busily writing or clicking away. By the time I finished, I thought I'd done a pretty good job. I lowered the mike for Jennie. She spoke for ten minutes about her prescription drug ordeal, her dependency, the car accident, the coma, and nearly dying.

"I was fortunate," she said. "I was given a second chance. After two days, I came out of my coma. It took me a year to recover, but I did. That was in Texas, but it could just as easily have been here or any other place in America. The problem is pandemic; the problem is the over-availability of legal, highly addictive drugs without enough oversight or education on how to take them. What I've learned is that drugs are drugs. Some are legal; some are not. But while the law has made some of them legal, it does not make them less deadly. Just because a doctor prescribes something doesn't mean it won't kill you. The sad fact is that it's easier for a doctor to write you a prescription than to take the time to deal with your health problem in a better way.

"I was fortunate. By the grace of God, I lived, so I'm alive to testify today. Hundreds of thousands of other people—every type of person—are not alive today. Next time, someone in your own family could overdose—a child, a spouse, a parent—or even you. Death from these drugs occurs every day, everywhere—about a hundred times *per day* in the United States, making this a crisis in public health. It's a national, state, and local plague, the number-one cause of accidental death. As a result, we have a moral imperative to work for change. That's why I'm here, asking you to support this legislation."

I stood beside her, proud and grateful, waiting for the press to respond.

For the next fifteen minutes, they followed up with questions—some to me, for example: "How did you become interested in this issue?" to which I answered that I chaired a study commission charged with finding solutions to the prescription drug problem. "But," I added, "I also have a personal interest in this subject because Ms. Boston and I have been friends since the first grade, growing up in Hickory."

But most of the questions were directed to Jennie. She answered every question honestly, but the more questions she took, the more personal they became. Now a reporter asked her: "How is it that you could just walk out in front of a car in broad daylight?"

"That's the whole point," she said. "When you're under the influence of a psychotropic drug, your mind is not your own.

You're not in control; the drug is. People on drugs do all sorts of dangerous and harmful things they wouldn't do otherwise, to themselves and others."

A great answer, I thought—still, probably time to intervene. I took the microphone. "We're approaching the hour," I said. "Thank you for your attendance and participation. We'll take two more questions, and then we'll close."

An unfamiliar young woman sitting in the front row, who had been scribbling assiduously in her notepad the whole time, said, "Ms. Boston, is it true, as has been reported, that you are planning a comeback tour?"

Jennie hopped to the microphone before I could stop her. "I wouldn't say I'm *planning* one—but I might be thinking about it." The way she said it made everyone laugh.

It would have been a good way to close, but I didn't, and then a question was directed at *Celia*: "And this question is for *Mrs*. Goodheart," that same reporter said. "Are *you* pleased to be on tour, giving concerts?"

I had no idea what Celia would say. She didn't give interviews, and she'd never attended a press conference, much less participated in one. She stepped to the mike—how proud I was to have her as my wife! I held my breath for her. "I'm not giving that many performances right now," she said. "We've been *awfully* busy the last two weeks." The entire room broke into laughter. When the laughter died down, she said, "But I'm pleased with the performances I'm giving. It's a labor of love."

Then a reporter sitting on the left side of the second row, a woman, African-American, in her early forties with short-cropped hair, raised her hand. I'd dealt with her for years, and her facial expression and tone never changed. As she was always professional and fair—in fact, my favorite journalist—I thought too much of her not to nod.

"Senator," she said, "since the subject has now been broached, by implication anyway, I think people would like to know, why would you have even thought—much less believed—that you would find what you found buried on an obscure island off the North Carolina coast? How could you be so convinced that you'd go, in advance, to the federal government for a permit to search?"

I was surprised that the direction of my press conference had been re-routed so radically, especially by this reporter. I hadn't given a full-blown interview on this subject, and I knew that whatever we said from here on out would go viral, making not just statewide news but national and international as well. But I couldn't blame these reporters for asking questions if I let them get away with it, so I had to decide whether to answer or cut off the news conference.

I thought to myself: *Maybe now, with all four of us here.*

"The four of us," I said, looking around myself, "became convinced. We were convinced there was a real possibility of something being buried on the Isle of Cats. I went through the Department of the Interior and the Justice Department to obtain authorization and an agreement because I wanted everything to be legal."

The legislative session had begun last Tuesday—on the 13th —and I was back on track with my legislation today, only two weeks after Opening Day. But two days before Opening Day, on May 11th, we—Croom, Bert, Ted, and I—had hit pay dirt. Now, I wasn't just a celebrity of sorts, but a celebrity, period. I couldn't go anywhere without people asking me about *it*—about what we'd found on the island. Since Croom and I hadn't given a full interview to the press, they were hungry for answers. Everybody wanted to know.

"All the clues seemed to point one way," I said.

When Croom stood up at the table at the Olde Town Brewery and announced that we were leaving, we'd spent, as I said, the rest of the evening—and night—in our den brainstorming. Eventually, Croom became so convinced there was something buried somewhere on the Isle of Cats, he insisted Celia and I accept a personal loan from him and Jennie to tide us over till we could pay them back.

"Anything to save Stately Oaks!" he joked.

"What kind of clues?" the reporter asked, her demeanor, as always, expressionless and professional. I looked to my left, to Celia, and my right, to Jennie and Croom. The three of them moved in closer.

"A story told for years in my family."

Croom leaned to the microphone. "And in mine."

"They've been friends since first grade, too," said Jennie, smiling at Croom. "My husband, Dr. Croom Westfall, IV."

Croom bowed theatrically, making the room laugh.

"Lifelong friends," said Celia.

"What was the story?" the reporter asked simply. The rest of the corps were deferring to her—at least for the time being—but making notes.

"The story always told in my family—"

"And in mine—" Croom added.

"Was that my grandfather had been cheated out of his

inheritance in a crooked poker game in college, and that, not knowing the game was rigged, he paid off in gold coins the student who beat him."

"Was that at Duke?"

"Yes." I smiled.

Groans and hisses from some in the crowd—UNC partisans, no doubt—but also good-natured laughs. I looked at Croom. "Croom's grandfather was a student at the same time. He was in the poker game, too, but pulled out, and the same story was told in his family. According to family legend, the cheating student's name was Hazy."

I saw no need to go any deeper with such details as our grandfathers' expulsions—and I definitely didn't describe our trip thirty-four years ago to the Isle of Cats over spring break.

Croom took the mike. "We looked through yearbooks—for the years 1912 through 1917—and found some group pictures with Senator Goodheart's grandfather, *my* grandfather, and a student named A.Z. Smiley. We did some research and tracked Dr. Smiley of Duke Hospital back to the Isle of Cats, an island he had bought and where he lived in the late 1930s and early 40s."

I thought Croom handled that pretty deftly; nevertheless, I stepped to the microphone. "So family stories led us to the Isle of Cats," I summarized.

A reporter well known among legislators for a creative weekly column appearing in newspapers across the state spoke up. I was surprised it had taken him so long. "There's a lot of land, even on a small island. How could you possibly have known where to dig? What other clues were there? It couldn't have been pure luck."

"We were on the island from May 5th to May 11th, seven days, six nights," I replied.

"We put in a lot of hours—hard work. Then—providentially—sheer good fortune helped us out. The last night we were there, Saturday, May 10th, a storm blew in and uncovered the top of a piling that had been buried in the sand. We'd been looking for a column of some type because we'd found on the island a small plaque with a message on it, written in Latin—"

"A map?" the young woman on the front row asked.

"No," I said, "but it led us to believe we should concentrate our efforts along a property line and look for a column. We knew the fed owned all the island except for the land under the house, and we'd contacted the Secretary of the Department of the Interior and the National Parks director and eventually were told that the private parcel was one-quarter-square acre as measured from the center of the house. The basement still existed, so we measured the property line ourselves. We concentrated all our digging in the area around that line, in a square. Then the piling showed up."

"Who was 'we'?" the columnist asked. "That wasn't the four of you, here—right?"

"Correct. Dr. Westfall and I went with my two sons, Bert and Ted."

"You didn't take your wives along?"

Celia stepped to the microphone. "Definitely not."

"Why not?"

"Digging in the sand from sunup to sundown on a desert island is not exactly my idea of how to spend a week's vacation."

Everybody laughed.

She looked at Jennie, who then took the mike. "I didn't want to get sunburned," she quipped. "Not with *these* freckles!" Everybody laughed again. "And I understand the mosquitoes on that island are as big as bats, and the no-see-ums are the size of microbes."

More laughter. She turned away but then added, "Besides, I'm allergic to cats!" The crowd roared.

I'd never seen Jennie more confident or smoother. Quite relaxed in front of the cameras and press—something she'd lacked terribly in her early years as a performer. It was the best news conference I'd ever been in.

"What message was written in Latin on the plaque?" my favorite journalist asked. I stepped to the mike. "At the end of the earth, marked by a column, lies buried a thesaurus."

She looked up from her notepad.

"Treasure," I said. "'Thesaurus' means 'treasure'."

"*Whoa*!" someone in the audience exclaimed. Some people gasped. Some clapped.

Everybody knew we'd found the treasure, but saying the word itself evoked awe.

"Who first hit the box with the loot in it?" asked the same reporter.

"I did," I said. The deeper we dug, the grayer and darker and firmer the sand had become. Since I was the tallest, I volunteered to go down into the hole and dig.

"I hit a hard object with my shovel. It was a metal box wrapped in several layers of what we think was a World War II-era tent. We pulled it out and opened it. There was another box inside the outer one, wrapped the same way. Inside the inner box were ten Ball Mason jars, two rows of five, each jar containing about one hundred and fifty coins."

The young woman on the front row said, "The figure reported as the value of the cache—is that accurate?"

"What was reported in the *News and Observer* and the *Charlotte Observer* was right."

"Are you going to share the money with your lifelong friend?" the columnist asked.

Croom stepped up. "He will not—I won't let him! My grandfather's initials are not on any of those coins. Every one of those coins was engraved with three initials: J.E.B."

That fact, along with the value of the find, had already appeared in the media all across the country: every coin was engraved with "J.E.B.," proof they belonged to my grandfather.

"Those are my grandfather's initials," I said. "His and his father's. They shared the same name. They stand for Jacob Emmanuel Beauregard. My grandfather's family and classmates called him Beergard."

"Can any independent third party verify that the initials existed on the coins when you found them?"

"Yes. There is an independent third party." It was Rudy Casper, but his name hadn't been mentioned publicly, and I didn't think this was the time or place to do that.

As for Croom not accepting anything out of the find, I'd convinced him to accept one of the coins, a twenty-dollar gold piece, as a keepsake.

"How much goes to the government?" another reporter asked.

"The fed didn't believe we would find anything," I answered him, "but our agreement says if we did find something of value on federally-owned property, they would have a claim if we couldn't prove it had been my family's property and that it had been taken from my grandfather illegally—through an illegal activity—gambling. But if we found it on private property, which is what happened, the government had no claim to it—other than taxes, of course—and if we could prove it had been my family's property, the only other claim to it might come from any heirs of Dr. Smiley. But no heirs of his survive."

"Who has the coins now?"

"My attorneys have them in escrow."

"What are you going to do with the money?"

Celia leaned to the mike. "Pay bills." Laughter.

Yet another reporter, who I knew was from Beaufort-by-the-Sea, said, "Growing up, we all thought if a treasure was ever found, it would be Blackbeard's. Of course, the loot on the Queen Anne's Revenge was his—by piracy, anyway—but *this* is a *real* treasure: buried gold coins. Would you say it's kind of ironic that the treasure isn't Blackbeard's or any other pirate's, but a state senator's grandfather's from near the mountains?"

"It's pretty ironic," I agreed, "but my grandfather used to say, 'Life is a collection of ironies.'"

He also used to say, I thought to myself, that "a person's whole life can be changed by an event that happens in a twinkling." How true I'd found that to be!

Croom stepped up, grabbed the mike, and said, "In that Doc Smiley stole the loot in the first place, in a crooked card game, he was kind of a pirate himself, collaborating with a foreign government, to boot. Doc Smiley steered our ships onto the rocks in wartime—among other things. You need to do some research on him; it makes for interesting reading."

I watched as the press corps scribbled in their notepads and clicked away.

"You're head of the biology department at S.M.U., aren't you?" one asked.

Croom nodded. "That's correct. On sabbatical."

The young woman on the front row raised her hand. "I have a question for Senator Goodheart."

I stepped to the mike.

"You know," she said, "you've acquired an image—behind the scenes, anyway, away from the Legislature—of being sort of a wild man, or at least a wild and woolly adventurer."

I looked around myself, from shoulder to shoulder. "Are you talking to *me*?" making the audience laugh. "You must be talking about *that* guy." I pointed to Croom, standing beside me. Croom smiled real big and held his fist in the air.

"*He's* the wild and woolly adventurer."

"So," she said, smiling, "you're not Indiana Jones. Okay—then how would you describe yourself?"

"Me?" I thought a moment. "I'm just your basic ordinary Joe. Wonderfully blessed." Not Indiana Jones, but Joe Jones. Wonderfully blessed.

I smiled, thinking of Rudy's continuing to call me by that name, even after he knew I'd made it up.

"So—" the young woman on the front row said, "does that mean?—is it true?—that you intend to run for Governor?"

I had no idea where *that* came from, but Jennie grabbed the mike. "*I* want him to!" Laughter. "I'll support him! I'm the one who told him to run for student body president in high school. And he won!"

Then Croom joined in. "I'll support him, too. I've been doing that for the last fifty years. Why stop now?"

The columnist spoke next. "What about you, Mrs. Goodheart? If Senator Goodheart runs for Governor, will you give up your career as a concert pianist?"

She stepped to the podium. "Things will be handled the same way in any event. Matt and I will talk everything through—and make our decisions together. But I can assure you of one thing, regardless of what my husband chooses to do, I will be there with him. He has always supported me. We're there for each other, regardless of what the future brings. That's just the way it is."

As her husband, I felt she'd hit that curveball past the outfield.

The front-row reporter then asked, "Is it true the four of you are really life-long friends? Is that possible?"

Croom answered. "I've put up with Matt—and tried to lead him in the right direction—since the age of six. It hasn't been easy."

Jennie followed. "We go back a long way. We grew up together in Hickory."

Celia finished up. "I came into the picture our freshman year of college. Very late in life." Laughter from the crowd.

"I have friends!" I said. Again, more laughter.

The sergeant-at-arms approached me at the podium. Putting my hand over the mike, I tilted my head toward him. "Excuse me,

Senator," he whispered, "but we've got to have the room; another news conference is scheduled in here in ten minutes."

I turned back to the microphone. "We need to let others use the room. I'll take two more, very quick questions; then we'll have to close."

"How does it feel to be rich?" the columnist asked.

"I don't feel rich. But I do feel blessed."

"Senator, to what do you attribute your success?" asked the young woman on the front row.

"Luck of the Irish."

"Are you Irish?"

"No." Laughter. "But I'm part Scots-Irish. That's pretty lucky." I paused. "I attribute any success I may have had . . . to . . ." I looked up and pointed—"His grace." More scribbling on notepads.

I thought, but did not say for fear of totally over-complicating the interview, *I've been searching my whole life. Finally, through His grace, I've found the gold in the darkness.*

Then that same young woman, smiling on the front row, said, "Have you thought about writing a book?"

I looked at her and smiled. "I'm glad you like to read. That's a key to a lucky life." Maybe it was time, now, to draw things to a close.

Again, the sergeant-at-arms was beside me. Again, I cupped the microphone. "Senator, we have to have the room." Just then, the building's emergency alarm went off, piercing the air in intermittent blasts. People in the audience grimaced and cupped their ears.

"Bomb threat," the sergeant-at-arms said to me. "Ten

minutes to get out."

I addressed the crowd. "Please evacuate the building. Go quietly and orderly to the nearest exit. Do *not* remain in the building. Leave the building immediately, in an orderly fashion."

43.

BURYING THE HATCHET

Since the interview was aired in parts on all the major television networks and was available in its entirety online, it was not surprising that Cindy Peppercorn saw it in Richmond. What *was* surprising, however, was that she made a point to visit Celia and me soon afterward to congratulate us on our good fortune—and to receive a word of thanks from us for her part in bringing it about. The three of us actually had a good visit, but I won't try to speak for Cindy—I was never very good at that—I'll let her speak for herself:

I guess if I were honest about it, I'd have to admit that I've been a little hypocritical in blaming Matt so severely for walking out on me and leaving me alone in the dorm, and in harboring resentment all these years.

What he did that night seemed like an act of betrayal, and it hurt me deeply, but to be honest, I'd have to admit Matt and

Croom did invite me, more than once, to go with them and Celia and her roommate. But the issue wasn't so much walking out on me that night as walking out on me, forever. But in all honesty, I'd also have to admit that Matt never liked me in the same way I liked him, and I *had* treated him unfairly on a few occasions over the years. I did and said some things behind his back to keep him away from other girls, especially Jennie. I kept her at bay in junior high and high school. Then Celia came along that night in college and took him away from me, forever.

Those three husbands I had didn't really have a chance: I compared each one to Matt, the Matt of my imagination. Of course, they didn't measure up. I was fixated on him, you might say.

All of that would be the truth if I were honest about it. But then again, honesty isn't what we humans are generally about, is it? Aren't we more about hypocritical self-righteousness? You know, we have a disagreement, and then it's all about I'm right, the other person's wrong, and there's no in-between. We behave as individuals in the same way as members of groups, only grouping us makes it worse. That unfortunate character flaw has caused a lot of wars.

Well, I'm Cindy Peppercorn, and as my last name indicates, I've got a lot of pepper in me; I'm the spice of life. Deep down within me, though, there's something more—the salt of the earth. It's taken me a lifetime to discover that, but I think I finally have. As such, I've decided to bury the hatchet regarding Matthew Goodheart.

I doubt we would have worked out anyway. After three husbands and striking out three times, I guess I have to admit

I'm not the marrying kind. I'm not much of a wifey. There's too much pepper in me.

Besides that, my whole life, I've sometimes seen or felt things that other people don't. I don't know how I know things—I just do. Does that mean I'm a sixth-sense person? I warned Matt about those people when we were in junior high and high school. I said, "Beware of people like that because they might be real or they might be frauds, and you won't know which. Besides, you might learn something about the future that you don't want to know, and that knowledge could change a person's whole life."

Well, it changed *his* all right—as well as Celia's, Croom's, and Jennie's. Matt should have had enough sense to listen to me—and thus protect the other three, as well. Instead, he fell for a screwy, old woman he'd never met before, and so did the other three. *That* was a mistake that cost them dearly!

Sometimes I see things in dreams. The first time was in elementary school when I had a dream about my brother Sim. I harbored a lot of guilt about that because I didn't try to intervene and protect him. I feel like that's when things might have started going wrong for me. Maybe if I'd had a trusted adult to talk to, things would have been different. But I had no one to confide in, until Matt came into my life in junior high school. He was my best friend. Then he dumped me for Celia.

I wouldn't want anybody to "see" the things I sometimes see. That can be too much of a burden. But recently, I've learned to consider it differently: God wouldn't have made me this way if he didn't have a purpose. Even if it's a cross to bear, it's a divine cross configured in the stars.

That's why, when I had the intuition that Matt needed to

go back to that island and search for answers, I told Celia. For me, that was a big breakthrough. Just dealing with Celia in a civilized way was hard enough—she had always been such a pill. Believe me, she was never tops on my hit parade, but I swallowed my pride and decided to talk to her to help out Matt. I guess I needed to do *something* nice, especially after I paid them that visit on Halloween with Jennie's diary as a present.

Of course, I had unsealed the envelope, read the journal, then sealed it back. I figured Celia would be so curious to know why Jennie would send her husband anything that personal, that she'd read it. I figured that what she read would infuriate her, especially since I'd seen in college that she had a real potential to blow her classy cool.

The dream I had about the old lady and the four of them in her house created a great opportunity for me to get some revenge on Matt and Celia for leaving me in the dorm, as well as an opportunity to do a little collateral damage to Croom and Jennie while I was at it.

Still, it's not that I'd been craving—plotting—revenge the prior twenty-two years. It's just that when my mother handed me Jennie's diary, saying it was private, of course I read it. Then it dawned on me: I had an *opportunity* for some mischief with a little revenge thrown in for fun. Why not take advantage of it? So I held onto the diary, waiting for just the right time. When my third marriage failed, and I was busy being hyper-upset about it, I had the dream.

I needed someone to blame and something to distract my thoughts. I'd just go visit Matt and the girl who stole him from me. Why not? So I visited them on Halloween dressed in a way that I thought would scare them and took Jennie's personal thoughts as a gift. I hurt Matt—and Celia—and I used Jennie, and to a lesser extent, Croom, to do it—Jennie, who'd already lost her baby, nearly been killed herself by a car, was on drugs, and was half-crazy for a while.

But there's more. In regard to the evening Matt was walking Pip and let her off the leash, I know more about that fateful night than Matt and Celia think I do. I was on the train that night, headed home to Richmond from Asheville, as it passed through the Olde Town section of Hickory. As I was looking out the window and thinking about how Matt and I used to lie beside the very tracks I was now traveling on—when we'd played Romilar, the Train Game—I saw the shadowy figure of a man and his dog standing near a street lamp. The man waved, and then he and the dog receded into the night.

A few moments later, the train stopped at the station, but I did not get off because I planned to go straight back to Richmond. As I looked out the window, people were getting on and off the train, but the only image I seemed to see was the man and his dog in the shadows of the streetlamp. The man waved, then the dog disappeared.

The train rolled out of town, and a feeling came over me, a feeling of sadness, then a wave of guilt, and I thought it was because we'd stopped in Hickory but I hadn't visited my mother. But as a few minutes passed and the feeling grew stronger, I realized it wasn't a daughter's guilt regarding her mother: it was much darker than that. Something told me a bad thing was about to happen to that man and his dog and if I'd gotten off the train and spoken to the man—talked to him for just a minute or so, then re-boarded the train—that bad thing would have been averted.

The image of the waving man and his dog haunted me for weeks, then I learned from my mom, who'd heard it from Jennie's mom, that Matt was walking his dog that night by the tracks at the very time I passed through on the train, and a few minutes later his dog was hit by a car and killed—and that a part of Matt seemed to die, too. But I wasn't sad when I learned that. Instead, I felt a sense of quiet vindication. He deserved it after what he'd done to me.

So you see, I haven't been the finest specimen of humankind ever to walk the planet Earth. But after a life of failed relationships, notably Matt and Croom and three husbands—not to mention Celia and Jennie—I have finally come to see, or at least *feel*, something different. I thought about it and remembered how kind, how very kind and sensitive and sincere, Matt had been toward me when Sim died, how Matt had listened when I had no one else who could—or would. He was quiet, gentle, and soft-spoken. My dad was so big and boisterous, my mother inaccessible.

That was long before Celia came into the picture and about the time I started falling in love. When Celia came along, I guess I kind of hated her. That's what jealousy will do to a person. You'd think Matt and I had been married and that he'd cheated on me, run off with another woman.

But the truth of the matter, when I'm honest about it, is that my imagination regarding Matt and me—and my envisioned future for us—was simply never his. Was that his fault? I was the one with the imagination, the longing for him, the love. He was just a guy who liked to pal around with people, and I was one of them, who just happened to be a girl.

So I've been working on straightening myself out, making myself a better person. It's never too late in a person's life to face the truth and deal with it honestly. So I've owned up to the fact that while I've been pretty special with dreams, I've not been so good with people. And I determined I could be better—I could be whole. Even in this, Matt has helped and is helping. He's my soulmate, even if he doesn't understand that. I can tune in to him. And I have.

I knew it was time for Matt to *go back* to where he'd lost it, and search until he found it. So I told Celia. And Matt did go back, and he did find it. That's how and why I went back to visit Matt and Celia this last time after they did that now-famous interview with the capitol press corps. I wanted to congratulate them on finding the treasure and congratulate myself on becoming a bigger person. But more than that, I wanted them to know how the change in me had taken place.

I can't answer the questions of the universe. I can't tell Matt if it was predestined for the four of them to visit that island and be forced by a storm—Nature—God—into that old lady's house and have their fortunes told. Or if it was happenstance. I don't know if she had any psychic powers or if she was just loony.

Everyone has to make those calls for him- or herself.

But when we're dealt a hand of cards, good or bad, we have to play it as best we can. It's not so much what happens to us as how we react to it. I do understand that now, even if I never fully understood it before. One way or another, God told me to tell Matt to "go back" and seek, and he would find. Well, Matt did go back, and he did seek, and yes, he finally found it. And when Matt found it, I did, too.

No, I can't explain how certain things work, like my being able to see things that other people don't see—or my being tuned in to Matt like we're soulmates—but I do know this: Now that Matt has found what he was searching for—and I have, as well—I've got a new attitude, and more than that, a new outlook on life.

And how does all this make me feel?

It makes me feel anew like my brain has been drained of poison and refilled with a spirit of gold. I feel more alive, more at peace, more confident, like my soul is infused with light instead of darkness. I feel like I've been set free, created to seize the day.

. . .

Recently, I've had another dream—this one about Stately Oaks. I dreamed there was a big garden party on the back lawn, and I was invited to it. It was a reunion of sorts with hundreds of people celebrating life. Since I've buried the hatchet and now have a sense of peace, I was good there at that party with people who at one time would have rankled the hell out of me.

Some of the dreams I've had over the years haven't been too good, and I would rather I hadn't had them. But this was a good dream, and I'm looking forward to that party and wearing a new dress. I know I'll look good in it, as good and new as I now feel.

44.

COMING TO TERMS WITH THE LEGEND

Two Years Later
June, 2010

This bench by the railroad track in the Olde Town section of Hickory was a good spot to chill in the morning with a cup of coffee and wait for the train. Gracie—Celia's and my Irish golden doodle, age two, forty-five pounds and energetic as a puppy—was sitting on her haunches at my feet, looking around as attentively as a sentry, her front legs long and straight and very furry, her coat a copper-colored chenille blanket.

About half the people who passed us asked me what type of dog she was. To the grandmother now standing in front of me, I answered, "She's an Irish golden doodle: half-poodle, one-fourth golden, one-fourth Irish setter."

"She's a giant puppy!" the little boy—I guessed age four—declared excitedly. "Can I ride her?"

"Better not," I said. "She might lick your face."

"I have a dog, and he licks my face. I don't mind."

"She might not want you to ride her," said his grandmother. "She might not be used to it. If you don't ride the puppy, I'll buy you a cherry snow cone." That worked; we visited a while longer, then they smiled and continued on their way to the snow cone stand.

The row of buildings facing me—old brick structures, three, some four stories tall—were well-kept and inviting looking; and with Independence Day next month, the Stars and Stripes fluttered from each one, appealing to my love of country and complementing my confidence in the future.

Ever since the 9/11, 2001, terrorist attack on the Twin Towers, we Americans had lived in a different world, security an issue where before it had not been. A bomb threat at the General Assembly during our news conference two years ago had been a false alarm, and over the years there had been others, of course, but in this post-9/11 age, bomb threats were taken especially seriously.

That morning news conference had turned into my first full-blown interview about the treasure, even though the program had been planned to promote my legislation, proposals which soon thereafter did pass, signaling a change in the right direction.

The treasure—about 1,500 coins appraised at over $10,000,000.00—was the largest cache of gold coins ever found in the United States. There were some five and ten-dollar coins, but the vast majority were twenty-dollar Liberties, minted from 1850 through the 1890s. The condition of the coins was quite exceptional, and the find included scarce coins from the 1850s, 60s and 70s, and rare dates from 1879, 1881, 1882, and 1885. Some had been minted in New Orleans.[13]

It had been my great-grandfather's money, tobacco money made on a huge farm after the end of The War Between the States. My great-grandfather, Emmanuel Beauregard, a farmer, had given it to his son, my grandfather Beergard, a college student. That money, over $30,000.00, was supposed to pay for Beergard's education, his living expenses, and give him a big head start in life, including business capital and a fine home for him and his bride-to-be and the large, prosperous family his father expected him to have. It didn't turn out quite that way.

It was still hard to believe we'd found it—almost a hundred years after Beergard had lost it.

Careful not to touch a single coin with our bare hands, we took photographs of every coin and catalogued each one. I contacted my lawyers, and together we consulted with the team of numismatists who'd worked with the Department of Cultural Resources cataloguing and appraising the coins salvaged from the wreckage of the Queen Anne's Revenge in 1996. By the time I gave the impromptu interview at the Legislature with Croom, Celia, and Jennie, the numismatists had had the coins only nine days. Totally in awe of what they were dealing with, they'd worked 24/7, so by the time of the interview, they had a reliable estimate of the worth of the cache. It was nearly impossible to keep a secret in Raleigh, especially if the story were sensational, and that figure got out to the press, though no one ever owned up to leaking it. Overnight, the news travelled around the globe.

Over the next couple of months, I considered various ways to sell the coins. The first thought was to auction them off through Sotheby's or Christie's, but then Celia and I asked ourselves Why, considering the high cost of the commission and the fact that thousands of people all around the country—and the world, for that matter—had heard about "the treasure." So we went online and advertised our own auction. The long and the short of it is that a rather eccentric multi-billionaire located in California got wind of the auction and decided he wanted our world-famous coin collection more than just about anything he could think of right then. To make sure he wasn't outbid by the other bidders, he offered to pay a purchase price we couldn't refuse.

He then flew us to the Silicon Valley where he put us up in a five-star hotel, no expense spared. We were chauffeured to his lawyer's office—dark-paneled walls, expensive furnishings, lots of glass, the whole nine yards—where we were presented with a contract. As we talked, another ultra-high roller called me with a superior bid, whereupon a bidding war ensued. Eventually, our benefactor, not to be outdone by his competition, did in fact offer us a deal we couldn't refuse. At that point, we signed over to him virtually the entire treasure trove for twenty-five million dollars. Needless to say, we were pleasantly stunned by what had transpired.

His driver drove him away from the meeting in the most expensive, high-tech, flashiest electric car he owned, and we were driven back to the hotel where we stayed two more nights. Our multi-billionaire got a new toy and conversation piece, and we got the financial backing to save, among other things, a furniture factory and all its employees' jobs.

Before I spent any of the money, I prayed long and hard. Acknowledging that there was an unlimited number of "good" ways to spend twenty-five million dollars, I decided to be a practical steward of the Master's talents. "Render unto Caesar," so I set aside money to pay federal and state taxes. And "Render unto God," so I gave to the church.

Then I paid back Croom and Jennie, and paid off the other debts caused by the embezzlement. Next, I used the money to make sure Tavern Craft was on a solid financial footing. After all, the money that had been stolen was from Tavern Craft. I figured since God wanted me to find the money, he wanted me to repay Tavern Craft and save all those jobs, 500 of them, most of which supported families.

Even at the height of the Great Recession, I hadn't laid off a single worker, a miracle of sorts in its own right. No employee had lost his or her job—or home. And neither had Celia and me.

Here I was, nearly one hundred years after Beergard lost his fortune, and I had a lot to be thankful for!

Since my fall from The Rocks, seeing The Light in Heaven, and being fished from the sea, Celia, Croom, Jennie, and I had done some serious soul-searching. Among other things, we'd sat down together and named any people in our lives against whom we held any grudge or ill-will.

We reminded ourselves of the adage that harboring hatred or resentment, even in small doses, is like drinking poison and expecting it to hurt the other person. Then we prayed to God to help us forgive them—and we prayed for them—and prayed that they would forgive us if the ill-will or grudge were mutual.

We'd concluded that if we—and other people—could forgive and forget, rather than judge and condemn, then the people of the world would be that much closer to the Light, that much closer to Heaven.

Three months after Annie was arrested, I went to court

on her behalf. I figured since I was a sinner and God had been merciful to me—he rescued me from the sea, saving me and giving me another chance—*I* needed to be merciful, too. And so, with the D.A.'s approval, I argued for a light sentence within the bounds of the law, restitution—though I expected I'd never see any of the money she'd stolen—community service, and probation with required therapy for gambling addiction. I agreed to pay for the therapy myself.

The judge agreed to the terms. It kept her out of prison and gave her a new chance at life, something I'd been given. Among other things, she doesn't gamble anymore.

But I didn't just think about people outside my own family. I thought about my children, too, and their families and my grandchildren, and set aside some funds to help them in the future. What father, similarly situated, wouldn't have? I also offered them jobs—except for Ted, who'd chosen to become a minister—because I wanted family at home, and I hoped to keep Tavern Craft running after I was gone.

I surprised BeBe, Stuart, and Kristen with gifts, though they expected nothing. But since they, too, were grandchildren of Beergard, I thought it was a nice gesture. They did, as well, since they weren't expecting anything.

All of that took a serious chunk of change out of my treasure trove. Still, I had enough left for some other giving, and at that point, I stopped to think about it because I wanted to be sure I did the right thing.

I decided to help Ted in his mission work. As part of that, I set up a foundation—mostly seed money I intended to grow—to help storm victims in North Carolina since we have a lot of storms, as well as people in South Carolina and Florida, for the same reason. And up and down the East Coast, too, and across the Nation, and in poor areas of the world, like the Caribbean, Central and South America, Africa and Asia. I named it Storm Purse. After all, we wouldn't have found the money if it hadn't been for a storm.

Funny, but even *finding* money could be a burden of sorts. Losing it was a burden for sure. But having it took work, too. Otherwise, instead of managing and spending it responsibly and morally, it could be squandered.

After all, Beergard had lost every dollar he had. And that was a lot of dollars! But I had to admire him for the way he'd reacted to what had to have been a trauma of life-changing proportions. I could only imagine how his *father* had reacted! Anyway, the colossal screw-up had made Beergard a man of God. He could have become a bum. And he could have become a bum even *with* the money.

"Life is a collection—a series—of ironies," Beergard used to say. He also said that life was often seriously unpredictable and therefore, "In any person's life an event can occur in a twinkling—or within a short period of time out of the blue—and change that person's life forever." I guess he found that out the hard way. I guess I had, too. And so had Celia and Croom and Jennie.

But now we knew the greater truth: Life is only 10% what happens to you—and 90% how you respond to it. The Smiley Factor, and all that.

I was determined to use my treasure in the most high-minded, as well as practical ways I could think of. It would take an abundance of additional thought and soul-searching—and prayer—to devise and implement a plan that would sustain itself and grow. But with God's help, I would succeed. I felt like I'd already accomplished a lot.

. . .

What I liked about the restaurant behind me—the old Southern Railway depot, converted and refurbished—was that someone would come outside and ask you what kind of coffee you wanted, then bring it to you right there on the bench, even though the city owned the benches rather than the restaurant. Today the waitress brought me coffee flavored with coconut. She reminded me of Elisa and Caroline when they were her age—late teens, early twenties—blond and pretty.

"Let me know if I can get you anything else. Are you sure you haven't changed your mind about the pastry?"

"I'm sure, but thanks, anyway." I handed her a tip.

She smiled, a pretty smile with perfect teeth. "Thank you, sir! And I'm here if I can be of any service—just let me know." She added, "I've always appreciated a person with good manners."

Surprised, I said, "Well—so have I!—thank you!"

"Oh, thank *you*," she said, her face beaming. She hesitated a moment, then, still smiling, walked away.

Something with a déja vu quality had just been said to me, but I wasn't sure what.

For the last year or more, I'd been giving a lot of thought to getting out of politics. After all, I'd been in the Senate for over thirty years. Over the last few months, I'd done a lot of praying about this. I knew we needed more good people in politics, not fewer, and I was a good person, but everybody is replaceable. A good person would come along and replace me.

Later today, workmen would be in the Square constructing a stage upon which a podium would stand. On July 4th, I would stand at the podium and deliver a speech in honor of America's 234th birthday.

At that Independence Day celebration, I was to receive from the mayor the Best Citizen Award, along with the Key to the City. It was supposed to have been a surprise, but Mayor Bryant told me on the QT, so I would be sure to be in town that day and show up. After I said I'd be there, he then asked me to be the speaker.

In preparation for an earlier July 4th, one of the newspapers had asked me, "To what do you attribute the greatness of America?"

I thought, now, about the quote I'd given them in response. Pulling a pen from my shirt pocket, I scribbled it on my coffee napkin: "The greatness of America is due to its people, its heritage, its religion, and its Constitution—not necessarily in that order. Knock down one of these pillars, and the house will crumble. Keep all of them strong, and America will retain its greatness."

Yes, that sounded like a good quote on which to base my Independence Day speech. That, along with what was written on our coins and currency: In God We Trust. "That's on all of our money for a reason," I would say this 4th of July. "God gives us every blessing we have."

I folded the napkin with my quotation and the national motto on it and put it in my shirt pocket. I'd flesh out the rest of my speech later.

I figured it would be my last Independence Day speech—at least as a Senator.

Sometimes when I sat on one of the benches next to the railroad track, I'd think of my dad: I'd imagine him as a little boy of six walking along the tracks selling candy bars out of a cigar box for a nickel—and for a penny, individual pieces of candy and packs of chewing gum. Even as a boy in the early 30s—at the height of the Great Depression—he was a born salesman and entrepreneur.

A young woman, walking away next to the track with a shopping basket on her arm, had made me think of him now.

And her polite demeanor as she'd spoken to me made me think of something else: the conversation I'd had with the young waitress. The words the waitress said to me—"I've always appreciated someone with good manners"—I'd heard before, in a strangely similar context, sometime long ago in my life. I could feel it. I was sure of it, though I couldn't recollect when or where.

Racking my brain, eventually, in a flash, it hit me: Miss Smiley had said those words to me right before she served me the plate of food. So now I realized: *I* was the one she'd chosen to serve first—I would have been the sole survivor.

Funny how the mind worked. Funny how the waitress's words had triggered that memory after all that had happened—drowning, being saved. Maybe it was just my dark side, a part of my human nature that stubbornly wouldn't go away. Or maybe it showed that my synapses were functioning properly.

At any rate, I didn't care. It wasn't so important what *might* have been—that I might have been the sole survivor; what was important was that I was *not* the sole survivor. We'd all survived, and far more than just surviving, the four of us had come to understand a great truth: What had happened to us, had happened for a reason—it was part of God's plan—and we were thankful for that. In God was our trust.

And at this point in my life, what did I think of the Legend of the Isle of Cats? Well, I didn't believe the bad part about the curses and all that dark stuff, but I did believe the good part, the part about the treasure. After all, I'd kept on searching and running the race, and thanks to the Light, I'd finally found the treasure of forgiveness and peace hidden away deep in the darkness. And I'd totally made my peace with Miss Smiley. And so had Celia, Croom, and Jennie.

The train swooshed past Gracie and me, pulled by four diesel engines, so I knew it would be a really long freighter, just like the ones Cindy Peppercorn and I used to seek out to test our courage when we played the Train Game and made our Romilar toast.

Cindy was one of the truly unique people I'd known in my life; she could see things other people couldn't. She could see that I had to return to the Isle of Cats, or I'd never find peace. And if I hadn't gone back, I doubt I would have fallen on The Rocks and been saved. And though she'd shown me her mean streak when it came to avenging a perceived wrong, she'd also proven herself a caring friend, and our last visit had been truly good.

Gracie was unique, too, not so much a dog, it sometimes seemed, as a small person dressed in a dog costume. When she looked at Celia and me with an intentionally expressionless face, that look, combined with her goatee and spiky hair, made us call her "the professor." You had to wonder what thoughts went on in the mind of a dog.

Pip used to love watching the train before her personality went home to Heaven with the others to wait for me and the rest of her family. I wouldn't say Gracie exactly loved the train, but she'd sit still for it, as she was right now, very erect, her head going back and forth while the train passed as if she were reading the boxcars. "Southern—serves—the South," she read, as an old boxcar, a picturesque anachronism, passed us, click-clacking along.

I counted the cars: 153 of them. At nine o'clock in the morning, I'd finished my coffee, and the last car passed us and disappeared down the track. I stood. Gracie, ready to go, wagged her tail.

I'd spent my whole life searching. Finally, "at the end of the earth," I'd discovered gold in the darkness. It was God's plan.

We walked around the block, then walked home.

EPILOGUE

Hickory, North Carolina 2012

2012 marked my second year in retirement from public office, and, as it turned out, exactly 100 years since Beergard's ill-fated poker game.

Those thoughts crossed my mind as I savored a cup of joe on the bench in front of the depot restaurant. It's not like all I ever did now was sit here by the railroad track, Gracie at my feet, and drink coffee. But I did like this spot on a balmy spring morning—to think, visit with people, and start my day.

I start my day before I get out of bed. When I wake up, I begin with thoughts of how wonderful it is in Heaven. Then, whatever I do, every day is a good day. Or, if it's not such a good day, thoughts of our Ultimate Destination keep things in perspective and make the day easier to deal with.

Gardenia bushes were in bloom on my side of a rustic wooden fence along the track, and with every gentle breeze, I caught their fragrance.

I wondered what the chances of my finding Beergard's inheritance were—a million to one? About the same chances as being saved from the sea, I guess. But the storm came, and so did the fisher. I'd come to see them both for what they were—gifts from God. Something I had to use for Good. Celia, Jennie, and Croom agreed. So the four of us had decided to make some public appearances together. After all, we'd done pretty well with that press conference at the Legislature. Why not go on the road with some of what we'd learned on the road of life?

To date, we've had a number of joint appearances, and each time, we've been well received. People are attracted to those who unearth buried treasure—that would be Croom and me—and people with talent: that would be Celia and Jennie. But folks are also attracted to people with a meaningful message. We've found that people like the way we interact when we're addressing an audience or being interviewed. Our bond is strong, and we seem to inspire people.

To loosen things up, Croom leads off. He always did know how to make people laugh, so he gets us started with a light-hearted anecdote or joke. Sometimes he tells audiences that many years ago, someone predicted he'd uncover a deep, dark secret. And he did. A treasure chest full of gold. Since our reputation as "the ones who found the treasure" usually precedes us, Croom's joking about it is both funny and exciting. Then Croom—Errol Flynn, Captain Blood—gives his rendition of the details.

Then Jennie sings. "Amazing Grace" is always special. As for Celia, she doesn't just please the crowds with her virtuoso piano accompaniment—she dazzles them. And she's versatile, so she can transition easily from popular to classical and back again.

When we speak to audiences, each of us has a unique take on things, and yet, we hold a story in common: We followed the wrong influence down the wrong path and got lost. Then we found the *right* path, and we definitely like the right path better.

Now our purpose is to go out and share the good news with people and offer them hope.

Those are our "joint appearances," and we love them. Sometimes I appear by myself, and Celia travels with me. Even so, this doesn't keep her from presenting her own classical concerts, and when she does, I travel with her. Her performances have never been better. Time and experience—and faith—have made her more relaxed and instilled her with confidence. She takes more risks; she's more willing to experiment.

Jennie is on tour again, too, singing her heart out in sold-out concerts, now preferring contemporary Christian. On occasion, she will bring a crowd to tears.

Croom, having retired from the university, is with her everywhere she goes. As he is happy to say, "I had a good, long run in academics. Now I'm proud and happy just to be the star's husband and biggest fan. And Wes's dad." Together, Croom and Jennie share a confidence and sense of security they never had before.

As for the gold, I concluded early on that I'd never get totally away from those coins. In terms of notoriety, finding them was worse than winning the lottery, so I decided to embrace the issue rather than hide from it.

That's why I'm not only happy to talk about it; I'm happy to make it crucial.

Last week in Houston, the four of us appeared in front of our largest gathering ever: 15,000 people! Celia played, and Jennie sang. Then Croom got things rolling with some humor and a brief description of hitting pay dirt. Then it was my turn. I have to admit it was stunning—at least for the first few moments—to stand before a crowd of that magnitude. I drew a few deep breaths, then prayed before I said a word.

Then I jumped right in. "What were the chances I could have found that treasure unless it was part of God's plan? What were the chances that a storm would roll in the night before our last day, rearrange the beach, and expose the buried marking that we were looking for because of the clues we'd been given? What were the odds—a million to one? How could it not have been God's plan?"

I loved to watch the people's reaction as I talked about the Fourth Plaque—our "treasure map" in Latin words—and finally, the treasure itself: the Jacob Emmanuel Beauregard coins.

As I looked out over the vastness of the audience, I thought of the sea, mostly calm, but also with some waves, stretching far to the horizon. A vast and diverse world spread before me, teeming with life. But beneath that mostly placid surface, I knew there was conflict, struggle, and pain.

That's three of the main things life on this Earth has to offer—conflict, struggle, and pain. I knew that many people lead lives of quiet desperation—their need, their yearning, both physical and spiritual. I knew that's what caused the waves. And sometimes tsunamis. I knew that what the sea before me needed and wanted in life was more than a mere distraction—or even entertainment. I knew that what the people wanted was: Hope.

We all do.

"I'll be candid," I told the audience. "I'm really grateful for that treasure. I'm very glad I found it. It was, as my friend Croom points out, my own grandfather's inheritance, and I desperately needed it, financially." I talked about the shock and fear of facing bankruptcy. "The gold saved me from that, and I've done good things with that money—and I plan to do more—and it's allowing me to speak to people like you around the country."

I said, "Everyone won't find a treasure chest full of gold, but aren't we all blessed by God in ways we never expected—or could ever deserve?"

I paused for effect. "But this is what I want to emphasize: While, yes, prosperity can be a blessing, all the gold in the world is worth less than the other treasure I found—the gift of restored, purposeful life, a life filled with hope."

I quoted Proverbs 3:13-14: "Blessed is the man who finds wisdom, the man who gains understanding, for Wisdom is more profitable than silver and yields better returns than gold." I also quoted Peter, who compared faith to gold, and said faith was of greater worth.[14]

I described my fall on the rocks. "It hurt like heck. I fell right on my tail bone, then hit my head." I described my fall into the sea. "It's horrifying to drown." And my being pulled toward the black hole surrounded by a ring of fire, my descent to the dead. "Separation from God is the ultimate punishment, the ultimate Hell."

I described my being saved by the outstretched hand of the Light.

Then, after pausing, I simply began to read—slowly, in a

deep, resonant voice—the following words: "In the beginning was the Word, and the Word was with God, and the Word was God. He was with God in the beginning."

The response from the sea of people was a hushed reverence as I continued: "Through Him, all things were made; without Him, nothing was made that has been made. In Him was life, and that life was the light of men. The light that shines in the darkness."[15]

I described the Light I had seen—dazzling, warm, loving, perfect. The glory of God. I described what I saw, how it felt, what I was told. "He told me the problem was sin. Sin is the problem. That humbled me and shamed me. But it also made me feel connected with everyone else—all other people. Because we all have sin in common, because we all are fallen. That made me feel connected, and in a good way because He also offered the cure. Himself. Sinful people were not condemned through Him; they were saved through Him.

"He was the cure—the remedy—for me and for everyone else who wants salvation. That's what Grace is all about.

"The dazzling light asked me if I wanted to follow him to be with him and the others forever. And I said 'Yes, I want to very much,' but he knew I was troubled about people I'd left behind, and so He said I could go back, since it was not for myself that I asked, but for others."

Then I told the sea of people before me about the fisher—the hooded man with the rod and boat—how he pulled me from the ocean and saved my life.

"The coins only saved my property—and the property of others. I've helped people with those coins, and that's all good, but the fall on the rocks into the sea, drowning and going to Heaven, the encounter with the Light, the fisher's mercy, gave me a second chance at life."

I paused, then, "Apart from faith in the Light," I said, "I have found that there is no hope in life. But through faith in the Light, His grace atones for sin, and there is hope. And when there is hope, there is life. That is what I found. The true treasure, not just mine, but everyone's."

Again, I read to them: "'To all who receive him, to those who believe in his name, he gives the right to become children of God."[16]

Looking up from the Scriptures, I said, "It seems to me, this is the truth, simple and complex at the same time."

I had some other things to say. "Life on this earth—in this realm—is an adventure, and more than that, a journey. Along the way, there will be all types of distractions, and sometimes they will get us off-track, and we will travel in the wrong direction. But that is part of life, too, part of the 'getting there.' Though there will always be distractions along the way, that doesn't mean they are all bad. There will always be duties and responsibilities, too. We just have to balance things.

"If we honor God and stay faithful, it's not so important to know where he is going to take us. We don't have to know how God is going to bless us. If we trust, we will be blessed.[17] The blessings may come when we least expect them, from people and events that don't appear positive at the time. The blessings may come as a surprise. At the time, they may even be unrecognizable.

"Since you never know when those blessings may come—or how—you need to keep a positive, receptive mind. A mind open to possibilities—and not so quick to judge.

"Jesus taught us: do not judge and condemn hypocritically. Forgive others."

I asked, "How many of you are looking for something?" I waited, repeated the question, and many hands went up. "The various demands of life shouldn't keep us from searching. The light is out there, knocking at our door. But we have to open the door and let the light stream into our hearts."

I paused. "All people are searching, but most just don't know that they are searching for the Light, the only thing that can lead them out of the darkness and satisfy their thirsty souls.

"'Ask, and it will be given to you; seek and you will find. Knock, and the door will be opened to you.'[18] Not necessarily according to your time. But in God's own time."

Again, I looked at Scripture, which I was holding in my left hand, keeping my right hand free. "Seek first the kingdom of God and his righteousness, and all the other things you need will be given to you as well.[19] This is the Gospel truth, the word of God according to Matthew." Smiling, I said quickly, "Not me, but Matthew the Gospel writer." The audience laughed. "From the Sermon on the Mount." I referred them to Matthew chapters six and seven.

Then I went personal again, saying, "I have always been a seeker, always searching, looking upward, reaching for God, always needing to fend off the dark side in me."

Yes, I knew people wanted to hear about the treasure and how it was found. That's why Croom had started things off by telling them about that, briefly, and I'd talked about the treasure, too, more at length. "I could have been washed out to sea, my corpse at the bottom of the ocean. That would have been the end. Instead, I was saved by the fisher and the Light of the Universe. The gift of salvation is worth more than all the gold in the world. Because of that time I spent in the depth of darkness, and in the presence of the Light of Heaven, I found my soul."

I paused, then said, "Many of you may be in a time of darkness right now. This could even be the darkest time of your life. Stay faithful. Good will eventually come of this trial."

This was heady stuff, speaking to a crowd of over 15,000 people. A month before, I'd spoken to 10,000. In contrast, in all my years in politics, I'd never spoken to anywhere near that many—one time, maybe a thousand people at the most. And on that occasion, they hadn't filled a hot gymnasium to hear my words of wisdom. They'd come to make sure I heard theirs. The bureaucrats in Raleigh during the worst drought on record had proposed an inter-basin water transfer from our water basin to the one next door, so the recipients of the transfer could build a water park for economic development purposes. The people who'd shown up to protest this proposal wanted me to know they were *not* happy.

Last week—and the month before that—they had come to hear my words of wisdom. And the virtuosity of Celia, the grand pianist—and the spirituality of Jennie, the superstar singer—and Croom, the good-natured humorist, who could also pray. For them. All of that was heady. We'd come a long way since the dark days of our fearfulness. All of *that* was why I was sitting on this bench. Because sitting here was not heady at all. The aroma of bacon and eggs and grits drifting my way every time the restaurant door opened was not heady at all. Neither was the smell of coffee. All of that was down to earth.

Celia's planning a garden party for the back lawn at Stately Oaks also helped me keep both feet planted firmly on the ground. She wanted me to help her be sure we didn't leave anyone, including Cindy, off of the invitation list.

That was down to earth, too. So was petting Gracie as she sat up straight as a sentry, anticipating the train.

I saw it now as it approached from down the track. It set off a deep blast as it passed through each intersection—like the foghorn on an ocean liner—until it was rocking and rolling in front of Gracie and me. She looked back and forth, as if she were counting the cars, or as if she were reading the side of them: "Southern—gives—a—green—light—to—innovations."

The smell of diesel fuel was in the air, churning in a breeze created by the train. None of this was heady. I liked it. I liked visiting with people who passed by or, as was the case now, those standing nearby, silent for the moment because the noise of the train commanded their silence.

Many years ago, I started out searching for the kingdom of God and the meaning of life. And I finally found it. Not quickly—not easily—not my way. But His way—in His time. From what I'd observed over the years, it was never too late for anyone to start searching. But a person did have to start—did have to open the door. *Anyone* could do that: after all, it was all a matter of grace, which was a gift.

I'd been to Heaven, and I was ready to go back. That's one of the reasons I started each morning with thoughts of how wonderful it had been in Heaven. But until He said it was my time, I didn't want to muck up things here. I wanted to stay grounded. I'd been at the gates of Hell, too. All of that had taught me a lot. But I didn't want to be heady about that. It was a gift. I wanted to have a servant's heart.

There was something additional on my mind as I sat on this bench, my dog at my feet: the question was how to end the novel I'd been working on for all these years. As someone once said, a novel is like a revolution in that once it's started, it's hard to know how and when to end it. That was the point, you see: This was all about the Light—and therefore Life. There *was* no end. But for purposes of a novel, a work of fiction, it had to end somewhere. As the author, I've decided, now's the time.

Hands covered my eyes.

"Surprise!" Celia said, standing behind me. She had approached stealthily, any sound she might have made, drowned out by the train. Even Gracie, facing away, hadn't sensed her. Then Celia kissed me on the cheek, her hands resting on my shoulders, as Gracie jumped up, tail wagging for attention.

The caboose passed in front of us. It soon would disappear down the track, and the train would be over. Unlike Life with the Light.

I figured Celia was here for the farmer's market.

She said, "I'm headed for the fresh produce stand. Come with me."

How pretty she looked in her long, floral, summery dress! And the light fragrance she wore was as pleasant as newly cut flowers. How bright were her eyes and smile! As I stood, Gracie, ready to go, looked up at us eagerly. I smiled and took Celia's hand. I looked to the sky. Those fluffy white clouds sure were softening the sea blue heaven. Hand-in-hand, Gracie at our side, we headed for the gracious display of fresh produce.

On a bright new day like this, it just seemed like a good thing to do. After all, when all was said and done, wasn't that a lot of what God was about—fresh produce?

Celia bought some things to fix for dinner, and I bought Celia a bouquet of flowers and some bulbs—Easter lilies. Gracie got a biscuit. Then, because the weather was so nice and the day so beautiful, we strolled around town for a while before we headed home.

In our front yard was a dogwood tree I'd planted five years ago upon my return to this temporal life. Now, in a circle around it, I planted the bulbs. As I was watering them, I heard off in the distance, another train passing through, signaling with the sound of a foghorn as it made its way through the downtown.

I smiled when I finished my watering, thinking how pretty the lilies would be when the Eastertime in all its newness rolled around in its heavenly orbit again next spring.

AUTHOR'S NOTE

The dog in this story whose name is Pip was in real life my dog whose name was Mady. I mention this because Pip's (Mady's) death, as depicted in the story, was in real life dramatic enough to make me feel a need to write about it. I wanted to make sense of her death: I wanted to show that something good could come from a painful personal loss that seemed totally devoid of anything good.

I know that many other people have used writing as therapy after the loss of a child or other loved one. While I would never, ever suggest that the loss of a dog is on the same level as the loss of a child, I just point out that in certain cases there may be some similarity regarding the trauma and heartbreak.

From the story of Mady's death, from which I began writing, evolved this novel. I started out writing about the death of my dog; I ended up writing about eternal life and the treasure of forgiveness and peace. From darkness came light. From death came life. From sadness and grief came hope and renewal. This is a story of God's grace, mercy and love.

NOTES

CHAPTER 15

1 Lucado, Max. *Just Like Jesus*; Chapter : "The Gold in the Garbage."

CHAPTER 34

2 Behanna, Gert. *God Is Not Dead.* [Speech from the mid-1950's, available on CD.]

CHAPTER 36

3 Matthew 15 and Mark 9.

4 Moody, Jr., Raymond A. *Life After Life*: Bantam Books, New York, NY, 1973.

5 Ibid.

6 Luke 10:41.

7 Hebrews 13:5.

8 Romans 8:38-39.

9 See: Young, William Paul. *The Shack*, 2007.

10 Moody. *Life After Life.*

11 Ibid.

CHAPTER 41

12 See: "Gold Country Couple Discover $10 Million in Buried Coins," Kevin Fagan, May 26, 2014. [Fagan is a SF Chronicle staff writer. kfagan@sfchronicle.com]

CHAPTER 44

13 "Gold Country Couple Discover $10 Million in Buried Coins," Kevin Fagan, May 26, 2014. [Fagan is a SF Chronicle staff writer. kfagan@sfchronicle.com]

EPILOGUE

14 1 Peter 1:7

15 John 1:1-5

16 John 1:12

17 Joel Osteen, "Peace With Yourself."

18 Matthew 7:7

19 Matthew 6:33

ACKNOWLEDGMENTS

A number of people have helped me with this book as I have written and revised it over the course of ten years. I would like to thank them:

First, for her patience and forbearance, I wish to thank my wife Judy. Ten years is a long time to hear about one prospective book. I couldn't have done it without her.

Next, I wish to thank:

Linda W. Hobson, Ph.D., who, early on, surprised me with the admonition, "To write a novel, you have to have faith." Her editorial assistance, advice and encouragement shepherded me through the first full draft.

The Hon. Judge Wes Barkley, who selflessly took the time to study several versions and who helped me narrow down my focus to a Christian theme.

Wayne Dow, friend from our college days, who offered incisive criticism that improved the protagonist as a character.

Lee Smith, a brilliant author and delightful creative writing teacher, who helped with some of the earliest material.

The following friends were kind enough to read some of the earliest drafts and offer advice and encouragement: Katie Perkins, Mayor Jeff Cline, and Tamara Coley. I appreciate all of them for their help and support.

And finally, I would like to thank the team at Redhawk Publications – Tim Peeler for his gracious and thorough editorial assistance, as well as encouragement; Patty Thompson for her enthusiasm and patience; and Robert Canipe, for his advice, insight and support.

And thanks also to Ethan Sehyun Park, who unscrambled a decade worth of word processing files.

Lastly, but not least, a thank you goes to Manley Fuller, whose life-long friendship has enriched my life with experiences I would otherwise have missed

ABOUT THE AUTHOR

Austin Allran—writer, attorney and elected official—has written numerous short stories, poems and newspaper articles. He has received awards from the N.C. Writers' Network (short story) and the Hugh T. Lefler Award (historical biography).

The Legend of the Isle of Cats is his first novel.

A life-long resident of Hickory, North Carolina, Austin lives with his wife, Judy. He is a proud father and grandfather.
Contact him at Isleofcats@gmail.com

Made in the USA
Columbia, SC
26 November 2022